GILDED

WICKED

MIRRORS

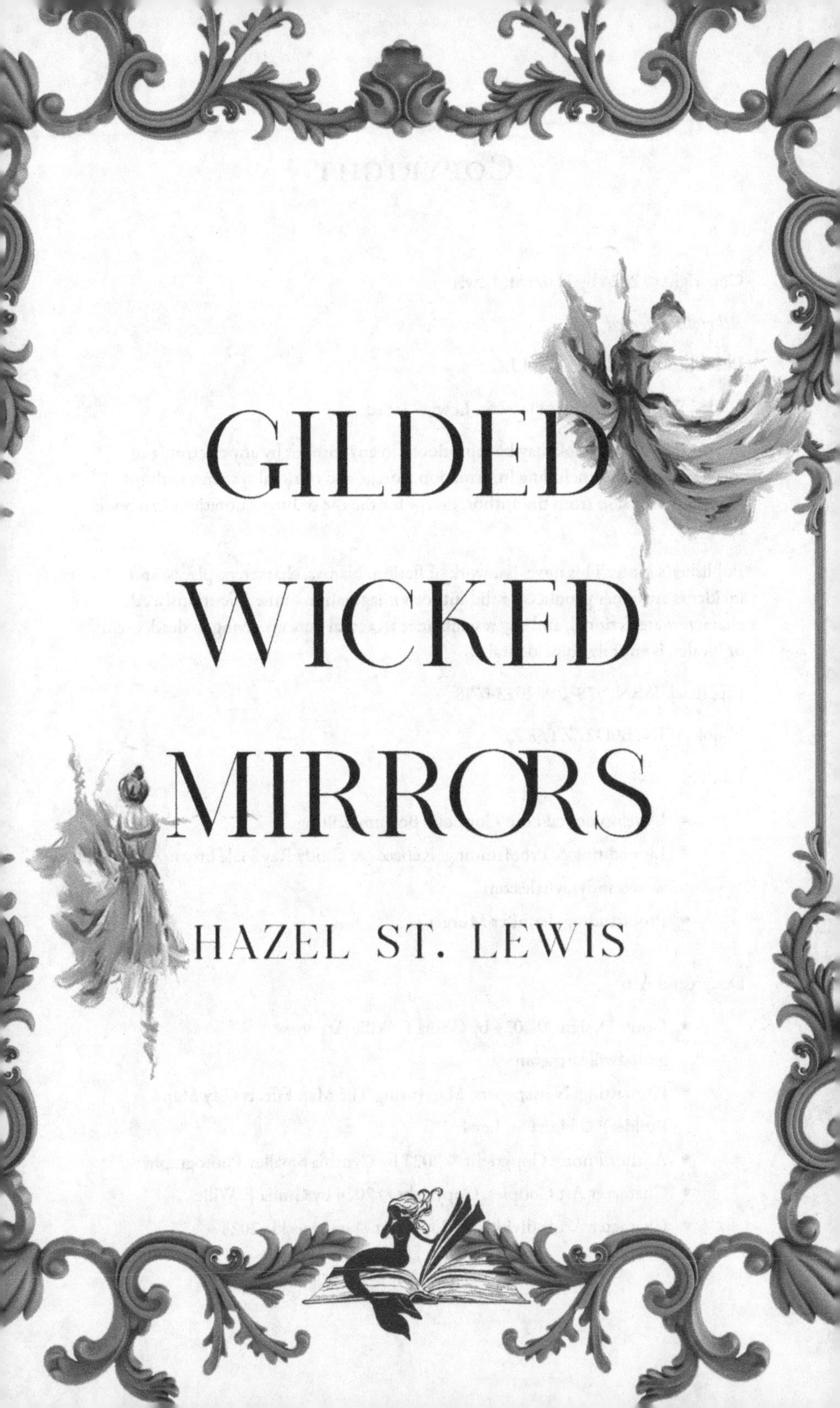

GILDED WICKED MIRRORS

HAZEL ST. LEWIS

Copyright

- Character Art Viridian Scene: Copyright © artsiidaisy 2024
- Character Art Tango: Copyright © 2021 by morgana0anagrom

For my Dad and Mom.

I promised I would keep this one clean... I did not. I have failed you.
Perhaps skip the latter half of Chapter 25 and Chapter 35.

Nature District
University Square
Castle Hill
The Grand Library
Art Sector

New Swansea City
Marina District
The Viridian
Pleasure District
The Royal Ballet
The Starling
Gold Quarter
The Russet
The Ruins
Estate District
Spirit Sector

AUTHOR'S NOTE

AUTHOR'S NOTE:

I finished the first draft of this book in 2019, and since then, I have called Emrys a Shadow Daddy. I just felt like I needed you to know that.

Everything from the murder mystery to Quinn's appearance, name, and role as a ballerina was written in 2019 *before* an incredibly popular book was published. All similarities are coincidental.

This book has characters with dyslexia and ADHD. All depictions of Quinn's learning struggles are based on my experience living with dyslexia. There is a moment in this book that closely resembles a scene from an extremely popular book. I also wrote the scene before realizing the similarities—apparently, we have similar minds—and I debated cutting it because of it. However, I felt that to be true to my dyslexia and Quinn's character, I needed to keep the moment in the book. Giselle's ADHD in the book is based on my experience with my own ADHD. All ablest terms used in the book, such as slow, dumb, idiot, stupid, crazy, annoying . . . etc., represent a realistic picture of what it was like for me growing up neurodiverse.

Gilded Wicked Mirrors takes place in a second-world fantasy, but it borrows the time period from our world, including technology and dress, from the late 1890s and early 1910s. I took liberties with some of the technology (like the inventions Giselle is working on), but 99% of the technology that shows up in this book was invented before 1912. For example, Cable Cars were introduced in San Francisco in 1873, and the Brownie Camera was the first portable camera and was purchasable for a dollar in 1900. The first ski lift was invented in 1908. Isn't it fascinating how many things were already invented in the early 1900s? One medical invention I took liberties with was medical gloves. While medical gloves have existed since 1889, surgical gloves like we know today weren't used until 1965. However, I did not feel the need to make this distinction in the book.

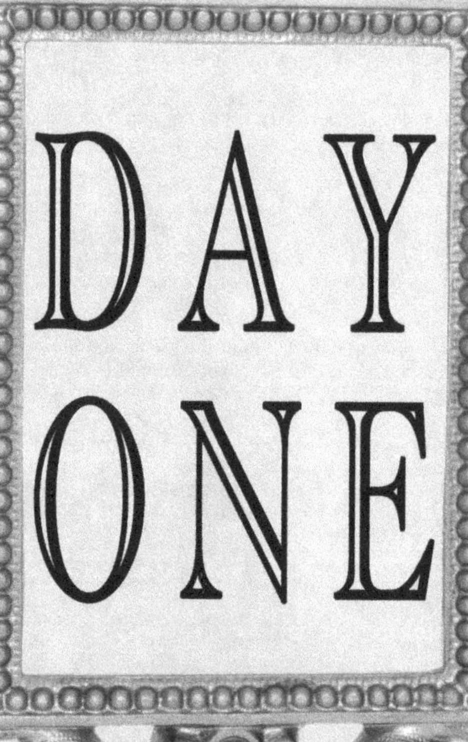

DAY
ONE

| BREAKING NEWS | # The New Swansea Times |

SUNDAY, NEW SWANSEA CITY, 90th DAY OF AUTUMN, 700AV

THE GOLDEN PRINCE RETURNS

Meet at the Marina for the Prince's Return and see History's Largest Steamship Dock

Tomorrow, Monday, the 90th day of Autumn, Prince Emrys will return from his venture overseas on the RMS Colossal. Docking a day early, he travels on the fastest and largest ship to cross the vast ocean, making history. The feat itself is a major deal, but the prince aboard makes the occasion all the more incredible and rarer—cont. page 2

GANG WARS WORSEN
the Mirror Blessed v. Human War continues with deadly consequences

Will the five Mirror Blessed gangs declare an all-out war on humans? Over the last fifty years, war has been kept at bay by the influence of Castle Hill. Although Prince Emrys is only in his mid-twenties, he's had a calming effect until now—cont. page 4

FIVE MORE FOUND DEAD
in the Nature District

Five more bodies were found drained of blood in the Nature District. The count to date of dead bodies has now reached a level—cont. page 8

ONE

It was highly inappropriate to run down the streets of New Swansea in a tutu. Not only was it indecent, it was utterly impractical. But Quinnevere Ashelle had no other choice. She was running late, and her life, her dreams, her everything depended on timeliness. It was the first day of auditions for the Royalle Ballet, and this year, she *would* make it into the corps de ballet.

She *had to*.

It was her last chance.

Steamship whistles blared obnoxiously overhead, grating against her ears. Thousands cheered and crammed the streets, wanting to witness the largest and fastest vessel to cross the Kardic Ocean. Children sang nursery rhymes and danced as their parents waved flags and jumped for joy, looking for the best view. Gramophones played classical music, and camera shutters echoed against cobblestones. The light from the flashbulbs reflected off the Mirror of Forgotten—the wicked magic mirror that loomed over the crowd. It stood stationary on Marina Hill, overlooking the docks. The majestic nature of it was meant to lure people near, drawing in individuals who were too cocky or foolish to listen to the warnings whispered throughout the town. This particular mirror was known for trading for people's most cherished memories.

But Quinn was no fool. She wouldn't be caught up in its beauty. Instead, she ran through the chaos, making her way to auditions with her necklace bouncing with her footfalls.

Panic rose in her throat.

The crowd was too dense, and time was not on her side.

Quinn was turning twenty-three tonight, and sadly, she was getting too old to join a ballet company. Apprentices were supposed to start at eighteen, but Quinn was five years behind on her dream, and unfortunately, she had to become an apprentice first to get her coveted role in the corps de ballet.

So, this year's auditions were her final shot—only shot.

Five. Years. Behind. Because of her uncle. He didn't see the value in non-practical things like dance, so he forced her to work as a junior medical examiner. But this year was different because Quinn was turning the age of majority, and she could finally make her own life decisions.

She could finally audition for the Queen's Royalle Ballet, and she wouldn't let the crowded streets of the Marina District destroy her future. The ballet was her ticket out of humble circumstances and into fame—and prestige. Respect.

But she couldn't accomplish her goal stuck in this horde.

"Oh, fucking mirrors," Quinn cursed under her breath. "Fuck, fuck, fuck."

Smashing down her scarlet tutu, she tried to weave through newsies and photographers—who would stop at nothing to get a picture of the rich and glamorous as they disembarked the grand ocean liner, the RMS *Colossal*.

This was the least opportune moment to make history. Why couldn't that godforsaken ship make port on any other day? Any other day when she hadn't overslept. Any other day when her whole life wasn't counting on it.

Just any other fucking day.

Quinn huffed, gripping her tulle skirt.

When she was finally about to get a respite from the chaos, a photographer elbowed her in the side, and she lost her balance. Quinn stumbled, hit a second man, and fell sideways. The world stilled. Time felt like molasses slowly dripping from a jar. The fall took an eternity—until it didn't.

Quinn's leg crashed into a miniaturized steamship souvenir, which sliced open the skin near her gastrocnemius muscle. Pain radiated through her bones as blood trickled down her calf, staining her tights and dreams in crimson. Quinn gasped. A mixture of untoward curse words escaped from her lips.

Her thoughts fuzzed, and her world changed.

All Quinn could focus on was external things because if she allowed anything else in, she would break. And she wouldn't break, so she turned her attention to the fog hovering over the brick-and-mortar shops like a veil slanted off a corpse bride's face. The icy autumn hurricane-like wind snaked through the streets, causing her cinnamon hair to fall out of her bun and dance down her chest. Storefront shutters smacked into rustic bricks. The coiling silver surface of the Mirror of Forgotten winked in the sunlight—mocking her. The nursery rhymes rotted, and screams pierced the morning dew.

Icy fire ripped through her leg; a burn so hot it felt cold. Quinn gritted her teeth, trying to brace herself for the pain. Dread sank into her stomach as blood gushed from her calf.

Dance. Auditions. It was all ruined. Now, she'd never make it to auditions on time, and her childhood dreams would wilt away like a cut rose—decaying. Her fantasies of traveling the world as a ballerina burned to ash between her fingers.

Quinn blinked as a bead of sweat glided down her temple. Sucking in a breath, she refused to give in.

This would not fucking end her.

She dug her fingertips into the coarse fabric of her tutu as she tried to ground herself. When that didn't work, she moved her hand to clutch her necklace. It was the only piece of her parents she had left. Quinn didn't remember much of their murders, but she recalled the screams and a shattered magic mirror—a piece of which hung on a chain around her neck.

After a couple of breaths, the panic subsided, and her rational brain took over. She knew how to suture a wound. And she would rely on her training. After all, Quinn was raised in the morgue, surrounded by rotting bodies and an eccentric uncle. Medicine, suturing, and blood were constants in her life. She was a medical examiner. In fact, she'd known how to sew since she was six because her uncle decided it was prudent and appropriate to teach a six-year-old how to close a corpse. So she'd assisted with his autopsies ever since.

This scratch was nothing.

The souvenir only pierced into the dermis. Which meant she barely had to stitch anything.

She clumsily stood up, and a man with a mirror-blessed tattoo reached out to steady her. The tattoo reminded her of the terrifying Mirror-Rite. The rite she had to make tonight on her twenty-third birthday or suffer severe consequences . . .

But she couldn't think about that now because she had bigger problems to deal with.

Like her shattered ambitions.

"Thank you," Quinn said, hopping to a storefront stoop as rivulets of blood soaked her tights and the street.

The man mumbled his reply and disappeared back into the crowd.

Once she sat down, Quinn reached into her pack and pulled out a small first aid kit. Making quick work of it, she threaded a needle before placing it between her teeth and ripping her tights off. The red staining her tutu nearly blended in with the maroon fabric, but her tights were as pale as her moon-white skin. Except, now, they were destroyed, caked with crimson streaks, and that would not do. It was better to go without tights than bloody ones.

Biting down tightly, Quinn sucked in a deep breath before pouring saline onto her left calf and lacing the needle into her dermis. She worked quickly through the pain as salty tears coated her cheeks. And Quinn hated herself for those tears. If it were up to her, she would never cry. She saw it as a sign of weakness. Showing emotion, showing how the world's cruelty affected her, only made her feel frail and out of control, like prey—like a victim. And she never wanted to be that. She needed to control her own destiny. So, she stifled her feelings and allowed no one to see them.

But it was impossible to hold in tears caused by excruciating pain, and sewing your wound on the side of a dirty street without morphine was, at the very least, painful.

Halfway through her stitches, the voice of a devil echoed through the chaos. "Hello, Ginger."

Quinn glanced up, and her eyes fixed on Emrys Avalon, Prince of New Swansea, her eternal adversary and the second in line to the throne. Her stomach coiled. The prince loved to make her life miserable and always showed up at the most inopportune moments. The needle in her fingers quivered as her heart turned into jagged icicles. Emrys was bad news incarnate, like nightmares made manifest. With his midnight hair and fiendish smile, he was way, way too attractive for his own good.

Disgustingly attractive.

She allowed her eyes to focus on him for a minuscule second before dismissively returning her gaze to her leg. But that moment was long enough to notice that he wore formal attire.

Formal attire at 6:30 in the morning.

He was dressed in a double-breasted pinstriped suit with a purple vest and silk cravat, which complemented his smooth, dark olive complexion. Topping the ostentatious outfit off was a gilded cane and a shiny black top hat with a grosgrain ribbon and a purple peacock feather. An outfit that screamed, *look at me with my expendable wealth and deep-rooted narcissism.*

No decent gentleman wore formal attire this early in the morning. But Quinn shouldn't be surprised. Emrys, the notorious rogue, only cared about wasting money, fucking, having a good time, and being surrounded by courtesans and booze. He was probably on his way to the Viridian or Starling nightclubs to continue his constant stream of partying.

Quinn sighed.

Focusing on her task, she felt his irritation in the shifting of his stance. No one ignored the Playboy Prince.

"What *are* you doing?" he asked the question in the sort of pompous way an aristocrat would ask a servant who had overstayed their welcome—like she had no right to be where she was and doing what she was doing.

Many untoward answers gathered in her mind, but she was suddenly aware of the crowd and cameras surrounding them. "I am suturing my leg."

"Would you like help?"

Her eyebrows crinkled. Emrys Avalon was not chivalrous. He only did things that suited him and his needs, and as he reached out a hand to help her, an echo of flashbulbs ignited behind him. Oh, that was the reason. He wasn't chivalrous, but he wanted to appear to be. In a society based on celebrity, it wasn't the truth that mattered. Appearances and gossip ruled the day.

"Have you ever sutured a wound before?" She turned her chin up to catch his gaze but nearly sprained her neck doing so.

Emrys towered above. He always towered over her, but the difference was stark when she was on the ground. She was a short, petite little thing, and he was, well . . . the ridiculous stereotype of a tall, dark, and handsome actor in a silent picture show.

"Would it surprise you if I said yes?" A devilish grin danced on his lips.

Yes. It would. But that was not what she said. She wouldn't give him the satisfaction of her surprise. "I am sure you've had many occasions to learn."

His smile widened further. "I am sure I have. Danger is a beautiful bedmate."

He moved closer as if to show his various skills, but she held out her hand to stop him. "Thank you for your offer, but I am perfectly capable of suturing a wound." With that, she turned her focus completely back to her task.

"Yes, clearly," he said. "I was merely suggesting that you allow someone to help you . . . in various ways."

Quinn gulped. What the fuck did that even mean?

Ignoring him and the question, she looped her final stitch, tied a knot, and wrapped her leg in gauze.

"Quinnevere, why are you wearing a tutu at the docking of the *Colossal*?" he asked as she returned her tools to her medical kit and placed them back in her pack.

She wanted to say, *why do you think I am wearing a fucking tutu? Obviously, I am going to dance.* He brought out the worst in her. But instead, she smiled through her teeth and said, "Queen's Royalle Ballet auditions."

"How is a junior medical examiner going to make it into the Royalle Ballet? Even if you had the talent, you wouldn't have the time to perform."

Did he realize how condescending he was? "I wouldn't do them both."

"But you're one of the brightest minds in the city. I assume you do more autopsies now than your uncle. Why would you waste that?" A baffled expression sparked on his bronze cheeks.

She wanted to say, *and how would you know? You never show up to the murder briefings, and when you do, you destroy evidence, mess with my investigations, and get me in trouble with all the physicians at University Square.* But she said nothing. Again, struck by the audience, hanging off their every word.

Castle Hill oversaw both the police and the Mirror-Blessed investigations. Murder briefings were the prince's responsibility—which was why Quinn had to interact with him so much—but Emrys only showed up to a handful of them. The last time the prince came to one of her autopsies, he burned all her notes and tampered with the lab results. It was so egregious that the entire investigation had to be dropped, and Quinn was blamed for allowing it to happen. He made her look like an idiot in front of her peers—and worse, the medical students. But the most egregious part was that even though the senior physicians knew Emrys was responsible, he never got reprimanded. Emrys could get away with murder, and no one would even bat an eye.

Perhaps Emrys was responsible for *that* case's murder. Why else tamper with the evidence? Unless it was to protect one of his lovers, like Harlowe Merriwether. Either way, it was infuriating.

Quinn hated to look dumb. She hated that he *made* her look dumb. While she didn't want to be a medical examiner, she never wanted to be bad at something, which is why she only slept three to four hours a night. She needed to perform her assistant duties while also training for the ballet. Her body and mind suffered, while Emrys wasted away his privilege, having absolutely no understanding or concern for the suffering of others. Her fingernails bit into her palms, her stomach broiling.

So she ignored him.

She set her jaw and tried to calm her thoughts. He was getting under her skin again, and that never led to good places.

And only dance mattered.

Quickly standing, she attempted to balance on her good leg. It did not go well, and she toppled sideways. But Emrys's hands were like quicksilver, sliding around her waist and steadying her like a partner in a dance. He flinched at the touch, and Quinn sucked in a breath and held it. The feeling of his firm grip soaked through the tulle of her tutu, making it feel like his fingers were stroking her naked body.

She shuddered.

"Here, let me help you," Emrys said, the heat from his words caressing her neck.

Tilting her chin up, she caught his chestnut gaze—which sometimes had a hint of azure blue in them. Temptation and dark promises lingered there. Promises like those hands stroking a different part of her body intimately. Quinn gulped, smashing down her traitorous thoughts. She'd never had a lover and never wanted one—she had no time for that—but she was starting to see why Emrys was so coveted in the bedroom.

Emrys released his hands from her waist, and Quinn stifled a protesting sigh at the loss of stability. *Get yourself together. You do not need him to steady you. Moreover, you do not want him to touch you.*

"I don't need your help." Her words were all wanton and breathy, and she pinched her eyes shut for a moment as shame stirred in her stomach.

Dammit. Quinn was better than this. *Pretty men are to look at, not to touch.* A great motto. She swallowed hard and brushed him off again. He wouldn't stand in the way of her dreams. Placing weight onto her bad leg, she tested her strength.

As she moved to leave, Emrys clutched her upper arm. "Let me walk you to auditions." A chorus of camera lightbulbs flashed, reminding her of how public and documented their interaction was becoming.

"No," she whispered, a little too weakly for her tastes. "No, I can do it myself." Quinn wrenched out of his hold and side-stepped him before making her way through the multitude.

Her tights were ruined, and her calf pulsed with pain, but none of that mattered. Rain or shine, hell or high water, Quinnevere Ashelle would make it to auditions, and if she had to dance with an injured leg, so be it.

Two

Quinnevere Ashelle tiptoed through the studio door twenty minutes late with no tights and a ruffled tutu. She sucked in a deep breath as mortification rattled her bones. The tardiness hadn't escaped the attention of the Queen's Royalle Ballet director or her close friend and ballet mistress, Jane Whitfield-Wryte. Quinn wilted under their scrutiny and mouthed her apologies as she ran to the side of the room and dropped her pack before quickly slipping into her pointe shoes and rushing to the barre.

Quinn took the spot beside Constance DeWinter, another one of her best friends and the best dancer in the room. Quinn knew all the other dancers there, and Constance was a shoo-in for an apprentice position.

"What happened? You're never late." Constance whispered while performing a plié.

"A titanic pain in my—" A glare from the ballet director cut Quinn off.

The last thing Quinn wanted to do after walking in late with no tights and a stained tutu was to anger the director further. So, with her mouth in a tight line, Quinn joined the rhythm of exercises, ensuring that her feet moved through first, second, and fourth positions with elegance and precision. Her calf burned in the first position and ached in the second position, and by the fifth position, she could ignore the pain and focus on other things, like the curl of cinnamon escaping her bun and clinging to the back of her neck. And how, as she warmed up, she smelled more and more like blood and street grime.

The music changed tempo as excited whispers twirled through the room. The ballerinas gossiped about the arrival of the prince and the Festival of Blood, a ten-day holiday celebrating the Blood Rebellion—the war that ended the tyrannical rule of all vampires seven hundred years ago. The holiday festivities culminated on Winter's Eve with the Royalle Suitor Ball. All eligible girls in New Swansea had received their invitations in the morning. When Quinn found hers in the mailbox, she tore it to pieces and threw it in the rubbish bin. No force in all the world would get her to attend a ball with Emrys Avalon.

"Prince Charming is back," Constance whispered out of the corner of her mouth, her deep olive skin shining with sweat.

"I saw. No one could've missed his colossal grand entrance," Quinn said, kicking her foot high into the air above her head, starting her last exercise, the grand battement.

"Funny," Constance said with a low, husky voice while maintaining a perfect arm position. "He will be hosting a ball to find a suitable wife on Winter's Eve."

"Yes, it's positively medieval." Quinn groaned, spinning and shifting onto her left leg.

Constance flashed a dimple with a devilish glint in her chestnut eyes. "I thought you would love that bit."

Quinn shrugged off the jest, but the idea still unsettled her. The mere thought of a suitor ball gave her the urge to gag. No self-respecting girl wanted to marry a man after only spending a night with him. At least that was Quinn's view, but according to the obnoxious whispers permeating the room, many did not share her opinion.

"I don't envy the poor girl who marries him," Quinn said. "I bet he stares at himself in a normal mirror for at least two hours every morning."

"Indeed." Constance's tone was low and brooding. She was always moody when she danced.

The ballet director cleared his throat and clapped. "Great warm-up. Let's begin today at the corps' first entrance. Remember, this is the Ball of Diamonds. It is a show filled with intrigue and romance. Make me feel the tension and excitement!"

The dancers split apart and moved into position—the girls on one side of the room and the boys on the other. They were to perform the Waltz of Roses.

"Girls, remember to act coy yet excited when your partners enter." The director walked to the front of the room and motioned to the piano. "From the top, please, Andrews."

The piano played a three-four tempo—the waltz tempo.

The dance began with bourrée steps to the center. The quick movements created the effect of floating atop the clouds, the magic of it erupting through Quinn's core and tingling on her skin as she glided across the floor like a fairy hovering above a lily pad, her steps light, delicate, and beautiful.

A fairytale come to life.

"One, two, three, not too fast. Watching your arms . . . . Left shoulder back and squeeze," the ballet director commanded like a drill sergeant. "Two, three into the passé, four lifting the knee, five arrive, six, hold . . ."

Quinn let the music flow, breathe, and live inside her body. Dance was a form of enchantment, and the movement, precision, and skill all filled Quinn's soul.

But a bead of sweat dripped down Quinn's temple as her legs moved in quick succession. Exhaustion gripped its claws into her side, and the intense fire radiating from her wound was all-consuming. Dancing on pointe forced her calf into a constantly flexed position that pricked her stitches and possibly loosened them. But she begged her body to continue—to fight. Her breaths became tight and restricted as they approached the boys' entrance.

"Gentlemen, find your partner, one; Quinn, feel that passion. You're stiff . . . You need to seduce your partner . . ."

Quinn's heart twisted, pounding like an untamable beast. She sucked in a breath and tried to calm down. She also tried to flash a seductive smile at her partner, Arthur. It came out far more like an uncomfortable grimace than anything sensual.

"That's not passion, Quinn," the director yelled. "You look repulsed by him."

Dammit. Quinn didn't understand passion. She didn't know how to look at a man with lust. Lust wasn't quantifiable. It wasn't science.

A sharp pain jolted through her calf as she spun into a promenade on attitude. A trickle of liquid rolled down her leg.

Shit, shit, shit, dirty mirrors, please only be sweat instead of blood, she begged.

"Alright, your final pirouette and a hold . . . five, six, seven, arrive."

The director clapped while the dancers stopped, the boys letting go of the girls' waists. Everyone tried to catch their breath. Exhaustion poured over Quinn as she clutched her stomach, trying to calm her nerves and heart.

"That wasn't bad. But girls, I want to see that sparkle in your eye when the gents come toward you."

Constance and Quinn shared a glance. Neither girl would have a sparkle in their eyes upon seeing a boy. But for different reasons. Constance preferred the company of ladies, and Quinn preferred . . . well, not a prince. Or a lord or a duke—but especially not a prince.

Princes were for looking, not touch—

Her thoughts were interrupted as the director said, "Especially you, Quinn. I need you to find your passion if you're going to make it into the company."

Her core solidified into unmoving, unyielding stone. She

needed to impress the director, so he'd choose her. The last thing she needed was to be singled out as the worst dancer in the room. This wasn't true because Quinn was a brilliant dancer, but she was adequate compared to the competition.

But not the worst.

Never the worst.

"Arthur, as usual, great work! Your lifts are seamless, and Mariam," the director continued his notes. "You have to control your constant mumbling. Your dancing is brilliant, but no one wants to hear your nonsense while you dance."

Quinn winced. Mariam was notorious for her bad deal with one of New Swansea's wicked mirrors. The deal's unintended consequence caused her to mumble, whisper, and never cease speaking.

Hundreds of mirrors known as the Bargainers lined the city, and the godlike souls inside of them traded for information, wealth, prestige, and magic at terrible costs. People negotiated to better their lives, but the bigger the ask, the bigger the cost and unintended consequence. And some people—the desperate people—bartered away their autonomy for a chance at a better life, and others promised a piece of their soul for magical abilities. Poor Mariam traded for magic shoes that allowed her to dance perfectly, but the cost was never to be silenced. The unintended consequence was that she could never stop talking. Ever.

Far too great a cost.

It was clear she deeply regretted her decision because her eyes grew red, and she looked like she wanted to cry, but Mariam simply said, "Yessir, I'll do better." But her voice cracked on the last word.

Quinn shuddered, her upcoming Mirror-Rite clawing at the back of her mind.

"Quinnevere, can I speak with you for a moment?" Jane asked.

"Yes, of course." Quinn swallowed, and her palms were suddenly sweaty. Nothing good ever came from that question.

Jane motioned to a corner, where they settled into a private nook. Fear stroked the insides of Quinn's stomach. It was never good to be pulled aside privately—even by a close friend. But Quinn greatly admired the other redhead and would take any correction she'd give.

"Quinny, you have wonderful technique, but you lack passion. I can see it, and the director can see it. You need to move the audience with artistry." Jane laid it out bluntly. It was her way, never pulling punches. But despite the harshness of her words, she flashed an empathetic half-smile. "We've talked about this many times, but now it matters. You have to impress the Royalle Ballet, and I fear that if you cannot show passion this week, you won't make the cut this year."

Quinn's throat felt as dry as the Kaldan desert.

It was not a new critique, yet it hurt as much as it did the first time—possibly because she'd spent the last four years trying to work on her acting and learning emotion. Quinn was precise and technical, rarely missing a beat. Her artistry resembled a steamship engine chugging away, working to a brilliant yet dull rhythm. And like her dancing, the machine was predictable and plain because it lacked all semblance of passion.

Unfortunately, Quinn didn't understand passion, nor did she know where to begin learning it. Long ago, to seek control in a chaotic and cruel world, she'd locked up her emotions in an impenetrable prison, and she no longer had the key.

"I know. I don't know how to change it." Quinn said as her heart was encased in ice.

"Try to feel something, and you will do fine."

That was easier said than done.

Pain soaked into the corners of Quinn's eyes, a stinging sensation pulsing through them, but she refused to let out a tear. Not for this. She would be strong and get through it. So Quinn merely nodded, not wanting to speak, not wanting anyone to see her upset.

What she needed was to get away.

"I can help you tonight if you would like." Jane's lips slid into a soft smile. "Maybe we could practice at the Viridian after your Mirror-Rite."

Quinn's stomach plummeted, and her hands shook at the reminder.

In New Swansea, on a person's twenty-third birthday, they reached the age of majority and were legally allowed to bargain with the mirrors, and over time, it became a tradition to challenge a mirror with a small, innocuous deal the night one turned of age. Urban legend said that if somebody refused to do the ritual, they would have seven years of bad luck. So, while Quinn hated the idea of the rite, and it was the last thing she wanted to do, she couldn't risk bad luck. Not with her week long auditions.

Jane placed a hand on her friend's cheek. "You look like you might be sick."

Of course, Quinn looked sick. People lost their souls to bad bargains. "Deals are scary, I mean you—" *lost your ability to dance to one.* Quinn cut herself off before she could finish. Jane's bad experience was never openly acknowledged. She'd been the brightest dancing star in the city until one day, mysteriously, she couldn't dance anymore. As far as Quinn could tell, Jane didn't have anything physically wrong with her; she just couldn't dance. Everyone knew it had to be a mirror, but no one ever mentioned or asked about it. It wasn't kind to ask about mirror deals gone wrong. But Quinn desperately wanted to know if her inability to dance was the cost of Jane's deal or the unintended consequence.

Did Jane know what she was giving up before she made the deal? Or was it a surprise?

Quinn sucked in a breath. She didn't want to become like her friend. She didn't want to regret her rite for the rest of her life—because after her rite, she never intended to make another mirror bargain ever again. The world was full of bad mirror deals, and Quinn had no intention of becoming yet another victim.

She shivered and clutched her necklace tight. "I'm fine."

Jane examined Quinn, and it was clear that she didn't believe it, but she decided not to push it. Instead, she changed the subject. "There is one more thing . . ." Jane's voice trailed off, and she glanced around the room hesitantly—nervously. In a whisper, she continued, "I was wondering if you might know anything about a Blood Mirror?"

Quinn's eyebrows crinkled. She knew about most bargainers, but she'd never heard of a Blood Mirror. But the name made it sound like something she'd prefer never to meet. Mirrors could not be trusted.

"I've never heard . . ." Quinn began, confusion twisting her words. "Why would you ask me?"

Jane ran her fingers through her hair, her eyes darting around the room as if she were afraid someone would overhear them. "It's just that your necklace—" She stopped mid-sentence when she caught Constance's eye. "Never mind, you wouldn't know."

Jane's red locks bounced as she shot one more hectic glance at Constance before turning on her heel and walking into a crowd of dancers.

"What was that about?" Constance asked, walking up to Quinn, her eyes following their mutual friend as she vanished into the bathroom.

"I have no idea." Quinn rolled her shoulders, trying to release both tension and confusion. "She asked me about a Blood Mirror."

"I've never heard of it, but it sounds like something to be avoided like the plague."

"Very true."

THREE

Dread was an aria pulsing through Quinn's stomach, the music notes stirring inside her and causing nausea to climb up her throat.

Her Mirror-Rite was upon her.

And now, with her four best friends in tow, she disembarked the Cable Car that brought her to the Spirit Sector—the quarter that housed her chosen mirror—and her torture. The Spirit Sector also housed the religious chapels, temples, and abbeys of the five major religions of New Swansea and was home to five infamous mirrors: Beautiful Decay, Midnight, Noon, Winter, and Skulls—although many other mirrors decked the streets.

As Quinn approached said mirrors, one burned with the rays of a dying star, and another one was so white she couldn't make out any image except a barrage of snow—an arctic tundra. The third frame was composed of sixty stacked skulls, and its surface showed mangled skeletons languishing under the liquid silver, hissing and calling Quinn's name.

The mirror's surface previewed the realm hidden within— some of the time. It all depended upon the mood of the creature trapped inside it. These mirrors were gilded prisons housing the most powerful deities in existence. Still, the only way for them to use their magic was to lure willing souls into their realms, and when the god was asleep or presumably not in the proper mood, the surface of the glass prison was merely reflective like a typical mirror. Hence, these deities became Mirror-Gods or Bargainers— most people interchanged the names when referencing them.

"I can't do this," Quinn said, but she didn't have a choice because her Mirror-Rite *had* to be completed.

Seven years of bad luck was no joke in New Swansea City. It was a place filled with grandeur and danger around every corner, and one did not test their luck here.

"Of course, you can," Giselle Reyes-Vega said, her chestnut brown hair bouncing and framing her dark olive skin. But of course, Giselle would say this. She barely worried about anything. One of her favorite pastimes was collecting, and her entire room at the Viridian—a courtesan club and cabaret—was riddled with trinkets from all over the city. Bells, clock hands, boxes, jewels, books, pillows, blankets, statues, and scrolls all glittered in messy piles around the room.

"We have all challenged a mirror and survived unscathed," Giselle amended, as though she noticed the mood was still sour.

Quinn's eyes instinctively traced to Jane, who very much had severe consequences from a mirror deal, and the attention didn't go unnoticed because Jane added, "I didn't get my consequences from my Mirror-Rite. I can't dance anymore because of a foolish bargain with the Looking Glass."

Fuck.

The entire group gasped, horrified. The Looking Glass—also known as the Mirror of Nightmares—was said to be the oldest and most powerful god in the entire country.

"Why the fuck would you ever bargain with him?" Jevon Yale asked, his eyes wide as he ran a hand through his unruly blond locks. He wore worry like a police badge over his ruffled single-breasted frock coat with a purple feathered pocket square. As usual, his state of dress left much to be desired, and his blond hair was a moppy mess. The man couldn't keep the wrinkles out of his clothing even if he wished for it upon a mirror. Yet there was still something dangerously handsome about him.

Something in his silent fidgeting and brooding made girls flock to his side.

Jane's resulting glower could turn someone to stone. "Do you think I would have done it if I had a choice?"

"Why wouldn't you have a choice?" Constance asked.

Jane crossed her arms. "Can we focus? This isn't about me. It's about Quinn's Mirror-Rite."

Yes, Quinn should be focusing on her own deal, but Jane had never before offered up so much information about her bad deal, and the entire group was fascinated and wanted to know more. Quinn had about fifteen questions she wanted to ask, but Jane's monstrous glower meant there was no more broaching that subject, so Quinn turned her focus back to her own task.

Anxiety twisted in her stomach as her eyes traced back to the Spirit Sector's mirrors.

Nope, nope, nope. Fucking nope. She was not doing this.

"We should just leave." Quinn's neck stiffened, suddenly aching. "Maybe I should accept the bad luck and move on with my life."

"You can't afford it," Jane said, rubbing at her temples. "You're going to be absolutely fine. I promise."

"Mirrors are evil. They try to make rotten deals all the time." Quinn's eyes shifted to Beautiful Decay, the second most vicious mirror in the city, just behind the Looking Glass. Its surface was flickering molten silver, and it moved like waves crashing in the ocean. Wisteria petals skated in the liquid like ice dancers during a performance, and belladonna flowers and thistles formed the frame. Beautiful yet deadly.

Beautiful Decay was known as one of the worst mirrors in

New Swansea. He made terrible deals and punished those who dared bargain with him with long-lasting and gruesome consequences.

There was a reason he was referred to as Poison.

Quinn rubbed her face and stepped toward the mirror she planned to challenge. Midnight. A purple galaxy shimmered underneath the glass, and lapis blue danced like the corps de ballet in Starlight Falls. The frame was made of swirling shadows and shooting stars. The Mirror of Midnight was one of the more harmless ones, speaking only in creepy, useless riddles and rarely harming anyone.

Sometimes, Quinn would watch the god talk with passersby on the street. Like a prison, the gods could communicate with the outside world, talking, luring, and doing their best to get people to enter their realm because the only way for them to make a deal was for a person to enter their mirror.

Midnight tried to talk to people on the street, but she wasn't very successful at it. People tended to avoid her. She was just *so* creepy.

"At least she's awake," Quinn said. Midnight also seemed to sleep far more than her counterparts.

"True," Jevon whispered as if afraid she'd overhear him. "It's strange how much she sleeps." He whispered because the mirrors could most likely overhear them, which was probably why they were so good at their deals.

All mirrors were tricksters, but some were worse than others.

"What if Midnight tricks me and traps her inside her surface forever?"

"She won't." Constance scrunched her nose. "It's true once you're inside the mirror, you're at its will, and it could trap you inside, but none of them do. If they did that, no one would ever come back to bargain with them."

"And for some reason, the mirrors need the bargains as much as we do," Giselle added.

Her friends' words made her feel better, but getting trapped was still a possibility.

The worst deal anyone could make was trading their soul with a mirror. It was so terrible that no one should ever do it, but desperate times made hundreds of people take desperate measures. The numbers were easy to track because each time someone traded their soul, a new mirror formed in Trapped Souls Row.

"You're going to be fine." Giselle clutched her friend's hand. "The Mirror-Gods won't hurt you because, again, no one would ever come back. It's why no one even trades with the Looking Glass anymore. He hurt too many people, and now no one dares to mess with him—except apparently Jane."

"Once again, I didn't have a choice." Jane crossed her arms.

"Anyway, my point stands," Giselle said. "No one trades with him either for the same reason." Giselle pointed to the Mirror of Beautiful Decay. They have consequences for their actions, too."

Quinn sucked in a breath, her hands shaking. The mirrors' magic only worked inside their mirrors and in deals. Meaning the only way a mirror could use magic—for or against her—was if she entered it or entered into an agreement. And Giselle was right. Most of the gods needed the bargains and wouldn't unwillingly trap someone inside. While their power seemed limitless, it wasn't. The Mirror-Gods were only powerful within their realms, and once a deal was made, the gods were bound to it. Quinn knew all of this, but she couldn't keep her heart from quaking and her mind from splintering. Because once a bargain was set, a mirror could bend the magic however they wanted, creating whatever costs they desired. Quinn said as much aloud.

"You'll be fine." Jevon swished an unruly blond lock out of his eyes. "They can't really bend the costs like that. It's more that they can trick you into a worse cost. Like for example, if someone made a deal to have enough money to feed their family and the person wasn't careful enough with their words, the cost might be that the mirror kills one of their children because it's one less mouth to feed, ergo, now they have enough money to feed their family."

"I don't think that example is helping, Jevon." Giselle shook her head.

It was a terrible reminder of how someone's deal could affect the ones they cared about and could bind more than just themselves to consequences.

"I guess it was a scary example." Jevon shrugged. "But it's not like Quinn is going to trade for eternal youth like that one boy who lost all his empathy to the mirror." Quinn stiffened, but Jevon didn't notice and continued, "She'll be fine. I've never met someone more careful."

"That's also not helpful either, Jevon." Constance scrunched her nose and glowered at him. "You are the worst at cheering her up."

Quinn gulped, and she clutched her necklace for comfort, taking another step toward Mirror of Midnight. If this deal were to happen, she needed to suck it up and jump head-first into danger.

But a frisson of fear rolled down her spine, and Quinn's heart stormed, so she clutched the nearest hand she could find.

It belonged to Jane. Her grip was sturdy and comforting.

To perform the rite, she needed to walk into the mirror, and Quinn didn't want any more time to think—to talk herself out of it. She was doing this to negate the bad luck. Doing it for her ballet auditions, and that was all she needed to think about. That was all that mattered.

Ballet.

Always ballet and only ballet.

Without another thought, Quinn stepped forward and touched the mirror.

It felt so cold it burned, so she ripped her hand away, and shock sank into her core. Her heart hammered like bourrée steps —quick and unrelenting, sweat dripping down her temple because her body was responding. And the panic gripped her so tight her lungs burned with the tension.

Jane's eyes stormed as she said, "I think this is a mistake. You're choosing poorly." Before Quinn could respond, Jane wrenched her into the *wrong* mirror.

Into one of the wickedest mirrors in all of New Swansea.

Beautiful Decay.

FOUR

Quinn sucked in a breath as the mirror portal's texture cascaded over her. The sensation felt like bathing in roses, almost as if a mixture of silk and velvet were caressing her naked skin. It was warm and inviting. Yet, she couldn't figure out if it calmed her nerves or made the experience more terrifying.

Because all that glitters isn't gold. Sometimes it's rotting flesh . . . or in this case, gilded wicked mirrors.

Stepping out of the barrier, Quinn fell onto a pile of wisteria petals, and with a huff, Jane landed beside her.

At least her friend was in this horrible realm, too.

Fucking mirrors.

Although, technically, Mirror-Rites were supposed to be done alone. But Quinn didn't know if that was a rule or a suggestion. Some things about the mirrors were so obvious, while others were infuriatingly vague.

"You shouldn't be here." Quinn rounded on Jane. "It's my Mirror-Rite."

"That's not a real rule," Jane said, grasping Quinn's arm. "You're going to be fine."

"Fine," Quinn whispered through gritted teeth. "This is Beautiful Decay."

A shiver crashed through Quinn's body as she took in the realm of the second most evil mirror in the city. It was a sea of color. A sunken garden, but not a real one. The hues were too bright and the foliage too pristine, lacking all imperfections. And the flowers . . . they created a tapestry of poison: lilies, oleander, wolfsbane, and nightshade danced in the morning breeze and sang a song of bewitching death.

It was funny how most beautiful things in nature were deadly. Kind of like how beautiful men were deadly—at least for Quinn's resolve not to *want* them—

Fucking magic spells. This place lured her into a calm, dream-like state and made her forget Jane's betrayal. Because once someone was in a mirror, the god had full control.

"What the fuck was that? Why did you do it?" Quinn rubbed her temples to calm herself down, but hurt still held up the scaffolding of her heart.

Jane held up her hands. "I'm sorry, but I couldn't let you bargain with Midnight. She accidentally causes permanent consequences."

"Are you out of your mind? Beautiful Decay is—" *evil.* Quinn said the last bit in her head, suddenly realizing that she probably shouldn't say it out loud where the god could hear her.

Jane visibly swallowed. "I know how it seems. Nightshade is known for cruel bargains, but he's my friend."

"A friend?" Quinn's voice pulsed with fascination and utter confusion. Humans weren't friends with mirrors. It just wasn't done. They were monsters, not drinking mates.

"Do you trust me?" Jane's tone was a plea.

Quinn hesitated. If Jane had asked that question a couple of minutes before, she would have said yes. She would have said she trusted Jane with her life. But now . . . she wasn't so sure.

"I swear he won't hurt or take advantage of you. He only

punishes the bad—the people willing to trade anything for selfish gains.”

“Coming from the person who made a deal with Nightmare, that’s *the* Looking Glass, Jane.” Quinn’s body was a thousand fractured fireflies buzzing and burning inside of her. “He’s responsible for everyone’s nightmares in the city.”

Thirty years ago, the Royalle House made a deal with the Looking Glass. The deal was simple: the mirror would power the city’s electrical grid, but the cost was nightmares—every person in the city would experience them, often nightly. Because the Royalle House represented everyone in the city, they could bind everyone to deals too.

“Nightmare not *as* bad as he seems either.” Quinn bit the inside of her lip as Jane continued, “I wouldn’t bring you in here if I thought you’d be harmed.”

Jane had lost it—completely.

Beautiful Decay *was danger incarnate*.

Everyone knew it. It was common knowledge that the sky was blue, rainbows followed the rain, and Beautiful Decay and Nightmare were never to be trusted.

Unwritten fact.

Jane wrung her hands, and her sleeves fell down her wrist, exposing the small intricate tattoo of a stemmed-looking glass on the outside of her right thumb. Another secret. A Mirror-Blessed tattoo. When someone traded for magical abilities, the tattoo was burned into their skin.

Trading for magic wasn’t forbidden, but it was seen as taboo. So taboo, in fact, that groups of non-magical humans hunted down the Mirror-Blessed for sport, torturing and killing them.

A metallic sensation coated Quinn’s mouth. It was like she tasted ash and smoke. She thought she knew Jane, but she’d never mentioned being Mirror-Blessed. Technically, Jane hadn’t lied about it, but she also hadn’t been truthful either. They were supposed to be best friends—*supposed* to be honest with each other.

Jevon and Constance were honest about their Mirror-Blessed tattoos that they covered with mirror cosmetics—makeup that erased any blemish. If someone had enough money, they could buy them. While expensive, the cosmetics didn't require a bargain from the wearer because once a mirror object was created, anyone could use it. Deep down, Quinn wondered if people who wore mirror cosmetics too often had unforeseen consequences like sunspots and wrinkles—faster aging. Mirrors were sick monsters. It would be just like them to create a product that forced a dependence upon it.

Had Jane used the cosmetics, too? Used them to hide secrets from her friends? With all these new developments, how much did Quinn truly know?

"This is going to be okay, I promise. I'd never do anything to hurt you." Jane wrung her hands and didn't instill the comfort she was trying to evoke.

Quinn gulped. None of this felt okay. "No, it won't," Quinn whispered, glancing around, trying to get her bearing.

They were in the center of a lawn with a sign that read, *No shoes on the grass.* Not wanting to anger the mirror minutes after entering its domain, she slid off her shoes and let the grass squish between her toes.

The garden smelled of sweet flowers and pure tranquility.

Butterflies pirouetted, and birdsong set a chipper and secure tone.

But was it a false feeling?

The hairs on Quinn's arms rose, and a regimental drum pounded in her ears. Her heart worked overtime, palpitating, and causing her breaths to grow short and tense.

This was foolish. Jane was insane. Absolutely insane. This place was a trap. Turning on her toes, Quinn frantically searched for the exit. Thankfully, a door—the one they'd entered through—hovered over the grass, waiting for her to leave. She ran toward it but halted abruptly.

A figure appeared on the path in front of her.

"Leaving already?" A sinister smirk rose on one of the most beautiful faces Quinn had ever seen. "We haven't even started yet. You don't want to ruin all the fun." *His fun*.

The Mirror-God raised a devilish eyebrow and crossed his muscular arms. Crow black hair shimmered in a ray of the rising sun, and his eyes swirled a liquid silver—the shade of a reflecting mirror. He wore black slacks and a white button-up shirt with the top three buttons hanging askew, exposing the top of his chest. His outfit lacked a vest, tailcoat, and cravat. It was utterly indecent for polite company.

The muscles in Quinn's back clenched, and she ground her teeth to keep herself from saying the wrong thing to the villain.

He didn't look evil, but sometimes evil came masked as pretty gentlemen.

Although he had unnatural eyes, the man appeared fully human. This wasn't so strange. The murals painted throughout the city depicted mirrors as living creatures with humanoid features. And all the ones she'd seen staring out of their glass seemed humanoid, too.

But it was still *unsettling*.

The mirror cocked his head, and his eyes examined her sideways, tracking from her red hair to her peacock dress and then landing on her green eyes. "Hello, Quinnevere Ashelle, a friend of Jane Whitfield-Wryte and the Daughter of Blood. I've been waiting for you."

Quinn swallowed hard, her hands growing clammy. What did that even mean? He had been waiting for her? That meant he knew she was coming, and if he knew that, what else could he know?

"I—" Quinn started but was distracted by her necklace. It buzzed. The shard of glass liquified into a flaring crimson metal that swirled to a legato rhythm. It was a ballerina twirling on attitude. As it pirouetted, it spilled out of its cage—

But as soon as it started to morph into something else, it froze, reversed, and solidified into a ruby, almost as if something had blocked its magic.

"I do not allow other magic in my domain." The mirror's voice slithered like an asp waiting to strike. He'd blocked the necklace from becoming . . . what exactly?

What the holy fuck was happening?

"Nightshade, stop scaring her." Jane folded her arms.

The god cocked his head like an eagle, amused but deadly.

Quinn's heart raged as she turned her eyes back on the male. "Is that your name?" All the Mirror-Gods in the city had titles like Beautiful Decay. But Quinn hadn't realized until now that they might have actual names, too.

The side of his lips turned up. "It's one of them." He turned back to Jane. "You will remain silent for the rest of our adventure."

It was a command, but was it magic?

Jane smirked. "As you wish, oh Terrifying One."

Nightshade glowered, clearly not amused. "Now, you." He angled his head, his gaze devouring Quinn like prey.

Snakes of shivers coiled over Quinn's arms and legs. She swallowed past the lump in her throat and glanced at the exit again. Now that she'd actually met him, she knew there was something very wrong with Nightshade—something that verged beyond sinister, and Quinn needed to get out now. She turned to do just that, but the mirror appeared in her way again.

"You've come here to avoid getting bad luck, so what do you want?" Nightshade asked.

Quinn's head felt hot and tight. She was way out of her depth. "How do you know that?"

"I am a god, little ballerina. The things I know would rattle your bones and rip apart your heart."

Okay, that was it. This was a terrible mistake, and Jane was unhinged. "I think I should leave now."

A muscle in his jaw feathered. "If you leave now, you will

incur the seven years of bad luck, and you and I both know that you wouldn't make it into the ballet if that happened."

Quinn's lungs burned. She didn't want to follow in her uncle's footsteps as a medical examiner. She liked corpses because they didn't talk back, because they had no emotions, and because they were simple and scientific, but she didn't like them that much. She loved science and medicine, but her *life was dance*.

"Fine." Quinn gritted her teeth and sucked in a breath. "What do you offer?"

"What do you want?"

She wanted to trade for a spot in the Queen's Royalle Ballet but imagined the cost would be far too much, especially from Nightshade. She wanted to dance, but she also didn't want life-long consequences from it, like diamond eyes or frozen hair—like the infamous Harlowe Merriwether. "Aren't you going to offer to make my dreams come true? To give me unending beauty or eyes that make everyone fall in love with me or a life filled with no pain or wealth that won't dry up or magic or something?"

A wicked sneer climbed up his face. "I could give you all those things, but why would I offer you any of that when I know you wouldn't accept it?" He cracked his neck almost as if irritated with how much of his time she was wasting. "You've come here, so what do *you* want?"

Quinn curled her toes in the grass, trying to ground herself, and she asked a question instead of answering his. "Is Jane truly your friend?"

"Yes."

"She pulled me in here so I wouldn't get horrible consequences."

Jane opened her mouth to respond, but Nightshade narrowed his eyes at her, and she closed her mouth.

"Interesting. That would depend on how well you can bargain." Nightshade's answer was a slither, like a snake homing in on its prey. The words were friendly enough, but the tone promised poison. "What is it you want?"

She didn't know what to say or what she desired other than to get this horrible rite over with.

"What do you want?" he asked again, spinning his words into an enchantment that latched onto Quinn's soul.

It was like he reached out and grasped at her deepest desires. "I want to have emotional expression in my dancing, but I am not willing to pay the cost and the consequences for that." She crossed her arms protectively over her chest.

Nightshade rubbed his chin in thought while glaring at her. His concentration was so fierce, like a visceral pulsating thing, that she refused to move or speak a word to interrupt it.

Eventually, he said, "Here is the only deal I will offer you. I will give you the ability to express emotion in dance. I will give you such incredible artistry that no one can look away—even better than Jane once had—if and only if you passionately kiss the prince you despise so much before the stroke of midnight."

"Nightshade, what are you doing?" Jane cut in, her eyebrows crinkling.

"Quiet, Red," the god growled.

Jane threw her hands up in mock surrender but said under her breath, "I thought you two had settled your issues."

Issues? With Emrys? Why?

"Anyway, Quinnevere"—Nightshade's voice was rough whiskey—"kiss the prince with passion, and I will give you everything you want."

"I can't kiss Emrys," Quinn gasped out.

"And yet, it is the only deal I will make with you." His grin sharpened like the edge of a broadsword. "Take the deal or receive seven years of bad luck."

"Why would you ask this of me?" Quinn shivered. "What do you get out of it?"

"Torture." A sneer twinkled in Nightshade's eyes. "I know you hate him above all others for making you look like a fool to your medical superiors."

How the fuck did he know that? Mirrors were horribly creepy. Quinn shivered.

"I want to torture you a little bit." Nightshade smiled. "And I want a fun show for me—being trapped in this glorious cage can get rather boring."

Could mirrors see beyond their portals? That was terrifying. Perhaps they were truly gods watching over the city, ever-present, always knowing.

That was a wretched thought. Gods or devils?

"I think you may enjoy your torture, my sweet, innocent Quinnevere Ashelle."

Never. She'd never enjoy that. Kissing Emrys would be more than torture. It was embarrassment and devastation wrapped up in one little bow because the prince had never met a heart he didn't break, and Quinn refused to be just another girl on his long list of conquests. Not that she'd ever let him close enough to break her heart.

Yes, what Nightshade was asking of her was pure torture. But that was the point. Some mirrors just liked to watch the world burn. Clearly, Nightshade was one of them.

"And if I fail your task?" Quinn stuttered, her voice quivering. "What happens then?"

"If you fail, you don't reap the rewards of our deal."

"And the consequences?"

"Kiss him passionately, and I won't give you any—"

"Nope," Jane interrupted, "this is where I step in. He can't promise you that because it is not the Bargainers who determine mirror consequences."

Clearly, his command of her silence earlier was merely a suggestion.

Nightshade rounded on Jane. "For the love of all the gods. Stop giving our secrets away. The Looking Glass should know better than that."

Jane scoffed. "While he has told me that, it was your lover who told me it first. If you want your secrets kept, speak with

Lowe about them."

As much as Quinn was fascinated by their interaction and its implications, there were more important things to focus on. "Who determines the consequences?"

"The magic," Jane said. "Whatever force exists beyond us, that is greater than the mirrors. The cost is upfront. It is determined during the deal by the god." She pointed with her thumb at Nightshade. "The consequences are unknown, and it is possible to get none or horrible ones."

Oh, that was fascinating and petrifying all at once. "So how do I avoid having horrible consequences or visible ones like Harlowe Merriwether?"

Harlowe Merriwether was the most famous Mirror-Blessed person in all of New Swansea—infamous for being addicted to mirror bargains and having physical and life-altering consequences. It was rumored that she even disappeared for seven minutes every hour without warning.

At the mention of Harlowe's name, Nightshade's eyes darkened, but it was Jane who cut in. "A lot of her consequences were costs that she knew about before making her deal, and she trades for powerful magic. That always carries harsher consequences." Jane touched the god's arm as if calming him. "What Nightshade is offering won't carry that kind of consequence."

All of that was a lot to take in. The entire night was too much to take in.

"Will you stop helping her now?" Nightshade pulled out of Jane's grip.

"She's family to me," Jane said. "You know better than anyone else. We *always* help family."

Warmth spread in Quinn's chest. *Family?* Was that how Jane truly saw it? Both were orphans, and to Quinn's knowledge, Jane didn't have any family left alive, while Quinn had her uncle. Although, people often confused them as sisters because they both had red hair and light-colored eyes. Jane's were a brilliant blue, and Quinn's a hazel green. But they weren't actually sisters.

Yet when Quinn was younger, she had wished it. She'd wanted more than anything for the confusion to be true.

But people didn't often get what they wanted in life.

"Fine." Nightshade gritted his teeth. "Back to your deal. Do you have any questions before you accept it? So we can stop pretending? We all know you will accept the deal."

A snake coiled in Quinn's stomach. It wasn't a foregone conclusion, and she hated that he thought it was.

"I could leave and not make any deal at all."

"Then you would get the bad luck."

"I know stubbornness is a trait of redheaded ballerinas, but if we could just get this done, I have places to be."

"Stuck inside a mirror?"

"You've seen my realm." He motioned to everything around them. "Maybe I want to frolic through the fields."

Now, he was being a condescending prick like Emrys. But if he wanted to get rid of her, that was a good thing because it meant he wouldn't trap her inside his realm.

So Quinn decided to move on, let it go, and focus on the implications of the possible deal. "What if I can't kiss the prince with passion?"

"Then I assume it will be a very disappointing kiss."

Jane snorted, and both the god and Quinn flashed her a glare.

All the possible outcomes and potential issues with the bargain filtered through Quinn's head. It was torture. The cost was unimaginably cruel. But if she accepted the deal, even if she failed to kiss Emrys passionately, she wouldn't get the bad luck. If she succeeded, she would have the key to her auditions. Besides being extremely painful, it seemed like a win-win for her. So then, what was the catch? She voiced the question out loud.

"There is no catch." He ran a hand down his face as if he were exhausted by her. "You're Jane's family. I will give you a good deal. Kiss the gentleman, and you will get your artistry. Fail, and you incur whatever consequences the magic has for you."

Quinn inhaled sharply. It was foolish to trust a mirror, especially Beautiful Decay. But she wanted to trust Jane, and Jane trusted this strange Bargainer. Quinn ran logic loops in her head, tracing all the possibilities and traps in his words. But it seemed straightforward. Besides, the alternative was seven years of bad luck, which just couldn't happen.

She nodded again and said, "I accept your deal."

"Wonderful." He clapped his hands. "Oh, and remember, dearest Quinnevere. If you don't at least try to kiss Emrys, you will receive seven years of bad luck. Trust me, your life is about to fall apart, and you probably won't survive it, even with good luck."

FIVE

"All aboard," the cable car conductor yelled at the Spirit Sector Cable Car Station.

A daze had settled over Quinn's mind, and she wasn't even sure where Jane had led her after they'd left the mirror. She'd accepted the deal, but instant foreboding filled her blood. Had she been tricked? Nightshade said, *your life is about to fall apart, and you probably won't survive it with good luck, let alone bad luck.*

Did he give her terrible consequences, or did he simply foresee the future and warn her? No one truly knew how mirror bargains worked, and Nightshade was the worst among them. But maddeningly, it was unclear whether he was helping or hurting.

Yet somehow, he was Jane's friend.

"All aboard," the cable car conductor yelled again. "On or off, but we are leaving."

Leaving. Quinn blinked, and the world returned to focus on the cable car in front of her.

"We can't leave. Giselle hasn't come back yet," Jevon Yale said, his eyes wild and worried. "She went to buy machinery parts while we waited, but she's not back."

"The next car comes in thirty minutes," the conductor informed them. "Either you get on now, or you wait or walk."

Fuck. They had to get on the cable car now. Quinn had to kiss Emrys by midnight. Fuck. Why did she agree to that?

"We need to leave," Jane said as she slid onto the cable car's redwood bench. "Quinn has a deal to accomplish, and I have to get the Viridian and meet Emrys to—" Jane swallowed, cutting herself off. "Giselle will catch up to us."

"Wait." Quinn rounded on Jane. "Why are you meeting with Emrys? Is it about my deal?"

Jane's eyes caught on the row of mirrors they'd just left but then turned back to Quinn. "No, I need to talk to Prince about Castle Hill business. It's really just silly matters about ballet studios and other nonsense."

"This conversation can wait. We need to get on the cable car," Constance said, grasping Quinn's wrist and pulling her into the car.

"But Giselle's *so late*," Jevon whispered.

Constance shrugged, making her way to the far back of the car, perching on the side of the rail.

The conductor signaled the gripman with one bell, and they began moving. Gears clicked into place, and the car glided up the massive hill on Passion Avenue—the street leading to the Passion District. New Swansea was a city of hills, cliffs, and dense fog. A sparkling azure bay encased the city on three sides, and cable cars and flying gondolas twinkled across the city like soaring diamonds.

Quinn swallowed and tried to focus on the Giselle problem and not her pending kiss or possible mirror consequences.

"The car is moving," Jevon said as he tapped his fingers on his vest. "And Giselle isn't here."

"Just wait. I promise she will miraculously appear." Jane folded her hands in her lap and leaned back into her seat, playing with the feathers on her dress.

Giselle was always late. It was an affliction at this point. Even with a wristwatch, a pocket watch, and a radio in her room, the girl never managed to show up on time. Only a miracle caused her to be early.

"How long do you think it will take her to catch up—" Jevon stopped as a shout pierced the air.

"Wait." It was Giselle, skirts billowing as she ran in the car's wake. "Wait."

"Stop the car." Constance glared at the conductor.

"I am sorry, mistress," the conductor said. "I cannot stop the car until a scheduled stop."

"I bet two sienna's that she will try and jump." Quinn stuck her head out and watched as Giselle stormed after the car.

A mischievous expression painted across Jevon's ivory cheeks. His worry finally settled. "That would be a silly bet to take."

"Indeed," Quinn agreed. She folded her arms and sat back as Giselle sped up and prepared to jump. Quinn might've been concerned if she hadn't seen Giselle pull off far more dangerous stunts on numerous occasions. Giselle performed with the acrobats and tightrope walkers at the Viridian Club just for the thrill of it. She had an addiction to adrenaline.

And just as predicted, with a strange grace, Giselle grand-jetéd and launched into the air before her fingers gripped the handrail. Graceful and skilled as always. But unfortunately, a rip sounded as she pulled herself into the cable car.

"Ugh, nearly perfect execution." Giselle's golden-brown eyes swooped over her torn crimson skirt as a bead of sweat dripped down her dark olive cheeks. "And this dress was so beautiful." She groaned as she dropped into the spot next to Quinn.

"You're late," Quinn said, not to shame her friend but to kindly remind her of the importance of timeliness—a constant argument between the girls.

"I might always be late, but at least I always show up." A warm smile crossed Giselle's lips. This was her typical response to the endless perfectionism.

Quinn sighed and returned the smile.

The girls were opposites in nearly every way, yet they fundamentally understood each other.

"Giselle, I am impressed with how fast you ran." Constance's voice was laced with snake venom mixed with chocolate macarons. Sweet and vicious. But she picked nonchalantly at the embroidered micro-sequins adorning her iridescent silver silk dress. The combination of expressions was striking in their discrepancy. But that was Constance. Hot and cold.

"Just because I'm not a ballerina like you three doesn't mean I don't have skills." Giselle motioned to the other girls. "Or were you implying that I shouldn't be able to run with all my extra curves? Because I am fat?"

Constance and Giselle's relationship was confusing. At one moment, they were the best of friends, and at other moments, they were entirely at odds. The tension usually came when Constance was in one of her more hyper moods because, in those moments, they were far too similar. Constance had two moods: energetic or brooding.

"I am pretty sure she meant nothing like that. She was just trying to compliment you," Jevon said.

"I am an asshole, but I'm not that big of one." Constance rolled her eyes. "I was merely saying I was impressed because it was fast. I don't even like running at all."

Quinn sighed and ignored her friends. They argued like this all the time. Instead, out of a hidden pocket in her dress, she pulled a small first aid kit, which doubled as a sewing kit.

If Quinn could keep her mind and fingers busy, it would distract from the anxiety settling in her bones. So she motioned to Giselle, who slid the torn part of her skirt over.

"I'll read while you work then." Giselle pulled out a small book from her cleavage and began to read. If Giselle could manage it, she would bring a library everywhere she went. Knowledge was her power.

"What are you reading?" Quinn asked as she used a tricot stitch to meticulously repair the silk.

"A book on the old vampire gods that I *borrowed* from the Grand Library," Giselle said, turning the page, her nose deep inside the tome.

At the word *vampire*, everyone reacted. Jane stared vacantly forward with her fingers steepled beneath her chin. Horror dashed across Jevon's cheeks, and Constance sat up straighter, leaning in but also trying to lace a disinterested expression on her face so as not to show Giselle she actually cared.

The girls were rivals in nearly every way, yet somehow, they still liked each other—or they pretended to like each other in Quinn's presence. It made for some interesting moments.

"And have you read anything interesting in your stolen book?" Constance asked.

"It's mostly *borrowed . . .*" Giselle paused her reading to shoot Constance a look so icy it could sink the RMS *Colossal.*

Quinn laughed and then said sarcastically, "Borrowed like all the other library books you will eventually give back?"

"Precisely."

"I don't get you at all," Constance said. "You're a daughter of a Countess—or so you say—and you don't need to *steal* them. You could buy them."

Giselle was a lady and extremely rich, but she refused to tell her parents' last names. She even took on a fake last name to hide their identities because she was so ashamed of them. After her father was sentenced to prison for murdering someone, she never talked about him again. And she hated her mother for unknown reasons.

"I barely do anything because I *need* to. Besides, who doesn't *keep* library books?" Giselle's nose flared. "Anyway, do you want to hear about my book or not?"

"Eh, not particularly, no." Constance wiggled an eyebrow.

"Well then, I shall definitely tell you now." Giselle's ruby lips rose into a wicked smile. "I was reading a story about the Bloody Countess . . ."

"Oh, fucking mirrors," Constance cursed under her breath.

"Now, you've started it," Jevon added in.

"A vampire who used to prey on men." Giselle ignored them and continued, "She bled them dry and hung them from gentleman's clubs in horrendous positions. She loved to use stakes. Many, many stakes."

A shiver crawled down Quinn's spine at the words, and she absentmindedly stroked a finger along her forearm, tracing the bleeding painting that was inked into her skin. Quinn performed many autopsies, but some things were even gruesome enough to churn her stomach. "Well, that's a bit of light reading."

"Did it give a reason for the murders?" Constance asked, a trill of excitement pouring from her tongue.

"Is there ever a good reason for murder?" Jane wrinkled her nose.

Constance shrugged and clicked her heels, flashing a naughty grin. "I could think of a couple."

Jevon let out a low laugh.

"Like wha—" Giselle's voice trailed off as ghostly screams pierced through the night fog.

The cable car approached Trapped Souls Row.

Quinn's stomach dropped. They represented the worst future imaginable. The worst mirror costs.

And it only served to remind Quinn of her deal and the future she had awaiting her if it soured. She wouldn't be turned into a mirror, but there were other terrible consequences.

Fuck.

This car needed to hurry because Quinn had a prince to seduce. *Fuck, fuck, fuck.*

She was far outmatched because not only was Quinn a virgin —dance and dead bodies took up too much of her time to lure and fuck men—but she had also never been kissed. At twenty-three. Again, not for any other reason than being far too busy.

But now, Quinn was beginning to believe she might be missing something. She'd pleasured herself, and she was adequate at it. But all her friends had many partners and experiences she never had.

Fuck, Giselle had nearly fucked an entire baseball team at this point, sleeping with a new man every week. It was unclear if she was a courtesan or just simply bored. Either could be equally true, and she had no shame for any of it—nor should she. But sex wasn't something the girls discussed.

Quinn wished she could be that free with passion, but that wasn't how she was made. Quinn wasn't free with anything. She was an uptight nightmare.

A scream cut through the night, and Quinn jumped.

One of the mirrors of Trapped Souls Row let out a banshee call and pulled Quinn back into the moment, her eyes falling on the haunted things. Some were screaming, some were frozen in slumber, and others waved sadistically, their eyes tracing Quinn like chalk lining a crime scene. Some even banged on the glass and begged to be set free.

Unlike the other mirrors of New Swansea, these ones decayed. Their metal rusted and crumbled at the seams. Moss grew along the rock walls and snaked up through the cracks like the tentacles of an octopus. They were so different from other mirrors that they were housed in an equally sinister part of the city, where no one dared enter. They were the entrance to the Ruins, a place covered in twisted shadows that resisted the light from the sun.

A place reserved only for ghosts.

If someone wanted to enter the Ruins—which no one would —they would have to walk through Trapped Souls Row.

Quinn looked away from the tormented place.

She didn't want to feel for these people because if she let it in, a flood of all her unfelt emotions would be set free. And that couldn't happen. *Ever.* It was far better to be in control—far better to avoid emotions and focus on something else.

Quinn tried to do this by sewing Giselle's skirt, but she just couldn't drown them out.

"Quinny, your necklace is . . . glowing." Constance pointed, and in her umber eyes, a glowing red light reflected.

Quinn lowered her chin and took in her necklace. Inside the iron casing, the shard of glass liquified into a flaring crimson metal that swirled to a legato rhythm. It was a ballerina jumping and dancing.

Shock rattled through her core. It was the second time the necklace had come alive. But it shouldn't happen. It was a shard of a dead mirror, and Quinn only kept it because it reminded her of her parents—of the life they would never have together.

What was going on? She rubbed her temples and glanced up at the Ruins and trapped souls. There was something about this place or these souls that spoke to the necklace. Something that revived it.

Like it had been during the rite.

She'd passed Trapped Soul Row hundreds of times, so why come to life now?

Was it because of the rite? Had something changed the necklace when they were inside Nightshade's realm?

Lost in her thoughts, Quinn didn't notice when Jane reached out and touched the necklace until it was too late. The other redhead jumped back and nearly fell out of the car and would have if Constance hadn't grabbed her dress, catching her.

"It burnt me," Jane breathed and stared at a coined-sized burn in the center of her palm.

Jane's expression sparked with recognition, and it was almost like her thoughts twirled in her eyes like a scene playing out on a stage. Quinn had no idea what her friend was thinking, but it was clear that the necklace coming to life meant something. And it became even more clear when Jane whispered, "So it's true."

"What's true?" Quinn asked, protectively pulling away from her friend.

Jane's hand fell into her lap. "What?" she asked as if coming out of a daze.

"You said it's true while staring at my necklace." Quinn

gripped the jewelry in between her fingers, the lattice cage digging into her flesh.

Jane bit her lip, and instead of answering the question, she said, "Did you get the mirror shard when your parents died?"

A strike of lightning surged through Quinn's core. There was no way anyone should've known that. She was the only person to survive the murders—murders that included a mirror.

Her fingers tightened further around the necklace as she contemplated telling the truth. "I—" Quinn started, realizing she'd been silent too long. She blew out a breath and finally chose to share this piece of her soul with someone else. "Yes," Quinn breathed.

"But that's not possible. When a mirror breaks, the pieces shatter and dissolve into nothing, leaving a mirror stain in its place." Jevon rubbed his hand and stared at her like he was trying to solve an impossible math equation.

Quinn sucked in a breath and swallowed down her emotions —deep down, never to see the light of day. She wouldn't allow what she was about to say to affect her. "When I was four years old, my parents were murdered in front of a mirror. They were in the wrong place at the wrong time. But when they died, the murderer shattered the mirror, and I grasped a sliver and hid. By the time I came out of my hiding spot, the shattered glass had dissolved. All except the shard in my hand. I don't know why it stayed. I barely know anything about that night at all. My memory is split into pieces. I don't really even remember my family or anything that happened before that moment."

Constance and Jevon's eyes met, and Quinn couldn't quite decipher what emotion was shared between them—if it was horror, curiosity, or empathy.

"I think they were guarding a Blood Mirror," Jane whispered to her lap, wringing her hands. "Which means it's a piece. Maybe it could find the thir—" she cut herself off, and her eyes darted over her shoulder. She stiffened, suddenly noticing her other friends hanging off her every word.

"Jane, are you okay?" Giselle asked, sliding her book into her corset.

"Yes, sorry." Jane flashed a false smile, squeezing Quinn's hand. "It's nothing. I was just surprised by the necklace moving. That's all."

Silence cascaded over them like a tidal wave, and the five of them sat huddled yet separately.

Quinn's thoughts turned back to her parents as she stared at the necklace.

She never talked about her parents. Ever. Preferring to pretend the murders never happened, but it didn't work. She heard their screams in her dreams and saw blood pooling on the floor—too much blood.

She cracked her neck and stared down at her fingers. She still hadn't finished fixing Giselle's skirt. Picking up the needle and thread, Quinn continued and tried to the best of her ability to erase her spiraling thoughts and emotions. It all just needed to go away.

When they had finally passed the Soul Mirror Way, her necklace stopped glowing and settled back into its original form, and a trickle of terror coiled in Quinn's stomach. The necklace never acted like this, and it was deeply unsettling.

Everything was falling apart, and Quinn had a sinking feeling that it was all about to get so much worse.

Six

The Viridian's grand ballroom pulsed with magic and possibility as Constance pulled Quinn by the arm into the festivities and closer to her dreaded deal—closer to midnight too. Jane said Emrys would be at the Viridian tonight, so if Quinn were going to kiss him, it would have to be in the infamous nightclub before or after Jane's meeting. Why Jane was meeting with the prince was just another mystery that needed to be solved.

But not now, because the mere thought of kissing caused an anchor to drop in her stomach. Everyone Quinn knew was *experienced* except her. Constance and Giselle both lived in a burlesque club and courtesan den—although from what Quinn had gathered, neither of them partook in that particular profession. Regardless, Giselle had a new *man* weekly, if not nightly. And Constance was more than skilled in the art of seduction. Even messy, clumsy Jevon fucked new women all the time.

All of Quinn's friends partied and truly *lived* while she was too busy dancing and working.

Now, she feared she was getting too old to be so sheltered.

Granted, Quinn had probably seen more penises in her life than any of her friends. But dead penises didn't really count. She'd even seen a broken penis once, but again, it didn't count—

except to be utterly scarring. Because Quinn had never used any . . . or touched them outside of a medical lab.

And the kisses she'd had in the ballet were pecks—for show. None of her experiences would help her seduce the Playboy Prince and kiss him passionately.

Fuck Nightshade. He'd set her up to fail. Kissing Emrys Avalon was madness. It was torture—and Nightshade knew it. He'd said as much, and that's why he chose it.

"You look worried," Constance said, pulling Quinn and their friends out of the rush of people. "Is it about kissing the prince?"

"Of course it is." Quinn's voice quivered. "I don't have any real experience."

"You don't really need experience. Emrys will do most of the work for you." Constance winked. "I'm sure it would be his ultimate pleasure."

Quinn groaned. She, too, was certain he'd love to kiss her. The man was known as one of the biggest rogues in New Swansea, but Quinn would still need to corner him and put the idea in his mind, and that wouldn't be easy.

"If it's possible, her face just got redder," Jevon fake whispered to Giselle, who stifled a giggle.

"You're going to be fine," Giselle said with a hand muffling her face.

"Yes, you will," Constance added. "He's been practicing for ages. I'm sure he's even deflowered a virgin or two. You'll be in great hands."

"Ages?"

"It's a metaphor, Quinn," Constance shook her head. "And of all of the rogues I *know*, he's probably the most skilled and patient."

Know. The way she said *know* . . . "Did he deflower—" Ugh, no, that was a ridiculous word. "Have you fucked him?"

"No, and yes."

Before Quinn could get any more answers to that fascinating

riddle, a group of young revelers pushed in between them. Terrible timing.

"Don't be so glum," Constance yelled over the crowd. "It's your birthday. Enjoy the splendor. It will be fun to lose yourself to handsome, handsy gentlemen."

"Handsy gentlemen?" Quinn's heart stumbled. She truly hoped Emrys wouldn't be handsy . . . or did she? Fuck. Maybe it was the night to experiment and learn.

Fuck. Quinn didn't know. It was all too confusing. Trying not to show her fear . . . again, Quinn played along with Constance, saying, "I am pretty sure the words handsy and gentlemen do not go together."

"Oh, I think they go perfectly together." Constance winked.

Jane's lips drew up at the corner. "Oh, they do."

"See, even our serious, boring friend knows how wonderful hands can be used in the proper ways."

So, Constance was in one of those moods. The girl's spirits flipped on a sienna coin. She would sometimes be elevated, talkative, and reckless, and other times, she would brood like the long-extinct vampires. A coin, once tossed, no one knew which side they'd get. The calm, rational, and relatable side or the crazy, fun, reckless side.

What was strange about tonight was that the Viridian usually placed her in a rotten mood.

In fact, Quinn couldn't remember the last time Constance was chipper at the club.

It might've had something to do with the cost of the Viridian's illusions—performance. Kordelia, the owner of the Viridian, made a deal with a mirror to create the club, and now those inside the club were bound by that deal. As long as the Viridian dancers, singers, and acrobats performed, the mirror created a world of intrigue and fantasy where everything was a game designed to induce pleasure. The unforeseen consequence of the Viridian deal was that the performers could never stop. Someone had to be on stage *always*. And Quinn was also pretty sure the building messed with people's memories—erasing them, warping them, and consuming them.

Constance was particularly susceptible to the club's effect.

Anxiety bubbled in Quinn's belly, so she tried to focus on the living, breathing nightclub. The Viridian was one of the seventeen sentient structures in the city, with walls that cried when they were upset and rooms that morphed of their own accord. And it had a personality. It was vain, like a bird prancing and preening.

The theme of the club revolved around peacocks—beautiful, ostentatious, and rich. It embraced the definition of exuberance and pride. Tonight, everything in the grand ballroom sparkled with enchantment—a viridian watercolor, blending, dancing, and breathing life into the room. The ceiling twinkled like the night sky. Fairy lights mixed with strands of white feathers that fanned out across the ceiling, forming a peacock's tail. Even the building's roof was themed with two massive peacock statues—with their feathers spread down the side of the building like a windmill's rungs—that could be seen across the city.

And even those peacocks moved with a glamour and looked alive. Everything in the place danced.

"Jevon darling, go get us some drinks." Constance snapped her fingers, and Jevon flashed a glower so deep and dark that the Obsidian Canyon would be jealous.

"Yes, princess," he mumbled under his breath and shrugged, flashing a helpless grin before walking away.

Constance was a star, and she liked planets to orbit around her. And Jevon, by far, was the most subservient planet. Quinn sometimes complied, and Giselle very rarely did, which was why the two had underlying tensions. But in many ways, Constance was the sun of the group because she was the one who introduced them. She met Quinn and Jane in ballet, knew Jevon from primary school and Giselle from her work at the Viridian.

Constance was the group's connective tissue.

"Wonderful." She clapped. "I'll be right back. Giselle, Jane, I assume you can watch after the birthday girl and make sure she gets into loads of trouble while we're gone?" Constance didn't wait for an answer before she disappeared into the crowd.

"I can manage trouble." Giselle grinned, the smile so devious it painted sinful red blossoms across her bronze cheeks.

Quinn groaned. Not Giselle, too. *Traitors, the lot of them.*

"Want to find a spot to watch the performance?" Giselle asked.

Not really. Quinn wanted to find the prince, lure him into a dark corner, and quickly kiss him. All of which would fundamentally ruin her birthday and every interaction with him in the future. Not like it would change their dynamic because every interaction she'd ever had with him was pure torture. But after kissing him, she'd never be able to go to a murder briefing again—at least not without turning bright scarlet.

When she didn't respond, Giselle grasped Quinn's hand and dragged her through the crowd, a couple of people elbowing them as they went.

Not fully watching her steps, Quinn accidentally ran straight into a guest in a dark charcoal suit as Giselle's hand slipped out of hers.

"Sorry, I didn't mean—" she started but stopped when she saw who she'd hit.

Emrys Avalon.

Well, fuck. She had been looking for him, but she hadn't meant to find him *this* soon. Her mind went blank, and all the sound emptied from the room because now her entire attention was focused on the rotten nerves tangled in her stomach.

Nope, she couldn't do this.

Running away was the far better option, right?

"Hello, Ginger." He raised an eyebrow as the corner of his lips twitched.

The raven-haired Emrys Avalon was dressed to the nines in a pinstriped suit with silk lapels that looked to be weaved from spider silk. He dressed like a gangster, terrifying yet alluring, and power radiated from his skin like an aura of magic.

Hanging off one arm was the beautiful and flirty Countess Teagan Atwater. The girl's walnut hair lay in perfect finger waves adorned with a feather and pearled headband. Her dress fell to her calves, the fringe composed of beads and pearls. The dress probably cost over one thousand siennas. On his other arm was the current prima ballerina of the Queen's Royalle Ballet and one of the biggest celebrities in the country, Nia Cross. Where the countess was hard edges and scrutiny, the dancer was soft lines and compassion. Her midnight hair was tightly braided and laced around a ruby headband that perfectly complemented her umber skin's jeweled undertones. She was dazzling and embodied grace.

Quinn swallowed, and anxiety bubbled in her stomach. Emrys, surrounded by his paramours, never boded well.

How was she to seduce him and steal a passionate kiss while he was dripping with accomplished women? Quinn could never measure up to that.

So, running. Yes, that was the far better solution.

Glancing around, Quinn searched for her friends for help, but they had already traveled on without her, leaving her to face these demons alone.

The countess waved down a waiter and ordered a cocktail before turning her attention back to the obstacle in front of her, glaring. Her eyes searched Quinn from her toes to the tight corset of her green gown. A disgusted expression flashed across Teagan's face but was quickly covered up with a sensual tilt of her lips. "I see the trash dressed up tonight. Who did you steal your frock from?"

Quinn clenched her teeth and smiled through a breath, nervously glancing down at Teagan's dress. Feathers dripped from the bodice like dried wax, falling down the skirt like teardrops. It was beautiful and looked expensive.

The aristocracy always turned their noses down on the lower classes. The titled and rich generally had enough money and privilege to avoid the Bargainers and were never desperate enough to make costly deals, yet they still benefited from them.

As a medical examiner, Quinn was considered part of the working class, but as soon as she made it into the Queen's Royalle Ballet, she would join the highest ranks of society. New Swansea's currency was fame and fortune. And the most revered groups in the city were ballerinas and silent movie stars. The aristocracy were only figureheads, and their only real power rested in their titles and wealth. But as the century turned, a lot of their wealth was draining, and the business tycoons were taking over.

Emrys, of course, had both fame and fortune, placing him squarely at the top of society.

"You look dazzling tonight, Quinnevere," the prince said with a velvet-smooth voice.

The countess suppressed a snort.

Quinn stilled. It was unclear if he was making fun of her, too. He had the ability to make his insults appear as compliments.

"I—" Quinn started, trying to figure out the right words to escape the situation. She needed to regroup and figure out how to trap him alone . . . preferably where no one would see them.

"Are you enjoying your birthday?" Emrys's gaze cut into her with the intensity of an earthquake.

Quinn's throat tightened. How the fuck did he know that? She tried her best to hide it from her friends, let alone the people she disliked the most in the world. "It is unsettling that you know that, Emrys."

"What?" He shrugged. "I keep tabs on all my enemies." A playful smile danced on his lips, but a chill slid down her spine. "Still . . . it's your twenty-third. *The big year.* Are you going to perform the rite?"

Yes, and now I have to seduce you.

"I—" Oh, Quinn needed to get away as soon as possible. She was falling apart. Words weren't even coming to her anymore. Taking a big breath, she glanced around the room, looking for an excuse, anything to escape. "Oh, look . . ." She pointed into the crowd. "Jane. I must go."

"Miss Ashelle." Emrys nodded his head with respect. Quinn nodded back before darting into a group of festive people.

Fuck. Fuck. Fuck. That went as terribly as she could have possibly imagined. She wanted to drown in a frozen lake. *Oh, mirrors, you're pathetic, Quinn. You can't even talk to the prince, let alone kiss him.*

As if adding to her misery, the clock struck eleven. *One hour.* Shit.

But she needed to regroup and get her friends. It didn't take long for her to find them on a ledge. They usually watched the shows in one of two places. A private booth or the ledges surrounding the room.

"Constance said to get you in trouble, but I define engineering as trouble. I know she wouldn't approve, but then she shouldn't have left you in my hands." From out of Giselle's dress pocket, she pulled out a camera.

Quinn laughed. "Is this one of your new inventions?"

"Yes, it's a camera with a portable darkroom, and it worked the other day," Giselle said. "I want to test it again tonight, but it's definitely better than what a mirror could create."

Giselle didn't like mirror deals for technology because they always left humans far more reliant and beholden to them. She much preferred to make her own things.

"It truly worked?" Quinn sat up a little straighter. Giselle was known for her inventions not fully working as intended.

"Well . . . It mostly works." Giselle took a picture and showed Quinn. After a couple of minutes, a distorted picture printed out from the bottom of the camera. "See, it's not perfect, but it works."

"It's amazing, G."

Their conversation was cut off because the lights grew dim, and the dance floor cleared of patrons. With a loud pop and an explosion of blue fire, the show began, and dancers gilded in, feathers grazing the floor. Quinn was exhausted watching them. It was like they were shot out of a cannon, running and dancing, quick steps and kicks designed to expose as much of their petticoats as possible.

"Do you see their emotional expression?" Jane asked, pointing at the dancers, and keeping her promise from earlier to coach Quinn's artistry.

Quinn rubbed her palms together. Of course, she could see it, but she couldn't do it. "Yes."

Jane squeezed Quinn's hand empathetically, knowing the depths of her friend's struggle. "As dancers, we are also actors. And in order to act, we need to have access to either true emotions or imagined emotions."

Quinn loosened a breath. "But that's the problem. I can't access my emotions."

Jane smiled kindly. "Yes, you can. In the four years I've mentored you, I've seen you connect with your emotions on numerous occasions. You can do it. You just don't *want* to."

Fuck, Jane was right. She saw into the depths of Quinn's soul. And that was terrifying because Quinn didn't want to feel. She couldn't afford to.

"If it helps, pretend to be a different person with a different past," Jane said. "Sometimes, letting go can be the very thing you need."

Quinn sighed and fiddled with her fingernails, watching the dancing. Could she let herself go? Was it possible?

Jane pulled a small box from her pocket behind the bustle of her dress. "I got you a present." It was a bracelet with a single charm on it. A gold ballet pointe shoe with a heart inside. But not a cute heart that a schoolgirl would dot her I's with, a human heart—the organ—cradled in a pointe shoe. To anyone else, it would have been utterly ridiculous and creepy, but to Quinn, it was perfect. She said the last bit aloud.

"I know your ballet is your dream, but I also know, deep down, you love carving up dead bodies. You love being smarter than everyone else, and there is a world in which you can have both of your passions." Jane rubbed a wrinkle in her skirt.

"They aren't both my passions."

"Sure, sure." Jane nodded, but it was clear she didn't believe her. "One day—" Jane cut herself off, her eyes focusing on someone in the crowd. "I have to go . . . There's a meeting . . ." Jane jumped down from her perch and misjudged the distance, stumbling and falling. Before anyone could help her, she sprang back up and disappeared into the crowd.

Quinn tried to follow her disappearing form, but an explosion of fire came from the ceiling, and out of it appeared a woman in a deep red costume. The feathers started from her bodice and traveled up her chest, finishing at her throat like a choker necklace. The dress had a deep V-neck that exposed the skin to her belly button, and the skirt was shaped like a tutu. The dancer floated down from the ceiling like a falling star.

Constance.

Her toes touched the floor, and she balanced fully on pointe. At the precise moment she touched, the ground and the air lit up with golden fire.

Quinn squinted, and on closer look, the fire was thousands of glowing butterflies flying and dancing in time with Constance as she performed the Sable Swan variation mixed with cancan and seductress moves. The butterflies moved and morphed into shapes in the sky as Constance moved.

Quinn looked up to share her excitement about the dance with Giselle but discovered that she'd left. She was so absorbed in testing her invention that she had wandered off taking pictures and was entirely across the room.

Quinn was alone with her thoughts. Never a good thing. So she stared down at her necklace, clutched it, and remembered her Mirror-Rite.

A frisson of anxiety gathered in her core and crystallized.

The only way to keep her mind from unwanted emotions was to do something, whether it be work, a puzzle, or dance. Something, anything would do. She decided to find Emrys and get this over with.

Through the crowd, she spotted Jevon's blond hair. He stood, his shoulders slightly slumped with a frown on his face, holding two refreshments and surrounded by a group of fawning girls—far too polite to excuse himself and find freedom.

He needed to be rescued.

But Quinn would have to do that later. She made it three steps before she froze in her tracks. Behind her, in one of the curtained-off alcoves, an argument was brewing between familiar voices. She turned on her heel and tiptoed to the purple curtain blocking the room.

Perhaps she had fantastic luck because the object of her search simply fell into her lap.

Slowly, Quinn opened a curtain leading to a hall with a set of four little alcoves—designed for midnight assignations. The voices came from the farthest one on the left, so she tiptoed up to it, placed a steady finger on the fabric, and moved it oh-so-slightly enough to give her a view.

It was the meeting Jane had run off to.

Emrys spoke in dark tones and boxed Jane in. He was with two other men. A tree-like man, tall and slight of frame, in a pinstriped, immaculately tailored suit and square-rimmed glasses that framed his face. On his russet-brown skin behind his left ear rested a gang tattoo of a mask with a snake coiling through the eyehole.

A Les Fantômes tattoo.

The second man was spun in a suit of midnight black that matched his hair. He was also tall and conventionally attractive, but his eyes were a haunting deep brown-nearly-black with silver rings around his irises.

"You have to tell me where it is," Emrys Avalon said fiercely to Jane, nearly shaking her. "We need to know. It's life and death."

"I can't tell you." Jane folded her arms and stood her ground.

The man with silver-ringed eyes cocked his head. "But you do know where it is?"

It? What could be so important that both Emrys and this man

were threatening Jane? The hairs on Quinn's arms rose. *Jane, what have you gotten yourself into?*

Jane's gaze jolted to his, and she said, "Shouldn't you already know exactly where it is?"

"It doesn't work that way," the silver-eyed man said. "Peri might be able to find it, but she's more talented with knowledge than I am."

"Then ask Periwinkle, not me."

"This isn't a game, Jane," Emrys snarled. "I need to know where it is."

"No one should ever know where it is." Jane crossed her arms. "It's too dangerous—and so are you."

A storm of questions laced Quinn's mind. The scene was more than just shocking. It was disturbing. Jane was clearly involved in dark matters. A prince, a gang member, and a mysterious Mirror-Blessed were not people anyone would want to mess with.

Quinn shifted slightly, and the wooden floorboard beneath her feet cracked.

Dirty fucking mirrors.

Fuck me. The last thing she needed was to get caught eavesdropping on Emrys. Quinn slowly stepped deep into the shadows, hoping the prince hadn't seen her. But as if summoned by bad luck, Emrys's eyes latched on to hers and stole her breath.

"Filthy, nasty mirrors," she cursed under her breath. "*Fuck.*"

"Hello, Ginger." His smile was wicked but not disturbed. He clearly didn't care that she was listening. Instead, he walked toward her as if she were prey. Fear spiked in her body, chilling her bones.

"I am sorry . . ." Quinn sputtered. "I didn't hear anything."

"You are a terrible liar." Emrys's eyes sparkled with amusement and mischief, and his mouth curved farther with sinister delight. "It's okay. We weren't talking about much of interest. You should just forget about it." His voice was laced with sugar, and

Quinn's mind twisted and melted, as if magic's claws were digging into it.

Jane rushed up, grabbed the prince, and harshly said, "No. Don't you dare!"

The prince's lips turned into a hard line. "As you wish." He waved his hand, and whatever enchantment he was spinning unraveled.

Was he Mirror-Blessed?

Jane glanced back at the silver-eyed man. "Remember, Darcy, hurt her, and I'll hurt you."

"You're worse than my paramour, Harlowe." Darcy rolled his eyes. "Besides, what's done is done. It is her actions that will decide her fate."

"And yours, it would seem." Jane stepped forward, laced her arm through Quinn's, and guided her away from the scene.

The entire exchange left Quinn reeling, and a shiver coursed through her bones. Jane had a lot of explaining to do, and as soon as Quinn completed her rite, she would get those answers because none of it made sense. But the one thing abundantly clear was that something was terribly wrong—like Quinn had walked into a secret underworld of peril and mystery.

SEVEN

"Wait," Quinn said, pulling out of Jane's grip. "You are going to tell me what all of that was about, but first, I have the Mirror-Rite to complete." Before Jane could stop her, she'd turned on pointe and strode back to the alcoves.

Twenty minutes. Jane could wait . . . for now.

Jane's voice called after her. "I can't follow you in this, Quinny. You're on your own."

"I understand."

The curtains were closed again, but the voices still escaped the alcove. The three men spoke in hushed, serious tones. Quinn tiptoed up again with no plan other than parting the curtains, which were like scarlet waterfalls dripping from the ceiling.

"I'm worried about her," one of the male voices she didn't recognize said.

"Jane is used to danger."

"Yes, but this one is personal, and we all know when it's personal, it gets messy."

"Unfortunately,"—this time, it was Emrys's voice—"it is personal for all of us."

"So, it's just a messy situation then."

"Precisely."

"And life and death," Emrys said. Quinn shook her head. Whatever they were wrapped up in was too dangerous, and they all needed to get out of it, but especially Jane.

At the slight noise, Emrys's entire body tensed, and she swallowed a silent curse. It was one thing to get caught eavesdropping once, and it was another to have it happen twice. Unrecoverable.

Shit.

She pinched her lips together. Acting without a plan was utter foolishness. Dammit. She slowly took a step backward and ran her hand through her hair, unsure of what to do. But she needed to trap him and kiss him.

That was easier said than done.

For fuck's sake. She inhaled sharply, trying to think, and the only thing she could come up with was hiding in the alcove next door and ambushing him when he came out, hoping he was the last to leave.

It was the only semblance of a plan she had, so she went with it.

The neighboring alcove was pitch black, so Quinn whispered to the room, "Can I please get some light?" But like all sentient buildings, it had a mind of its own and refused to aid her.

Letting out a huff, she ran her fingers along the gilded walls, trying to feel for a light switch. But instead of finding a wall sconce or switch, her finger hit human flesh, and she jolted. The other person stiffened as if in pain.

"Oh, shit," Quinn said, "I am so sorry. I didn't mean—"

Before she could finish her sentence, she was thrown off balance and pinned to the wall. Her breath came out in a rush as the massively tall frame trapped her within its hold. His—for the pure size of the figure made her believe it was either an impossibly tall woman or a tall man—hand curled around her throat but didn't squeeze.

"Truly, I am deeply apologetic," she breathed. "I didn't know anyone was in here, and I never would have come in if I did."

The figure ignored her. "If you wanted to touch me, all you

had to do was ask." It was the voice of the devil. All at once, Quinn was relieved and horrified because not only was it Emrys Avalon, which was both good news and bad news, but once again, he was touching her in ways she enjoyed. And that *was* horrifying.

Although the excited pounding of her heart or the honeybees buzzing against the velvet lining of her stomach was answer enough.

"I believe you are the one touching me."

He loosed a low chuckle. "Technically, yes."

"Well, it's always prudent to be technical."

"Is it really?" he asked. "How enlightening. Although, I do think some things are enjoyed far more in the absence of perfection."

Quinn scoffed. She couldn't think of a single thing that benefited from a lack of precision.

"Ginger, I know you are obsessed with me—"

"I am not obsessed with you." Her cheeks heated, and she was suddenly very happy he couldn't see her in the darkness.

"But why are you eavesdropping on me twice in one night?"

"I wasn't."

"Then what do you call skulking around outside of a private alcove when people are in the middle of very important conversations?"

Quinn bit her lip and blinked, wishing she could see him better. Her vision was slowly adjusting to the dark, but he was still only a blur of strong masculine muscles. "Alright, I will concede that I was outside your meeting, but it wasn't with the intent to listen in."

"Yet you did." His grip shifted on her neck, and he tilted her chin up as if he were looking into her eyes, which would have been impossible unless he was Mirror-Blessed with the magic ability to do so. Given that he tried to spell her earlier, it was a high possibility, which was a horrifying thought to consider.

"I simply wanted to ask you for help."

"Oh?" She couldn't see him, but she imagined his midnight-manicured brows rose at this. "Ask away."

His thumb stroked along her jawline, and she tensed, her breath hitching with excitement and terror. What she was about to ask would have negative consequences because no matter what he said in return, she would be mortified.

"I wanted to . . ." She simply couldn't say it aloud. It was wrong of her to consider ambushing him, but that was what she wanted to do. It was also impossible. She couldn't reach his lips without his help.

"Wanted to . . ." he repeated. Not helping in the slightest.

Oh, bloody mirrors, was he truly going to make her say it?

"I would like you to teach me . . ." Quinn swallowed. Possibly, if she presented it as a teaching opportunity, he might be willing to help her. What was she kidding? Emrys kissed a new girl every night. It was his way. He'd be more than willing to help.

"Teach you?"

Could he stop merely repeating her? Quinn's heart slammed in her ears like it was a bird trying to escape a cage.

"Passion." The word was so low only a long-extinct vampire would have been able to hear it.

"What?"

Quinn placed her palms against the wall, bracing herself. There wasn't much else she could do.

"Would this happen to be about your lack of passion problem?" Emrys said loudly, the sound brushing her earlobe as if his lips were nearly touching her.

"What?" *How could you possibly know that?*

Thankfully, he answered her unspoken question. "After our conversation this morning, I asked Jane why you've never made the Royalle Ballet before, and she said it's because you lack passion."

A wineglass shattered in her stomach, jabbing into her core. "Oh."

"Is that what you want me for?" His hot breath stroked her

neck, and his fingers slid into her hair, now cupping her head instead of her jaw.

The movement sent a sensation of pleasure down her spine. There was something about the way he touched her neck and hair that caused her to completely unravel.

If this was her body's reaction to a simple touch, she desperately wanted to know how it would respond to a kiss. It could be a fun science experiment. Quinn might not want to be a medical examiner like her uncle, but she loved the scientific practice. It made sense.

It was logical and precise.

Two things she desired above all else.

"Because I am known as a perennial rogue, you want to learn from me," he asked, sliding one finger down the column of her neck, and resting above the crest of her breast.

"Yes," she said, wanton and desperate for more of that liquid fire touch.

Every movement of his hand caused her nerve endings to erupt in sensation. And it was beautiful. Magical.

"You want me to touch you here?" His finger slid further south, and her breath hitched as it slid down her bodice. "Ginger, you must verbally answer me."

"Yes." She gulped. "I want that."

"You feel like velvet." His lips touch the spot just under her ear. Quinn gasped. "You want me to kiss you here?"

Words weren't forming to answer him because she was so overwhelmed with stimulation. She'd touched herself before, but it was nothing like this. It was all more exciting because she couldn't see anything, and she had no idea what was coming next. Tension licked at her spine as she waited for him to make his next move.

It was to place another kiss up her neck. His lips were hot against her skin, and his hand traveled farther down her bodice until he completely cupped one of her breasts. "You like this."

Too much. "Yes." She pinched her eyes shut, hating herself for admitting it—hating herself for all of it. He was her enemy and off limits, not even a thought on her mind until today. Quinn did not lust after young gentlemen and certainly not princes.

Lust. Yes, that was precisely what was happening. *Fuck.*

But if this was happening, then it needed to happen fully. "I need you to kiss me."

He nipped her neck with his teeth and followed up with his tongue, touching where his teeth had marked.

"Oh . . ." Her fingers dug into the wall to keep her from reaching out and touching him.

"Is this not enough of a kiss for you?"

"No," she whispered, "I need you to teach me true passion."

"Like I am your little whore?"

"Yes," she said without thinking, "I mean, no. Of course not."

"You want to use me?"

Yes. But how could he possibly have a problem with that? His moniker was the Playboy Prince for a reason.

"Do you, Ginger?"

"Yes."

"How very enterprising of you." His voice was fire, both harsh and passionate. "There is a forbidden part of you that wants me to touch you everywhere."

Yes.

He flicked a finger across her nipple, and her entire body tensed with anticipation.

"I want you to kiss me." *Please, Emrys, for the love of all the mirrors, just kiss me so I can complete my rite before midnight . . . and because now it's the only thing I desperately want.*

His lips hovered over hers, and with his free hand, he titled her chin up. "You want me."

Now, that was an utterly too broad question, and she wouldn't answer it because her goal was within reach, so close. Quinn wasn't willing to wait anymore. So, without any skill, she leaned forward and touched her lips with his.

But as soon as she did it, he pulled back. "No."

"What?"

"No." The word was a nail in her coffin.

"Why?"

"One day, I will kiss you thoroughly, but it will not be today." And like lightning, he disappeared into the shadows.

She reached her arms out, feeling for his body, but he was gone.

Truly gone.

Placing her hands back on the wall, she cursed.

"Emrys, please come back," she whimpered, pathetically because she knew he wouldn't, and that only meant one thing.

The sound of the clock striking midnight reverberated through her bones—like a dagger twisting into her soul.

She'd failed.

Ten-thousand-fucks.

She hung her head, her fingers clawed into the wall. One thing was certain—she felt it in her bones—she was going to incur terrible mirror consequences.

DAY
TWO

PRICE 2 CENTS

BREAKING NEWS

The New Swansea Times

MONDAY, NEW SWANSEA CITY, 91st DAY OF AUTUMN, 700AV

RMS COLOSSAL DOCKS EARLY

PRINCE IS BACK

The Ten Day Festival of Blood has arrived and it's time to Celebrate!

The docking of the grand ocean liner kicks off the ten-day Festival of Blood, which celebrates seven hundred years of peace since the Blood Rebellion and the slaughter of all vampires. The celebration will culminate in the Royalle Ball, where Prince Emrys will announce his betrothal to one lucky girl in attendance—cont. page 2

Golden Prince Snubbed by Beautiful Ballerina

In a colossal mistake, a pretty red-headed ballerina insulted Prince Emrys only moments after he disembarked the grand ocean liner, the RMS Colossal. She refused to let him aid her and spoke to him as if he were a lowly commoner—like herself. It is unclear what the consequences will be for the pretty, petite dancer, and so far, the palace has refused to comment—cont. page 3

MORE DEAD PILE UP in the Nature District

The homeless are dying at a much higher rate than usual as the winter frosts barrel towards us. More than five a week now. When will the death toll stop, and what if it doesn't—cont. page 8

EMRYS'S BALL INVITATIONS have gone out

All eligible women in New Swansea have been requested to make an appearance at the palace —cont. page 6

EIGHT

Blood and screams coated Quinn's nightmares as she jolted awake.

The Looking Glass had worked extra hard last night, causing nightmare after nightmare after nightmare, all filled with vampires murdering her or terrible mirror consequences. Consequences like her kisses cause men guttural pain. Apparently, that was one of the infamous Harlowe Merriwether's consequences.

But one thing was certain: the Looking Glass was taunting Quinn.

She was used to these types of rotten dreams, living in the City of Nightmares, but they were still jolting from time to time —especially today. Every morning, Quinn cursed the Royalle House for making their stupid deal with the Looking Glass.

Fuck.

Drums pounded at Quinn's temples. The world tilted to the side, and Quinnevere Ashelle tumbled out of bed, shaking the dividers of her makeshift bedroom, and falling into the pile of ballet attire.

Quinn and her uncle lived in a humble one-bedroom apartment above the morgue at University Square. Because sharing a room was improper, they converted the living room into a cobbled-together bedroom of wall dividers, stacked boxes, and hanging curtains.

It looked far better than one would expect. But then Quinn was a perfectionist, so even under meager circumstances, she would make the room orderly.

She groaned and sat up, and a ribbon stuck to her cheek.

She had landed on the pointe shoes she'd laid out the night before. Even when one partied, it was important to be ready and prepared. Therefore, Quinn always chose her clothing well in advance and neatly laid them out so as not to get wrinkles.

Oh fuck. She was running late again.

Well, at least her birthday had been . . . absolutely, horribly, and gutturally confusing.

Quinn bit her lip, remembering the rite and remembering that mirror consequences awaited her future. At least her lips actually touched his, so she wouldn't incur the seven years of bad luck. But there were worse results of a mirror deal gone wrong, and she knew in her core that something truly horrific was about to happen.

Especially after Nightshade's warning.

Quinn stumbled around, hopping on one foot as she tried to dress. It would be the second time that she would run down the streets of New Swansea in a tutu, but at least this time, there'd be no crowd.

Her headache only grew worse throughout the morning, and her body was slow and lethargic. The world swam and tilted on its axis. Two hours into dancing, Quinn felt like her body might give out, but she pushed through it. Athletes didn't give up, and they certainly never gave in.

The night before was an intense blur. She barely remembered

partying with her best friends, her jarring rite, and catching Emrys threatening Jane—who was strangely missing from class this morning.

An anchor of unease sank in Quinn's stomach.

Quinn turned on pointe, trying to keep her dancing accurate and beautiful. It was quite a challenge.

I stayed up too late.

IIt didn't matter if Quinn felt like she could throw up from her lack of sleep. She would dance the Captured by Death pas de deux from the ballet *Lover's Lost*. The dance took place in the third act when the main character, Isadora, tragically died in her lover's arms and was pulled into the underworld by Death. It started with quick bourrée steps to symbolize Isadora running from Death. But eventually, he captured her. The majority of the partner dance was done between Isadora and Death.

The dance was mesmerizing lightning, but for Quinn, it was an exhausting rain. With every move, she felt a pulsating stab in her calf.

A bead of sweat hovered over Quinn's eyebrow as she spun into a partnered pirouette. Wrecked with fatigue, she measured her arm movements and made her feet move at precisely the right time. But Quinn missed steps—a rarity.

When the music slowed, her partner whispered, "So you're hungover. I heard you were partying at the Viridian last night."

Shit. Who else knew that?

She had drunk one—or seven—too many drinks after her deal failed. Quinn groaned and whispered a not-so-pleasant curse back at him. Arthur chuckled and pulled her into a lift.

By the time the dance was almost finished, Quinn had missed her arabesque seven times, and her lines were wonky from the pain cutting at her leg.

I will never party again. Or challenge another mirror.

The morning passed like wildfire. Quick and destructive. Quinn danced for three hours before meeting her uncle in the morgue.

Stepping into the lab, Quinn placed her pack down before walking over to meet her uncle, who examined a corpse.

Uncle Matias Thyssen was her only living relative and her mother's younger brother. He had ivory skin, dark green eyes, walnut hair, and an eccentric personality. He lived and breathed corpses, choosing to spend even his free time studying brains and rotting flesh. He mumbled to himself incoherently and hated uncleanliness of any kind. For all his knowledge about the human body, he knew very little about feminine issues and how to raise a child.

But he was the only family she had, and despite his many quirks and flaws, Quinn loved him—except when he told her to be practical and be a medical examiner instead of dancing ballet or when he reminded her that at twenty-three, she was entering into her spinster years.

It was in lectures that she longed for her parents or Gideon. Gideon was her father's best friend, who was like family. She'd never met him because he died in his mid-twenties. But even a fake, non-existent relative sometimes felt better than her real uncle. Apparently, Gideon was a rebel, endlessly charismatic, and deeply kind. He probably would've loved Quinn's passion for dance and cherished it. But he died far too young, and his death rocked the family to the core.

But, of course, everyone ignored his death.

It was a family trait. Refusing to acknowledge death, emotions, or hardship.

"Anything interesting?" Quinn asked, making her way over to the exam table. From afar, Quinn only saw the left side of the victim's face, which was bashed in and unrecognizable. A brutal murder.

"No. Just another dead gang member," Uncle Matias said, tilting the victim's head so that only the left side of her face was visible. He pointed behind her ear. "She has a Les Fantômes tattoo." Quinn stepped in and inspected the marking of a mask with a snake coiling around it. "No need for an autopsy. We need to write up a report and send her on her way."

New Swansea was a city filled with so much crime that when a gang member died, the city refused to waste resources on an investigation. If someone chose to belong to a gang, they decided to live outside of the law—in turn, so would their death. That was the risk and deterrent of joining a gang.

At least that was the official reason for not pursuing gang investigations, but the real reason was far more sinister and because of the police's foolish mirror deal.

The institution of the police bargained to be able to solve any murder instantly, but their unintended consequence was that they were forbidden from acting on Mirror-Blessed murders. They couldn't arrest the murderers or even tell the victims' families who did it. People could bargain with a mirror as a group, and everyone belonging to that group was a party to the deal. That's how the entire city of New Swansea was bound to the Looking Glass's nightmares, and the police were tied to this shit one, which left a third of the population utterly vulnerable. But not just vulnerable. Mirror-Blessed were hunted.

So, the five gangs of New Swansea emerged as bodies to protect those with magic.

And because the police were forbidden from investigating Mirror-Blessed killings, cases were assigned to medical examiners' offices and were rarely looked into. Unfortunately, murder was so rampant in the city that there weren't enough resources, so the royals—who oversaw all crime—agreed that the medical examiners would only solve non-gang-related murders.

But the royals didn't stop the gangs from investigating and seeking their own justice.

Uncle Matias started to wheel the victim into the cooling cell when Quinn noticed something strange. Puncture wounds under the slice marks on the neck.

Like a vampire's marking.

"Wait." She put a hand on his shoulder. "There is something off about this corpse."

"It doesn't matter, Quinn. It's gang business. Leave it alone." Uncle Matias continued wheeling the corpse to the cell.

"I know, but can I take a look to appease my curiosity?" Quinn asked.

The punctures resembled a vampire bite, and Quinn's insatiable need to understand things ate away at her core. She *must* know how things ticked.

Vampires were extinct, and it couldn't possibly be their markings, but it was far too interesting to pass up.

"Fine." He sighed. "You can have a quick look."

"Can I do the autopsy by myself?" Her uncle cocked an eyebrow. "It would be a perfect way for me to practice without any stakes. If I mess up"—which she wouldn't because she'd spent eleven years helping with autopsies and four actually performing them, but it always made her uncle happy when she volunteered herself to do them—"the stakes won't matter."

His face creased in thought. He probably weighed the cost-reward split. Quinn rarely volunteered to do an autopsy on her own. She enjoyed them, and she was good at them, but she'd always preferred to be dancing, and her uncle desperately wanted her to focus on a "real career" instead.

"Fine. But you have to perform the autopsy after our briefing," he said. "You can do the external now if you want, but you must save the rest for later. And you won't under any circumstance use the information you gather for any other reason than studying."

"Agreed." Quinn flashed him her best attempt at a studious smile that said, *look at me. I'm trying to make you proud.*

She pulled on rubber gloves and started a quick external examination of the corpse. The two slices across the victim's throat were given postmortem based on the lack of blood flow, but the puncture holes in the jugular occurred while the victim was still alive. *Interesting*. Why cut the throat at all if the puncture wounds killed her, and why postmortem? To hide the punctures? Quinn traced her finger along the wounds.

Along the woman's wrist was a painting tattoo. Just like Quinn's. Strange.

What could it mean?

Gently, she turned the victim's head to see the other side of her face and throat.

Quinn jerked back and crashed into a tray of tools, which went flying, the metal clinking against the ground as they fell. Bile rose in Quinn's esophagus. She was going to be sick. Racing to the sink, her heartbeat erratically, and she braced her hands on either side of the metal and let out the remnants of her breakfast into the drain.

Then Quinn sank to her knees on the floor.

The body was *Jane Whitfield-Wryte*.

NINE

G ray concrete lined the walls, and wooden chairs layered the room in stadium seating. At the bottom, a solitary podium was perched in the rays of an artificial spotlight. Top members of the police force and Castle Hill were scattered in the chairs, waiting for the briefing to begin.

Quinn sat huddled with her best friends in the hallway, peering into the room. A broken silence mingled between them, and tear stains laced all but Quinn's cheeks. She wanted to cry. She wanted to let out this unbearable agony, but she couldn't afford the tears because if she let go, if she let herself feel the emotions bubbling in her belly, she wouldn't be able to breathe. She wouldn't be able to endure.

So, instead, her eyes stung, and her mouth hurt from the weight of her unshed tears and her clenched jaw.

The first thing she did as soon as she regained composure was inform her friends. All of them immediately dropped everything to come to the morgue. Of the friends, Constance seemed the most inconsolable. A sea of agony coursed through her, and her face was a haunted shipyard devastated by a severe hurricane. From time to time, she sprayed herself with a mirror-enchanted perfume that was supposed to calm her nerves. It worked for about ten minutes before it wore off, and she'd have to use it again.

"Quinn, it's going to be okay." A gentle voice danced in her ears. She blinked, realizing she had zoned out, and found Jevon tapping on her arm. "Are you okay?"

Tap, tap, tap sounds reverberated on her arm to a perfect four-four tempo. It was strangely soothing.

Jevon, despite his near silence, always soothed her. He was a steadying source. Based on his ruffled and unkempt demeanor, he shouldn't have been so soothing. Untamed blond locks swooshed across his forehead. His attire was ruffled from his lack of care and the way he adjusted and readjusted his cuffs and tie, which was in tight contrast to Quinn's charcoal medical examiner uniform that she ironed meticulously every night before bed, keeping them perfectly tailored and uncreased.

His presence should have grated against her need for perfection, but instead, he was precisely what she needed.

Staring at his still-tapping fingers, her mind twirled into place. "It's not going to be okay. I killed her."

After gaining her composure, she remembered her deal. She failed and was bound to have consequences from it. Jane's death couldn't be a coincidence, could it? Quinn was normally rational, but in this, her brain was broken. It wasn't thinking straight. There was no concept of straight anymore.

"I killed her," she let out a whispered whimper.

"No, you didn't," Constance said softly. "You didn't murder her."

"No, but I failed to complete my mirror deal, and this is the consequence."

"Or it is a coincidence?" Jevon said, squeezing her shoulder. "You can't know it was your fault. Think of it rationally; Jane had been cagey for weeks now. It's very possible she died for completely unrelated reasons."

A mix of emotions licked across Quinn's skin, and she let out another whimper. She hated how well her friends knew her and how she couldn't hide from them. Jevon knew she held rationality above all else, and he clocked that her thoughts were straying from reason. She wanted to hate him for it. But how could she?

Friendship was about seeing the rough parts of one another and working through them.

And as much as Quinn wanted to lean into reason and Jevon's words, she couldn't. Because what if she was responsible? Would she ever be able to forgive herself? "This is all my fault."

Jevon's azure eyes locked on her, and he squeezed her arm again. "Your brain is quite fascinating, Quinny. I just saw you acknowledge I could be right, and then you fell back into a black hole of guilt and shame."

"Stop being so damn observant. I hate it."

"If it makes you feel better, only he can see that," Constance said, "otherwise, you're excellent at hiding how you are truly feeling. I often find you an impossible nut to crack. I often have to ask him to interpret you to me."

It did make Quinn feel better because she didn't want anyone to see her brokenness.

"Giselle is the same, by the way." Constance pointed at the brunette with her thumb.

Giselle scoffed. "I am far more observant than you."

"Yet we all missed whatever was happening with Jane." Jevon's eyes darkened with sadness as he rested his head against the wall.

The friends descended into a silent tableau of sorrow. Jevon's face paled to the color of falling snow. Giselle's shoulders sagged like a deflating balloon as she opened the book in her hands, and Constance looked like pure devastation.

Jane was more than just a friend to Constance.

She was an idol.

But she wasn't just Constance's idol. Every ballerina loved her and wanted to be her—except for her terrible deal. Jane was the best ballerina to grace the stage of the Queen's Royalle Ballet. Her artistry was unmatched. But more than that, she was a friend.

Someone people could count on in their hardest moments. Someone who understood hardships and was so much more than a teacher. If anyone needed to cry, Jane was there.

She was warm, passionate, and beautiful. She was a light. And now she was gone.

Quinn swallowed; her throat was on fire from the pain of holding back tears. "It's still possible I did this without holding the weapon."

"Stop it. Someone else killed her." Giselle slammed her book closed. "You cannot hold the blame for that."

"The only thing I can do now for her is find the blade. Find the person who killed her. I owe her that much. I am going to perform an autopsy. But she has a gang tattoo—" Quinn trailed off at the gasps from her friends.

None of them knew it because Jane hid so many things from them—far too many things. Possibly things that got her murdered.

"What?" Both Jevon and Giselle said at once.

Quinn's shoulders slumped, and she picked at her shirt cuff. "It doesn't make any sense."

A vein in Constance's neck budged as she said, "But that means she'll have no justice."

"I know," Quinn breathed. But she wasn't willing to let her friend die without justice. She would do something, anything, to ensure that. Now, ballet and the morgue and Mirror-Rites held no importance.

The only thing that mattered was getting revenge for Jane.

Constance wrung her hands. "Screw the gang law. Jane deserves justice. We'll just have to find the person responsible and make them hang for it."

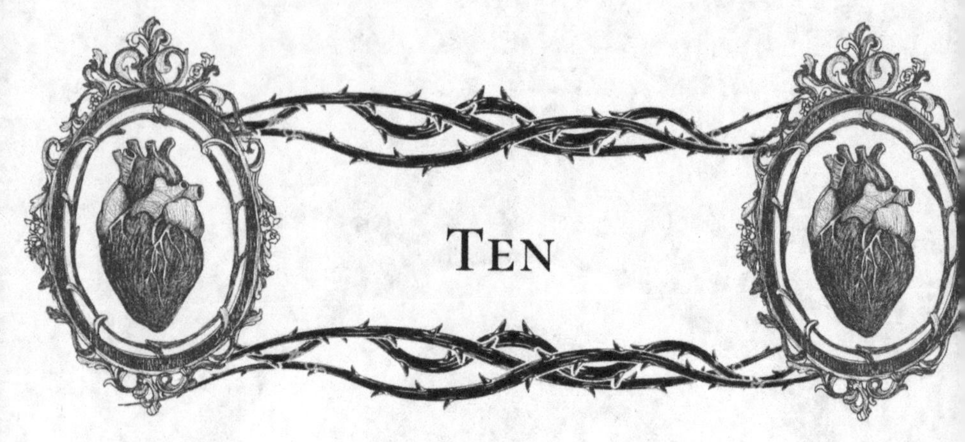

Ten

The scents of decomposition and formalin hovered like a cloud over the room, caking Quinn's pores with rot. Formalin stung Quinn's nostrils, making the already pungent smell of rotting flesh more concentrated and invasive.

Quinn didn't mind the smell so much, but Giselle's normally bronze cheeks faded into a shade of dark olive green, and she kept making gagging noises from behind her book—which she wielded like a sword.

Jevon's complexion was ashen, and Constance seemed to be wholly undisturbed. Ever since she vowed to find the murderer, something inside her changed. It was like she flipped a switch and buried her devastation within her. That or the flask that she kept drinking out of did the trick. She was almost certainly drunk at this point, and it was entirely possible that Constance was drinking Mirror-Blessed wine. She sat on an exam table, swinging her feet to an invisible beat, and chewed on charmed macarons—the owner of La Pâte Rouge made a deal with a Bargainer for the ability to bake without calories or cavities.

Autopsies never bothered Quinn. Growing up in the morgue and having her hands deep in a chest cavity was normal. But this one shook her. This one was personal, and the only way she managed to push through was to pretend that it was a nameless victim.

Otherwise, Quinn would completely fall apart.

A nameless victim. Quinn pinched her lips together and turned her eyes to the external examination. She tried her best not to look at the face. Slowly, she removed the clothing and examined the body.

But the whole while, her hands shook oh so slightly. Quinn could pretend everything was normal, but her body knew it wasn't.

On the *nameless victim's* left arm was the tattoo of a painting dripping with blood—the same one as Quinn's. Another secret. So many secrets. The victim also had a Mirror-Blessed tattoo on her thumb and the Fantômes gang tattoo behind her ear.

"Where was she murdered?" Constance asked.

"My guess is she was killed somewhere and then dropped at the docks." Quinn's words were matter-of-fact. Scientific. Rational. She would only use ration for this autopsy. *She would.* She had to.

With a mirror-spelled thermometer, Quinn checked the body's temperature. 72.3 degrees. The precise temperature of the room. So, the body was fully equilibrated with its surroundings, which meant, "The victim died at least twelve hours ago."

"Like at the Viridian?" Constance asked.

"Yes, possibly," Quinn said tentatively. She didn't like guessing without proper evidence. "We know that the victim was at the Viridian the night of her murder. Her dress is caked in mud and blood . . . and a substance that seems to be glitter. Tucked into a piece of her red hair was a fragment of a purple feather and silver sequins typical on Viridian dancers' dresses. It's possible she was killed at the Viridian before being dumped in the Marina District. Additionally, there doesn't seem to be any water damage to the body. So, the killer either didn't want to dump her in the bay or was unsuccessful. However, the most significant evidence so far is the bloody fingerprint found on the victim's corset. But I'll have to check it later and see if it's hers."

"Which means the killer was in a rush?" Giselle poked her head out of her book, her eyes still laced with tears.

The sight caused Quinn's throat to bobble. It was a reminder of the truth. A reminder that she was about to cut open the body of one of her best friends.

Quinn placed her hands on the exam table for stability. *Fuck, this is hard.*

"Or that they were interrupted," Jevon added, his shoulder slightly curved and a dark expression lingering in his eyes.

"Yes." Quinn's voice wavered, but she swallowed down her emotion and continued. "There are many possibilities. Maybe we should go down to the docks and ask if anyone saw anything." Quinn examined the bruises covering the *victim's* body—*nameless victim. You can do this.* The bruises seemed to occur both pre-and-postmortem.

"Maybe we should do that when you're done?" Constance asked.

Giselle glanced at the corpse before placing a hand in front of her mouth and gagging again. "Yeah, that, or we might want to go talk to the leader of the Les Fantômes gang. I could do that now." Clearly, she wanted an opportunity to leave the morgue. Giselle's father used to run the gang, so she probably knew who to talk to and how to get answers. But then again, she only lived there for the first ten years of her life before her mother forced her to leave and learn how to be a lady.

"No one should go anywhere in this investigation alone. It's not safe," Jevon said cautiously. Calm, practical, and observant. Three traits Quinn adored.

"I agree," Quinn said.

"Doing things alone is how people end up dead in this city," Constance said. "What do you think the time of death was?"

Quinn glanced down at the body. It was in a state of full rigor mortis, which took roughly fifteen hours. The state of the maggots found on the body also suggested around fifteen to eighteen hours of decompensation. "I'd say approximately between two and three am." It was not as precise as she would like, but it'd be more accurate after examining the stomach and intestine contents.

Which meant she needed to open the corpse.

Quinn pinched her eyes shut. Fuck, this hurt, and she was struggling so much to compartmentalize. So utterly unlike herself. *Get yourself together. You need to do this for her. Do it for Jane.*

Yes. I can do that.

With a scalpel, Quinn made the preliminary incision—the Y-shaped cut that ran from the shoulders to the sternum. For a female, the incision was a bit different. Instead of a straight Y, Quinn cut under and around the breasts and up to the shoulder joint.

Blood should've flowed from the incision and drained off the exam table, but the corpse had a complete absence of postmortem lividity and drainage. No blood left to remove. Quinn hypothesized that blood loss was the cause of death. The two slices across the victim's throat were given postmortem, but the puncture holes in the jugular occurred while the victim was alive.

The holes were five millimeters wide, and Quinn was unsure what object caused them. If she had to guess—which she frowned on doing, accuracy was currency in science—they belonged to either a letter opener or a set of pointed teeth. The implications of the latter were terrifying.

Fangs could mean the wound was inflicted by long-extinct vampires.

Was it possible?

They were the most powerful creatures in the world at one point. What if they hadn't vanished seven hundred years ago? What if one survived?

Survived to create more.

Survived to feed on and murder people.

Gooseflesh crawled down her arms. It was a horrifying thought.

Cracking her neck and rolling her shoulders, she tried to release the tension in her back before focusing on her task. But it was so fucking hard. Made even harder by the fact that her eyes suddenly learned how to produce tears, which she was forced to hold back, and the entire process of doing so stung and was utter agony.

Focus.

Quinn pinched her lips together and cracked open the ribcage, and gagging sounds were heard from over Quinn's shoulder. Jevon and Giselle.

With her arms wrist-deep in the chest cavity, Quinn's sliced at connective tissue. She needed to remove the organs to examine them. With her scalpel, she sliced along the spinal cord, the bladder, and then the rectum. This separated the remaining organs so that she could take them out all at once before placing them on a table.

Without having a diener—assistant—Quinn needed to close the corpse herself quickly. The stitches were rushed and far less precise than she would've wanted, but she didn't have the time—a fact that scratched at the back of her perfectionistic brain.

"Do you know how many ways a vampire can kill a person?" Giselle asked, her nose still deep in her book.

"Why are you so random?" Constance let out a belabored sigh and picked at her nails.

Giselle shrugged, not looking up from her book. "Just so we are clear, I am still heartbroken, and I have no idea what to do, so I am trying to deal with my grief through facts. So please indulge me."

"You're so weird," Constance said.

"And clearly, you're heartless."

Quinn cleared her throat, trying to break up an argument that was about to start. "There are hundreds of ways to kill a human.

So I would gather it is a couple more than that," Quinn said as she examined the stomach.

"Hmmm, good point," Giselle said. "Well, this book says there are 472."

"How would the book even know that?" Constance scoffed. "That is such a specific number."

While meticulously cutting into the stomach, the door slammed open. Quinn jolted, trying to keep the tip of the scalpel away from the fragile intestines. She didn't need the contents of the bowel bursting into her face.

Quinn's heart pounded in her ears, and sweat gathered under her corset. No one was supposed to enter the lab, and she definitely shouldn't have her friends here. Her uncle would have her head for something like that, and he would be extraordinarily angry, knowing that the four of them were very much going to investigate this murder.

Glancing up through her lashes, Quinn saw . . . a villain. And possibly a murderer.

Emrys Avalon.

The gate and cadence of his footsteps were long, proud strides. The kind of walk that screamed, *I own this room and everything in it, including you.*

Her stomach turned to delicate glass—glass that could shatter at any moment. He was the last person in the world she wanted to see. Not after last night. Not after she'd begged him to kiss her, and he refused, instead taunting her with passion. He was just as much responsible for Jane's death as she was. He forced Quinn to lose her deal.

Not to mention, he'd threatened Jane last night. Fuck, he threatened Jane last night, and now he was in her lab. He only came to destroy evidence or mess with her investigations. She would not let him do that to Jane.

"Are you here to cover up your murder?" Quinn spat.

If Emrys was the killer, he had all the access he would ever need to destroy evidence. The palace was the law in New Swansea City. When Emrys had destroyed her autopsy records and obscured the evidence, she'd reported him. Her uncle simply shrugged and said, *He owns this building.* But worse, all the other physicians blamed her and removed her lab privileges for three months. If she hadn't reported him, she wouldn't have been punished for his crimes.

Because only the victim got in trouble when powerful men were at play, and Emrys *was* the power in New Swansea. If he had killed Jane, there was nearly no recourse to punish him.

"Get out." Her words were nearly a growl. "I won't let you tamper with my evidence. Not on this case."

"Hello, little Ginger." Emrys flashed a smirk and a dimple. "I am not sure what you are accusing me of. But trust me, if I murdered someone, I wouldn't need to cover it up."

"Of course, you wouldn't; you'd probably parade the dead body down the streets."

"Perhaps in another decade, that might have been my recourse, but I promise you, Quinnevere Ashelle, if I murdered you, no one would ever discover your corpse."

Quinn froze, and she stifled a full-body tremble. "Probably because you would devour me whole."

The side of his mouth ticked up. "Oh, most definitely." His eyes locked onto hers, and she glanced away quickly, unable to hold the contact. "But I might do that just for a good time. Isn't that what you wanted last night?" Her eyes flashed back to his, horrified.

"I hate you." Quinn's fingers quaked, and she had to very slowly remove them from the victim's bowels so that she wouldn't rupture them.

"We can have fun with hatred, Ginger." He slowly slid his hands into his pockets and turned his attention to everyone else. "Are we having a party in the morgue?"

Quinn's friends collectively stiffened. They knew they weren't supposed to be in the lab.

"Are you jealous you weren't invited?" Giselle asked.

At the same time, Constance said, "We were just leaving. Quinn was kind enough to demonstrate an autopsy for us, but now we must get going."

Constance's entire demeanor changed. She jumped up like she couldn't get out of the room quickly enough, and she glared at Jevon, sending him a message *to get out quickly.*

"Yes." Jevon cleared his throat. "We were just leaving."

"Right." Giselle closed her book. "We learned so much. Thank you for teaching us."

And with that, her three best friends left her to be devoured by the big, bad—murderous—wolf. *Traitors,* Quinn thought as she watched her friends scurry away. Now, Quinn would have to defend the lab from his tampering alone.

ELEVEN

With a fiendish smile, Emrys strolled over to an empty counter across the room, his every step long and showy like a peacock strutting its feathers.

An ember of fire licked at the back of Quinn's eyes as she met his shrewd gaze. He leaned against the counter in his extravagant pinstriped suit and purple vest, a devilish grin lacing his perfectly proportionate tawny face. Annoyingly perfect face.

Nonchalance and confidence poured from him like smooth liquor.

Fury burned in Quinn's core as she watched him. One way or another, Emrys was responsible for Jane's death, either by killing her at his own hand or by refusing to kiss Quinn. Both scenarios were rotten.

Clearing her throat and breaking eye contact, Quinn asked, "Are you here to gloat about Jane's death?"

He said nothing, but his jaw locked, and a muscle jumped. Then, a stilted silence met her as he took his top hat off and placed it on the counter. His nonchalant demeanor slipped away at the question, and only darkness remained.

But Quinn couldn't quite make out the nature of that darkness—the tone of it.

She swallowed, frustration hollow in her stomach. Emrys had power. And there was nothing she could do to stop him from whatever he was going to do next. Her only way forward was to gather as much information as she could from the autopsy before he ruined everything. So, she returned her attention to the body.

Quinn dumped the victim's stomach contents into a bag and labeled it. Then, she put the major organs into formalin jars to preserve them before moving on to inspect the intestines.

"You think I murdered Jane . . ." he said slowly, lingering on each word.

"Yes," she seethed, her eyes trailing to the hem of his pants.

"Why?"

"Why are you here?" she said through her teeth.

"Perhaps I enjoy watching you play with bowels. Perhaps it is the highlight of my day." His mouth fell into a hard line.

Quinn's lips pressed together, and it took all of her strength not to throw something at him. "You have very sick hobbies then."

"Conceivably."

"Like murder." Quinn sucked in a sharp breath. "Why are you trying to cover up this murder?"

Emrys glared at her, and the muscle in his jaw ticked. "What I do is no concern of yours."

Oh, he didn't like to be questioned. Not with all that power. People simply did what he wanted.

"You don't deny it?"

He let out a low chuckle. "Deny what? Watching you do a job that my house oversees? Watching you do your job is my job."

Quinn's nostrils flared. "That's rich, considering you barely ever take an interest in *my job*. And when you do, you destroy evidence and get me in trouble."

"Trouble?"

Quinn shook her head. Like he didn't know. The man radiated bullshit. Of course, he knew. As he said, his house oversaw the entire city. "Never mind, why don't you go back to being uninterested in my job? That would be far more enjoyable than your presence."

He scoffed. "You know, you're right; I shouldn't take an interest in you. But then you should drop your obsession with me."

It hit like a punch to the stomach. Because he was clearly referencing the night before, making her mistakes abundantly clear. She had never been obsessed with him and never would be. It was a foolish, rotten deal, but she couldn't say any of that out loud.

"I hate you."

"Right now"—his voice was low—"the feeling is mutual."

It all hurt and was too much, but damned if she let him get to her. Quinn inhaled sharply and refused to look at him. "You were at the crime scene. Why?"

He dodged the question with one of his own. "Why are you performing an autopsy on your best friend, who happens to be a gang member?"

A trickle of unease crawled up her spine. He knew things he shouldn't, like that Jane was in a gang. Even Quinn didn't know that, and Emrys was standing too far away to see the tattoo.

"Why do you refuse to answer any questions?" Her blood bubbled as her frustration rose into her tone.

"Why do you assume that I went to the crime scene?" The side of his mouth ticked as his gaze raked over her.

She was over the back-and-forth question game. "Your attire is disheveled, which is uncharacteristic of you." *Disarmingly disheveled* at that. She spoke clinically and without looking up. "And you're wearing dress shoes that are scuffed and covered in mud. Your hem is also coated with mud, your right cufflink is missing, and the collar of your shirt is ruffled. A splotch of dirt runs from your neck to behind your ear. I can't imagine you were playing in the mud for fun." She bit her lip, the fire in her belly bouncing to a three-four tempo. "So, I ask again, why are you tampering with evidence and trying to cover up this murder?"

Silence coated the room like coagulated blood. He sucked in a breath but said nothing. Perhaps he was shocked by her deduction.

"I am not tampering with evidence nor trying to cover up the murder," he said finally.

Lies. It was all lies. The guilt was plain to see on his clothing.

Emotions bombarded Quinn from every angle, and she could no longer keep them hidden and trapped in the deep prison inside of her. They spilled out when she said, "You're such a liar." The words came out more as a sob.

"I'm not," he nearly growled. "I want to solve this murder. I need to."

"Because you feel responsible?" She spat out, "Because you threatened her last night."

"Because I care." His voice was hollow.

He sounded sincere, but Quinn had never known him to care about anything other than having fun. He attended the Viridian at least three times a week and had the nickname of the Playboy Prince. He was callous and spoiled.

So, it was hard to believe he cared. Emrys Avalon didn't care about anyone.

Even if he didn't kill Jane, her death was not a spectacle. It was not an opportunity for a bored royal to play with or demean. Quinn wouldn't allow it.

"That is the last thing in the world I would ever believe," she said. "You don't have the ability to care."

Every muscle in his body went preternaturally still. "You're so right. All I am is a rogue to be used and abused."

Used and abused, right. She scoffed. "Who is Jane to you?" Quinn glowered.

"Perhaps I enjoy ballerinas, Quinnevere." Emrys cocked his head. "Maybe I like the taste of them, the smell of them." His devil-may-care smirk returned, but it was covered in rot and anger. "Maybe they're my type." His voice was a soft, unnerving velvet like the insides of the intestines. "Maybe I fuck them and then kill them." His broken smile stretched wider. "Maybe you're next."

He took a vicious step forward, and without thinking, Quinn picked up one of the tools on her tray, and she hurled it at him.

The next events seemed to happen in slow motion. The edge of his lips quirked up as the blade carved through the air.

She'd thrown a scalpel.

Oh fuck, a scalpel. She'd thrown a knife at his throat, and it would hit and slice through his carotid artery at its current projection. *Shit*, Quinn didn't mean to do that. Was she now to be a murderer as well?

"No." The word slipped from her mouth.

The last seconds were the worst because he hadn't moved, and Emrys Avalon, prince of New Swansea, was going to die.

But—

But he didn't. In the last second, Emrys moved his hand and caught the blade between two fingers, a centimeter from his skin.

"What the fuck?" Quinn breathed, stunned.

Emrys was not . . . normal. She was certain of it now.

"I see *you want* to murder me," Emrys said, lowering the knife from his throat.

She did. Metaphorically. Never in reality.

"How in all the mirrors did you do that?" Quinn asked. "You'd have to be Mirror-Blessed." It wasn't a question anymore. With a move like that, it was undeniable. The prince had magic.

"I know you've always wanted to hold a knife to my throat, Quinnevere"—his anger dropped, and his voice was back to his usual dark and sensual tones—"but this seems excessive."

"I didn't mean to do that."

"It seemed like you very much meant to throw the knife."

"I—" she stammered. "Yes, I . . ." Frustration's claws dug into her core. Oh, how she hated him. "Actually, no. I meant to throw a tool at you, but I never meant for it to be a knife, and I never meant for it to get anywhere close to you."

"I mean, if knife play is your thing . . ."

"Emrys."

"What? I don't kink shame." He raised his hands in mock surrender, his joking demeanor back. Apparently, it only took her trying to murder him.

"And what is your kink? Almost being murdered?"

A dimple flashed. "It's certainly one of them."

"Then it would seem we are perfectly suited." She placed her hands on the table, exhausted.

"In solving this murder, we most certainly are."

"That's only if I believe you want to solve it." Quinn glanced at the exit, her heart punching into her throat. "You were threatening her last night."

"I was." Emrys slowly walked toward Quinn like a lion observing its prey. He didn't stop until he was uncomfortably close. She refused to look, but she felt him hovering—towering next to her. His presence sent shivers down her spine.

"I think you should leave." Quinn returned to examining the intestines.

"And I think you should look me straight in my eyes and tell me I am a murderer."

"I've already told you that a handful of times." She felt his dark chestnut stare raking and assessing her.

"Now tell me to my face."

"Is this another kink?" She turned and tilted her head up to find his eyes. "I think you are a murderer." She tried to keep her voice steady and mechanical but failed spectacularly.

He slid a gloved finger across her jaw, and his body tensed, pain flashing on his face for a moment before it disappeared. "Jane and I—"

"Don't say her name." Tears coiled in Quinn's eyes. "Just don't . . . please."

He stepped closer, his vest grazed her arm, and he tilted his chin down to better meet her. "I did not kill her. I needed her help, and now I need your help to find her murderer." The words made Quinn gulp. "I know that you think I'm a careless, rich fool who spends all of his time partying and wasting my life away—you made that abundantly clear last night—but perhaps there may be more beneath that facade."

His presence tingled like energy in the air between them. And although she didn't want to admit it, something was shining through his mask of indifference, but she couldn't decipher exactly what. Maybe he was a narcissist and able to manipulate people and their emotions easily.

She wanted to ask why he needed Jane's help, but instead, she said, "I think you should leave." Then Quinn turned back to the intestines.

"Think of me what you will, but I'll search for Jan—her killer, with or without your help."

"I don't want you here." Quinn's chest rose in tight breaths.

"Trust me. If it were up to me, I wouldn't be here with—" *you*. The last word hung in the air unsaid. "I cannot let the killer roam free. It's—" He cleared his throat and stepped back. "I'll watch from over here. You have more work to do."

His audacity. Oh, he was so frustrating.

Emrys strolled to the closest counter and leaned against it, sliding his fingers into his pockets, and striking a devastating pose.

But he was right. She did have work to do, so ignoring him, Quinn pulled out the top of a long worm from inside the small intestines. She pulled and pulled and pulled, and the worm kept coming. White and slimy, the tapeworm was nearly three feet long. Considering how long they could grow to, this one was rather small.

"What in all the mirrors is that?" Emrys cursed, his expression one of pure disgust.

"A tapeworm." Her words were clinical and unimpressed.

Emrys's face lit up with horror and shock. "What? That's disgusting."

"It is a tapeworm. Some girls used to swallow an egg to try to get the tiny waists that you would see on some of the Starling

Ladies, and many courtesans do it, too," she said. Starling Ladies were high-class, high-fashion ladies.

But why would Jane use one?

Quinn thought she knew Jane, but as the minutes ticked by, she realized she understood nothing about the other redhead.

"I didn't know that girls were still doing that." Emrys stepped closer to get a better look at the worm.

"I didn't know people still held suitor balls. I guess some people like to keep up their archaic traditions." Quinn shook her head at his hypocrisy.

Emrys opened his mouth to respond but then abruptly shut it. He visibly swallowed before finally saying, "Why do it? The beauty standards are changing. There is no need to do this."

"Some girls still feel a lot of pressure to be skinny and to look like the 'ideal woman.'"

"But—"

"Or perhaps the Fantômes gang requires their girls to look a certain way," Quinn said clinically.

"That is . . . excessive."

"Indeed," she agreed. "Or perhaps it was another mirror deal gone wrong. Clearly, I know nothing about Jane."

Emrys's eyes darkened, and he let a long pause linger before he said, "How did she die?"

"Blood loss."

He took a hesitant step forward. "Drained entirely of blood?"

"Yes," Quinn breathed. Her hands shook, and dread crawled up her throat.

"What do you think killed her?" he asked.

Quinn shuddered and pretended to examine the bowels, but in truth, she didn't want to say that her best hypothesis was a vampire. It sounded ridiculous.

"Do you think it was a vampire?" His voice was wary.

Quinn bristled. It was like he read her mind. Or, possibly, he believed it. She faced him. "Vampires are extinct." She was a machine devoid of emotion.

His only response was to place his hands in his pockets and nonchalantly rock on his feet. Quinn glared up at him, a snake coiling around her heart and baring its fangs. He was so annoying. Emrys only suggested it to get under her skin—to toy with her.

"Can you please leave? You are too distracting." Quinn returned to her task.

"I can be quiet."

"No. You should leave. You are too distracting even with your mouth shut, which by the way, is always preferable."

Part of Quinn craved the distraction, though. Because she had to admit that since he entered the room, her devastation was held a little bit at bay. She was too focused on the prince to acknowledge her broken heart, and that made the autopsy easier.

But he was still an irritant.

Emrys chuckled. "You are refreshingly honest."

Were people not generally honest with him?

"And you are not quiet." She flashed a glare at him that could cut deep wounds in his chest.

He raised his hands in silent defeat and went back to leaning against the counter in a pose that must have been on purpose. No one leaned like that on accident. He looked like a hero in a silent film.

Quinn huffed. He was too distracting. Distracting because she hated him but also because his face disturbed her. She changed her mind. His presence was no longer useful. She'd deal with the devastation instead of whatever this was. "You are too diverting. Please, leave."

"How am I diverting if I am silent?"

"Your face is unsettling." Quinn grunted. "It is too perfect. Perfectly proportionate, with sharp cheekbones and sculpted eyebrows. Your nose is just the right size to fit your face. Your lips too full. Your eyes are too golden brown to be naturally human, and even your ears are just the perfect length, like they were gifted to you by a mirror. It's all too distracting. I want to measure it and study it."

Emrys's face flickered with an emotion Quinn couldn't read. "Thanks?" he asked hesitantly.

Quinn sighed. "Perfect does not equal beautiful. Beauty is in the flaws. Which you have none . . . unless you count your charming personality."

Emrys laughed, and Quinn gathered samples from the large and small intestines before preserving them in formalin. Then she packed up and cleaned the body.

As she was nearly finished, Emrys asked, "How was your birthday?"

Quinn glowered. "I much prefer the company of corpses. They don't talk bac—"

Her voice drained of all its power as she pulled a note out of an intestine. It was paper, and it should have been eroded by stomach acid, yet it wasn't. It was perfectly intact. It had to be mirror-spelled. Quinn's brain swirled with emotions and letters, and it took all her concentration to read the words.

Find the second Blood Mirror by the Suitor Ball, or you will be my next victim, Quinnevere.

She gasped and dropped the note back into the bowels. She felt the blood draining from her face, and every muscle in her body was as taut as a harp string. Whoever killed Jane knew that Quinn would do the autopsy. They knew she wouldn't be able to resist, which meant the killer either knew her or was watching her *very* closely.

Shivers coursed through her body, and she trembled.

The note gave her nine days to find the second Blood Mirror. An object she knew absolutely nothing about.

Her heart pounded, and beads of sweat rolled down her temple.

"Are you okay?" Emrys took a hesitant step toward her.

Quinn sucked in her emotions, sewed a smile on her face, and lied through her teeth, "Yes, everything is fine."

Emrys couldn't know about the note. Because if he were the murderer, she didn't want him to see her find it. And if he wasn't the murderer then . . . then she didn't know what, but she needed the note not to exist, and maybe if she pushed it away, it wouldn't.

Emrys cocked his head. "You don't seem—"

"Everything is swell. Truly, I should probably be finishing up." Her nostrils flared as she rolled the victim's body toward the negative temperature chamber.

Emrys's eyes narrowed for a moment before trailing down to her wrist automatically, almost as if he was expecting something to be there, and when he saw the tattoo, he oh-so-slightly cringed. Quinn felt naked and had the sudden urge to hide her marking. But at the same moment, she was curious to know what he knew about it.

Jane had the same one. It was a clue, and Quinn could use all the clues she could find.

So, instead of hiding, she decided to be straightforward. It was the most practical thing to do, after all. "What does my tattoo mean?"

Quinn had hers since before she could remember. Her entire family had them, and she never knew why. No one was alive to tell her.

Emrys crinkled his eyebrows in false surprise. "I have no idea what it means. It's your tattoo."

"You're a terrible liar."

"It would seem we both are." Emrys's lips slowly curled into a cruel smirk, and then he did something genuinely abominable. He strolled over to Quinn's process notes and started reading.

"Don't look at that." Her voice cracked. She tried to grab for the notepad, but right as she was about to reach out, she remembered body juices covered her hands and apron.

Emrys stepped back—taunting—his eyes still on the paper.

Shame pierced at the back of her throat like falling icicles. The last thing that Quinn wanted anyone to do was to read her notes. Because if they did, they would finally know. The girl who couldn't read. The girl who couldn't spell. The girl who would never succeed, no matter how hard she tried.

The slow, stupid, foolish girl.

At the age of six, Quinn was diagnosed with word blindness, a disease that caused her to be unable to differentiate words and sounds. Sounding out words, understanding meaning, and decoding sentences seemed impossible. Everything blended together and became a scrambled mess. She was unable to break down the sentences and words into smaller parts to learn them.

She'd managed to keep it secret for most of her life, but if Emrys read her notes, he would figure it out.

"Everything is spelled wrong. You really can't read, can you? That's why you refuse to do the murder briefings now?" His smile disappeared like crumbling ash.

Quinn gulped. "I can read." Her voice was far smaller than she intended it to be.

"But you certainly can't spell." There was the mocking she expected. He smoothed the silk lapels on his suit jacket before taking out a pen and writing something. "Can you read this out loud?"

Reading aloud. The number one enemy. A muscle twitched in her jaw as she decided if she would humor him. If she didn't read it, he would certainly think she was an idiot. But if she did, he would also think she was stupid because it would take far more effort than it should. Quinn huffed and jerked the paper out of his hand.

It had a sentence composed of many words she hadn't yet memorized. She knew how to read it. She knew the majority of what the note said, but she couldn't understand the words she hadn't memorized, and she was unable to break them down into more understandable chunks. Her uncle had taught her how to take apart words and sound them out, but sometimes it was so hard. But she had an excellent memory, and once Quinn learned a word, she would know it forever.

The sentence read:

> *Quinnevere Ashelle wants to help Prince Emrys find the murderer, and she thinks he is devilishly attractive, and that's why she wants to fuck him.*

Quinn refused to read it out loud and instead tossed the paper at Emrys's face. "I think you've made your point. Can you please leave now?"

"I don't understand. You're clearly brilliant." Emrys waved his hand at all the samples and the room. A fire burned at her cheeks. "How do you do all of this if you can't spell or read?"

Quinn rubbed at her temples. He was getting on her last nerve. "I can read. It's just . . . that it's hard. The words and the sounds don't make sense in my brain. But I have a good memory. And I don't want to help you do anything. Ever. I can read it, as you can see. It just sometimes feels like an impossible task."

"Oh."

A stilted quiet danced through the room to the beat of a three-four waltz as Emrys stared at her. She returned to her task but still felt his eyes prickling on her skin.

"You *are* brilliant, you know," he said, causing her to whip her head in his direction. An incomprehensible emotion gathered on his perfect face. "I need you to help me solve these murders. I am a great detective, but I can't solve this case without your expertise."

These murderers? There was more than one?

Quinn swallowed, not knowing what to do with these words. She didn't—couldn't help him. Especially not when he was a suspect.

"I am not going to stop, and I don't think you are either," he said. "Let's work together."

Quinn wasn't sure if she could trust him. This was the

famous Emrys Avalon, who only cared about having fun and ruining things. Over the last five years, Emrys had gotten caught in three scandals that tarnished him and the crown's reputation. He even burned down his country house in Aberdare.

Trusting him was foolish. He could be the murderer. "No," she said. "I don't trust you."

"You will." Emrys bowed his head in respect and said, "Good day, Ms. Ashelle."

"Mr. Avalon. I mean, Your Highness." His honorific felt foreign on her tongue.

His exit was swift and confusing. He refused to leave, yet suddenly, he couldn't wait to get away. The hairs on the back of her neck tingled, and she wondered if she'd accidentally agreed to something she shouldn't have. She'd refused to help him, yet somehow, she knew it wouldn't matter. He'd worm his way into her investigation.

And that was dangerous.

Any time spent with Emrys Avalon was a terrible mistake.

TWELVE

The smell of fish was suffocating.

Quinn and her three friends were knee-deep in mud by the docks, trying to find clues. It was where Jane's body had been found. So, it was the best place to start an investigation.

Action kept them all from breaking down. If they kept moving, maybe they wouldn't have to acknowledge the truth of Jane's death.

"Why is it so cold?" Giselle shivered and rubbed her arms to try to keep warm. "It's only autumn."

"Because a New Swansea City autumn is winter everywhere else." Constance folded her arms and glared at the mud as if it might physically harm her. She did not shiver. Constance never appeared to be cold, despite never wearing any overcoats.

Jevon moaned. "The cold is not doing good things for my temperament."

Quinn laughed. *His silent fidgeting, brooding temperament?*

The wind howled a cruel song, and fog hung over the Marina District like toxic gas, invading the grimy streets and clinging to Quinn's pores. But beyond being irritating, it was also contaminating and possibly washing trace evidence away. Not to mention, high tide was inching closer and closer.

Sea lions barked at the frigid air, creating a symphony of ear-grating annoyance. Quinn huffed. This was a forensic nightmare.

With every gust of wind, Quinn cringed a little, not only because evidence was drifting away but also because if she didn't solve this murder, she might be the next victim.

She would have solved the murder anyway, but now she couldn't afford not to. Nine days. It wasn't enough.

Quinn inhaled sharply and caught Giselle staring at Pelican Isle, the small island prison in the middle of the bay that held her father captive. The place was impossible to escape.

Sometimes, Quinn wondered if her friend wanted to break her father out.

A shiver ran down her spine. Quinn hated breaking rules because she couldn't control the consequences. If there was one lesson she learned from watching her parents die, it was that Quinn never wanted to be powerless again.

Which was precisely why she needed to get this investigation under control.

Quinn rubbed her necklace, asking it for support. It was a portal to a Mirror-God, and somehow, despite everything, she still wanted it near.

Sailboat rigging clinked against masts, each ding sending a jolt through her. The sun grew tired and slipped closer to bed, night beckoning. Seagulls flew over the brick-and-mortar shops as fish vendors started to pack up for the day. The ferry building, normally bustling with patrons and boats, also began to clear. The marina at night was not a safe place to be, and no one wanted to stay past sunset.

"Look what I found." Jevon held up a piece of a purple peacock feather that possibly matched the fragment found on the corpse.

Quinn swallowed and closed her eyes before whispering, "Don't touch it with your bare hands." She didn't want to reprimand Jevon, but he'd put his fingerprints all over it and possibly contaminated the evidence. "Here, place it in this bag." She waded over to him and hoped for the best.

"What are you doing down there?" a man called from the street above. Jevon jumped and nearly dropped the feather back into the dirt, Giselle cursed under her breath, Constance narrowed her eyes like a tiger measuring its prey, and Quinn jolted.

Shooting a glance at each of her friends, Quinn climbed up the hill. The man had salt and pepper hair, wrinkles at the corners of his eyes, and leathery, beige skin from staying out in the sun for prolonged periods. He wore an apron covered in what Quinn could only assume were fish guts. He was most likely a seafood vendor, which meant he spent a good deal of time on this street and around the waterline. It was also possible that he lived in the fish merchant row houses nearby.

Quinn straightened her shoulders and tried to look both older and more trustworthy. She needed this man to comply and not dismiss her. "We are investigating the murder. I am with the medical examiner's office." Quinn's tone was both clinical and authoritative. It was the voice she practiced every time she had to present her findings on an autopsy to the police.

The man's brows creased. "But I heard it's a gang murder."

How had that news already made it out to the public? Was it Jane's tattoo? Was it seen by onlookers before the body was brought to the morgue? "Perhaps, but we have reasons to believe this case is not that simple." Quinn sucked in a breath, and she tried to keep her hands from trembling.

"Oh, I see." The man grunted as his eyes raked over her friends. "And you're all with the medical examiner's office?"

"Yes," Quinn lied. "Do you know if anyone saw something out of the ordinary yesterday?"

The man contemplated her question for a moment, his eyes tracing all of them again. He seemed to be weighing their validity, concluding that it would be worse to hinder them because he turned and called down the street. "Johnny, come over here."

A boy roughly three years younger than them lifted his gaze and stopped working. He'd been packing up a roadside stand. Slowly, he walked over and met the merchant and Quinn.

"Tell this young lady what you saw last night before discovering the body," the older man said.

"I saw a star, miss." The boy averted his eyes. He was either scared or trying to be respectful to his superior. The latter thought made Quinn's skin crawl. She was no better than this boy. She was probably far poorer in all the ways that counted.

"A shooting star?" Quinn asked. "Like in the sky?"

"No," he said, roses blossoming on his cheeks. "On the ground. I saw a fast-moving, shining object that looked like a shooting star. It lit up the night, and then it was gone. I am betting the killer was Mirror-Blessed, ma'am."

"It was on fire?" Quinn asked tentatively.

"No." He shook his head. "It was simmering like glitter caught in the light of a chandelier."

Shimmering like glitter?

It could be a Mirror-Blessed persona with a magical power. Or a person who made a bad bargain and ended up with sparkling skin, but—and this was incredibly unlikely but considering the puncture wounds on Jane's body—it could have also been a vampire moving at super speed with reflective clothing. But that last possibility was incredibly far-fetched. Quinn still didn't want to believe that vampires were back, but it was a distinct possibility. Most likely, the murderer wore sequins or something else of that nature.

It seemed to be a big possibility because Jane was most likely killed at the Viridian nightclub.

"Did you see anything else?"

The boy sneezed and flicked out of existence for a moment. Disappearing and reappearing in an instance.

A mirror consequence? Or a mirror cost?

Many vendors in the Marina made deals with mirrors, mostly for things like a never-ending supply of fish or food that would not spoil. It was possible that he traded for something practical but settled for a terrible consequence.

But he barely looked of age. Maybe twenty-three at the oldest.

"No, ma'am, I promise that is all I saw." He winced, and his shoulders sagged.

"Thank you for your time." Quinn nodded to each of them in turn before rotating back to the crime scene.

Once they were gone, Constance said with her usual sarcastic jubilance, "So a shooting star killed Jane?"

"Let me add that to my list of ways humans can murder each other." Giselle grimaced as she tried to lighten the mood.

"Or to the list of ways vampires can." Quinn's voice hung on the frigid air.

At her words, Jevon gulped, Constance paled, and Giselle pinched her lips together in deep thought. None of them wanted to believe vampires could be back. But Jane had vampire-shaped puncture wounds in her neck.

"So, what do we do now?" Jevon asked.

It was the question of the hour. So far, their only evidence was puncture wounds, glitter, a fingerprint, and now a feather. But they had no suspects.

"I think we should look into Jane's past," Quinn said. "We need to pay a visit to the Fantômes."

THIRTEEN

After the crime scene, Quinn and her friends split up to wash off the mud and get ready to go to the Russet, the Les Fantômes gang's casino.

Dripping wet and holding a towel, Quinn froze in her tracks.

At the center of her bed was a small white box, the size of a croissant. Slowly, she approached, her body on full alert. It could be from the killer. After all, they'd already sent her a threatening note.

Maybe it was insurance.

Sucking in a breath, Quinn opened the box, her fingers trembling. Two items rested inside. A key and a note. The key was bronze with intricate loops carved into the handle. And the note read:

My Dearest Quinnevere,
If you're reading this, it means I am dead.
I've spent the last couple years trading in secrets
that were meant to be kept buried. If I am right,
then you are in grave danger. I am sorry for all

the riddles, but I cannot write clearly in case this
ends up in the wrong hands. I am so sorry to
involve you in this.
        I leave you my inheritance and my secrets.
This key will lead you to both.
        Your Loving Sister,
        Jane
        P.S. Keep your necklace close.

Translating the words to meaning took far too much effort because the handwriting was curved and rushed. Quinn's brain had to work four times as hard to understand, and when she did, she fell on her knees to the floor. Unshed tears licked at her eyes and burned.

Quinn crumpled the note between her fingers and threw a pointe shoe at the wall, then a ballet slipper. Agony building in her chest, she threw anything she could get her hands on. Tutus, anatomy books, pillows, clothing. One of the pointe shoes hit the makeshift wall of her bedroom with the force of a small boulder, shaking it.

But she didn't stop. She hurled books, clothing, and bed sheets around. Her heart was a crescendo, and her breathing became stilted.

Jane was dead, and Quinn couldn't cry.

Jane had called her sister. She'd thought of her as her true family, and Quinn couldn't even cry.

There was something fundamentally broken inside her. Normal people cried. Normal people could read without struggle. Quinn was such a fool to believe she could solve her friend's murder because she would never be smart enough or good enough to do it.

And if she didn't solve the murder, she'd die.

Nine days.

To solve the murder or uncover the mystery of the Blood Mirror.

Nine fucking days.

It wasn't enough.

Quinn huffed. She was surrounded by chaos, yet she felt empty. She shivered at both her ineptitude and the mess. Disorder was the enemy.

Everything was so out of control.

"Quinnevere, what are you doing in there?" Uncle Matias asked from the other side of the makeshift wall. "Are you okay?"

"Yes," she called back but pulled her legs into her chest and let her head rest against the wall.

He slid open the divider and said, "You don't look okay." He eyed the scene, disgust flashing on his cheeks. He did not tolerate disorder either. "You look like you got into a fight with the ballet."

"I may have." She shrugged off the evidence of her emotions.

"Should I be concerned that auditions are not progressing as you had hoped?" he asked, holding a tray of food. "I hope you're doing well," he added to her continued silence.

His expression seemed genuine, but it was hard to tell. He desperately wanted Quinn to set aside her *foolish pursuits*—his name for dancing. After all, he never wanted her to audition in the first place. In his mind, she *must focus* on the morgue.

"It's going fine, except tomorrow's auditions are canceled because of the . . ." She inhaled sharply. "The murder. The Royalle Ballet director loved Jane, and he wanted to postpone a couple days to respect her memory."

A letter had arrived saying as much before Quinn's bath.

"Oh, I am sorry. I know you cared for Jane." Uncle Matias's voice was a melodic tenor as he placed his tray down on the kitchen counter.

A wellspring of emotions gathered in her throat, and she was unable to speak, so she simply nodded.

He rubbed his hand, clearly not knowing what to say or how

to comfort her. He settled on practicality. "Well, I do hope you clean up this mess."

Perfectionism ran in the family. As did the lack of emotional expression.

"And, Quinn, you better not be looking into that murder."

Quinn stilled. "Why?"

"Because I said so." And as usual, that was the end of every argument between them.

The group was running a half hour behind to Les Fantômes's gang casino because Giselle was late. As usual. On the way, Quinn told the group about the threatening note she found during the autopsy, and she showed the group the key. It didn't make sense to keep things from them. No one knew where the key came from. So, they decided to check the casino for something that might fit.

The plan was that Constance and Jevon would ask around about Jane at the bar, and Giselle and Quinn would search for a door that fit the key.

When the entire group had finally arrived, they walked to the entrance.

In keeping with its mysterious, enchanted theme, the Russet entrance was in the back of a dark, dank alley. The rickety mahogany cellar doors creaked as Constance lifted the latch, exposing a set of claustrophobic stairs leading to darkness and shadows. Although Quinn had been to the Russet many times, the hairs on the back of her neck rose. There was something about walking into pure darkness that deeply unsettled her.

Constance, on the other hand, bounded down the stairs like it was nothing. Following, Quinn held the rail so tightly that white spread across her knuckles. Giselle and Jevon made up the rear; neither of them seemed to mind the dark at all.

As Quinn stepped onto the landing, a glowing light confronted her senses.

"What has a head, a tail, is silver and has no arms or legs?" asked a petite bouncer with vibrant purple waves that danced a Lindy-Hop atop her head, bouncing and twirling in a manufactured wind.

Was it a mirror consequence or wish?

Quinn shuddered. Either way, magic always unsettled her. They reminded her too much of the mirrors and what they could do. Nightshade purposely set her up to fail. He wanted her torture.

Dirty fucking mirrors.

The only way to enter the Russet was to solve a ridiculous riddle. Quinn appreciated good riddles but often found them to be useless and trivial things. As she pondered it, the light emanating from inside the cave blinded her. The vast difference in the atmosphere, temperature, and surroundings caused her vision to blur, and her knees buckled under newborn fawn-like legs.

"A sienna coin," Giselle said in a disinterested voice, as if the riddle was the easiest and most boring thing she had ever heard.

"Welcome into the land of sin. Best of luck on your adventures herein," the tiny girl said with a triumphant yet mystical voice that made Quinn's insides burn.

The group stepped into a vast, watery cavern. Clinging from the cave roof were stalactites formed like crystal icicles, dangling like stars' tears falling through the sky. Lighting up the entire room were thousands of magical fireflies buzzing across the ceiling and the water glowed with a gradient blue and purple pattern, illuminated by the Russet's enchantments.

The place glistened like a river of ornate diamonds.

A jazz singer graced a wooden stage, singing a somber and smooth melody, setting a calming yet chilling ambiance. Wooden walkways allowed patrons to cross the cave to platforms housing liquor, tables, and gambling. Gondola boats floated on the water as couples shared romantic moments.

Quinn turned to her friends. Giselle's eyes were wide, and she visibly shook. "You okay?"

"I . . . it's been fifteen years since I've been here," Giselle said, nervously, her eyes darting around like a trapped rabbit. "A lot has changed. My father is in prison, and I don't even know who is in charge."

It was rare to see Giselle shaken, and Quinn was at a loss for words. This wasn't in Giselle's nature. She was addicted to danger and adrenaline, and she never faltered. So Quinn had no idea how to help.

"It's going to be okay. You won't even have to speak to anyone," Quinn said, trying to give comfort in some way.

Giselle nodded but still looked utterly uncomfortable.

Quinn wrung her hands. "Constance, make sure you are discrete."

"Discrete." Constance laughed before completely changing the subject. "Shouldn't you be the one looking for the Fox?" Constance glared at Giselle. "He's your old friend."

Many of Les Fantômes went by code names, and Fox was the name of Giselle's childhood friend that she hadn't seen in fifteen years. Not since her mother forced her to leave the gang at ten.

"So would you like to be the one to pick the locks?" Giselle asked.

A smile soaked in golden mischief spread on Constance's face. "I'm sure I would enjoy trying."

"I'm sure you would give up after a second," Giselle said under her breath.

Constance rolled her eyes. "Fine, we all know I am much better at forcing information from people anyway."

Quinn clenched her eyes shut for a moment. "You did hear me say discretely, right?"

Constance merely winked at her friend before pulling Jevon by the hand onto a bridge that led to intoxication and excess.

That did not bode well.

"Shall we go?" Giselle's gaze tracked her friends.

Quinn nodded with a gulp, and anxiety built in her stomach. She was about to break into Les Fantômes' private rooms. Something that went far out of her comfort zone. She was a bitter rule follower. She didn't break in, lie, or steal.

All of which she would have to do tonight.

The wood creaked beneath Quinn's feet as she walked across a bridge past the Shadow-Prince tables. Her skin tingled. She longed to play the cards. Quinn was uniquely good at Shadow-Prince because she'd learned to spot patterns in the cards at the age of six. She might be a terrible reader, but she was uncommonly good at recognizing patterns. Her brain worked in sequencing. She saw things others did not. She understood things others did not. So much so that people often accused her of jumping to conclusions too quickly. But more often than not, her original guess was correct.

The girls walked the darkened path behind the stage. Along it were nooks, presumably for a lover's tryst. The songs echoed off the walls and dampened any spoken words. As the path continued, the stalactite crystals formed deeper, and Quinn had to maneuver her head around the crooked daggers slicing from the ceiling.

"There are wooden doors over here." Giselle pointed to a fork in the walkway.

When they reached the doors, Quinn pulled the key out of her pocket and tried to match it to a lock, but none of the doors worked. So instead, Giselle pulled the pins out of her coiffure, chose a door at random, and picked the lock. In seconds, she had it open.

"Shall we?" Giselle said, her hair falling down her shoulders.

Inside was a brilliant blue, yellow, and orange thermal pool. The heat and steam radiated off the water. Across the cavern, ice crystals surrounded boxes—thousands of boxes.

The juxtaposition of the extreme heat and cold was jarring. And magical.

But there was no visible way to get to the boxes.

"We should take a peek, don't you think?" Giselle walked over to the side of the cavern. Before Quinn could respond, she hooked her feet into makeshift foot holes on the rock wall and began to traverse the cave.

"Giselle, that pool's probably hot enough to melt your skin off."

"Well, what is living if you don't take chances?" she called back, still fully focused on her task.

Quinn clenched her teeth, causing her face to hurt. Her friend was insane and watching stunts like this was always nerve-racking. But within seconds, Giselle had made it entirely across the room, jumped down onto the ledge, and started opening the boxes. Giselle was all curves, but with her years of acrobatic training, she made climbing look as easy as breathing.

"What is it?" Quinn called.

"Blood bags. Hundreds and hundreds of blood bags." Giselle held one up.

"What in all the fucking mirrors?" Quinn whispered.

But she didn't receive an answer because the door burst open, and five Fantômes poured in and pointed their guns at Quinn.

FOURTEEN

"Y̲ou're trespassing, and do you know what Fantômes do with people who interfere in their business?" A tall brunette man in his mid-twenties with russet brown skin asked. He wore a deep purple pinstriped suit with an olive-green cravat, purple feathered pocket square, black glasses, and a smile that would make the gods jealous.

Something about him seemed familiar.

"Oh, probably something horrifying," Giselle said sarcastically.

The man pointed his gun across the clearing. "How did you get over there?"

"I climbed," Giselle said as if it were the most obvious thing in the world. "How do you get across?"

"The bridge." The man matched her tone. "Would you like to come join your friend?"

"Not particularly." Giselle smiled. "I don't see a bridge."

"It's invisible." The man took two strides into the room and held his gun up to Quinn's temple. "Please join us."

Quinn rubbed her necklace for support as her heart screeched like a violin string off-key, and her teeth chattered. She was going to die. And worse, her friend would be murdered with her.

Giselle threw her arms up dramatically. "While I don't believe you'd actually do it, I'd prefer not to risk it."

She maneuvered the climb just as quickly as the first time. If Quinn didn't know for a fact that Giselle didn't possess magic, watching her acrobatic skills would make anyone believe she did.

"Hadleigh, bring her here," the man with glasses said to a brunette girl. She wore a dark maroon pinstriped pantsuit and walked over to Giselle with her gun at the ready.

Hadleigh did as commanded, grabbing Giselle and roughly throwing her at her friend. Quinn caught her and stumbled back, her face coming dangerously close to a crystal. Clasping hands, the girls stared at the Fantômes in a silence so deep the cave threatened to swallow it.

"Why are you riffling through our things?" the leader asked.

Quinn's tongue seized up, and no words formed. She had no idea what to say. So she clenched her hands into fists and tried to feel her feet upon the wood. A grounding exercise. She needed to get her breathing and heart rate under control. It was the only way to fight.

Instead of answering, Quinn finally settled on, "You're blood traffickers?"

"Yes," he said slowly, playing with his pistol.

"You're vampires." As she said the words, she knew they didn't make sense. First, vampires were extinct—although the building evidence might suggest otherwise. And second, all of them had both a gang tattoo and a Mirror-Blessed tattoo. They couldn't be vampires . . . unless vampires could bargain with the mirrors. Right?

That was a horrifying thought.

"No." He smiled; a grin filled with toxins. "We are the supply. It's a very profitable business model."

"Supply for vampires?" Quinn's fingers shook as she grasped onto Giselle.

The man shrugged. "All things are possible in the land of mirrors."

It was not an answer, and Quinn knew she wasn't going to get one, so instead, she asked, "And the casino is a front?"

"The casino is, as it turns out, a casino." His eyes had a wicked twinkle. "Although perhaps we might also do some Mirror Market business from time to time." He winked. "Do let me know if you are in the market for anything forbidden." That last bit was definitely directed at Giselle, and Quinn was fairly certain it was some kind of innuendo, but that was Giselle's specialty, not hers. "We have many things in the market that might be to your tastes."

The Mirror Market was a black market for highly dangerous mirror magic goods that were banned by Castle Hill and the police.

Turning to Giselle, Quinn asked, "Did you know about the role in the Mirror Market?"

"No—" Giselle pinched her friend in a way that said, *shut your mouth now, please.*

"Why would she know about it?" Hadleigh asked.

Giselle's nostrils flared, and she ran a finger along her necklace, thinking, "I am a private investigator. My job is to uncover secrets."

The leader's lips turned up. "You seem too *obvious* to have that type of job. There isn't a room you would be in where I wouldn't notice you." His eyes flashed for a moment over her curves.

"And you seem young to run a gang. I much preferred your old leader," Giselle spat back.

His smile grew larger. "I grow tired of you. Maybe we should throw you in the pool." The man faked a yawn. "Or maybe I'll just shoot you and leave you for carrion birds."

"Carrion birds in your casino? It doesn't even make sense."

"Do you have a death wish, girl?"

"Are you going to murder me? Really?" Giselle squared her shoulders and glared directly into the leader's eyes. "You can't, can you? We aren't gang members. The police would instantly know if you did, and I am sure they are dying for a reason to lock you away on the Rock with your old leader."

He let out a deep laugh and strolled up to Giselle, putting his face in hers. "If I wanted to kill you, girl, I'd do it and brand you with our symbol after you were dead." Fire crackled between them, but both remained resolute. Either Giselle was not afraid of him or wouldn't allow her fear to show on her face. He grasped her by the chin. "Or maybe I would do it before you died so that I could watch you scream. Not all our members get their markings from a mirror. Some take the iron."

"I am sure you would enjoy me screaming," Giselle said with a soft, dangerous lilt. "Maybe we could schedule another time when I could reciprocate the favor."

He let out a low chuckle, and a glimmer of warm delight danced in his eyes. "I am sure I would enjoy that more than I would like to admit." He sighed. "But alas, I have to kill you. You know our secrets."

Quinn's heart pounded in fast violin strokes, but she pulled upon Giselle's bravery and said, "No one would believe we joined a gang, and even if they did, the branding wouldn't be healed, and no decent medical examiner would miss that. They would suspect you planted it."

"Good point." He turned his coal eyes on Quinn. "Maybe I'll just hold you hostage long enough for your marking to heal. Meanwhile, I'll torture you and your pretty friend."

"I am sure I would enjoy the torture too much, and it would devalue the whole point of doing it." Giselle held her chin high, still intensely studying him.

The man's gaze dipped to her chest, and his smirk turned feral. "You do make rather a good point. Perhaps you would be more valuable to me alive."

A dangerous tension jolted between them, running on an electric current so hot sparks chipped off, threatening to consume them in flames. Giselle flashed a vicious smile and winked. And the two engaged in the most inappropriate of staring contests.

Hadleigh cleared her throat. "Francois."

That name felt familiar.

"Right, you are, Haddie. Where were we?" he asked, stepping back and composing himself a bit.

Giselle let out a snort and defiantly crossed her arms. "I believe you were threatening to torture us. So why don't you get along with that?"

Quinn's head swung to her friend. What in all the mirrors was Giselle thinking? Admittedly, she was brave and had a sheer lack of fear in the face of uncertain circumstances, but now she was goading this man—Francois—on.

But something was off about the Fantômes and the situation, and it gnawed at the back of her mind. It was almost as if they were play-acting. As if this is how they were expected to appear.

After a prolonged moment of silence, Francois laughed, and his face lit up with pure enjoyment. "Touché, perhaps we'll wait on the torturing for now."

Quinn loosed a breath, but Giselle only rolled back her shoulders and said, "I thought the new leader of Les Fantômes would be scarier." Giselle glowered at him, the energy between them palpable.

"While a fox might not be scary, I find that they can outmaneuver almost everyone." He ran a finger down his silk lapels, straightening them.

Giselle tensed and tilted her head once more, studying him intensely. "Almost everyone."

"You're the Fox?" Quinn blurted out.

"You know of me?" he asked with a raise of his brow.

"We were loo—" Giselle stomped on Quinn's foot before she could say anything else.

Clearly, Giselle didn't want him to know who she was. But why, if they were once friends? And if they were friends, how did he not recognize her? It'd been fifteen years, and it was possible that Giselle looked utterly different after growing up, but why wouldn't she want him to know?

Francois slightly shifted on his feet, waiting for an actual answer. His shadow danced against the wall, reminding Quinn of a Viridian illusion.

Illusions . . . Quinn let out a gasp, stepped back, and nearly fell into the thermal pool. "Francois," she whispered. "It was you. You were with Jane the night she died. You must know more about her death."

"Oh, that's why you've come. You're the little redheaded medical examiner I've heard so much about." Francois rubbed his chin, his entire demeanor changing—softening. "I wondered if it was on council business, but this makes more sense."

Council business? And he knew about her? From who, Jane?

"And before you ask, we had nothing to do with Jane's murder," he said, his tone and demeanor utterly shifted. His "gang" mask fell away, leaving a less intimidating version of him underneath. "Jane was family, and we don't kill family even when they step out of line. I assume you're investigating the murder because you cared about Jane, and while that doesn't make us friends, it does place us on the same side."

Hadleigh shuffled her feet and averted her eyes slightly, clenching her fists. If Quinn hadn't been staring right at the girl, she would have missed it. But it was clear Hadleigh didn't want anyone to see what rested in her golden irises.

Did she care about Jane—maybe loved her?

Quinn released some of the tension in her shoulders and loosed a breath. She chose to believe, for now, that the gang didn't want Jane dead—at least until she had solid evidence pointing toward them.

But now that Francois was talking, she'd take advantage of it. "Stepping out of line?"

"Jane was acting cagey lately," Francois said.

"How so?" Giselle asked.

Hadleigh opened her mouth to respond, but Francois held up a hand. "We are not in the business of charity. If you want information, you'll have to trade. Tell me about the autopsy, and I'll answer your questions."

Quinn swallowed. Francois knew too much about her, and she knew barely anything about him. It was unsettling, but then maybe Jane told him. But she needed a lead or a clue to a killer. The best option was to trade. So Quinn listed the facts of the case but intentionally left out precisely what was found on the body, in case the gang only wanted the information to cover up the murder.

None of them spoke. Silence and heartbreak were their only companions, their demeanors hollow and shaken. Either they were excellent fakes, or they cared.

Francois was the first to regain his composure. "Thank you for telling us," he said, a tiny quiver in his voice as he slipped his gun back into his jacket. "Ask your questions."

"Alright," Quinn said slowly, unsure if she was falling into a trap. "She was acting cagey?"

Hadleigh frowned. "She was sneaking and hanging around places she normally wouldn't go—"

"And before you ask, she means like the Viridian." Francois darted a glance at his friend. "It's an unwritten rule for rival gangs not to mess with the Viridian."

"No one wants to mess with Kordelia Shone," Hadleigh said. "Most of us would rather die than endure her form of torture."

Torture?

Quinn knew Kordelia was dangerous and very, very powerful. She was terrified of the Viridian's owner most of the time. Still, she never assumed Kordelia would harm someone.

"What about someone in her life who might have a motive to kill her?" Quinn asked.

"No one in the Fantômes would dare, and the only person who would from her past was her husband, but he is dead now." Hadleigh's throat visibly bobbed.

Husband. That was right. Jane had been married. It was another thing she barely talked about, and the only reason Quinn knew about it was because she'd done the autopsy on the vile man. When asked about it, Jane refused to answer. At the time, Quinn didn't want to pry, but now, she wanted to know everything.

"Why did Jane join your gang in the first place?" Quinn asked.

"Because her terrible dead spouse gambled away all of her earnings, life savings, and livelihood, and then he wagered her off as well." There were warmer blizzards than the frozen lake of Hadleigh's words.

"What are you saying?" Quinn asked.

"He offered her to his enemies as collateral." Francois placed his hands into his pockets and leaned against the wooden railing. "After a couple of nights of what I presume to be a living hell, Jane went to the Looking Glass and asked it for three lifetimes full of riches."

"What did she trade?" Giselle asked sternly.

"It's unclear; her deal with Nightmares has always been private information," Francois said pragmatically. "But something did happen in that mirror that caused her never to dance again, and she somehow became tied to Nightmares because after that first deal, she visited him weekly, sometimes daily."

"We know she got some money out of the deal because we know she paid off her husband's debts and freed herself from the Cobra Lilies. When her husband eventually died—" *Was murdered.* It was one of the investigations Emrys tampered with and got Quinn in trouble. "Jane came to us for refuge."

Acid frothed in Quinn's esophagus, and a sudden wave of heartburn hit her. The entire story was tragic. How could Jane have remained so positive and happy with everything that had happened to her? It was like she didn't know Jane at all. And this new information slanted Quinn's worldview and made her question every interaction she'd ever had with Jane.

"And what did you do?" Giselle asked.

"I allowed her to join my gang in a business capacity," Francois said. "She was a stunning and talented woman, after all."

"So she traded one gang for another?" Quinn bit out. "You took advantage of her vulnerability."

The corner of his mouth quirked upward. "I take advantage of anything that will let me."

Quinn swallowed her disgust. "How chivalrous of you."

He stood up straight and caught her gaze in his midnight-fire eyes. "If you want civility, I wouldn't ask me . . . or your prince."

Quinn jolted. This was the last thing she expected to hear. "My prince?"

"Haven't you seen the papers this morning? Your face is all over them." Francois motioned to one of his cronies, who ran out of the room and reappeared with the paper in his hands. With a jerk of the head from Francois, the boy handed the newspaper to Quinn.

The headline read, *Golden Prince Snubbed by Beautiful Ballerina*.

"You have got to be kidding me," Quinn said. The last thing she wanted was to be in a newspaper next to Emrys. If she were to be in a newspaper, it would involve accolades for her dancing.

She crinkled the paper before handing it back to the boy.

Francois let out a deep chuckle. "Apparently, you were quite rude. All the gossip columns are covering it. And speaking of your pretty prince, he was hanging around Jane a lot recently. The two always sneaking away."

Quinn shouldn't be surprised by this information because Emrys had said as much himself, but it was still startling. But she didn't have time to think about that because a voice sounded at the door. "She was no more rude than she usually is." Emrys appeared at the alcove's entrance.

He wore a midnight black double-breasted tailcoat accented with emerald green trim, a silk cravat, and a gilded cane. He'd left his top hat at home. His ink-spilled hair framed his face and drew focus to his sparkling chestnut eyes, which blazed with mischief, humor, and entertainment. He looked like trouble dancing a tango with joy.

Apparently, he found Quinn surrounded by wicked gang members quite amusing.

"Ah, there is your prince now." Francois beamed as he met Emrys's stare. "We summoned a demon."

"Don't call him *my* anything," Quinn murmured and dropped her gaze to her feet. She did not need to peer at his deep arrogance.

Ignoring Quinn, Francois asked, "Do you appear anytime someone talks about you? Is that your power?"

Quinn's heart stopped. Francois knew that Emrys was Mirror-Blessed.

"Often enough to keep you on your toes." His words weren't dark, but the way they trilled off his tongue made it feel like a threat. Like his words were a pool of darkness drowning her.

"That sounds intoxicating," Francois said ruefully. Their dynamic was strange. Deadly yet friendly like they were two devils playing tricks on each other. They both basked in power and influence and could enchant with a smile.

"Well, I hate to ruin your fun, Francey, but I need to speak to our little ballerina." Emrys was a picture of ease and power.

Quinn scoffed. She didn't want to talk to him. Ever. Rogues might make other girls melt, but she was not interested in his playboy nature.

"Wait, I have one more question," Quinn said. "Why was she asking about the Blood Mirror?" Quinn threw all caution to the wind. She needed to know this information.

Emrys's hand stiffened, and shock jetéd across Francois's sculpted face before he cooled his features. "I have no idea," he lied.

Interesting. So, the gang knew about the Blood Mirrors.

"A word of caution, Quinnevere Ashelle," Francois said. "I may let you investigate Jane's murder, but you should stay far away from anything else related to Les Fantômes' business. Do you understand me?"

Quinn simply nodded. There was no point in arguing with a

deadly gang leader. But he was threatening her, and that was information. It was a clue. And if he knew about the mirrors, maybe he knew about the tattoo.

"Do you know about this?" Quinn lifted her own arm, showing the bloody painting.

Francois paled and tossed a glance at Hadleigh. "No," he lied again.

"Great!" Emrys flashed a fake prince charming smile. "Then the three of us will get going."

The prince escorted them out with one hand curled around her right bicep. His touch shot fire through her body. But as soon as they were out of earshot, Quinn spun around and pushed him against the wall. He hit it with a thunk. "I didn't need your help."

A gilded grin painted his lips. "Yes, that seems to be a pattern for you. It was clear that you had the situation fully under control."

"Why do you want to speak with me?" Quinn said, crossing her arms across her silk evening dress.

"To solve a murder."

A murder she still wasn't sure he didn't commit.

FIFTEEN

"**W**hat have you discovered here?" Emrys's voice, usually a dark-devilish-honey, now sounded like a bothersome gnat.

"Nothing I plan on sharing with you," Quinn said, turning her back on him and walking into the center of a wooden pathway, a crossroads of sorts that led to four different paths. The glow of the cave's fireflies illuminated their faces, and the water dampened their conversation.

Emrys turned his inscrutable gaze on Giselle. "You seem the more practical lady. Are you willing to share what you have learned?"

Giselle snorted and covered her mouth with a hand, trying to stifle her laughter. "You clearly don't know us at all."

Emrys smiled wide and bright, showing a dimple. "Yes, Lady Reyes-Vega. I was desperately mistaken. Quinnevere's blood streams with practicality."

Giselle laughed harder. "I like him."

"Sometimes, you're impossible." Quinn glowered at her best friend, who simply shrugged.

"Does this mean that you'll tell me the information you've gathered about the murder thus far?" Emrys asked Giselle.

"Tell me why you were with Jane, and we will tell you," Quinn said defiantly, crossing her arms. "You don't seem like the type of gentleman who settles on one dalliance, so I don't believe you were courting Jane."

"No, I wasn't *courting* her." His eyes sparkled as he emphasized the word. "Jane was like my sister."

Quinn sucked in a long, belabored breath. "Then, why did you need her *help*?"

"I cannot tell you that," he said, leaning against the wooden rail and striking a pose.

Ugh. He loved to do that. And it was irritating. And distracting.

She swallowed and tore her gaze away. "You're asking me to trust you with vital information, that you aren't her killer, that you have her best interest at heart, and yet you're unwilling to trust me with your truth?"

"It's not a matter of trust." Emrys visibly held something back.

"It certainly seems like it is," she said under her breath.

Before he could respond, high-pitched feminine laughter floated across a path. Jevon appeared with both a clearly intoxicated Constance and the ever-regal Countess Atwater on his arms. The glee on Constance's lips faded as her eyes locked on the prince. And before Emrys could turn his head to glimpse her, Constance disappeared into an alcove like a wraith clinging to darkness.

That was strange. It was like she purposely was avoiding Emrys.

Was that one of Constance's mirror abilities, too? The ability to disappear quickly?

Unfortunately, Countess Atwater continued on and bounded across the paths with a terrorizing expression on her face.

In what world did Jevon think this was appropriate? He knew Quinn hated the countess. Teagan Atwater was the devil incarnate, and she took every opportunity to mortify people.

Quinn respectfully bowed to the prince. "Goodnight, Mr. Avalon." She couldn't avoid the countess and her plans for torture, but Quinn could bow out as quickly as possible, steal Jevon away, and ask him what he was thinking.

"Technically, it should be goodnight, Your Royalle Highness," the countess corrected, staring daggers at the other girls.

Quinn clenched her fists and said through gritted teeth, "Goodnight, *Your Royalle Highness*." Without hesitation, she stalked to Jevon, clutched his arm, and pulled him away. Once they reached Constance's hiding spot in the alcove, Quinn turned on her friend. "Jevon, what were you thinking escorting Teagan Atwater?"

"He was thinking with his cock—" Giselle started.

"While I often think with my cock"—Jevon waved a hand in the air—"I was distracting Lady Teagan with my considerable talents so she would stop asking around about Jane. She was being far too obvious and would ruin our plans."

Constance's face slightly soured. She hated the countess and probably hated the thought of Jevon entertaining her. But Constance was ever the actress and always hid her true feelings behind jubilance and liquor. Just like she was currently hiding her current grief behind the alcohol. Quinn couldn't fault her for that because she was also hiding—behind work and always being busy.

If she didn't stop, she wouldn't have to feel the pain.

"Teagan was asking about Jane?" Quinn's brow furrowed.

"Probably on the prince's behalf, but I thought I would intervene," he said, his shoulders slightly slumped.

"Yes, good thinking." Quinn nodded. "Did you learn anything on your adventures?"

Constance held out a hand. "Wait, wait before we go on. We need more drinks." Then she led the group to a seating area with cocktail waitresses.

Once they were served, the friends traded stories. Jevon and Constance discovered that Francois was the Fox but were unable to find him. They also learned that Jane was a well-respected member of Les Fantômes and lived in the row houses above the casino.

The group talked and drank for a couple of hours. Losing themselves to the buzz of alcohol and the excitement of the casino. They danced the lindy-hop and let loose, which was admittedly hard for Quinn, but she needed something to keep her from thinking about the threatening note, the murder, and the fact that she had no suspects or true leads in the case.

She needed something to keep her from breaking down. So, she drank and partied . . . until Jevon pulled her aside.

"How are you doing?" Compassion painted his face. "I know you loved Jane."

"I am fine." Quinn hiccupped as she slumped down onto a bench next to Jevon. The world was a bit blurry now that she wasn't in motion.

"Well, I know that is a lie." He squeezed her hands. "You're like my little sister, Quinny. I know when you're hiding the truth."

"Truly, I'm fine," she fibbed. "I am okay."

"You're allowed to mourn," Jevon said. "I don't know if I ever told you this, but I lost my brother. I know what it is like to grieve."

"What?" She breathed. "I didn't know you had a brother. I'm so sorry."

Shock rattled her core, eating away at her composure. Jevon never talked about his family before and certainly never told her something like that.

He pinched his lips together. "He wasn't blood, and we weren't related at all, but he was my brother. I am not sure if that makes sense."

"It makes sense." Quinn nodded. "It's like how I feel about all of you. You're family without being *my family*."

"Yes, exactly," he said. "Anyway, I get it. I know what it feels like to have complicated feelings about the ones we've lost, too."

Quinn rubbed her eyes to keep tears in. "I don't wanna feel, and I know I'm a terrible person for it."

"I understand that well. Sometimes, I hated my brother." He tensed. "But I also loved him, but he died because he tried to murder me, and I unfortunately fought back."

She gasped. "He tried to murder you?"

"He became obsessed with fixing what he deemed to be a massive mistake I made. He wasn't alone. He convinced my other best mate to join him in his delusions. They didn't like that I traded with the mirror and thought that I'd become a monster that needed to be exterminated. Because of their obsessions, they lost track of who they were." Jevon's voice was hollow, and his eyes were distant, as if he were remembering it all again.

"What happened to your other best mate?" Quinn asked.

"After the dust settled and our friend was dead, we made peace, but we've never talked since that day."

It was all horrible. Quinn couldn't imagine what it would be like to be so betrayed by her family. Jevon was strong.

He was being utterly vulnerable. Was she even worthy of this level of trust? "Thank you for sharing with me." Quinn gulped, her throat burning with unshed emotions. "I know it wasn't easy."

Jevon opened his arms for a hug, but when she bristled, he dropped his hands into his lap. Quinn didn't hug. "Thank you for allowing me to share it."

His words cut to the core and both warm and sad feelings stirred inside her. But she still refused to cry.

After the conversation, the night continued, but she couldn't help the dread pooling in her stomach. Jane was murdered, and it was somehow linked to Blood Mirrors, but she had absolutely no way of getting information about them.

The Grand Library had archives, but it didn't keep a history of mirrors because the Bargainers forbade it. If someone wanted to learn their history, they had to bargain for it. This was another way the mirrors kept the city dependent upon their deals.

None of the current evidence pointed to a suspect. Even if Quinn pulled prints from the feathers and cross-checked them, all she would have would be a match with no suspect. There was no feasible way to test every citizen's print to find a suspect.

So, she had nothing useful. No real clues.

She was stuck, and her life depended on solving this case in the next ~~nine~~—eight—days. The killer would strike again before the week was out.

DAY
THREE

PRICE 2 CENTS

| BREAKING NEWS | # The New Swansea Times |

TUESDAY, NEW SWANSEA CITY, 92nd DAY OF AUTUMN, 700AV

THE PRINCE WAS SPOTTED WITH THE BEAUTIFUL BALLERINA AT THE RUSSET

****Editor's Note: Prince Emrys is taller and more handsome than depicted.*

Is there a romance building between our golden prince and the disrespectful ballerina? The prince was seen with the girl at the gambling den in a dark corridor. It is unclear if they did more than talk, but from the look on the ballerina's face, she seems to be falling head over heels in love. Maybe she is trying to worm her way into his heart before he announces his betrothed at the Royalle Ball—cont. page 3

cont. page 3

HAS THE PRINCE ALREADY CHOSEN HIS NEXT BRIDE?

Second Day of the Festival of Blood Starts

Art and wine will litter the streets as the second day of the Blood Festival arrives. Tradition dictates the second day of celebrating is hosted by the Art Sector. For one day, the bohemians will take over the city, filling it with a torrent of color, scandal, fun and naughty festivities. Some say that this is the best day while—cont. page 2

cont. page 2

INFAMOUS BALLERINA JANE WHITFIELD-WRYTE DEAD

Jane Whitfield-Wryte was found dead covered in mud and fish guts in the Marina District yesterday morning. But the legend had a gang tattoo and so her murder will not be investigated—cont. page 8

cont. page 8

Sixteen

A knock pounded at her door, and Quinn awoke from the nightmare that dripped with blood—she watched as her father was murdered on repeat. Oh, how she hated the Looking Glass—the Mirror of Nightmares—and its stupid deal. She hated waking up every morning in cold sweats.

Quinn rubbed the hilt of her palms into her eyes, groaning. She had a massive headache snaking up the back of her skull. Drinking last night had been a terrible mistake.

Her head pounded again, louder, and more irritating this time.

"Ginger, open your door. We have a murder to solve," a male said with a voice like liquid magic. Smooth and intoxicating. And she knew that voice, but her muddled mind couldn't quite connect the dots.

Quinn groaned and smashed a pillow into her face. "No."

"Little ballerina, I would like to speak with you, and I would prefer if you didn't run away from me this time," the man said again, his tone as dark as shadows. A tone that dripped with arrogance and power. The tone only royalty could muster.

Emrys Avalon.

Quinn groaned again and pulled the covers over her head, mumbling, "No. Go away."

"I'd rather not."

"Go away." She mumbled into her pillow for a third time.

"You know I can pick a lock, right?" Of course, he could. Quinn couldn't see the prince's face, but she imagined he looked rather proud of himself—a preening peacock.

"Uh, fine." She rolled out of bed and stumbled to the door. "How may I help you, your grand, glorious majesty?" she asked sarcastically as she opened the door to the impeccably dressed prince.

Thank God her uncle was already in the morgue. She had no idea how she'd explain this to him.

Emrys's eyes raked over her, and he laughed. "You're hungover."

"I am not."

"So, you're hungover and a liar."

"I'm pretty sure you are the liar and murderer."

"I very well may be a liar, but I am certainly not a murderer." The corner of his mouth lifted into a roguish smirk that could compete with any hero in a silent picture show, which was fitting considering that he escorted beautiful actresses to one of the Pleasure District's clubs every night.

"Why are you here"—Quinn glanced at her grandfather clock —"at six in the morning?"

Quinn finally got a day to sleep in because ballet auditions were canceled for the next three days to honor Jane's death, but this irritating prince had to ruin that.

"Can I come in?" he asked, his hand on the door as he peered in.

Quinn crossed her arms and shot him a glare so hot it could melt the Arctic. "Absolutely not. It would be utterly indecent."

A lazy smile laced his tawny cheeks. "Fine, we can have this conversation in the hallway then." He leaned against the door jam.

"What do you want?" Quinn crossed her arms in sad resistance. "What is so important that you must wake me up early in the morning, banging on my door?"

He glowered. "I want your help to solve the murder."

Quinn forced her head high and stood up to him even though he was far, far taller, and stronger than her. To anyone watching, it must have looked like a cat cornered by a mouse. But if she were a mouse, she'd be a fearsome one to behold. "I'll help you if you tell me why you were spending so much time with Jane."

"I can't tell you that."

"Then I can't help you."

Emrys folded his arms in response to her stubbornness. "If I could tell you, I would. But I cannot. I am bound—" He cut his words off, and a flicker of something akin to pain thundered in his eyes. "I cannot tell you what Jane and I were discussing. However, I can say that the murder may be connected to secrets that Castle Hill and the Royalle House must protect at all costs."

"Including the cost of murder?" Quinn asked.

Emrys shifted a hint of desperation in his stance. "Do you know the Graham Knight novels?" he asked, switching the subject.

"With the detective who is always wearing a deerstalking hat?" Quinn ran a finger down the doorframe, hoping that the sensory stimulation would cause his change in subject to make sense.

"Yes. Have you read *The Knight and the State Secret*?"

"Of course not." If he thought she read for fun, he was far stupider than she ever imagined.

"Right, well, the story is about—"

"—I said I didn't read it, not that I didn't know the story."

"Right, so then you know that the murder in that book has to do with state secrets and national security, and if Knight and his medical examiner partner Briggs don't solve the murder in time, hundreds of people will die?"

"Yes. . ." she said slowly. "Are you saying that hundreds of people will die if you don't find the murderer?" Confusion burned a hole in her stomach as Emrys nodded and leaned in slightly.

If Jane's death was linked to a larger conspiracy that Castle Hill and the queen knew about, then Emrys might know about the Blood Mirrors. And if he did, it would speed up the investigation.

"Would this national conspiracy have something to do with the Blood Mirror?" Quinn asked, curling her fingers around the door.

His reaction was physical. Every muscle in his body tensed, and his face slightly paled. "I can neither confirm nor deny—"

"Of course, you can't." She scoffed, but then she narrowed her eyes because that was a physical reaction, not just a verbal one.

"But let's speak hypothetically for a moment. If there were Bloo—" His words broke off as the vein in his neck budged. Quinn cocked her head, watching him. "I'm sorry, I can't."

Something, probably magic—there wasn't much else that would do it—was keeping him from being truthful. So, how could Quinn get around it? Have him tell her without him saying it.

"So you can't tell me anything." Quinn sighed. "That's going to make solving a murder difficult. It's like asking me to fight a duel with my hands tied behind my back."

"I know." He visibly swallowed.

"I presume you can't tell me why you can't tell me as well?"

He nodded. "If there was something, let's say, that I couldn't speak about, perhaps you might be able to find the answers without me telling you."

"And how would you suggest I do that?"

"Either the Grand Library or a mirror."

"You want to take a girl who cannot even read to a library?"

Emrys shrugged. "Eh, so you can't read. Big deal. I can't sing, and I am still considered a gentleman . . . mostly." His lips rose in a silky smirk. "Reading might be hard, but I know you can do it. You are quite brilliant."

A library. He must really hate her.

She glowered; her arms crossed protectively in front of her chest. Eventually, she rolled her shoulders back and decided to humor his metaphor. "If you were Knight in this scenario, would that mean you would wear the stupid hat?"

Emrys moved closer to her. She stepped back in rhythm with him, but her back hit the doorframe. He was so close that the warmth of his breath caressed her neck.

"Would you enjoy that? Maybe I can wear only the hat . . . and nothing else." He winked. "I do believe you still need lessons in passion."

Butterfly wings tickled her stomach, and her foolish heart sped. She had forbidden the lessons in passion to continue, but a horrible piece of her wanted his hands all over her again—wanted him to teach her everything. She swallowed. No. Strength, Quinn. Finding Jane's murder was all that mattered. No foolish, indecently handsome, and charming princes.

Quinn measured her voice and made it sound clinical and uninterested so that her lust wouldn't show. "You did not need to say, 'and nothing else.' The 'only' implied that you planned to be naked."

He chuckled.

"Besides, I already told you there would be no lessons in passion anymore." Her eyes tracked for a mortifying moment down to his cock and then back up to his chestnut eyes.

His chuckle deepened. "It's interesting your mouth is forming words, but your eyes are not agreeing with them. If you truly don't want to use me for passion, then try telling your eyes to stop caressing me." He stepped closer, his proximity indecent. "Your eyes feel a little bit like this." He trailed his thumb down the column of her neck. His jaw was set tight as if the act pained him.

Shivers radiated through her entire body, and she inhaled sharply, wishing he would do it again . . . that and so, so much more. But he didn't. Instead, he stepped back, freeing her. And it was the one instance where she longed to be confined again.

"But you forbid me from teaching you passion," he said, "for no discernable reason."

Quinn gritted her teeth from frustration and anger. The anger that emerged every time she remembered why Jane was dead. "Perhaps you should deploy your charms on someone who might want to spend time with you." Quinn dug a verbal knife into his arrogance.

It caused the opposite reaction than she intended. Emrys's arrogance grew.

"But they will work on me," Giselle said, stepping up next to them and causing Quinn to nearly jump out of her skin. "Come on, princey. The Grand Library sounds like a great idea, and I don't mind you tagging along."

"You are not serious," Quinn whirled on Giselle.

"Yes, I am. If the prince insists on being a part of the investigation, it only wastes our time and energy resisting him."

Giselle was an abnormally good judge of character. Maybe Quinn should trust her friend. "Fine." Quinn sighed, knowing that she had lost this round.

He chuckled and grasped Quinn's left wrist, rubbing a thumb over her tattoo as a wince prickled on his features. "I am bound from telling you the truth," he whispered. "But I won't prevent you from discovering it yourself."

Thirty minutes later, Quinn stared at the Grand Library's turrets, which climbed to the sky like claws piercing the heavens. Nerves rattled in her stomach. She'd never been in the opulent building before because she avoided reading like the plague. And she never particularly wanted to meet the Looking Glass.

The Looking Glass was the most famous mirror in the Art Sector, the part of the city filled with bohemian treasures, galleries, artists, writers, musicians, and actors—people living on the fringe. But it also housed the Mirror of Untamed Talent, known for bestowing artistic talents on those brave enough to challenge it.

Most of the mirrors were legends in the city, but the Looking Glass was probably the most iconic for its sheer size and the rumor that it was the first mirror discovered.

The Grand Library was designed to house the four-story-high mirror and was itself a grand masterpiece of architecture. Flying buttresses lined the walls with twisted, intricate designs and supported the towers, allowing them to pierce the sky. This feat of engineering was like no other.

The library rivaled the gods in technology and decor. Colonnades lined the perimeter, and sculptures of the old vampire gods were etched into each column.

Above the entrance, a sign read: With Every Death We Grow Stronger, a slogan of the old vampire gods.

Emrys cleared his throat. "Are you planning on gazing upon the building all day, or would you like to see what lies beyond?"

"I—" Quinn absentmindedly patted her skirts.

She clenched her fists and forced herself to focus on meeting the Looking Glass. An evil, vindictive mirror that killed her nightly in her sleep.

Every night, covered in blood and surrounded by screams. Every night, a different version of her parents' murders or hers. All because the Royalle House bound every citizen with their terrible deal to get electricity.

Her palms grew clammy as she stepped up to the gilded entrance. Emrys turned the handle and held open the door.

"Just don't look at it," Constance said, sensing Quinn's worry. There was something almost magical about Constance's ability to gauge when Quinn was worried, upset, or even happy, almost like she was an empath.

"You'll be okay." Giselle squeezed Quinn's shoulder.

Quinn nodded and hesitantly stepped through the door, followed by her friends.

The outside of the Grand Library was nothing compared to the opulent interior. Sparkling augmented light shined patterns into the marble floor. Massive murals of the stars and the vampire gods were painted across the ceiling. Some original vampire paintings were coated over, but others remained, causing a disjointed tableau.

But the light emanating from the mirror forced her eyes toward it, despite Constance's warning. Quinn's jaw dropped, and her stomach grew sick with dread. The mirror's presence pulsated energy—thick and sticky. As the jeweled centerpiece of the room, it was rimmed with gilded gold embroidery, and its molten silver surface swirled with the warm hues of dripping watercolor paint.

It was transfixing and impossible to look away from.

Quinn's breathing turned ragged as she felt her limbs go heavy. Her heart rattled in her chest like a beast trying to escape a cage. Stuck and unable to remove her gaze. Frozen in both fear and awe. Enthralled.

In an instant, or maybe an age, Emrys appeared before her and blocked her view, his hands on her face. It took an eternity for her to blink and gain functioning over her body again.

"You looked," he said softly with his glistening eyes that twinkled like brown sapphires at midnight.

"I—"

Fire twirled in her core. Or maybe it was butterflies. Or poison.

It was hard to tell with Emrys.

She sucked in a breath and stepped back and out of his hold. He was nearly as mesmerizing as the stupid mirror. Both made her blood boil. Averting her gaze, she noticed the statues surrounding the room of people with their heads turned up to the mirror.

"Does it turn people to stone?" Her voice shook.

"It can't turn people into statues," Giselle said, also eying the stone people.

"No, not people." Emrys visibly swallowed and turned to Constance. "Shall we move on?"

Constance's face twisted in horror as she tried not to look at the mirror. "Yes, please." A vein in her neck pulsed.

All of them struggled against the mirror's magnetic pull except Giselle. She merely peered at the mirror with defiance and shrugged.

"I don't get it," Quinn said. "Giselle, you come here so often. Why would you risk it?" It was a stupid question. Giselle was addicted to risk. It probably colored her soul.

"Its power no longer works on me." Giselle's smile played on her lips like she knew the secret to the universe. "The trick is, once you know what the mirror wants to do to you—that it wants to entrance you and keep you frozen forever locked in nightmares—its power fades."

Once in a separate room, Giselle and Emrys ran off to find books. Emrys didn't say what he looked for, but Giselle found books relating to tattoos and anything that might relate to the Blood Mirrors. She came back with a pile stacked up to her chin.

Jevon grabbed a stack of recent newspapers covering the last few years and began reading the murder reports while tapping his fingers on the desk.

Giselle opened a small book with a leather cover, and Emrys plopped a tome before Quinn.

She jolted out of a daze and turned her eyes to the massive book in front of her. "What in the dirty mirror's name is that?"

Emrys flashed an arrogant smile. "New Swansea history of the royal family." He patted her on the back in the most condescending way. "Have fun!"

"Why in the world would I need to read about the history of *your* family?" she asked him incredulously.

"Trust me. It is relevant."

"Because you're a narcissist?"

He slid his hands into his pockets and shrugged. "Possibly. But even so. Let's say there was a secret involving Castle Hill and the coun—" He gulped. "A secret that I was unable to tell you myself, but you needed to know to solve Jane's murder."

Constance eyed him warily. And Giselle muffled her giggle and pulled a book to cover her face.

"And it is in this book?" Quinn asked.

"Possibly."

Quinn narrowed her eyes, her heart quickening in her chest. "You have got to be kidding me. That *thing* . . ." She emphasized the word thing and pointed at the tome. ". . . Could eat twenty New Swansea history books. I am not reading it. I *can't* read it."

Quinn's blood bubbled with anxiety. It would take her twenty years to read that book. Emrys merely shrugged, which burned her blood even more, frustration coating her soul. "You know I have reading issues, right?"

Emrys flashed a dimple, his tawny face lighting up with amusement. He certainly liked to provoke. "A lot of the newspapers have pictures. Look for something about blood. I am fairly certain you know how to spell blood. You'll do fine."

Condescending prick. Of course, she knew how to spell blood . . . maybe. That wasn't the point. The point was that he was insensitive and obnoxiously rude.

"You know what? Sometimes you're so charming that I can barely contain my knickers," Quinn said. "All the girls must find your arrogant condescension so utterly swoon-worthy."

He dared to chuckle and shrug again like every word she said was accurate. "Thank you. Now, get to work." He pointed at the book.

"And what will you do?"

"I'm going through gang records."

"And why can't I do that?"

Emrys wiped his hands together like he was removing dirt. Nonexistent dirt. "Because we need you to guard that history book."

Frustration's claws burrowed a hole in her heart. Oh, how she hated this arrogant, stupid, insolent man. She glared at the book. "Right." She rounded on her friends a little too harshly. "What are you two reading?"

"I'm looking through old murder briefing reports. It's possible Jane wasn't the first victim," Giselle said.

Constance flipped open a book. "And I'm trying to search for anything to do with your tattoo and Blood Mirrors." Since Jane shared the same tattoo on her wrist as Quinn, it made sense for one of the friends to investigate that while they were here.

Turning a few pages, Quinn grunted. This was a torture designed specifically for her. Her eyes clouded over as she turned the pages in the book. Not only was this task utterly dull, but it was also strenuous. The words jumped from page to page and danced a tango. None of the letters wanted to behave. It felt like a ballerina jumping grand jetés in her brain. Her temples throbbed, and her overall mood could only be described as a tornado mingling with a forest fire.

Quinn's legs stung, and she tried to stretch her toes and did relevés with her feet to relieve the pain, but numbness curled up her legs like the talons of a vicious tiger. The exhaustion from drinking, ballet auditions, and all the stress of the murder lingered in her body. A rotten apple soured in her core as she carelessly flipped over another page.

Hours into the search, she gave up and rested her head in the tome.

"Eyes on the book, Ginger," Emrys said as he leaned against the wall four tables away.

"Stop calling me that. It's not accurate. My hair is reddish-brown." It was just indecent to continue to repeat the same inaccuracy over and over again.

His signature, devilish smirk crossed his lips. "As you wish, little ballerina."

Quinn sighed. At least that nickname was accurate.

Eventually, she focused back on the book and pretended to be very involved just to prove him wrong. Moving quickly, she took his advice and only looked for the pictures, which was how she stumbled upon something spectacularly strange.

A photographed painting of Emrys, but it couldn't be the Emrys standing across the room. It was too old. In the painting, the king held a staff, and on his middle finger, he had a strange freckle. It was on the inside of the finger where it shouldn't have been visible to the sun. It was odd and unique.

Quinn bit the inside of her cheek and examined him as intently as a dead body. The portrait was identical but painted at least seven centuries before. She squinted and tried to read the information. It was a handwritten news sheet for a wedding announcement.

Emerson Avalon married Elody Wittfield in the year 50 AV. The new princess who was chosen at the Suitor Ball is enjoying life at the palac—

Quinn stopped reading because the rest of the article was about the ceremony. She turned the page and found another marriage announcement.

Ezekiel Avalon married Charlotte Davies in the year 75 AV.

It must have been Emerson's son. The next page similarly was another announcement.

> *Edmund Avalon married Yasmin Perez in the year 100 AV.*

She flipped the page.

Page after page, Quinn turned to marriage announcements for the royal family. The articles changed from written news sheets to printed newspapers, but they were all similar. Quinn caught the pattern almost immediately. All the weddings took place twenty-five years apart. All of the married couples had a son, and each of their sons had a name that began with E.

Following the announcements were articles announcing the death of the princes.

> *Prince Emerson Avalon died on the fifth day of Summer 66 AV.*
>
> *Prince Ezekiel Avalon died on the fifth day of Summer 91 AV.*
>
> *Prince Edmund Avalon died on the fifth day of Summer 116 AV.*

The princes died precisely sixteen years after their wedding on the same day. Every. Single. Time.

The hairs on her arms rose.

Was the royal family cursed? Cursed to repeat the same marriage and death cycle over and over again? Could a mirror cause that?

Was this what Emrys wanted her to find? And if it was, how could it possibly have anything to do with Jane's murder?

It was an impossible pattern. How had someone not noticed before? Unless they had . . . and a mirror erased their memories. As soon as the thought hit her, it vanished, as did everything she'd just read.

Quinn shivered, fear dancing in her stomach, turning it hollow. She shook out her arms and tried to relax. Something was missing from her mind . . . but what?

"Is the book that horrifying?" Constance asked, noticing the discomfort.

"It's a book."

Giselle chuckled, her nose still in her own book. "I have something else you could look at. I found these from the night of the murder."

Giselle passed Quinn a pile of pictures, and Constance returned to her task.

One picture captured a tableau of passion and delight. A crowd of twenty people danced, partied, and swayed to the music. Illusions floated above and painted a watercolor of magic and a sea of excess. Everyone glittered and shone under the light of a thousand peacock eyes.

The Viridian.

The most noticeable thing about the picture was the people who weren't moving—who weren't shining in their joy. With a frown on her face, Jane talked to Emrys, who held her arm like he was about to pull her away. His expression shadowed with danger like he was threatening her. It was not a scene of friendship or alliance.

This picture painted a different idea altogether. One of danger and possibly murder.

Squinting her eyes to get a closer look, she noticed purple feathers on his pocket square. Purple feathers like the fragments she had found on the body. He was the last person Quinn saw with Jane before she died. And he had mud caked on his dress pants the morning after the murder. All the clues led to Emrys, and she gulped.

But if he were the murderer, why did he bring her to the library and point her to . . . what had she learned?

Nothing added up, and she was far more confused than before.

Anxiety crawled over Quinn's skin like a thousand tiny ants. Sliding the important photo into her skirt pocket for safekeeping, she turned her eyes to another shot.

Jane's glamorous crimson hair stood out. She was alone in a crowd, searching for something. Nearby was Constance in her silver sequined dress, talking to a blond man with his back to the camera. It could be Jevon possibly. He had the same yellow curls as this man, plus it made the most sense.

Constance's eyes weren't on the man in question. They seemed to be on Jane.

A strange coincidence.

And she wasn't the only one. There were three other people in the crowd staring at the former ballerina. The prince. Francois. And Hadleigh.

Also strange. All the photos seemed focused on Jane, as if the photographer were following her.

Odd.

Why would Giselle be so pinpoint focused on Jane?

It didn't make sense.

But the photos spoke a thousand words, and it would seem that one of the people in these pictures—or many—was a liar.

"I found something." Giselle poked her head up from behind her book.

"What?" A chorus of voices sang at once, all four hovering around Giselle.

"It's a murder briefing from nineteen years ago. All the victims were drained completely of blood, and all of them had the same tattoo as Jane."

"What?" Quinn said as Emrys nodded as if something clicked and came together in his mind.

"And all five of the bodies were found in front of a dead—red —mirror stain." Giselle poked her head out of her book, and a big smile was on her face. "It has to be a Blood Mirror. Why else would it be red?"

A jolt of memory hit Quinn in the chest. Physically and

viscerally. "My necklace is named Blood. Wasn't that what Night-shade and Jane had said?"

Her necklace was a Blood Mirror.

"Oh shit." Giselle paused, reading, her eyes trailing up to Quinn. Her normally tawny olive skin turned polar white.

"What?" Quinn tilted her head, her fingers curling tightly around her book.

"I don't think—" Giselle's voice cracked, and a tear leaked from her eyes.

"What?" Quinn asked again, more insistent.

Giselle shook her head as more tears gathered with the first. "I don't think you should see it."

Quinn gulped. "I need to see it, Giselle. It will be fine no matter what it is."

Pushing the book in Quinn's direction, Giselle looked like the haunted in Soul Mirror Row—devastated and tortured. Turning the book toward her, Quinn peered down at the words. The letters were loopy and hard to read, but eventually, she saw what caused Giselle's reaction.

The names of the victims included Quinn's parents.

SEVENTEEN

She stopped reading and tuned into petrified wood, unmoving and unblinking. She stared down as the letters spilled together like pooling blood. She held her breath until her throat burned.

Time dripped and ticked together into a blanket woven of silence and sorrow.

It was unclear how long she sat unmoving and unwilling to process the information she'd just read. Eventually, she slammed the book shut and pounced out of her chair. She ran without knowing where she was going and without caring either. A robed librarian yelled at her, but she didn't listen. She just needed to run to physically process the pain coursing through her veins.

When she finally stopped running, she clutched at her chest and gulped for air.

Emotions bombarded and attacked like the cavalry in a medieval vampire army. Her hair rose at the base of her neck, and her heart burned with devastation.

It hurt like a thousand splinters cutting her heart. There was a reason Quinn chose to push her memories down into a bottomless dark pit, never to be seen again.

So, Quinn ran. Ran out of the library and to a place she felt at home, her lab. She needed to throw herself into science or dance. But dance reminded her too much of Jane.

When Quinn got lost in her work, she didn't have to feel. It had worked in the past, and it would now, too. Refusing to cry, Quinn pulled Jane's body from the preservation cabinet. It had been two days since her death, and unsurprisingly, the newspapers barely ran the story. A couple of lines was all she got. Gang murders happened far too often to be considered news to the city, but Jane deserved to be remembered. She deserved more.

But no, the newspapers were too enthralled with writing about Quinn insulting Emrys, which happened far too often to be news.

Trying to avoid thinking about everything she learned at the Grand Library, she decided to check if she could extract any other fingerprints. Using ink, Quinn painted each of victim's fingers black before pressing each down onto a piece of paper. Once she finished, Quinn cleaned Jane's hands and methodically transferred the bloody fingerprint onto paper. With all eleven samples, she compared the prints to see if there was a match. Every person in the world had a unique set of prints on each finger. If the print didn't match the victim, it most likely matched the killer.

Quinn's lower back ached as she refused to feel emotion. She had to be impartial and distant.

It was the only way to do this job.

She checked and cross-checked the samples four times until she concluded that the bloody fingerprint was not Jane's, which meant that Quinn held the best evidence that could identify the murderer.

Unfortunately, she needed samples of their prints to identify them.

Next, she placed the feathers' fragments next to each other and tried to extract fingerprints from them. She managed to pull a print from one of the feathers. Quinn was pretty sure it was the one found on the body. Cross-checking it with the bloody print, Quinn found a match.

The fingerprints matched.

So the purple feather came from the murderer? Maybe.

"Hello, little Ginger," Emrys glided beside her. "Did you want to talk about it?"

Of course, Emrys would be the person to find her. It was just her luck.

"What?" She swallowed, her throat tight and sore.

"Any of it." Emrys leaned against a cabinet, and his brown eyes sparked with compassion or pity. Both of which made Quinn cringe.

"No," she whispered.

As if sensing that she needed a distraction, Emrys said, "So what would you like to talk about? I can talk about anything, but I do prefer talking about myself."

A soft laugh escaped from her lips. Emrys's chestnut eyes twinkled like a kitten who discovered a roll of yarn. It was contagiously charming.

"But I gather that you would rather not like to discuss my narcissism today?"

"Come here," she said, using her head to point at the gloves. "I want to show you something."

Emrys pulled gloves on and strolled to the other side of the exam table. "As you wish."

Quinn gently pushed back Jane's hair from her face and pointed at the puncture wounds. "Jane died from blood loss, most likely from these puncture wounds. These slash marks were made postmortem." She ran her finger across the cuts. "It's all connected. Isn't it? Jane was killed because of her knowledge of the Blood Mirrors or because of the mirrors. And so were my par—"

He grasped her hand and squeezed. "Yes. It is all connected." He flinched as if in pain, as if he couldn't say any more.

The beast in her heart banged against its cage, and her hands trembled. She needed to pull herself together. She rolled her neck and cleared her throat, returning her eyes to the victim. "I think we need to read those reports."

Without another word. Quinn rolled the corpse into its storage chamber and pulled off her gloves. Swinging open the door, she called behind her, "Are you coming?"

Three minutes later, the two were piles-deep in the evidence room, sifting through autopsy reports. Quinn still didn't trust the prince, but Giselle was right. It took far too much energy to fight his presence.

When they finally found the Ashelle murder files, it was almost impossible to gain any new information from them. Most of the report was redacted, leaving only the cause of death and physical findings untouched by black ink. All of the investigation, motive, and circumstances of the murders were covered up.

There were six Ashelle murder victims, but one of the bodies was missing. The other five all had two puncture marks covered up by the lacerations—just like Jane—and their bodies were completely drained of blood. The victims also had the same tattoos as both Jane and Quinn. Under some of the retracted ink, the words *guarding a Blood Mirror* were shown through.

"So, a serial murderer is killing people with a connection to the Blood Mirrors." Quinn ran a finger along one of the reports as a strand of her cinnamon hair fell into her face. "But someone is covering up the facts of the crimes . . . why?"

"Not someone, something," Emrys said before clutching his head in pain.

"Something, meaning an organization, or something, meaning a monster?" Quinn asked. Emrys visible gulped, and the vein in his forehead budged. "Should we be searching for a vampire?"

Emrys watched her hand, circling the report. "It's possible." He winced again.

"Right." Quinn sucked in a breath. "Why can't you speak about any of this?"

"It's—" Pain flashed across his face again.

"Magic," she guessed. He tilted his head by a fraction and squeezed his eyes tight momentarily. "Okay, so how do I find the answers without forcing you to endure pain."

"I thought you enjoyed causing me pain." He flashed a smile and a sensual wink. At her glare, he said, "Perhaps we could start here." He pointed to a newspaper article that accompanied the reports.

On the margins of the article, someone wrote, *I think you're right, St. John. It looks like vam . . .* The last word was smudged, but it was definitely the word *vampires.*

"Who is that?" Quinn asked.

"A reporter," Emrys answered. The prince knew everyone who was important.

Quinn stilled as she stared at him, a mixture of emotions circling inside her. This reporter might have answers to who and why someone wanted people connected to Blood Mirrors dead.

EIGHTEEN

After taking two separate cable car lines, Quinn and her friends assembled in the Gold Quarter, searching for the reporter's apartment. She didn't want to go with only the prince.

The streets glittered, the gold surface shining in the sliver of sunlight that poked out from behind the clouds. The metal appearance was created by the Mirror of Molten Gold.

The streets were also filled with celebration from the second night of the Festival of Blood. Everywhere you looked was art, dalliance, and wine. The bohemians of the Art Sector hosted the event, but all parts of the city joined in on the fun, from the rich of the Estate district to the craftspeople of the marina.

On Quinn's left was the Queen's Royalle Ballet, gilded in all of its glory. She always imagined herself standing here in the company of the rich and famous. She imagined standing in this very spot, being honored and respected. She wanted to be the greatest ballerina the Royalle Ballet had ever seen. Then, she would finally be enough. She would be accepted. She would be whole. The world would know her name.

Deep down, she always wanted the Playboy Prince to respect her, too.

"I think his apartment is somewhere around here," Giselle

said, scrunching her eyebrows and looking at a map. Directions were not her forte.

Quinn shook her head. She never should've allowed her friend to navigate. They could be in the completely wrong district. "Let me see the address," Quinn said, holding a hand.

Within seconds, she pointed them in the correct direction. The reporter lived in an opulent apartment building three streets off Union Square.

When they arrived, without hesitation, the group rushed into the building and presumably up the elevator with the attendant's assistance. But Quinn's shoes were glued to the golden street, her palms sweaty, and her heart racing like a cheetah trying to catch its prey. Her bag gently fell off her shoulder and sank like an anchor dropping to the sidewalk.

The Gold Quarter might shine with glamour and merriment, but Quinn's soul fractured with dread.

Starring up at the tall building, she gulped. Anticipation siphoned at her self-control. The reporter might be the key to unlocking Jane's murder. Unlocking—

No, she wouldn't let herself think about the rest. Quinn needed to focus on either catching Jane's murderer or finding the second Blood Mirror because if she failed either task, Quinn would be the next victim.

Noticing that she hadn't followed, Emrys stepped back through the rotating doors.

Slowly, as if walking on shattered glass, he approached. "We will go in together."

"Together," Quinn whispered back, took the offered hand, and forced her feet to move.

Without another word, they entered the building and the elevator. The operator cranked nine floors up before opening the doors and letting them out. Emrys flipped a sienna at the attendant as he exited.

Halfway down the hall, a door hung ominously open. Unease gathered in the shadows around the door. Something was terribly wrong, or Quinn was overreacting. Her friends being inside was probably why the door hung ajar. Tentatively, Quinn stepped through the entry and was met with disaster.

It was like entering a windstorm. Papers littered the floor, creating a sea of disorder. Books, picture frames, and clothes, among other items, were stacked high on the couches. Every surface of the apartment was covered in some type of mess. It made Giselle pristine in comparison. Excrement laced the floor, and jars of yellow liquid sat on shelves. This room was an explosion of chaos.

Giselle knelt in the middle of the room, poking through a box with a pen. Even she was disturbed by the disaster. Constance stood stunned at the kitchen entrance.

"Where is Jevon?" Emrys asked at Quinn's side.

"He's searching for the reporter." Giselle didn't glance up. Instead, she searched through the box's contents, looking for something. "I think he is in the kitchen."

As if summoned, Jevon stepped out of a doorway, his complexion ashen and eyes wide. Quinn was immediately on edge because of the unfamiliar expression on his normally bored face. His mouth worked as if unable to communicate his thoughts to the rest of the group. Instead, he pointed into the room.

Quinn rushed past and stopped in her tracks as she spotted what stole Jevon's words.

A dead body lying face down on the kitchen's marble floor.

NINETEEN

Quinn held her arm out, blocking her equally curious friends from entering the room and contaminating the scene. Everything needed to be handled appropriately.

"Emrys, find a telephone and ring my uncle," Quinn said before turning to Giselle. "Do you think you could find a camera?"

"Yes." Giselle scurried off and out of the room.

Quinn continued to bark orders like a highly skilled admiral, and everyone listened, even the prince. "Jevon, guard the hallway and make sure no one enters. Constance, I need you here to help me gather the evidence."

Slowly, not trying to disturb the scene, Quinn walked into the hallway, searched for her medical kit, and dropped her bag next to the door. She tied her cinnamon hair into a tight ballet bun and slipped gloves onto her fingers. Once everything was in place, Quinn retraced her steps and carefully tiptoed over to the body.

Her hands shook as she reached out to grasp the man's wrist. Inhaling sharply, she tried to steady the hailstorm of emotions cutting at her core. This man was the one person who had answers, the one person who might be able to lead them in the correct direction.

He was the key, and now he was dead.

As she slid her fingers across the victim's wrist, she was struck by how warm his body felt. If the body was this warm, it meant that his time of death would've been less than an hour before.

The human body lost temperature at the rate of 1.5 degrees per hour, and although she didn't have a mirror thermometer on her, this body felt nearly alive. But she would need Uncle Matias's equipment to confirm.

The killer was one step ahead of Quinn. Ruining her chances of discovering their identity. It was almost as if they watched her and knew precisely what she'd do next.

A chill crawled down her spine.

It might be possible to have a mirror object that could spy on people, but the cost of an object like that would be astronomical. Quinn's heart rattled. The type of person willing to make that large of a bargain scared her.

No lacerations, no puncture wounds. No tattoos. This body didn't fit the profile, but it was too coincidental that he showed up dead right when they sought answers from him. The only logical reason for killing the reporter was that he might know the murderer's identity because if his information had led to a Blood Mirror, there was an incentive to keep him alive and let Quinn get closer to finding the information.

Worse still, there were no longer any good suspects. Emrys was with her all morning. He couldn't have killed him.

The victim, a roughly middle-aged man, seemed to have died from a broken neck. The victim's head was tilted to such an inhuman degree it looked like it was barely attached to the body.

Someone—or something—incredibly strong killed this man.

At the morgue, Uncle Matias started the autopsy on Sir Andrew St. John, a wealthy aristocrat who had turned freelance reporter. The body's internal temperature was ninety-seven degrees, which placed the time of death likely minutes before Jevon discovered the body.

Emrys was the only one observing the procedure because her friends were not allowed in the lab.

Wringing her hands and contemplating the best way forward, Quinn stared at the corpse on the exam table.

"So, child, what were you doing at the crime scene?" Uncle Matias asked.

Oh, scratched mirrors.

She placed a false smile on her face. "We were . . ." Quinn tried to come up with something clever to say that would get her out of trouble, but she was the worst liar. Lying was not practical, functional, or helpful on most occasions. It usually caused more problems and led to a lack of control. And because she hated trouble, she had no idea what to do or say.

"Quinnevere Igretta Ashelle, I know you are lying to me." Her uncle shot a withering glare with his hands, wrist deep in a corpse. "Please don't tell me you are investigating the gang victim."

"I—"

"Igretta," Emrys whispered to Quinn with a raised eyebrow.

She flashed him a look that screamed, *shut your mouth, or I'll devour you*, which was met with a low chuckle.

Her cheeks warmed outwardly, expressing just how caught she was, and of course, her uncle's shrewd gaze noticed everything. "I specifically told you that you were not allowed under any circumstances to investigate her murder."

It was true, but it was abnormal for him to forbid investigations. Something was off. "I—"

"Dr. Ashelle." Emrys tilted his head as if acknowledging a gentleman of higher rank. Of course, no gentleman in all of New

Swansea out-ranked Emrys. "I asked Quinnevere to look into Jane Whitfield-Wryte's murder. She's helping me. That is all."

Emrys rolled his shoulders back, power and arrogance pulsating from his pores—it was real and physical. It was like he lit a flame of magic, and no one or nothing could look away from his tango of dominance. Her eyebrows creased.

"Oh, I see. Castle Hill business, then?" Uncle Matias asked.

"Yes."

"Perhaps you should let Quinn work on the investigation while you continue your autopsy." Emrys's voice buzzed with enchantment, each word coated with magic and force.

Uncle Matias rubbed his left forearm and clenched his teeth. "You could ask. You don't have to do that." A chill rushed through her body, and she gaped at Emrys as her uncle turned back to the corpse. "Well then, Quinnevere, get to work," Uncle Matias said as he pulled organs out of the chest cavity.

Quinn's feet felt like concrete blocks. She didn't know what to do. She bit her lip, her eyes flashing between the two gentlemen.

Emrys had used magic on him, and Uncle Matias noticed it but brushed it off. What in all the mirrors was going on?

Emrys prowled over and whispered, "Are you okay?"

She rounded on him and whispered back, "I am guessing you can't tell me about that either."

"No," he breathed, his eyes alight with shimmering enchantment.

"Wonderful." Her mouth grew sour. Even if he wasn't a murderer, he was insufferable. But if he weren't the murderer, then Quinn would need to visit a mirror, which she absolutely didn't want to do. The reporter was the last lead, and now that he was dead . . .

Quinn glanced at her samples and hurriedly asked, "Can I take your prints?" Hopefully, he wouldn't be offended, but it was important to cross him off the list of her suspects.

A side of Emrys's lips jerked up. "You think I am the murderer?"

"I would like to rule it out."

Emrys followed her gaze to the fingerprint samples. "You have a fingerprint from the murderer?"

"Yes."

He gave a slight nod. "Then you shall inspect my fingers, and you will know that I only mean to help."

She prepared the ink and paper for his samples. Reaching out, she clasped his hand, and it tremored. "You have magic."

"So it would seem." His words were hurt and clipped.

Quinn dipped his fingers in ink and methodically rolled them on the paper. Her heart danced in her chest, speeding up like bourrée steps. "So, you are Mirror-Blessed?" she asked, rolling his final finger on the paper.

"Or am I something else? That is the question, isn't it?" His eyes dripped with unreadable thoughts like an ocean of mystery.

Something else, like . . . a vampire?

Quinn was nearly convinced vampires were alive and well. Emrys had implied it before, and the markings on all the victims were too much of a coincidence. Plus, what would be strong enough and fast enough to kill the reporter before they arrived?

A vampire.

She shuddered as she placed the paper down next to the other samples. Quickly, she checked, cross-checked, and checked again.

The vein in her neck pulsed to the rhythm of a war drum. "Whatever you are, at the very least, you are not Jane's murderer."

TWENTY

The investigation was at a complete and utter dead end. Quinn needed to learn about the painting tattoos and the Blood Mirrors. She had to find answers, and it was clear that Emrys couldn't provide them.

Quinn's only true option left was to face another mirror or wait to be murdered. But she absolutely was not going to challenge Beautiful Decay again. So, instead, she would go to the Mirror of Midnight.

Quinn stood in front of the Mirrors of: Midnight, Beautiful Decay, Winter, and Skulls, trying to gather enough courage to go into another mirror. Her eyes focused on Midnight. A purple galaxy shimmered underneath the glass, and lapis blue danced like the corps de ballet in Starlight Falls. The frame was made of swirling shadows and shooting stars. Quinn's heart stormed in her chest, and she clutched her necklace for support.

But she had to do this. Her life depended upon these answers.

She stepped toward the mirror and without another thought, Quinn plunged inside. Its texture was like a million granules of sand that scratched at her skin and eyes. Ice crawled like spider veins up her arms and neck and encased her body with the freezing cold. Her breaths grew hollow and strained. There was no oxygen here.

Stumbling out of the barrier, Quinn fell to her knees and landed on a sea of glitter. No . . . it wasn't glitter. It was starlight. Purple and blue clouds circled her. She tried to touch one, but her fingers went straight through it.

From the dancing clouds, stepped a petite girl with cotton-candy pink hair. She looked to be slightly younger than Quinn. "Hello, Quinnevere Ashelle, daughter of Callan and Brielle and seeker of truth." The girl had eyes like blood diamonds and the voice of a seven-year-old child. Airy yet cheerful. "Daughter of the Blood Glass, Daughter of the Council, Daughter of Secrets, Queen of Mirrors, what is it that you require of me?"

Quinn shuddered, and confusion was a claw biting into her back. None of those titles made any sense to her. But then she remembered she was in the Mirror of Midnight, notorious for only speaking in childlike riddles.

"I—" Quinn started but was distracted by her necklace.

It buzzed, just like inside Beautiful Decay, but this time, it liquefied, spun on pointe like a ballerina out of its cage, and grew into a life-sized humanoid creature. The red metal melted off like dripping wax, revealing a raven-haired lady in her mid-twenties.

The woman's hazel eyes, far greener than brown, stood out with her dark hair and pale features. She wore an indigo blue gown that dropped from her shoulders, loose and elegant, and reminiscent of ancient times. It was simple, but in its simplicity, it almost seemed more commanding—like the woman's power radiated through the dress rather than overwhelming her.

"Hello, Quinnevere," the raven-haired woman said with a gentle smile.

Quinn gasped. All 206 bones in Quinn's body shuddered and froze. Her heart hammered in her ears—at the base of her skull—and each beat sent a different emotion pouring through her body.

The necklace spoke.

It actually spoke to her. Well, *she* spoke. And the necklace was a beautiful woman. Quinn shouldn't have been surprised because she knew she was carrying a Mirror Portal around her neck after visiting Nightshade, but it was still unreal to confirm it as fact.

The necklace Quinn had worn around her neck for nineteen years SPOKE.

Quinn didn't know if she felt faint, nauseous, or curious. It was all a little too much. Her knees buckled, and she started to fall, but the woman swooped in and caught her. Her grip was gentle and warm.

"Who are you?" Quinn asked, staring into the woman's green eyes. "What are you?"

"Oh, hello, Blood." The pink-haired girl pouted in a voice that made it clear that she was not happy to see the other woman.

"Midnight." Blood curtsied to the other mirror.

"Are you okay?" Blood asked Quinn.

"I—" Quinn gulped. "Ah. Yes . . . No." Her gaze raked over the necklace-woman again. "Who are you? Are you the mirror that was destroyed the night my parents died? Did you know my parents? What were they doing there?"

Quinn's questions slurred together and stormed from her mouth, one after the other, with very little thought given to them. It was like a cascading waterfall of all the unanswered questions she'd had in the last nineteen years.

Blood started to respond but was immediately cut off by Midnight's dramatic moan. "No, no, no. This is my realm, and I don't care about these silly questions." Midnight rounded on Quinn. "So, Quinnevere, what is it that you seek from me?" Without any warning, the girl hopped down into a cross-cross sitting position and clapped. It was a surprisingly graceful move, but it made her seem even more like a child.

Quinn swallowed but squared her shoulders. "I would like to trade for information."

"Hmmm, you seek only information, but I could give you a voice that compels all to love you, or I could change the colors of your hair with every emotion or grant you a kiss of death. I could give you the ability to compel anyone like a siren. Or I could give you a chest of the rarest jewels in all the land." The voice came from the clouds and the lightning, the shadows, and the stars. It came from everywhere and vibrated in the wind.

A tremor coiled in Quinn's core.

To her surprise, Midnight said in a lazy voice, "I control everything in here. It's like my dollhouse." Midnight paused, her red, ruby eyes cutting into Quinn. "I could give you the Queen's Royalle Ballet."

At this, Quinn paused. Her heart was a fast-flying hummingbird in her chest. It was what she always wanted, but . . . the cost. Nightshade's deal already killed Jane—probably. "I thought you could only give information." Quinn had only heard of people getting information from Midnight, but it made sense she could bargain for magic, too.

Red chrysanthemums blossomed on Midnight's cheeks. "I excel at information. It is my passion and my past-time, but like all mirrors, I can give you magic, if you prefer. I just might not get the ingredients quite right. I am not practiced, you see."

"You practice," Quinn repeated, not fully understanding what that meant.

"Yes, not all of us can be like the Looking Glass. He is so skilled he can project his costs and his magic outside of his glass cage. He makes everyone in New Swansea City have nightmares every night." Midnight tapped her long fingers on her knee as if she were playing a nursery game with herself. "I wish I knew how he did it. But he is ancient and won't tell me. At least four thousand years old and the same with Passion, Gold, and Greed. They're from long before the Blood Rebellion. That's why they can extract like they do."

During Midnight's monologue, Quinn glanced at Blood, who stood silently, watching and assessing. Upon catching Quinn's questioning gaze, Blood simply shrugged. But the shrug spoke loudly. It said *I am not responsible for her. She's gone a little mad.*

"Information is my magic," Midnight continued.

"It is definitely your greatest skill." Blood's voice was gentle, like a mother soothing a child.

"Oh, sssh, I didn't ask your opinion." Midnight glowered before turning back to Quinn. "I could give you the name of your parents' murderer or Jane's murderer, but that would take a big cost, not quite a soul level, but pretty big."

No.

The cost was too much.

Quinn needed to get out of this unscathed. "How much will it cost for clues for the investigation?"

"Clues aren't really worth that much. So, what will you give me for them?"

Quinn gulped. She had no idea what fair cost would be or how to go about starting the bargain. "Umm, uh, what would you like?"

"I like hair." Midnight twirled a finger through her waves. "I'll take some of your hair for every answer given." Shivers rolled down Quinn's arms. That was a creepy cost.

"What are you going to do with it?" Quinn asked.

Rubbing strands of her hair together, Midnight said, "Braid it. I like braiding. It is an art form, you know."

Quinn nervously reached for her hair. "How much of my hair?"

"Enough to play with but not enough for it to matter. You have thick hair. You'll have plenty left for you." Midnight's face was a tableau of excitement.

"What are the unintended consequences?"

Midnight smiled. "Oh, you're good. If you promise to come and visit me again, I will give you no unintended consequences."

Quinn sucked in a deep breath and thought about all the ways Midnight could try to twist the bargain. She combed through every alternative she could think of until she landed on the cost and the wording she was willing to be bound by.

"I'll agree to a small lock of hair taken from the bottom of my head for each question I ask." Quinn held out a very small section of hair between her fingers. "As long . . . as long as you never use my hair to spell me or to hurt me or use me in any way . . . or to hurt my friends. And when I come and visit you again, I can leave whenever I want."

Midnight furrowed her brow. "I don't play tricks on humans. I solemnly swear on my peach feathered wings that I'll never ever, ever spell you . . . unless asked." Peach-colored wings sprouted from her back with her words. "And I agree to all the other things you've said. You have a deal, little human."

Quinn couldn't see any more traps, but just in case, she refused to respond until she thought it through again. Eventually, she said, "I agree on the terms established."

"Wonderful." Midnight clapped her hands together.

"What are these tattoos?" Quinn asked as she showed her wrist and the mirror tattoo. She figured she would start with the tattoo and then ask about the Blood Mirrors.

Midnight's answer made absolutely no sense and started with eight horrifying words. "Your future is cloaked in blood and death."

Twenty-One

"Midnight, that is enough," Blood said as she rolled her eyes.

"That is not my name." Midnight pouted and crossed her arms in childlike defiance.

Ignoring the pink-haired girl, Blood said, "The tattoo symbolizes the Blood Council." Blood glanced over her shoulder before continuing in a rush. Almost as if she didn't hurry, the other mirror might intervene. "The Council is designed to govern and hide the existence of vampires through the laws known as the Vampire Accords."

Hide the existence of vampires.

A spider of fear surged down Quinn's spine. She was right! Her suspicions, all of the fang markings on the bodies, all pointed to the irrevocable truth that vampires were still alive.

Midnight glared a river of daggers at Blood and crossed her arms. "Hmph, you're absolutely no fun. You give her all the stupid answers."

Blood rolled her shoulders back and faced the other girl—mirror. "Your deal didn't say I couldn't. Perhaps you should have been more specific."

Quinn's insides churned as she watched the showdown

between the two powerful beings. As the truth about vampires stirred her insides and clamped her mouth tightly shut.

"Fine," Midnight said with a huff as she threw her hands up like a two-year-old having a tantrum. "You're technically correct. But next time, I'll muzzle you."

"Next time." Blood's smile was victorious poison.

Confusion raked through Quinn's blood. Why was Blood helping? But more importantly, could she trust the mirror? The mirror that she wore around her neck and seldom took off.

Quinn recoiled, and her muscles quivered with tension, and she tried to focus herself back on the moment. "I need to clarify: vampires are alive?"

"That was another question." Midnight wrinkled her nose with glee.

Shit, shit, shit. Quinn needed to be more careful, or she'd leave the mirror with absolutely no hair. Oh, and she really should've ensured her hair would grow back. It'd just be like a mirror bargain for it to be gone forever.

"I'll take your hair now." Midnight held out a hand.

"You never answered my question."

"You said every question asked. I never said I had to answer the question." Midnight's voice was a singsong soprano.

Blood cleared her throat, and she glared. "I thought you said you don't trick humans."

Midnight scoffed, clearly taking offense. "That wasn't a trick. I told her exactly what I would do. She failed to specify that I had to answer the question she asked."

"You're all the same." Blood shook her head.

"What are you like, nineteen?" Midnight's voice was suddenly older and as dark as a bottomless pit. "When you've been trapped in your cage for hundreds of years, you'll understand." Midnight's demeanor shifted again back to the joyous yet eccentric teen. "Plus, I am a nice mirror. I don't even ask for people's souls like most of the others."

Blood's eyes grew stormy—like an overcast, never-ending rainy day. "I am sorry, Midnight."

The teen waved away the apology. "If you must insist on your answers, then yes, vampires exist."

Quinn's knees buckled, and her muscles grew weak and faint. She let her knees fall to the cloudy floor. Fear coiled around her throat like a snake suffocating its prey.

"Are you all right?" Blood stood up and reached for Quinn.

"Yes. I am fine." Quinn panted as if she ran a race and lost. Before Quinn could think it through, she asked, "What are the Blood Mirrors?" Quinn knew they somehow had to be connected. Her parents had the tattoos and were murdered protecting a mirror. And Jane was murdered because of the mirrors, too.

"That's three questions now." Midnight tallied them on her fingers.

"The three Blood Mirrors house the vampires' only mortal weakness," Blood said. "And they are protected by the Council."

Quinn desperately wanted to ask about the weakness, but she'd already bargained away three chunks of her hair, and she still didn't know if it would ever grow back—and she didn't even know what Midnight meant by a "small lock." And it wasn't that Quinn was vain, but she did like her hair. It was one of her best features.

If she asked one more question, she'd probably be fine, but she was unwilling to let go of that much more.

But what question would lead her to the most answers outside of the mirror?

Quinn finally settled on, "How can I get more answers about the Blood Council and vampires without asking a mirror?"

"A council meeting will be held at the castle tomorrow night. You should be able to get more answers then," Blood said.

"I am assuming that was your last question?" Midnight asked, playing with a cloud kitten she'd created.

"Yes," Quinn breathed.

"Wonderful." Midnight's complexion lit up. "I'll have my prize now."

She held out her hand. With a slight pinch at the back of Quinn's head, the bottom half-inch of her hair fell out and appeared in Midnight's hand.

The teen kissed the hair and rubbed it against her face before saying, "Goodbye, sweet Quinn. I did enjoy your company. Do come back for a visit!"

Quinn stiffened. That was the last thing she ever wanted to do.

Red metal climbed up Blood's body. "It was an honor to get to see you, Quinnevere." A tear dropped from her eye as the crimson metal captured her. Once fully covered, the woman melted into dancing liquid and flowed back into the necklace's cage.

Then Quinn fell through darkness.

She hit the asphalt road with a thud. The mirror had tossed her out back onto the street. "Ouch."

"How did it go?"

"At least she still looks the same."

"She doesn't look too tortured."

Quinn's mind whirled, and she didn't know which of her friends belonged to which voice. She laid her head back against the ground and sucked in a breath. So much happened, and she was unable to process it all. The tattoo and Blood Mirrors and vampires.

It was all too much. She needed to forget about it. But she couldn't, so after a long pause to collect her thoughts, she sat up and told her friends everything.

DAY FOUR

DAY
FOUR

PRICE 2 CENTS

BREAKING NEWS

The New Swansea Times

WEDNESDAY, NEW SWANSEA CITY, 93rd DAY OF AUTUMN, 700AV

THE LOOKING GLASS CHRONICLES
LEARN MORE ABOUT THE INFAMOUS MIRROR

What is your favorite Mirror? Find out the Prince's on page 6!

Third Day of the Festival of Blood

The third Night of the Festival of Blood belongs to Pleasure. It is a night filled with normally forbidden desires. The streets will be overcome by the performers of the Viridian, the ladies of the Starling and the sin of the Russet. It will be a time of passion, decadence, and unruly dreams —cont. page 2

Ballerina Charms Prince with "Dance" Skills

Our glorious prince seems enamored by one of the top contenders to join the Queen's Royalle Ballet this year. But is the prince grooming her for a more valuable position? Or is she just a desperate girl in love? She wouldn't be the first fool to be obsessed with Emrys and get their heart broken. Our guess is it's the latter and desperation doesn't look good on anyone—cont. page 3

TWENTY-TWO

Ballet auditions were still postponed for another two days as an act of remembrance, but Quinn still needed practice. It was hard to dance now with Jane dead. It felt wrong. So much so that Quinn considered stopping altogether. But if Jane were alive, she'd force her friend to complete the week of auditions.

Jane wouldn't let her quit.

So, Quinn threw her hair into a bun, in the process scratching the bald area at the nape of her neck. She groaned. So that was real. She wanted to study her reflection and see the extent of the damage, but she didn't want to do it in front of her friends.

And if that's real, then so was the necklace. Quinn clutched it tight, its cage cutting into her skin. It was alive. A soul. A brunette woman. She shivered and pulled the chain over her head. Maybe she shouldn't wear an alive soul around her neck. After a moment, she pulled it back over her head.

Jane told her to keep it close. So, she would.

Quinn shuddered and turned her eyes to her friends. Emrys sprawled on the studio dance floor, flipping through autopsy reports that he inconspicuously "borrowed" from Uncle Matias. Constance rested against the studio mirror and sewed her deep olive pointe shoes to her specifications. Ballet dancers went through at least three pairs of pointe shoes in a week, and each new set had to be broken in and tailored to the specific dancer. Giselle had her nose deep into a book, and Jevon stood slightly in the corner, observing the scene, and flipping Jane's key through his fingers. As usual, he was quiet, reserved, and examining.

Quinn practiced with precision and grace. Her arms fluttered and floated, painting a nightmare across the room. A nightmare embodying death's embrace. Her dancing was like broken promises, last kisses, and shattered dreams. Her feet glided and glittered along a field of corpses clawing at her toes.

Everything matched the tone of the dance—everything except probably Quinn's face.

She gritted her teeth and tried to show her character's sorrow and horror. Unfortunately, Quinn's version of distraught felt more like a mild case of irritation.

Her left leg tingled as she finished her pique turns, sweat flowing down her body. The Realm of Death variation from Lover's Lost was taxing in almost every way imaginable.

"No. No, no, stop," Constance called, the needle in her hand still moving even though she wasn't looking at her task. "You need to feel terrified and devastated. You just lost your husband and will forever be trapped in the land of the dead."

"I am trying," Quinn huffed. "This is my devastated face."

"No, that is your constipated face," Constance said. Despite the harsh words, her tone was warm and soft. It was the somber calmness that she typically had when dancing. In fact, Constance always seemed to be in a less energetic mood around Emrys.

He chuckled, his face now deep in the Ashelle murder autopsy report.

"Perhaps it is *my I am gonna murder someone face*." Quinn glared at the top of Emrys's raven hair.

Giselle's ruby lips rose with amusement. "If that is your murderous face, it will scare absolutely no one."

Pain rippled through Quinn's calf. It wasn't until she stopped dancing that she felt the deep agony in her leg. She shook out her numb calves to try to release the tension. "That's probably true. Thankfully, I don't plan on being a murderer."

"No, you just plan on investigating them." Constance's maple wood eyes flicked back to her pointe shoes as she folded the toe, trying to break them in.

"Well . . . hopefully not," Quinn pouted. But even that lacked the proper childish emotion. Quinn didn't need to actually see it to know her acting was bad. "Hopefully, I'll be dancing in the Royalle Ballet for the next five years."

Emrys wrinkled his nose.

Constance's eyes narrowed. "Do you ever rest?"

"Of course, she doesn't," Giselle chimed in, turning a page of her book.

Quinn crossed her arms and huffed. "I'll rest when I am dead."

A wicked grin danced on Emrys's face as he looked up for the first time all practice. "Let's hope your death is more restful—"

Constance hit him with her shoe, cutting him off. "Let's stop talking about her death."

His entire body sparkled with mischievous amusement, and he shrugged as if discussing Quinn's death was as normal as discussing the weather.

Constance pursed her lips. "Back to work, Quinny. And try to imagine what it would be like to lose the love of your life," Constance commanded, still glowering at Emrys.

"Perhaps she needs to know what it is to touch a man before she can accurately pretend to lose a great love." Emrys winked before ducking his face back into his report.

All three girls glowered at him. He held up his hands in surrender. "If you are looking for a murderous face, you should copy the one you have right now. It is grand."

The fire burning inside Quinn deepened to a poisonous gas, spreading, and suffocating him in his place.

"See." His playboy smile grew. "Precisely my point, you're withering." Emrys's eyes returned to his book. "But you really should find yourself a gentleman and learn to . . . *love* from experience and return to your lessons in passion." He winked and emphasized the word love as if he meant an entirely different word.

Horror ruptured in Quinn's stomach while Giselle hit him over the head with her book. "Watch yourself, princey, and go back to your reading."

He shrugged. "I am just saying—"

"Why don't we go over what we know about the murders." Quinn cut him off. It would be an excellent way to put non-offensive words in his mouth.

"Great idea, Gingey," he said.

Quinn sighed. Again, with that stupid nickname. He was doing it at this point to bother her, and they both knew it. "Stop, calling me that. It is not accurate."

Her issue was the accuracy more than the nickname itself.

He held up his hands again in defeat. "So, Quinnevere, where should we start with the evidence?"

"From the beginning," Quinn said. "We know there is a serial killer out there, possibly a vampire, who has been killing members of the Blood Council and specifically members that have some connection to the Blood Mirrors." Once Quinn was finished, she started the variation again, dancing as the others continued.

"Blood Mirrors that hold the vampires' greatest secret," Giselle added, placing her book on the floor.

"So, the motive is the mirrors, but how does the key figure into all of this?" Jevon added.

As Quinn spotted him, she saw that he crossed a leg in front of him while leaning against the wall nonchalantly. Jevon was normally so still, so quiet, so observant that sometimes he blended into the scenery like a chameleon, which is why everyone's eyes except Quinn's landed on him.

Breathless and doing pas de bourrée steps, Quinn said, "I have no idea. Jane was trying to tell me something, so maybe it led to another clue. If only we could figure out where it goes."

"Can I see it again?" Giselle asked.

As Jevon walked to hand the key over, Quinn did a double pirouette that went into attitude, her leg high in the air before finishing in a plié with her leg still extended out. It was a hard turn to complete, but Quinn had no issues with the steps. No issues except the pain dripping from her leg like acid.

"Hmm, it looks familiar. It didn't open any of the rooms in the casino . . ." Giselle studied the key, sliding a finger across it. "Do you mind if I hold onto it for a while?"

"No, go ahea—" Quinn choked out as she jumped into a grand jeté across the floor. Quinn made the movement look smooth and elegant, but jumping with her legs in a full split across the floor took skill and dedication.

"Is there any evidence that might help us?" Constance asked, finally setting her shoes down.

Quinn ignored the question, running across the floor and trying to make her arms look as if she were chained and being dragged away. She poured every ounce of emotion into the movements. Stopping and clutching her side, she said, "Well, there is . . . the feather, sequins . . . and prints."

Quinn gulped for air, so out of breath that she was barely able to answer the question. One should not dance and speak. It was too much. She collapsed beside Constance, sweat dripping from her forehead.

Once she finally was able to compose herself, she told them about the matching fingerprint on the feather and Jane's corset, along with a print lifted from St. John's neck. The victims were killed by the same person, and they had the fingerprints to prove it.

"So, we're missing suspects. But you have the killer's fingerprints . . . so all we need to do is find some suspects and check their prints," Giselle said, rose buds blossoming on her bronze cheeks as excitement grew on her face. "You know what this means, Quinn." Yes, she did. Quinn gulped, knowing precisely what her best friend would say next. "We're breaking into Castle

Hill and attending that council meeting so that we can figure out a list of suspects."

It made sense to gather fingerprints at the council meeting because they had the greatest connections to the victims.

"Precisely what I was thinking," Quinn agreed, but her stomach churned with anxiety. She hated breaking the rules. But her preferences no longer mattered. "Not only can we get a list of suspects, but we could also gather fingerprint samples."

"No, we absolutely are not going to break into Castle Hill to watch a council meeting. If we get caught, we could go to jail." Constance stood up as if to make her position clearer.

"You know, Constance, sometimes you seem like two different people." Giselle glowered at her friend. "Most days, you would die for a bit of excitement and fun. And then other days you're just . . ." Giselle thought on the appropriate word, finally finishing with, "boring."

"I might be boring, but at least I am not foolish. We are talking about the palace and the queen," Constance said. "We're not going."

"I agree with Constance," Emrys cut in. "It is not safe to be at Castle Hill tonight."

The argument continued for a long time, and Giselle and Quinn finally agreed that they wouldn't try to sneak into the palace because the prince didn't approve. But knowing Giselle, they were absolutely going to break into the Royalle Palace.

Quinn crossed her arms. "If you don't want us to go, fine, but Emrys, you'll need to gather all of the fingerprints from council members."

"Absolutely, but for now, I must be off. Castle Hill business." Emrys bowed to the group before sauntering over to Quinn and clasping her hand. "Do remember to stay far, far away from Castle Hill tonight." He winked.

Lifting it to his lips, he kissed the back of her hand while simultaneously slipping a paper between her fingers. Then he disappeared out the door and into the night.

Quinn unrolled a parchment that held five words:

Red River.
Meet me after.

Her brain stumbled through the possibilities of what those words meant. Clearly, he wanted to meet her after the council meeting, but the Red River meant very little to her. It wasn't a place anywhere in the city or the country.

And then it hit her.

It must be the password to the golden gondolas that floated up to the palace.

Twenty-Three

If Quinnevere thought the city danced with magic before, it was nothing compared to Castle Hill. To reach the massive palace at the city's center, surrounded by cliffs on three sides and an enormous incline on the other, she had to ride a sky gondola that moonlighted as a star. Made entirely from molten silver with gold accents, the carriages carved through the sky like diamonds cutting glass.

Quinn rode a gondola every day to and from University Square, but those carriages were nothing like the ones streaming up Castle Hill.

The only other way up the cliffs surrounding the fortress was a narrow, sharp, zig-zag road that had so many turns it made drivers vomit from motion sickness. Thirty-three turns in all. The crooked, deadly road. Almost no one chose to take that path these days. Not with flying coaches.

But even the beauty of the moment couldn't dissuade the panic pooling in her stomach. Quinn fiddled with the fabric of her skirt as she rode alone up the midnight cliffs, the anxiety springing up her throat. Her hands were clammy, and her entire body constricted.

Every sound of the gears made her jump and squirm. All she

wanted to do was enjoy the magic and scenery, but the closer she got to the top, the more unsettled she became.

And she was alone.

Alone.

Giselle was late . . . again. She was always late, but this time it mattered. Because now Quinn had to figure out how to do everything.

The plan was to meet Giselle at the gondolas at the stroke of eight. Which would give them plenty of time to make the meeting by nine—its official start time.

When Giselle wasn't there after thirty minutes of waiting, Quinn had no other choice but to face her biggest fears—*alone*. So, she gave the operator the password and got into a flying carriage.

As the doors opened, she stepped out onto a glittering path leading to the palace. If she'd thought the gondola and road were impressive, it was nothing compared to the palace itself. A massive external rotunda acted as the entrance, with its domed ceiling carved from jade. Pergolas lined with colonnades snaked around the rotunda like a labyrinth of wonder. Lacing the palace on one side was a serene lagoon, and on the other was a garden of disorienting hedge mazes.

Quinn's heart pounded like exploding fireworks as she jumped behind a bush, trying to avoid the presumed council members on their way to the meeting.

Oh, shattered mirrors, this was bad.

She waited too long to take the gondola, and now carriage after carriage arrived, making it impossible for her to sneak anywhere.

It felt like hours passed as Quinn waited. Finally, after watching seven empty carriages arrive, she felt safe enough to try and enter again.

"There you are."

Quinn's heart jolted, and fear spiked through her body, bone by bone, sinew by sinew, and vein by vein. She was caught, and it felt like death—like her body would completely give out on her. Quinn hated getting in trouble with every fiber of her being. Her throat tightened, and she couldn't breathe.

It was too much. She gasped for air but didn't feel any flowing into her lungs.

Panic consumed her.

Small hands clutched her face. "You're okay. I am here. We're in this together." Giselle's gentle voice soothed the fear tangled in Quinn's limbs. "I'm sorry I was late."

When the panic attack settled, Giselle stepped back, also panting, and clutching her side. Quinn hadn't noticed the exhaustion in Giselle's voice before. But she was a mess, her clothing ripped and disheveled. Branches and leaves poked out of her hair, and mud laced her boots. She looked like she'd run through the Nature District to rescue her friend from a dark monster.

"Did you run up the crooked street?" Quinn asked.

"Yes. You never told me the password." Giselle's face hardened, and storm clouds gathered in her eyes. "Quinnevere Igretta Ashelle, you disappeared and rode the gondola alone."

Quinn swallowed, her neck growing tight with shame. "I'm sorry. You were late—"

"I am so proud of you!" Giselle bounded forward and laced her arms around Quinn's core, engulfing her in a massive hug.

Quinn bristled, and her body ached. No one ever embraced her like this. She didn't know what to do. Of course, she'd been touched, lifted, and even intimately embraced while dancing with her pas de deux partner. But that wasn't real life. That was an act —dancing.

This was different.

After a long moment, she allowed her muscles to relax, and she gave into the hug, even returning it.

"So, what do we do now?" Quinn whispered into Giselle's hair. "I have no idea how to sneak into a palace."

Giselle released her arms and pulled away, the smile on her

face indecently villainous. "We're going to walk in like we own the place."

"You have to be kidding." Quinn's mouth almost dropped in her shock, but she managed to pinch it shut and withhold any further amazement.

"You have the council tattoo," Giselle said. "I was watching, and that is the entry fee."

"And what about you?"

"I am rather good with a pen." Giselle flashed her wrist, showing a crooked and sloppy version of the marking. It looked like she had clumsily drawn it on herself, which, of course, was exactly what occurred. "It's fine. Trust me, if you act like you own the world, then people will think that you do. It is the only decent lesson my mother ever taught me."

At Quinn's protest, five minutes later, they were flashing their tattoos at the man guarding the front doors, and to her utter surprise, the man simply muttered his approval and let them inside.

Quinn stepped through the towering double arched doors, which led to a grand staircase and ballroom. Her Mary-Jane heels clicked against the marble as they glided through the palace. Room after room of gilded walls glazed with paintings, colonnades, chandeliers set with diamonds, and statues made of stardust.

They followed voices until they reached a domed room. Standing at the edge of one of the entrances, the girls peered inside.

Chairs and desks were set in a semicircle around the room, and at the front, towered three opulent thrones. The walls were lined with gilded carvings fit for a king, and the room vibrated with grandiosity and the smell of rosemary, mystery, and aristocracy—like the walls were dripping with power and influence. Some of the people in attendance were nobles, while others were industry moguls, but the most fascinating groups in attendance were the gang leaders and Queens of the Night—like Kordiela.

The ones who ruled the underbelly of the city with an iron fist—all mixing with the rich elite.

It was jarring.

From the side of the room, three figures entered, decked in finery. They swept in like ice skaters across the floor and gracefully sat on the thrones. Regal and royal, the queen and princess observed the room while Emrys sat with his legs draped over the side of his throne, a bored look painting his face. The crown on his head tilted so far off that it was surprising it even managed to stay atop his head.

"There is a balcony," Giselle said in a voice lower than a whisper and pointed to the top left of the room. Before Quinn could respond, Giselle swooped from her eavesdropping position and pulled her friend with her up a velvet staircase.

Within a matter of moments, they found the balcony that moonlighted as a spy nest. The queen gently clapped her hands, sending the guards into action. The announcer pounded his staff on the floor three times, silencing the room.

The groups sat down at their respective desks, allowing the girls to see many of their faces for the first time.

All of the air evaporated from Quinn's body when she spotted a familiar figure.

Directly below the balcony, Uncle Matias sat among seven empty chairs. His group was late . . . or missing.

Her uncle was at the council meeting, which meant he knew about vampires and her parents' connection to the mirrors. And he'd kept it from her.

Her legs trembled. She was so unsteady that it felt like her bones had liquefied. She backed up into the wall and slid down it into a sitting position as she held her knees. She tried to take a deep breath and calm herself.

He lied to her.

He *betrayed* her.

Someone cleared their throat and said, "As with every meeting so no one forgets, let's get started with a reading of the accords."

From the cadence and majesty in their voice, Quinn imagined it must have been the queen.

As her temples pounded with each beat of her racing heart, a new person spoke. "As signed into law on the Fifteenth Day of Spring in the Fiftieth Year AV . . ."

The timing didn't make sense. The Blood Rebellion was year zero. Why would it take fifty years to enact the laws, and why did New Swansea's history say that vampires were completely exterminated during the war if they'd survived?

"The Vampire Accords Agreement reads," the man continued.

> *Law 1. Vampires cannot kill a human without forfeiting their own life, unless the human killed was an execution sectioned by the council.*
>
> *Law 2. Vampires cannot create new vampires or mark a human.*
>
> *Law 3. Vampires cannot disclose any information about the Blood Council, Blood Mirrors, or the existence of vampires to anyone who does not already know the secrets.*
>
> *Law 4. Vampires can only feed to maintain their existence.*
>
> *Law 5. A vampire can compel a human but only to protect the secret or for the purposes of feeding."*

Halfway through the reading of the laws, Quinn slid on her knees across the floor to peek through the railing. A member sat to the right of the room, was holding up a scroll and reading from it.

> *Law 6. Vampires are forbidden to compel anyone to tamper with the Blood Mirrors, destroy them, or threaten them in any way.*

*Law 7. Vampires cannot compel a human to release
their painting from a Blood Mirror.*
*Law 8. Only human council members can enter the
mirrors and unbind a vampire. The cost of
unbinding vampires will be a soul.*
*Law 9. Council members must keep the vampire
secret or face imprisonment or execution.*
*Law 10. The council will choose its next leader, who
will act as New Swansea's queen. Every 25
years, a new human will be chosen from among
the council members as the princess who will
eventually become the queen.*
*Law 11. If the public finds out about the existence of
vampires, all vampires will be executed by the
Blood Mirrors.*

"This concludes the reading of the Vampire Accords." The announcer's words echoed through Quinn's mind, and her fingers bit into the cold metal railing. She felt the blood rushing from her head, dripping like crimson tears, leaving her face ashen and haunted.

Vampires were truly alive. She'd heard it before. She knew it, but it didn't feel real until this moment.

The monsters that haunted her dreams were real.

The only comfort was that they were bound by the laws and apparently unable to kill.

Did that mean a vampire was not behind Jane's murder?

The queen rose from her throne slowly, like a snake examining its prey. She was radiant. Age barely took any of her unnatural beauty. Although wrinkles settled beneath her eyes and her pale skin didn't hold its youthful tightness, she still managed to catch and keep every subject's attention. Her beauty wasn't in looks that faded, but in the power she emanated.

She strolled to the center of the room and faced a young man with brunette locks and square-rimmed glasses. Giselle stiffened and stifled a gasp. "We offer our condolences to Francois of Les Fantômes' gang for the tragic loss of your second, Jane." The queen's voice pulsated with a soft dominance and majesty.

Second? How had Jane become the second most powerful Fantômes in the city? That was a long way to rise.

Francois bowed to the queen. "Thank you, your majesty." The people surrounding Francois also bowed or curtsied.

A tangle of emotions churned in Quinn's stomach as she stared down at the gang members. Lies, so many lies. From the gang, from Emrys, from her uncle. Was everyone in her life lying to her?

Giselle tapped Quinn on the shoulder, tearing her out of her thoughts. "I am going to try and get a better view," Giselle whispered.

"A better view of what?" There was nothing else to see except maybe the papers on the table, and the girls were too far up to be able to make out any of the lettering. Not that Quinn ever could.

Giselle waved a dismissive hand. "Everything."

"Remember, our plan is to collect as many fingerprints as possible."

"Yes, I will be doing that too," Giselle said as she jumped onto the railing and began climbing a pillar to the rafters. Within seconds, she'd disappeared.

"It is a tragic day indeed to lose yet another council member," the queen said from below. "Medical Examiner Thyssen, please give us an update on Jane's murder."

Uncle Matias approached the center of the room with ease. There was always a sway and rhythm to the way he moved, the way he spoke. Soft but commanding and utterly terrifying with his subtly.

He cleared his throat and launched into a report. He compiled the same evidence that Quinn had with similar results. Jane had lacerations across the throat and puncture wounds. The only new information Uncle Matias provided was the alibis of the seven vampires who were unbound when the first Blood Mirror was destroyed. Most of the names on the list were unfamiliar, but Countess Teagan Atwater's name struck with the force of a falling cable car.

Teagan Atwater. The girl who made Quinn's life a living hell *was a vampire*. A vampire unbound by the Vampire Accords. Vampire who could kill.

However, according to Uncle Matias's report, the seven were monitored and forced into routine check-ins with a parole officer daily.

Uncle Matias ended with, "As of now, we have no viable suspects or motive for the murder."

Emrys snorted, his legs still dangling off the chair like he had no cares in the world. "The motive is clearly the Blood Mirrors."

Matias Thyssen returned to his seat as a middle-aged lady with a countenance of daggers stood and walked to the center of the floor. She was all sharp edges.

She made a sound of pure disgust before saying, "No human or vampire will ever find the last two mirrors. They are hidden from our memories and far out of our reach, cloaked by mirror protections. Not even our pretty prince can find them, and we all know you've tried for nineteen years."

Nineteen years. Quinn stiffened.

Emrys slightly raised his head, showing a modicum of interest. He yawned before saying, "I've only searched for them as a means to find the person who murdered my friends and stole my family's paintings."

"And how has that gone?" the angular woman asked, her tone an insult.

"As you have clearly pointed out, I don't possess the talent for hunting." Emrys stroked a leisurely finger down his lapel as if the lady's words meant nothing. "Regardless of my skills, it doesn't change the fact that someone far more talented than I am is hunting down those mirrors and killing anyone who gets in their way."

"They must not be that talented," the lady said. "It's been

nineteen years, and no one's found the other two mirrors. You need to let this obsession go. The mirrors are protected."

"Those protections won't last forever." Emrys's words were a haunted, hollow warning.

"By then, the killer will be dead." The angular woman stood taller, making her display of dominance known. Quinn wasn't sure if this woman was human, Mirror-Blessed, or immortal, but she certainly was an even bigger narcissist than the prince.

"And if they're not? What then?" Emrys rose a brow. "I have lived many lives, Lady Annabelle Ravenscroft, long enough to know that one does not need to be a vampire to live forever."

Lived many lives . . . One doesn't need to be a vampire to live forever. Quinn gulped. Emrys was immortal, but was he Mirror-Blessed or a vampire?

Quinn blinked and clutched her head, suddenly feeling an ache accompanied by her lost memories from the library. They came back!

The royal family's curse. But . . . maybe it wasn't a curse. Maybe the prince was trying to show her all the different lives he's lived. Because . . . because he was a vampire.

Emrys adjusted his crown as if reminding the lady it was still there. "We all remember Gideon."

"I remember you plunging a dagger through his heart," Lady Annabelle said.

"Yes, and ending his reign of terror, but if I hadn't, he would still be eternally young like a vampire."

Francois cleared his throat and stood up. "Lady Ravenscroft, are you suggesting that we allow this murderer to kill us off one by one?" Francois's expression was wildfire. "Seven council members are dead, and one reporter."

"Someone is after those mirrors," Hadleigh, Francois's new second, said, her voice slightly unsteady. "And they killed Jane because of it. We cannot let this go."

Jane was killed because of the mirrors, and the gang knew. This would have been important to know about earlier.

"We have no new evidence or suspects. What are we to do?" Lady Annabelle asked. "We must stay the course. The mirrors are protected, and that is what matters."

"Except Jane found the second mirror," Emrys said as chatter broke out through the hall. "She told me the night she died but refused to tell me where. If we let this go and do nothing, we're doomed because while we might've forgotten about them, the murderer certainly hasn't."

That was the conversation Quinn overheard. Things were finally starting to make sense.

"Someone wants to steal our paintings, destroy the mirrors, and, in essence, destroy the accords," an unknown young man said.

"Maybe the accords should be destroyed." Every set of eyes turned in unison to Countess Teagan Atwater as she held her head high and shoulders back.

In a blink, she was at the center of the room. Quinn gasped but tried to stifle it with her hands because no one else was remotely shocked by the woman's vampiric speed.

"Perhaps the laws are too strict. Death to all vampires if the public learns our secret? Come on, even you have to admit that is going too far." Countess Atwater said the last bit directly to Emrys.

"The laws keep vampires from our worst impulses like human laws restrict their worst impulses," the unknown young man said, also disappearing and reappearing in the center.

"The difference being that if a human gets drunk and mouthy and tells their secrets to the world, they don't get themselves and their entire kind executed for it," Teagan said. "Not to mention, it's not just the vampires who can't tell a soul. Every single person in this room must remain silent. If any of you were vindictive enough, you could print the secret in the papers, and within seconds of the truth escaping, we would all be dead."

"Don't give them any ideas," the unknown man muttered.

"We are bound by the accords too. If one of us let slip the

secret, it would be our heads, too," a woman from the center of the room, presumably a human, said.

The argument went on for what felt like hours with no resolution. Vampires stood for and against the laws, but not a single person had any clue to any major suspects for the serial murders.

But Quinn's suspect list was growing. It now included:

Francois and Hadleigh, the unknown young man, Countess Teagan Atwater, and Lady Annabelle Ravenscroft.

All of them seemed to have some motive for either destroying the accords or framing vampires.

Eventually, the conversation turned to other topics.

"Lady DeWinter, how does your operation fair?" the queen asked, clutching the arm of her throne.

DeWinter. There was only one person Quinn knew who went by the name DeWinter.

Constance.

A cloaked figure ambled to the center and slowly removed her hood, allowing her midnight locks to spill down her shoulders and her mahogany eyes to sparkle in the sconce light. "As always, the Viridian's true business thrives as well as its ostentatious one."

Constance's voice echoed through the chambers of Quinn's heart, slicing tiny lacerations with each wave of sound. If she weren't already on her knees, Quinn would have crumbled to the ground. The force of this betrayal was visceral and disorienting.

Constance. One of her closest friends had lied to her and kept one of the most important secrets imaginable. She was a council member, and this whole time, she'd known about the tattoos and the connections to the murders. She'd known everything and withheld it.

"Good, and all of your shipments are running smoothly?" the queen asked.

"In the last four hundred years that I've run the Viridian, have we ever let this council down?" Kordelia, the owner of the Viridian, prowled to the center, her voice liquid fire.

"No."

"Then that is your answer." Kordelia scowled before clutching Constance's arm and leaving the center.

The meeting continued as Quinn's mind stormed, betrayal and confusion dancing a pas de deux.

Eventually, the meeting adjourned, and the council members trickled out of the room, except Uncle Matias, who remained glaring at Emrys, who still lounged on his throne.

When everyone was nearly gone, Uncle Matias rounded on the prince—slow and stalking like a bird of prey. "That stunt you pulled today in my lab will never happen again."

"I was having a bit of fun." Emrys smiled like a tiger.

"You and your fun. That's all you ever think about."

Emrys raised a brow, which clearly indicated that it was not all he had *thought about.*

"Stay away from my niece." Uncle Matias's anger, as usual, was dull and guttural—even more painful for its lack of sharpness.

"She is a council member, and now that Jane is dead, Quinn is the last of her line, and she deserves to know everything."

Uncle Matias raised one terrifying brow and said in a voice filled with danger, "She deserves to know only what I want her to know."

"Yes, you have made that clear many, many times." The words swished off Emrys's tongue in a leisurely, bored manner as he picked a piece of lint from his vest.

"Stay away from my niece," Uncle Matias said again, this time marking his every word with poison. "I do not want you anywhere near her."

"Yes, Your Majesty," Emrys said mockingly, giving an over-the-top bow. As he returned to his full height, his eyes flicked up to meet Quinn's, and she ducked once more behind the railing.

Shit. Shit. Shit. Dirty, broken fucking mirrors. The last thing she needed was Emrys catching her eavesdropping, even if he had invited her.

Twenty-Four

Quinn scuttled back and out of the balcony, making far too much noise. She landed in the hall on her knees and tried to get away from the council chamber as quickly as possible. Not that it mattered because Emrys saw her, and perhaps he'd known she was there the whole time.

After all, he was the one who gave her the password to the gondola.

But she needed to get away because her uncle couldn't find her. If he did, she'd be in a world of trouble. But more than anything else, she needed to get away because a weight of betrayal sank in her chest, and she needed to run from it.

It was too much to bear. Her uncle lied about everything and withheld the truth about her parents' murders. And Constance was a council member. Possibly immortal and definitely hiding a lot of secrets.

It was too much, and Quinn couldn't breathe. Betrayal was a poison suffocating her.

But running helped.

Dashing from one hall to the next, she got confused. It was such a big castle, and every room looked eerily similar with its over-the-top decoration, filigree, and gilded finishes.

After a couple of minutes of trying to find the exit, she was halted by the echoing of screams. Loud and unforgiving. Originating from down the hall. Normally, Quinn would have ignored it, but those voices were familiar.

Constance and Kordelia.

It was crossing some sort of line to listen in on her friend in a moment so tumultuous, and Quinn really should have ignored it, but she was so utterly frustrated. Constance was one of her closest friends, yet she felt the need to lie at every turn.

Quinn's chest swelled with hurt like an allergic reaction was smothering her innards.

"You cannot be serious." Constance's words were low and filled with dark astonishment.

This was followed by a lot of undistinguishable angry words thrown at each other back and forth. Quinn's heart was a caged animal trying to escape, angry and beating against the bars of her chest. She counted to five, trying to steady herself before she tiptoed to get closer.

"You forget your place," Constance said.

"I forget my place?" Kordelia spat.

"Remember who you're talking to." There was a pause before Constance continued, "You had no right."

"I had every right. I run the—"

"You only run the Viridian because I allow it," Constance cut back, a snake ready to strike.

Confusion slithered along Quinn's skin, leaving gooseflesh in its wake. Kordelia oversaw the Viridian, yet Constance controlled this situation like a judge's gavel. But then, the queen had asked Constance first about her business, not Kordelia.

Was this yet another thing she was lying about?

Only muffled sounds cut the air, and Quinn's human ears couldn't make out the words. She tried to peek through the crack in the door, but she only saw grey shapes.

"I am sorry. I should've let you handle everything." A cloud of blonde crossed in front of the crack as Kordelia humbled herself.

"Yes, you should have." Constance was softer, but there was still a sharp edge. "Maybe Jane would be alive if we . . ."

"Yes," Kordeia breathed.

"So, we are clear," Constance said. "I need you to tell me when suspicious things are happening at the Viridian. I know you can handle them, but with . . . with what the mirror took from you, you don't have the best judgment."

Quinn's heart rattled. They were talking about the murder, and they were withholding information from the others. So many questions slithered through Quinn's mind, but chief among them was why would Jane be alive if they . . . what? She desperately wanted her friend to end that sentence.

"Understood, your grace." Kordelia bowed her head in deference. The words were not condescending but sincere, which was puzzling. Why would she call Constance "your grace?" That would make her a duchess. But she never once told her friends that.

"Don't call me that." Constance crossed her arms, her face a mask of sorrow.

"Understood," Kordelia said with a coquettish grin. "Since you want me to tell you when there are suspicious activities at the Viridian, I think we need to talk about Seren."

Constance's brows crinkled. "What about her?"

"I thought I saw her the other night," Kordelia said.

"That's highly unlikely." Constance smoothed out a rogue feather on her costume. "She left twenty years ago, and if she were back, I'd feel it."

"You're probably right. I worry about you." Kordelia reached out and played with one of Constance's bouncy raven curls. The touch was so close, so intimate. Then she cupped Constance's face and kissed her. It was passionate but short-lived as Constance pulled away.

"Don't," she breathed, a struggle lighting up her posture. Her limbs were rigid, yet her body tilted toward the blonde. As if two sides of her warred.

"I'm sorry." Kordelia's voice cracked. "I am sorry for everything."

With her thumb, Constance caressed Kordelia's chin. "I wish . . ." Constance's thumb traveled south—a lover's caress. "I can't. I can't be with you," she said, letting her hand drop.

Kordelia reached for another raven curl, but Constance stepped away. A mask of indifference flooded across her face as she tried to keep her emotions in check.

"Because you don't trust me," Kordelia finished the thought.

"I trust you in every way but this." Constance rocked between her feet, not wanting to meet the blonde's eyes.

"I know," Kordelia whispered. "I wish that I had never ruined things between us."

"Me too."

"Just know, Constance DeWinter, I love you. I have always loved you, no matter what I've done." The words were so devoted and private that shivers ran down Quinn's arms.

Now, Quinn truly crossed the line. Despite her anger at her friend, this was not a conversation she should've overheard. It was an intimate fight between two lovers or ex-lovers or whatever they were, and it was not appropriate to listen in on.

As Quinn backed away and forced her feet to make no sounds, she heard Constance say, "I know."

Making her way down the hall undiscovered, Quinn felt terrible. Shame crawled down her spine and settled in her stomach. Eavesdropping on something like that was so wrong and felt like being covered in tar without a way to get it off—

A sonorous, velvety voice sounded from behind her ear. Quinn jolted out of her skin as panic writhed up her bones. "Hello, Little Ballerina."

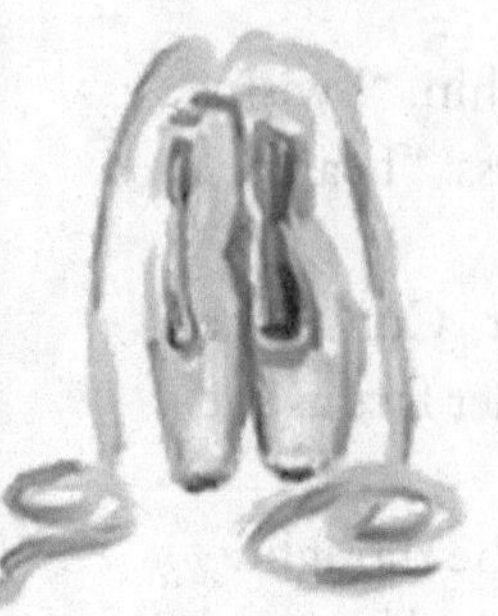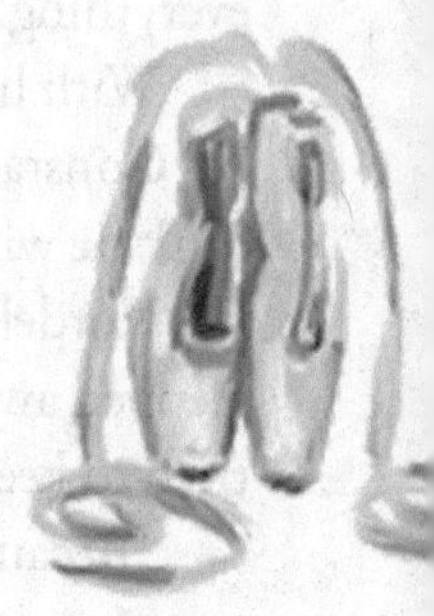

TWENTY-FIVE

The beast in her heart raged against its cage as she felt his hot breath on her neck. Emrys was immortal and powerful and most likely a vampire. Her whole body tensed, waiting for him to speak, to strike, to do something. But he only hovered behind her with preternatural stillness.

He was a vampire. She knew it in her bones. But would he hurt her? What did monsters do with maidens in all the fairytales?

"You are trespassing in a vampire's lair." His lips caressed her earlobe.

It was a confession.

"I believe I was invited," she breathed, her body trembling because he was the villain that plagued her nightmares.

His fingers hovered over her shoulder. "Hmmm, were you?"

Now, he was toying with her, but that's what monsters did. They toyed with their prey. Their food.

"Are you here to kill me?" Her voice was a shiver.

"No." She felt him bristle behind her.

This fear was unfounded. There was no reality to it. He'd never hurt her, and he couldn't kill her. She knew that, but it didn't keep her heart from pounding or her body from trembling.

She angled her head slightly to look back, and her red hair fell down her shoulders and mingled with the layers of her dress. Her breaths were stilted and filled with dread. She couldn't trust Emrys. He was a devil and a murderer. Maybe not Jane's, but he was still far too dangerous, and Quinn was in way over her head. She was just a ballerina. A silly little girl who dreamed of dancing and fame.

She never should have investigated this case or got herself tangled in this secret underworld. Not like she could run away from it now. Her life was on the line . . . in more ways than one.

His breath tingled against her ear. "I'm not going to hurt you."

"How can I believe you? You're—"

"A monster?" he finished.

She inhaled sharply. "Yes." She whirled around to face him, her back against the wall, his chest inches from hers.

A dark silence cut between them like a machete. His countenance was a dark and stormy night. He embodied a creature of darkness. A creature of death.

"More accurately, you're a vampire." Her voice was a lilting, withering soprano.

From down the hall, two people spoke in sultry tones. Emrys glanced around, the muscle in his jaw feathering. Worry colored his face. "Please, don't say that so loud," he whispered.

That was the last thing Quinn wanted to hear. A rich, powerful, selfish vampire did not tell her what to do. Her fear melted away and was replaced by anger. "I will say whatever I want when I want at whatever volume I want." The voices got closer. "VAMP—"

Emrys placed a hand over her mouth. He flinched slightly before pulling her out of the hall and into a room just as a maid and a footman stumbled by, intoxicated and exuberant. He closed the door so that they could have a more private chat.

"Stop it," she mumbled into his hand.

"You stop it." Emrys pinned her to the wall with his hand still over her mouth, a painful expression coloring his face. "You cannot say vampire out in the open like that. Your tattoo binds you. If you spill the secrets to a non-council member who doesn't already know, your tattoo will punish you. It won't kill you like it would me, but it will hurt you."

It would hurt her. So, the tattoo was as much a punishment as it was a boon.

Quinn opened her mouth to either respond or bite him when she noticed where they were. An extravagant bedroom with a four-poster bed draped in crimson curtains.

Oh, many gods. She was alone in a bedroom with the Playboy Prince. A clandestine meeting at night. It looked terrible. Not to mention, she'd never been so alone or so vulnerable with a man. She hadn't experienced much young adult mischief, if she were truly being honest. She was far too controlled—too sheltered. Plus, imagine the scandal. The newspapers would jump for joy to run a story about the prince and a ballerina meeting in a bedroom in the dead of night.

Her breaths came in a quick and unsettled pattern. She stared at his full lips, and an image of him kissing her danced through her mind. And all their previous encounters mingled there, too. Emrys was built for passion, and as much as she had resisted before, she wanted to know what it was like to kiss a wicked vampire.

Fireflies buzzed in her stomach.

Stop it, mind. Don't imagine yourself kissing a vampire. Are you insane? This is Emrys Avalon, your nemesis. Do not fantasize about him.

But the image didn't leave; it was like a foreign body in her mind—a parasite—that wanted to latch on and stay forever.

"You need to be quieter," Emrys said, his hand still resting on her lips, still silencing her. He flashed an expression that said, can I trust you enough to let my hand go?

She nodded, frustration lighting up her core. This stupid, arrogant man told—

He dropped his hand from her mouth, but instead of freeing

her from the wall, he instead placed his hands on either side of her face, boxing her in.

But she was having none of it. She may be a foolish human, but she still had weapons. As fast as she could, she reached into her skirt pocket, pulled out a knife—she always had a small medical kit with her—and slid it against his throat. "Please, get out of my way."

Quinn flinched. She was threatening a powerful immortal, and she chose to say please. It did not display confidence.

Emrys chuckled but didn't budge. "What are you going to do with that, Quinnevere?"

Her heart pounded in her ears, and she tried to pull together a logical plan, but she had none.

Infuriatingly, Emrys raised one of his raven eyebrows. "For clarity's sake, you think I am an immortal—"

"I know you are."

He sighed and raised his gaze to the ceiling. "Right. And you think I am a murderer."

"Yes."

"And your plan was to hold a tiny knife to my throat?"

Quinn gritted her teeth, her heart still raging. "This is a scalpel. It may be tiny, but it's very sharp."

"Sorry." His lips twitched. "You think your very sharp, tiny knife is going to be able to kill an immortal?"

"Well . . ." Quinn's knuckles curled tighter around the handle. "When you put it that way . . ."

This was going utterly horribly. Not only was she threatening a dangerous immortal, but he was taunting her—playing with her.

Like prey.

"So, to be clear"—his smile widened, and his eyes sparkled— "the great, brilliantly talented, brilliantly intelligent Quinnevere Ashelle hadn't thought this through? Is that right?"

Oh, he was so pleased with himself. The arrogant prick. Emrys loved it when she was wrong. Loved to throw it in her face.

With that spirit in mind, he leaned into the knife, and his eyes darkened with amusement as if he were saying, and what will you do now, little ballerina?

"What in all the fucking mirrors are you doing?" Quinn sucked in a breath and tried to steady her unusually shaky fingers. "I said it was a sharp tiny knife, and that is your fucking carotid artery."

"It is."

"Emrys."

"Quinnevere." He pulled her name out like he was tasting chocolate.

"I hate you."

"I know." He curled his fingers around the scalpel, plucked it from her grip, and slid it inside his impeccably tailored suit jacket. "You have mentioned this several times now."

Emrys finally stepped back, freeing her from the wall, but as he did it, she noticed the freckle on his middle finger. She froze like a glass sculpture.

Spiders of fear crept down her body, and she gulped. She knew he was a vampire, but it wasn't until she saw the freckle that it fully hit her. He was the Emrys Avalon from the Blood Rebellion. The human who led the war and became a king.

"How many people have you killed?" She stepped farther away from him, trying to get closer to the door. Her fear returned with a vengeance.

"Too many." His throat bobbed.

She moved again, now directly in front of the door.

"I know you didn't kill Jane, but . . . you're a—" Flashes of her nightmares returned. A vampire standing over her, blood dripping from his fangs. Her breath hitched, her fingers biting into the metal door handle.

"I am no monster." He took a hesitant step toward her. "At least not the type you are so afraid of."

She wasn't sure what to believe, but she wanted to believe him. "But you're a—"

In a blink, he pinned her against the door, his strength superhuman. Again, he flinched as if touching her physically hurt. With a hand around her neck, he hissed, "Yes . . . is that what you want to hear? Is this what you expect me to do?" In a blink, his fangs appeared, and before she could move or gasp, his fangs glided against her jugular. "Is this what you imagine I would do?"

"Yes." She trembled but held her head high. Fear spiked in Quinn's blood. If he wanted to kill her, there would be no way of escaping. Her heart played percussion in her ears.

His fangs retracted, and he was left with his lips on her ivory skin, the blue of her veins lining her neck. He softly kissed the spot before he loosened his grip and stood at his full height once more.

Dragonfly wings scraped along the lining of her stomach, sending a tingling sensation through her body. Her heart didn't believe Emrys was evil. She didn't believe that he wanted to hurt her, especially when he had every opportunity to compel her to do his bidding, injure her, or kill her.

She rubbed her neck, feeling a phantom sensation where his fingers touched.

He hadn't even left a bruise.

With all that power and speed, he showed intense control.

Quinn inhaled sharply before saying, "I believe you're utterly arrogant, but I hope you won't hurt me." She pinched her eyes tight for a moment and drew in a long breath. "I also believe you enjoy playing with people." Her voice cracked.

"That would depend." His words were an eerie lullaby.

Her chest rose in frantic beats. "Do you enjoy toying with me?"

"Always," he purred.

"You seem to have a talent for it."

He scrutinized her, his gaze traveling from her dark green dress to the shimmering makeup dusting her skin and landed on her green eyes. "I have many talents."

She placed a hand on the door handle. She wanted to turn it

and desperately escape whatever emotions were bubbling in her chest. But that's not what she did. Her insatiable curiosity got the better of her.

"Why did you want me to come here?" The question stormed from her scarlet lips.

Emrys pulled his features into a mysterious mask. "I wanted you to know the truth. I wanted to be able to tell you everything, and I couldn't do that until you already knew my secrets. I am bound by the Accords and couldn't say anything before tonight."

Quinn's hand dropped to her side. She no longer wanted to escape. Instead, she wanted to learn more of this man's secrets.

"You wanted me to know," she repeated as she suddenly realized he was the only person who trusted her with the information. Her uncle, the council, and even Constance wanted to hide everything from her, including why and how her parents were murdered.

"Yes, you deserve to know."

"Thank you," she said, biting her lip, trying to process how much it meant to her that he fought for her to know the truth. That he cared enough to tell her.

"Of course." He nodded, the mask slightly sliding, showing a vulnerability she'd never seen in his eyes.

If he wanted to tell her everything, she had questions. "How are you a vampire if you were the human who led the Blood Rebellion?"

He sucked in a breath. "The short version is that during the war, I was captured and turned as a punishment. I would become my worst fear." He grimaced. "It was their greatest mistake because as soon as I became a vampire, I knew our weakness." He ran a hand through his hair. "I used it to win the war. And when the dust settled, humans decided to let the five vampires who aided in the war live. We lived peacefully for a time until we created too many new vampires, and things got out of hand, and the Accords were created."

"And you agree with the laws?" Quinn asked.

"More or less." He shrugged. "I agree with protecting my people. I am the King of all New Swansea, not just the vampires. It is my duty to keep humans safe. I cannot always protect people from the mirrors, but I can protect them from vampires."

It made sense. If he never wanted to be a vampire, it would make sense that he spent his immortal life trying to protect humans.

"Will you tell me about Jane?" she asked.

"Yes." A muscle feathered in along his smooth jaw. "Jane and I were working together to solve the council murders. Her . . . parents were also murdered the same night as yours."

A surprised sound crossed her lips. They were called the Ashelle murders for a reason. "But that would mean . . ."

Shit. *Holy shit.*

"Jane wouldn't want me to tell you this, but she is . . . you're related to her," Emrys confirmed.

"She's my cousin?" There was no other reasonable explanation. Quinn didn't have a sister. She'd remember that. Wouldn't she?

Wouldn't she?

When Emrys didn't respond, Quinn asked again, "She's my cousin?"

He nodded. "Jane didn't really share much about herself or her family . . . even with me."

Fuck. *Her family.* Quinn *was* Jane's family.

She didn't know what to do with that realization. So she chewed on it for a moment before deciding it was better not to think about it, because if she thought about how Jane was her cousin and brutally murdered, the dam of emotions would break.

And that could not happen.

So, instead, Quinn asked, "Why were you fighting the night she died?"

"Jane found the second Blood Mirror but refused to tell me where it was." His voice sent a prickle of anxiety down Quinn's spine. It was hard and filled with immense sorrow. "I was too forceful and upset. I wanted to find the mirror to protect the paintings inside it. If the murderer gets to them first, it will mean disaster."

"What are the paintings? I gather they are the secret inside the mirror."

Emrys sucked in a breath and placed a hand on the wall beside Quinn's head as if he were steadying himself. "A vampire's life is tied to their Blood Painting. When a marked human dies, the blood spilled during death forms into a painting that contains their life force. It looks like a normal painting once formed. However, vampires must sustain their life force by drinking blood. The painting feeds off it. If a vampire doesn't feed, they will become weak until they eventually turn solid like a true painting or statue."

He stepped back, and his unfeeling mask slipped more. "To kill a vampire, you must destroy their painting."

"If the murderer gets to the paintings before we do, what will happen?" Quinn asked, her throat bobbing.

"They would be able to control us or kill us." Emrys's eyes sparked like thunder clouds gathering beneath a murky ocean of raging waters. "If someone holds our painting, they can compel us like we can with humans."

Quinn's veins pulsed with lightning, and her skin prickled as if thousands of fire ants stormed along the surface.

The killer absolutely could not get access to more of these paintings. It could be terrible. They were already an unstable murderer. What would they do if they could control all the vampires? "I'll help you find them and protect your people."

"Thank you, Quinnevere," he said with a whisper, his hot breath caressing her cheek. Emrys moved his face to meet hers, his amber eyes grasping and holding on to her like prey. No, not prey. It was a lustful embrace.

They stood so close. Her chest rose with the nervous beats of her heart, her stomach tumbling with fireflies.

"You're so beautiful." Emrys's eyes rested on her lips, and she gulped. "Your aid means more to me than you could possibly know."

He laced his fingers into her hair and tipped her chin up, tension eating at her core.

Silence hung in the icy air between them. A silence deeper than the greatest depths of the Kardic Ocean. Her chest quivered as she scrutinized his body, starting with his silk lapels and his purple cravat. She marked his unnatural existence scientifically. Surprisingly, he had a slight stubble on his chin, framing the hard edge of his jaw. Apparently, vampires' hair grew. Her study turned medical as she reached up and touched his jugular. Feeling for a heartbeat and then counted it as she felt it.

Unfortunately, he didn't give her enough time to figure out the beats per minute because his fingers curled around her wrist and pulled her away. Her fingertips grazed his chin in the process. Their attention focused on each other like a gentle caress, and his lips moved toward hers, hovering too close.

"Are lessons in passion still forbidden?" he asked.

Her breath hitched. All at once, she wanted him both to move closer and further. It was a strange battle in her mind—an unfamiliar one. "No."

His lips grazed hers. Soft and gentle, light and tender, exploring her and the moment. But shock stitched her lips together, tight and unyielding, until he ran a highly experienced tongue across her lower lip, and she gasped.

Opening her mouth to him, he deepened the kiss and pressed his fingers into her hair, cupping her head as he invaded all her senses.

Emrys tasted of peppermint and daydreams. He smelled like a mix of dry cedar, ginger, and longing.

Her body trembled, and she wondered if she was kissing properly. She was so inexperienced, and she didn't want to get it wrong, but he was a brilliant teacher, patient and tender. With every stroke of his tongue, he taught her and coxed out her bravery and passion.

Kissing was new and exciting, like the first time she'd learned a pirouette or walked on pointe. It was exhilarating and terrifying. But more than anything, she was lost in it. Her thoughts, her fears, her control faded away—locked in a deep cave, and she only knew this moment, and she melted into it.

His kiss was a spell, an enchantment consuming her soul.

Quinn whimpered as her hands curled into the small of his back, pulling him closer. He laughed against her lips, enjoying the pleasure he pulled from her. As he plundered deeper, his fingers stroked her waist, exploring and learning her body like an impossible puzzle.

The sensations he coaxed and the way his hands moved were like nothing she'd ever experienced before, and she should've been horrified, but instead, she was intrigued. It was a different kind of science experiment. A better, more tantalizing one.

Quinn's toes curled in her shoes, and she wanted to be even closer to him. He must have felt the same way because he lifted her up by the waist and pressed her against the door. Her legs wrapped around him, the process pushing her skirts up to her pelvis, allowing him to slide a hand up her nearly naked thigh.

He deepened the kiss with both his talented hands and experienced mouth. It was like pure possession, claiming her—all of her, and she wanted it and more. Emrys's hands cupped her ass and squeezed as he asked, "Do you want more of me, sweet Quinnevere?" His lips pulled away, but his eyes locked on hers, sparking with sensual delight.

Yes. Oh, mirrors, she wanted everything. She was a student of passion, and she needed to learn it all from him. She wanted to feel his hands touch her most sensitive parts. Quinn had studied her own body enough to know the magic of an orgasm, but she'd never allowed anyone else to give her one. Would it feel different if his mouth stroked her clitoris? Her hands were talented, but she imagined Emrys's tongue far outmatched her, especially after he had just used it to destroy her composure so thoroughly. But more than anything else, she wanted to experience his hard length inside of her. Twenty-three years was far too long to stay a virgin.

Yet all of it was still utterly terrifying.

But Quinn was in a curious mood, so she nodded. "Yes, I want so much more." She curled her fingers beneath his shirt, allowing them to climb up his bare chest, digging into his impeccably sculpted muscles.

Emrys's eyes held her captive, searching for something beneath her gaze. "There is a bed." His voice was dark, forbidden chocolate. "It probably wouldn't be best to fuck you against a wall for your first time."

Excitement stroked through Quinn's core. The words should have horrified her, but they did just the opposite, and she nodded again, unable to speak.

A low chuckle resonated from his throat. "The bed it is." Shifting his grip, he held her as if she were light as air—and to a vampire, maybe she was that easy to carry. Gently, he laid her down on the bed, her head resting against the pillow as he hovered over her. All the while, his lips claimed hers again. Now, instead of pressing her to the door, he was pressing her to the bed. And oh, how glorious it was.

As his hand traveled beneath her skirts, seeking her forbidden folds, his gaze latched on her—like he was asking permission with every new liberty he took. "This will be—" But she didn't hear his last words because they were covered up with her gasp. Emrys's hand was met with slick wetness as he circled her pleasure center with his thumb.

"Oh," she breathed as her head fell back, and she pinched her eyes shut. He plunged two fingers into her core, stroking her most sensitive spot. "Yes, you're much more talented at this than I am. I wonder if there is a scientific reason . . ."

"Stop talking, Quinnevere, and enjoy it," he growled before capturing her lips once more.

It wasn't easy for her to shut her brain down and simply be in the moment. But she desperately wanted to try. Passion was the goal, and if she could learn to do it with him, then maybe she could get out of her head while dancing.

Pinching her eyes shut, she focused only on the sensation of his fingers driving into her channel and circling her clitoris.

Emrys drove her to the edge of ecstasy and then pulled away, releasing his mouth and fingers. Once again, torturing her with pleasure and withholding it. "Please, Emrys."

"Only if you are good." Emrys bit her lip, and with a low possessive growl, his fingers returned to their ministrations.

"I can never be good for you," she sighed, the words only breath. Even in a sex-addled state, Quinn still had her priorities.

Emrys chuckled, increasing his speed. "I guess that's the appeal of you. Obstinance."

"Yes, obstinance." She released a moan as the waves of her orgasm began climbing. "Emrys, that's—" She didn't finish the words because she fell apart beneath his touch, trembling as wave after wave hit her, and his fingers kept striking, prolonging her pleasure.

A loud noise knocked against the outside wall as Quinn let out a final moan.

"Someone is coming," Emrys said, moving with human speed off the bed and away from her. "You need to fix your clothing and hair if you prefer not to get caught."

The space around her suddenly felt cold, his body no longer warming it, but also, the change was so abrupt, and she was not ready for it. The moment was breaking apart, piece by piece. Quinn panted, her chest rising in frantic passion-filled breaths, as she adjusted her drawers and swung her feet to the ground, her skirts tumbling down as she moved. The hardwood was cold against her toes as she curled them and tried to ground herself.

"What was that?" It all hit her. Everything she'd just done and allowed. Reality hit like a sledgehammer. Holy, fucking mirrors, she'd been about to fuck her biggest enemy. The reason Jane was dead . . . at least a partial reason. Anger flared in her blood, coating it with fire and fury. If Emrys had done that on her birthday, Jane might still be alive.

"I find myself . . ." He trailed off, pausing for a long moment, his eyes an unknowable midnight fire. Then he shrugged before straightening his cravat. "You're a very beautiful girl. A rake like me, well, I couldn't help myself."

Just like that, the remaining magic of the moment vanished and turned to ash in her mouth. She was another one of his conquests in a long, long list of conquests.

Nausea pooled in her stomach.

"Chin up, Quinnevere darling. Perhaps it will help with your dancing."

"You are very cruel," she breathed.

He flinched as if her comment disturbed him. As if he wanted to take his words back, but his demeanor remained rigid and distant. "But isn't that what you wanted me for? To teach you passion."

"No, it wasn't." Tears gathered in her eyes, but she refused to let them out. To let him see the pain he caused with his careless words. Yet the pain seeped into her chest anyway. Her first kiss, the first time she ever allowed herself to be so vulnerable, so open, so touched by another person, only occurred on the whims of a roguish prince. A cruel, hurtful devil.

She felt so foolish.

"I shouldn't have said that." He appeared in front of her and ran his thumb along her chin, his eyes softening.

Quinn licked her swollen lips, her chest unfortunately still rising in passionate breaths. His amber eyes traced and tracked her tongue, and she felt the sudden terrible urge to close the distance between them again—a stupid, stupid magnet drawing her toward—

"What in all of the mirrors are you doing?" Emrys and Quinn pulled apart at Giselle's words. "This is definitely not gathering fingerprint samples."

Quinn felt like red calla lily petals were blossoming on her cheeks as she cleared her throat and flattened her skirt. Emrys slid his fingers into his pocket and struck a devastatingly nonchalant pose—like it was normal for him to seduce sheltered girls.

Ever the Playboy Prince.

Giselle dropped through the window gracefully as if scaling walls and sneaking through palaces were second nature to her.

Giselle arched an eyebrow as if to say, *but you hate him?*

Quinn shrugged and silently responded; *I do. I think I do. Yes, yes, I hate him very much.*

Oh, broken fucking mirrors, she was so confused.

"In case either of you are curious, I gathered about fifteen fingerprints, and I finally figured out where I'd seen this key before." Giselle held up said key like a prize.

Twenty-Six

"I should have known the moment I saw the key," Giselle said. "It unlocks the vaults at Russet Row."

Russet Row—the houses above the Russet casino that were owned entirely by Les Fantômes gang. A place where danger lurked, and midnight monsters ruled. Not monsters like Emrys. No, these wore pinstriped suits and smelled of mirror magic.

Of course, Giselle knew about the key. She grew up at Russet Row for the first ten years of her life, until her aristocratic mother got bored and decided she'd try her hand at parenting. It was unsuccessful, seeing that her daughter ran away to the Viridian six years later.

"Then perhaps tomorrow we can put your skills at breaking and entering to the test?" Quinn rocked on her feet, avoiding the prince's caressing gaze. "But right now, I need to speak to my uncle."

"He's in the cigar room." Emrys's lips curled into a lazy smile.

Five minutes later, Quinn was met with eccentric fury. First, it was pointed at Emrys for deliberately disobeying Uncle Matias's earlier decree, and then the anger was inflicted upon her—for sneaking onto the golden gondolas, trespassing on Castle Hill property, but worst of all, eavesdropping on the Blood Council. All egregious acts in her uncle's estimation.

However, only one of the accusations was true but her uncle didn't care much for accuracy, which was intolerably infuriating. Precision was always next to godliness. It was Uncle Matias's motto, for fuck's sake.

Utterly hypocritical.

Usually, facing his ire made her cower. Quinn hated so much to be in trouble. But after all the lies and deaths and everything that happened, she'd had enough, and her blood churned with fury too. Her uncle lied to her. He sheltered her and withheld the one thing she needed. *Answers.* Quinn's wrath didn't end with him. Constance lied too, and Emrys was cruel.

He'd made her feel things, he'd touched her, seduced her, kissed her, and then made her feel like a common rag one uses to satiate a need before tossing it away.

Quinn snorted. "That's rich coming from you, Uncle. You're angry at me for sneaking around and trying to find answers when all you have ever done is sneak around and lie? Were you ever going to tell me the truth?"

"No." His expression was cold and unmoving. Quiet and forbidding. His fury was never loud. Instead, it was subtle and small like a single thorn on a rose or a porcupine's needle. But that made it more terrifying. But even in his stillness, the vein in his forehead slightly feathered. "You never needed to know."

Quinn fingernails bit her palms. "I never needed to know that vampires might have killed my parents and are after me?"

"Oh, don't be dramatic, Quinnevere." He tapped his thigh with his pinky finger, followed by his index, followed by his middle, then his pointer and thumb. He repeated the pattern three times. It was his grounding technique to keep him from getting too emotional. "No vampire would bother with you."

A massive lie. A vampire had invited her to the palace and . . . kissed her. What he'd done with his hands would certainly qualify as a bother.

Her cheeks warmed, and she tried to cover up her embarrassment by turning away.

What in all the mirrors was happening to her?

Eventually, she answered, her voice a bit hoarse. "Jane warned me about the Blood Mirrors and my possible danger the night she died. I am pretty sure that would count as a bother." She deliberately left out the threatening note. "You should've told me everything. I shouldn't have to learn that I performed an autopsy on my cousin from a passing comment from an arrogant ass."

Uncle Matias started tapping again and turned to Emrys who was standing in the doorway, silhouetted by the glimmering light behind him. He looked like a god. "You told her Jane was her cousin?"

"I told her something like that." Emrys's answer was short and pointed.

"Quinnevere and the Ashelle family are none of your business." Matias's voice was a deep pit filled with poisonous snakes.

An equally deadly smile brushed across the prince's lips. "I do believe the Ashelle family is entirely my business. As I recall, Callan personally asked me to protect his daughter if anything happened to him. Not you."

Quinn's heart lurched, and her breaths became unsteady. She didn't know what to do with that information, or what it possibly meant.

"Your misplaced friendship with my brother-in-law means very little to me, Emrys Avalon," Uncle Matias said. "Besides, why are you acting so chivalrous now? In the last nineteen years, you've done nothing. You acted like she didn't even exist."

Emrys shrugged, and it spoke volumes. Because to him, she

didn't exist . . . until very recently. Until she got in the way of what he wanted.

"I have legal authority over my niece, not you."

"You did, but I do believe she is twenty-three now and can legally make her own choices." Emrys strolled into the room, radiating power as if it pulsed from his pores. "I don't want any authority over her. I merely want her to make her own decisions."

"She lives in my house and follows my rules."

"She doesn't have to live in your house."

"And where would you have her live, the palace?" Uncle Matias scoffed.

Emrys shrugged. "Sure, if she wanted to, but she is also going to make it into the Royalle Ballet and can live there."

Uncle Matias smirked. "If she *somehow* makes it into the Royalle Ballet, then that is another discussion, but as of this moment, she has yet to achieve that goal, and she is under my protection."

Quinn's throat ached as she pulled in a deep breath. She always knew her uncle had little confidence in her dancing, but it was another thing to hear it.

Emrys shuddered, his cool mask sliding for a tiny second. "I guess I have more faith in her vast abilities than you do."

It was enough. "She can actually speak for herself," Quinn spat, and both turned sharp gazes on her. "I think I would like to leave now. Giselle, would you mind if I stayed with you for the night?"

Giselle who'd silently watched the play unfold, said, "Yes, absolutely. Stay with me as long as you would like."

With that Quinn stood and strode out of the room, completely uninterested in what either gentleman thought. Neither of them deserved to tell her what to do. Not tonight, and not after all the lies.

This might be the first and bravest choice she'd ever truly made for herself, but it was time to face her fear. It was time to walk away from the lies and go with the one person who'd always had her back and never lied to her—never toyed with her.

Giselle.

The sky sparkled with stardust, creating a tableau of fantasy and glorious dreams, the gondolas a jewel among the stars. New Swansea at night was a painter's masterpiece. It was pure magic and mystery. It smelled of sea salt and crisp ocean air and tasted like a triple creme dessert.

Yet the only thing Quinn tasted was rotten, decaying relationships rife with confusion.

While her brain should've spiraled about all the lies and information about the murders, the only person on her mind was the stupid, alluring prince and the dam he broke inside her—the sensations she never knew she wanted.

Quinn had never thought of Emrys as someone she could desire. Before, she considered him a massive, spoiled inconvenience with a pretty face. But now that he'd kissed her, and more . . . all she thought about was desire. Of the way his lips felt, and his skilled hands . . . and his tongue. Oh, bloody mirrors, he was the plague in her mind.

She touched a finger to her lips.

Stupid, stupid gentlemen. This was precisely why she avoided all entanglements or possible distractions until now. Men were not practical. Distractions were not practical.

Stupid kisses and orgasms plaguing her mind were not practical. But worst of all, men could not be controlled.

They were dangerous. Unpredictable and messy.

All things she could not abide.

"Well, that was an interesting night," Giselle said, her eyes fixed on Quinn's fingers. "Which part would you like to talk about first?"

"He kissed me," Quinn breathed. *And did a bit more.*

A devious smile danced on Giselle's dark olive cheeks. "Yes, I know."

"And I think I kissed him back." Quinn stared at her friend like a doe trapped in the headlights of one of the new automobile inventions.

"You think?"

Quinn sighed. "I had absolutely no idea what I was doing."

Giselle tittered, roses twirling on her cheeks. "Yes, but did you enjoy it?"

"I . . ." Quinn sucked in a breath, not knowing what to say. "I, um . . ." She swallowed. "No. No, I didn't enjoy it. He's a monster."

"Hmmm, right." Giselle's words were pure amusement and filled entirely with disbelief. "Monsters can be great kissers."

DAY
FIVE

PRICE 2 CENTS

BREAKING NEWS

The New Swansea Times

THURSDAY, NEW SWANSEA CITY, 94th DAY OF AUTUMN, 700AV

THE DISREPECTFUL BALLERINA PERFORMS PRIVATE DANCE FOR HIS ROYALLE HIGHNESS

Sources say that the prince watched the Disrespectful Ballerina perform a seductive and sinful dance—just for him—in the University Square dance studio. It is said the performace lacked all sense of respectability and was just short of fornication on the dance floor. So far, the palace has refused to comment on the couple's most recent interaction, but we here at the New Swansea Times speculate that the two will soon be doing far more scandalous acts together over the coming days—cont. on

What is Known About the pretty Ballerina?

So far, not much. Here is what we do know: Her name is Quinnevere Ashelle, and she descends from the previously esteemed— now nearly extinct— Ashelle family. They were once a wealthy house but now seem to

Day Four: the Festival of Blood Welcomes the Ritual of Blood

With the Royalle Suitor Ball days away, we celebrate the Festival of Blood with the traditional Blood offering. Tonight, people will prick their fingers and honor those who died at the hands of the centuries-long rule of vampires. We do this as a sacrfice to keep the dead from—cont. page 2

Nature District: Teen Girls Found Drained of Blood

Three young, vulnerable runaway girls were found drained entirely of blood. No one wants to say the word vampire, but it could be possible. But what would—cont. page 8

TWENTY-SEVEN

The morning played out like a Looking Glass nightmare, except instead of being covered with blood and fighting vampires, it was covered in a pending dramatic altercation with one of her closest friends.

Quinn needed to confront Constance's lies. Unfortunately, when Giselle pounded on the dancer's door, there was no answer. Constance DeWinter avoided them.

"Come on," Quinn said. "We have to get going."

She only had six days to find the mirror or the murderer, or die. Her time clock was running out.

"Yes, and timeliness is next to godliness." Giselle yawned. "The words I so lovingly woke up to this morning."

"Seems like you are enjoying your new roommate." Jevon leaned against the wall across from the door, biting into a croissant and silently examining the situation, his fingers tapping as usual. His hair was tousled like he'd just woken up from an eventful night filled with glitter and many mistakes. He was not as much of a rogue as the prince, but Jevon often found himself surrounded by female company. He was just so sweet and brooding, and girls fawned over it. On occasion, he gave in to the temptation.

Quinn scrunched her nose and crossed her arms, not amused. "Someone has to teach Giselle how to show up on time."

Thirty minutes later, Quinn hovered over all the fingerprint samples that Giselle and Emrys had gathered. Giselle didn't care to elaborate on how she'd gathered the gang's samples, but it was most likely using her charm or the skills she learned when she lived with her father. Giselle picked locks better than most professional thieves.

Using the list of who the fingerprints belonged to, Quinn cross-checked them as she lifted the samples and tried to find a match.

So far, nothing.

Her friends were doing their best to help. She taught them how to dust and pull prints, which proved to be helpful because they had 130 to check.

"What did I miss?" Constance sprang up behind them, scaring everyone.

Quinn clutched her chest. "Mirrors, Constance, you do know how to terrify."

"I believe that is my middle name, Constance *Terrify* DeWinter." She crinkled her nose, and merriment lit up her cheeks.

"Oh, and here I thought your middle name was *Liar*." Giselle's glower was so dark it rivaled the shadows.

Constance's eyebrows crinkled into a plié, her chipper demeanor slightly slipping. "I am not sure what you mean by that."

Giselle scoffed. "I am sure you do."

"Would you like to enlighten me?"

Quinn cut in, slightly afraid of what Giselle might say next.

"You told us not to go to the Blood Council meeting, but then you were there with Kordelia."

Constance jolted, her spine becoming ramrod straight. "I was at the Council meeting?" The words seemed to slip from her mouth as if she didn't mean to say them.

Quinn side-eyed Constance. Something about her was off.

"And now you pretend like you weren't." Giselle shook her head, and the vein in her forehead pulsed.

"I—" Constance's mouth worked. "I . . . yes, I was at the Council meeting with Kordelia." She chewed on the words as if the longer it took her to say them, the more clarity it would bring her. From her reaction and general demeanor, it truly seemed to be news to her.

"So, you are a liar," Giselle said.

"I forgot. I am not sure how, but I didn't remember going last night." Constance's eyes were drowning in confusion. She was typically forgetful, but this was a new level of absent-mindedness. "Maybe I drank too much, or the Viridian mirror is getting to me again." She rubbed at her temples.

"The Viridian mirror never gets to me. Perhaps you've been faking it." Giselle's voice was a silk cravat fashioned into a noose, trying to strangle her friend.

"That's not entirely fair. You're the only one of us not affected by its memory warping, G," Quinn said.

Giselle glowered. "Fine but blacking out is not an excuse. At any moment since Jane's death, she could have told us about the council and vampires."

"But I . . ." Constance trailed off, lost in thought, an unreadable expression storming on her face. She glanced at Jevon as if asking for help. He slightly nodded as if giving her encouragement. "I couldn't have told you anything. The Accords bind me just like they bind vampires. I wanted to tell you. It's been torture watching you try to solve the murders and not being able to say anything."

Quinn fiddled with the fringe on her dress. It made sense. If

Emrys couldn't tell the truth and she couldn't, then how could Constance? All of Quinn's pent-up hurt fizzled and melted. How could she be mad at her friend for something that she couldn't help?

"She is telling the truth," Quinn said. "I've seen the pain cross Emrys's face as he's tried to tell me about the Accords."

"Then why keep us from going to the meeting?" Giselle asked.

Constance shuffled her feet, her face a deflated hot air balloon. Tears gathered in the corner of her eyes and threatened to fall at any moment. "I don't know."

Giselle was a frozen sculpture, but some of her ice seemed to be slowly trickling off. "Is there anything else you would like us to know?"

"What do you mean?" Constance's brows crinkled.

"You don't have a council tattoo."

Constance glanced down. "I do." She held out her arm, and the tattoo blinked into existence. "I keep it hidden with my mirror abilities."

The illusion was so real and persuasive. Quinn knew her friend was powerful, but she'd never realized until this moment just how much Constance must have given for magic that was convincing. Maybe that's why the Viridian mirror affected her so much more than others.

But then, the Viridian seemed to affect everyone's memory except Giselle. There was something eerie about that, but Giselle never knew why either.

Perhaps she was keeping secrets, too.

After another ten minutes of cataloging the prints, Constance ambled up to Quinn's side. "I'm very sorry about the lies." She seemed to be still worrying about the easier conversation.

Quinn set down her dusting brush. "I understand why you had to lie about the council meeting, but you've been acting strangely lately. You always forget things, you lie, and you act like a completely different person around Emrys."

"I know." Constance wrung her hands. "I hate lying to you. I hate it." The vein in her neck feathered. "Sometimes I don't know what the truth is. I feel like I'm going crazy. The Viridian is slowly destroying my mind."

Quinn also lost time and memories at the Viridian, and she was hardly ever there. She couldn't imagine what it was like for her friend. "Why don't you leave?"

"It's not that easy." Constance loosed a breath. "Kordelia is tied to the Viridian; she can't leave for long periods of time, and I . . ."

"You love her." Quinn finished the sentence.

Constance nodded. "Wouldn't you do almost anything for the person you love?"

Quinn didn't know. She didn't love anyone romantically like that, but she could see herself going to the ends of the world to fight for her friends. "Yes."

Constance's lips rose in a defeated smile. "And as for Emrys, I do act like a different person around him because we have a complicated relationship."

Quinn raised a brow.

"We used to be . . ." She cleared her throat. "Lovers."

"What?"

"Keep your voice down. I don't want everyone to know." Everyone being Giselle. "Emrys and I had a . . . *fling*." Constance swallowed, her face flushing, and she looked utterly uncomfortable.

"But I thought you only liked girls?"

"Well . . . it's complicated. Constance likes—" She cut herself off. "*This* version of me only wants to be with girls, but I had an experimental phase."

Quinn nodded. She understood the urge to experiment. That's what she told herself she was doing with Emrys last night . . . just experimenting.

"When I ended things with Emrys, he was devastated, and now things are awkward, and I don't know how to behave."

Constance bit her lip. "I sometimes think he still has feelings. I think that's why he dallies with so many girls now."

"Oh . . ." Quinn gulped. Girls like Quinn.

And as if summoned by his name, Emrys stepped into the lab, his usual arrogance on full display. "Did we find anything? Match any prints?"

Quinn averted her eyes, the embarrassment a tightrope in her stomach. How did one look at a person after they'd done such improper acts together?

But Emrys seemed to have no qualms because while she squirmed, he was all ease, confidence, and the manifestation of dark desires. Every time she glanced at him, she remembered the feeling of his lips and her deep mortification—and her fury. He used her as his new shiny toy.

That was what grated against her heart the most. She was not a plaything or a girl who wanted to be seduced.

She was practical and focused.

Realizing he asked a question, she finally said, "No, and we only have five more prints to check."

"So, another dead end?" he asked, sliding his hands into his pockets and striking a pose.

Shivers danced in her stomach, and she looked away again. "It would seem." She played with her brush, letting her thoughts decay into rotten roses—moldy and covered in mistakes.

"So, what do we do now?" Emrys asked, jolting her back to the present.

Quinn placed her brush down slowly before looking up. "We need to find a way to break into Russet Row and figure out what Jane left for us in the vault."

"How—"

"Your vampiric illusions, how good are they?" Quinn asked, cutting him off. Everyone knew about a vampire's four main abilities: their glamour—which gave them the ability to change their appearance. Their compulsion—which allowed them to control a human's mind, their pervasive illusions—which allowed them to create images that were nearly impossible to see through, and their inhuman strength, speed, and senses.

He cocked his head. "What do you mean?"

"Could they turn us invisible?" Quinn asked. "Could we use them to get into the house unnoticed?"

He rubbed his forehead in thought. "Yes, but I don't think I would be able to cover all of us efficiently, but if—"

"That's okay," Constance cut in. "Jevon and I don't have to come in with you."

Constance really did try to avoid him.

Emrys's brow furrowed, and he examined Constance like he was asking an intensely hard math question. He appeared to come to a conclusion because, eventually, he shook his head and shrugged off the worry lacing his brows. "Alright, so Giselle, Quinn, and I will go in."

"Sounds like a plan," Constance smiled.

An hour later, Emrys, Giselle, and Quinn arrived a block away from Russet Row—the beautiful row houses that laced the edge of the Gold Quarter.

"This might feel strange," Emrys said as he lifted his fingers, and what felt like ropes of darkness encircled her. It tingled but wasn't wholly uncomfortable. "Now, ladies, you're invisible. But you still need to be quiet because there will be lookouts."

The three entered the street of tall, narrow row houses.

Despite their lack of side-yard, the houses were bathed in glamour. Each carved with gilded gingerbread trim, featuring decorative towers and dormers. Porches lined the fronts with ornamental spindles and brackets. Everything about the buildings screamed power, wealth, and extravagance.

If Emrys weren't a prince living in a castle, he certainly would have lived in one of these houses.

"So, which one do we enter?" Quinn asked.

Giselle pointed to the house at the dead center. "But we have to be careful because five Fantômes are on the roof." Her eyes pivoted to the nook and crannies on the housetops—the shadows.

Confidence coursed through her stance as Giselle pulled the pins from her coiffure. Making quick work of it, Giselle picked the lock and slowly creaked to open the door. As she did it, her eyes settled in the shadows on the roof.

She slipped into the doorway and motioned for them to follow.

In a blink of silence, Emrys had the door closed behind them. "So where to, little phantom?"

"Don't call me that." Giselle glowered. "The top floor."

The house opened to a grand entrance with a spiraling staircase at the back. The place was filled with ornate mahogany and rosewood carvings, as well as luxurious crimson and black fabrics. All the wooden panels throughout the house were filled with curling vine patterns and snakes.

Giselle shivered and touched her temples for a moment. Her eyes looked haunted, and she seemed to be struggling.

Was this her childhood home?

But before Quinn could ask, Giselle slowly made her way to the stairs and climbed. Quinn followed until they reached the top landing and a solid silver door. Giselle knew the place. She found the vault too quickly, and she did not know exactly what she was looking for.

Giselle slid the key from inside her corset and into the lock.

The door opened to a night terror.

A pulsating mirror.

It was the only thing in the entire room. It must be the mirror that gave the Fantômes their tattoos.

The mirror's surface rippled, and at its center, appeared a man with a sinister face crying liquid darkness.

"Well, that's not ideal," Emrys said, stepping up behind them.

"What mirror is it?" Quinn asked.

"The Mirror of Unbound Terror." He smoothed out his lapels. "It's the mirror that the Fantômes stole and used for all of their bargains, but I believe it also holds their secrets, and in order to reach them, you must walk through your deepest fears."

"If it's secrets you seek, come take a peek." The mirror's voice was death personified, and it rattled through Quinn's bones. The hairs at the nape of her neck rose. "So shall we?"

The clock on Quinn's life was slowly ticking toward its conclusion. If she didn't find the murderer or the mirror soon, she'd become the next victim. There was no time to waste on fear.

Besides, this mirror couldn't be that much more terrifying than Nightshade . . . right?

But Giselle beat her to it. Without any hesitation, the brunette stepped through the liquid shadows and into the portal.

As Quinn moved to join her friend, Emrys appeared like a lightning strike in front of her, blocking her path.

"We need to talk," he said, clutching her hand.

She forced a fake smile. "I can't let her be alone in there." Quinn tried to step past him.

"Even if you went in with her, your paths would be split," he said softly. "You can't help her now."

Quinn cracked her neck, but she believed him. After all, he'd once bragged about going into all of the mirrors. "What is it you want to talk about then?" She huffed.

"I shouldn't have—"

"We really don't have to discuss that." Quinn interrupted him. She couldn't bear being so embarrassed again. He'd used her. He made it clear yesterday exactly why they kissed, and she absolutely didn't need to hear it again. "We really don't need to talk about it. As you said, you're a rake and the . . ." She stuttered, not wanting to say it. Swallowing, she gathered her strength. "The kiss meant nothing."

The room suddenly dropped its temperature, turning the

place into an ice cave. Or maybe it was Quinn's heart freezing over and guarding itself. She *couldn't* care for this spoiled, selfish man. And she absolutely couldn't want to kiss him again.

"I shouldn't have—"

"It was just a kiss. I thank you for teaching me." Her breath hitched, and she forced her smile to grow bright and filled with a thousand lies. "You're right. It will probably help my dancing."

A cloud grew over his countenance. "I shouldn't have done that with you. You're not . . ." He started but trailed off. Oh, what she'd give to hear those final words. But she could fill them in . . .

You're not appealing.

You're not rich.

You're not titled.

You're simply not enough.

Not that she ever wanted to be enough for him. She didn't want him.

He stroked a hand through his hair and tried again. "I just don't want you to—"

"I understand that I was just another girl on your long list. Don't worry. I know you'll never have . . . feelings for me, and I certainly will never be fond of you." Her words tasted like rotten raspberries left in the sun for days.

She understood that she'd never be enough for a guy like him. She was poor, far too thin, and entirely unappealing, not to mention utterly broken—illiterate.

Emrys simply laughed.

And her blood boiled. "We need to help Giselle."

She didn't wait for a response. Instead, she pushed past him and stepped through the glass. Emrys was on her heels, and he clutched her hand as they walked through.

The mirror's surface felt like being suffocated by a thousand snakes. She held her breath, her muscles quaking, and stepped farther inside. There was a slight reprieve from the horrifying sensation until Emrys's grip disappeared, and the real terror started.

One moment, they were together, and the next, they were ripped from each other and plunged into darkness.

All alone, she had to make it through the next part without any help.

From the darkness, a creature silhouetted by screams greeted her with an evil smile. "Hello, Daughter of Ash. If you want Les Fantômes secrets, you must walk through the seven layers of your fears."

Quinn swallowed and rolled her shoulders. "Fine."

The creature held an arm out and motioned to a door. "Make it through all eight doors, and I'll give you the information you seek."

As she stepped through the first door, her leg snapped, and she crumbled, the bone rupturing through her skin, causing a deep agony to radiate through her body. Quinn's stomach lurched, and her hands grasped the leg, blood seeping through her fingertip and coating her tutu in crimson. The color of shattered dreams.

Pain pooled at the corner of her eyes, begging to be released. And this time, the tears were too heavy to hold in.

Her life as she knew it was over. Ruined. *Forever.* Ballerinas couldn't come back from an injury like this. The bone would never set correctly, and even if it did, there was nerve and tissue damage. Medicine just hadn't come far enough to fix a wound like this, not for a top athlete.

It was a ballet career-ending injury.

An agonized cry slipped through her lips. Ballet was the one thing Quinn loved. It was her heart, her life, her dreams, her everything. And now she would never be able to dance again— probably never even able to walk without pain. But this injury wasn't only the death of dance; it was the death of her freedom. There would be no escape from this cruel world of mirrors, vampires, and murderers.

Her life as she knew it was over, and there was nothing she could do about it except reverse time or trade with a mirror. But could she? How big of a cost would that take? But she knew a mirror was her only—

Mirror. A mirror. Quinn was inside the one in Jane's room.

So perhaps this injury wasn't true. It was fear. An illusion. Right?

But it felt so real.

Quinn glanced down to the wound to check, her fingers hovering over the bone, but the injury was so gruesome that she passed out from the pain, her body sensations finally catching up with her thoughts.

When she woke up, the pain vanished; her wound healed, but in its place, she cradled a completely uncalloused foot. Then, the scene was replaced by her clutching her knee. All the tendons were ripped apart. Vision after vision, scene after scene on repeat.

Her fear of not being able to dance manifested itself into physical pain.

There was something about the mirror that made Quinn forget it was all fake. The visions were so real and so consuming.

It was unclear how long she spent repeating injury after injury. It felt like forever, but eventually she sucked in a breath. Yes, a career-ending injury would destroy her heart, but it wouldn't destroy her. She'd *survive.*

On the thought, she gathered her strength and hopped to the door, leaving the first chamber behind.

In the second she was attacked by her ongoing Looking Glass Nightmare.

Vampires.

Fangs sliced into her neck and ripped out her throat. She didn't even have the chance to scream. Just like the first scene, once she died, the vision repeated.

And repeated.

And repeated.

And repeated.

. . . Until she was able to fight the fear just long enough to reach the next room.

Panting, Quinn stepped into the third chamber, and she turned into a vampire, her fangs and claws bursting out.

Fear gripped her soul, and time spilled.

She didn't know how long it took to reach the next door.

It felt like an eternity and just moments.

In the fourth room, Quinn simply cried, showing her emotions to an entire newsroom filled with cameras. Everyone saw her vulnerability. It was unbearable.

She lost all control over her life, situation, and emotions.

It was pure torture, having no control.

But it was the fifth room that gutted her.

A vision of Jane appeared and said, "The Queen's Royalle Ballet Director has made his final decisions, and the list of new apprentices is posted on the wall."

A volcano of bad luck erupted in her blood, and she knew without even checking the list that she hadn't made the cut. It was her instinct, and it was never wrong.

With steady feet, she trekked to the crowd gathering around the board.

Only three names glimmered like glorious comets.

Arthur Florence

Scarlet Jones

Constance DeWinter

Quinn's name was not there.

Devastation rattled her bones, piercing its fangs into her core. She wasn't special. She wasn't great. She wasn't worthy. She wouldn't get fame or glory or a better life.

She'd have no control and no prospects.

Quinnevere Ashelle was useless and pathetic, just like Countess Teagan and the police always said.

She couldn't read.

She couldn't solve a murder.

And she wouldn't be a ballerina.

She was a failure.

An utter despicable failure.

Quinn crumbled to her knees and let the agony consume her. It was unclear how long she stayed on the floor, rolled into the fetal position, refusing to cry. Eventually, she pulled herself off the floor to face her next fear.

But with each room, the fear elevated, and in the sixth room, Giselle appeared.

"Oh, thank the gods," Giselle said and flung her arms around her friend. "This place is horrible, absolutely horrible." Her voice cracked.

"Yes, it is." Quinn sunk into the comfort of a friend.

The hug eased all the residual fears lingering over from the previous rooms. Giselle's presence would help her get through whatever came in the last two rooms.

But pain ripped through her core, and she jerked. Her gaze fell to the knife protruding from her chest. Her knees buckled, and a vicious Giselle caught her limp body.

"Why," Quinn whispered, blood bubbling from her lips.

Giselle cocked her head like a bird of prey. "Didn't you know you've always been the pathetic one? Never good enough to be with us." Jevon and Constance appeared at Giselle's sides; their smiles equally feral.

The scene repeated, each time a different friend stabbed her in the chest and betrayed her.

The last room was the worst.

The last room was pure devastation.

Giselle, Jevon, Jane, and Constance's lifeless bodies rested in a pool of blood, their eyes staring sightlessly at the sky. Quinn ran in and cradled Giselle to her chest. Tears freely rolled down her cheeks, and she rocked back and forth, whispering sorrow into her best friend's ear.

Quinn was inconsolable, her hands shaking, and her heart shattered into a million pieces. She wanted to crawl into darkness and never return. She wanted to die and trade her life for her best friends. She clutched Giselle's icy pale hands as a guttural scream escaped her lips.

Giselle was the strong one. The rock. The one who kept them all together. The one person Quinn allowed to see her most flawed pieces.

This couldn't be reality.

The thought tore Quinn from the vision, and she suddenly remembered that it wasn't true. It was a wicked mirror.

Time poured out as she tried to get herself to move. Knowing something was false and believing it were two different things.

She'd felt the body in her arms. It felt so real.

So true.

But eventually, Quinn sucked in a silted breath and reached for the final door. As she turned the knob, the mirror spoke sinister words. "Four of your greatest fears will come to be. Perhaps next time, you won't come to me, for every mirror bestows a consequence."

The final room appeared to be a normal messy bedroom with papers strewn all over. On one of the walls was a map and prison escape plans and on another hung a painting of a ballerina center stage at the Royalle Ballet.

After spending about ten minutes examining the plans and the painting, Quinn was at a loss for what it all meant.

It was another dead end.

Another lead that went absolutely nowhere.

A pulse stroked up Quinn's bones but not from fear, shock, or surprise. Jane said that the key unlocked her secrets. That it would lead her to the truth.

The Royalle Ballet.

The only object not associated with a gang plan. The only thing that didn't fit was the painting of the ballerina. It was a clue wrapped in lies. To anyone else, they would just assume it was a painting, but not Quinn.

"The second Blood Mirror must be at the Royalle Ballet," Quinn whispered.

Quinn shuddered as Giselle—the real Giselle—appeared beside her. "So that's where we need to go—" Giselle's words were cut off as she glimpsed and fixated on the second wall. "It's plans for a prison break."

Giselle's face paled as if she'd seen a long-lost ghost.

Quinn sighed and shut her eyes tight. She knew her friend was in pain, and it killed Quinn to hear the vulnerability in her friend's voice. The only person valuable enough to the Fox to spring from the Rock was Giselle's father.

It was complicated and cruel knowledge.

Giselle loved her father, but she also hated him for abandoning—

Suddenly, the world fell out from beneath them, and both girls were thrown from the mirror and were dispensed onto the floor.

They had the information they came for, and the mirror no longer wanted them.

Emrys was missing, possibly still fighting his own demons inside the mirror.

But now that Quinn was out, her fears and the awful prophecy the mirror spoke hit her all at once, and she started shaking as tears leaked down her face. Four of her fears would come true.

It was the mirror's promise as an unintended consequence.

But which four?

"What do you need?" Giselle asked and crossed the room with tentative steps as if she were scaling across shattered glass. And she was. She was traversing Quinn's haunting emotions, across the vast expanse of feeling that she'd never let anyone see.

It was a small and delicate thing.

"I don't know," Quinn whispered as she reached up and touched the liquid fire still flowing down her scarlet cheeks. It was wet and precious, like a secret had been first spoken. She swiped a teardrop onto her finger and stared at it like it was magic.

But her awe was splintered as the door swung open, and the Fox entered, his face a nightmare covered in scorpions and the promise of poison.

Twenty-Eight

Quinn froze as Francois's fury danced on his face. Behind him stood his second with a pistol at the ready.

Quinn's fingernails bit into her palms as a spike of fear raged through her body.

Francois's gaze flicked over her for a moment, but it settled on Giselle, devouring her whole, his eyes lingering far too long on her chest. Instead of cowering under his scrutiny, Giselle slightly tilted her head and raised one taunting brow.

"Are you here to make me scream?" He winked, his glasses highlighting his angular face.

Quinn was pretty sure it was a carnal reference, but she wasn't entirely certain. She needed Giselle to interpret these types of things, but it didn't seem like the time to ask.

"I did say we could schedule another time for it." Giselle's voice lilted and fell into a purr.

Quinn swallowed, embarrassed, and Hadleigh cleared her throat.

"Right, you are, Haddie." Francois shifted his gaze to Quinn. "I told you to stay out of Fantômes business, and here you are, breaking into my vault."

"We aren't very good listeners," Giselle answered.

"Clearly." His lips rose slightly in amusement. "How did you get inside unseen, and where did you get the key?"

An enchantment filled his voice, and a siren song interrupted Quinn's thoughts, humming in the air, and pulsating through her bones. Her mouth moved without her permission and formed the words, "Prince Emrys used his illusions to get us inside unseen, and Jane gave me the key."

The rhythm of Quinn's heart sped up into a stampede of terror. The man had compulsion magic like a vampire, but she was fairly certain he wasn't one.

This was very bad.

There was no way to fight against this type of magic. The girls were sitting ducks. That's why vampires were so dangerous in the first place.

Quinn glanced at the mirror, begging Emrys to return. She didn't know if his compulsion would be stronger than Francois's, but she hoped it would be.

Either way, Emrys was a vampire and would be able to help. Quinn needed to stall just long enough so the girls would have a fighting chance.

"Where is Emrys now?" Francois asked again with his siren tones.

Quinn opened her mouth to respond, but Giselle cut in. "Why, do you like princelings?"

Francois's lips flattened into a straight line. "I don't remember asking your opinion. You will not speak another word until I request it." An enchantment twirled off his tongue and captured hold of the beautiful brunette.

Giselle opened her mouth and formed words, but nothing came out. She leveled a poisonous glare at the man. Quinn knew Giselle too well, so well, she knew the fire in her eyes was a promise. When she wasn't trapped by his magic, she would devour him for that.

"Where is Emrys?" he asked again.

The spell claimed Quinn's voice. "In the mirror."

He chuckled softly and shared a silent exchange with Hadleigh. "Oh, I bet he's hating that."

"Terror has never been fond of him." Hadleigh leaned against the wall, a ray of light dancing on her pale cheeks. On her exposed forearm was a large tattoo of a black cat. Quinn's eyes lingered on it because it was unusual to have a non-mirror tattoo. They were considered bad luck, and often, people mistook them for mirror tattoos. Some people were mistakenly killed because of them.

"He could have asked us instead of breaking in," Francois said to his second.

Hadleigh folded her arms. "It would seem the prince does not fully trust us."

A jolt of energy shot through Quinn. They were talking as if they were chummy with Emrys, as if they had a deeper relationship and connection to him. Almost as if they were *friends*.

"It's in his best interest not to fully trust us." Francois smiled. "Where is the key, Quinnevere?"

"Giselle has it." Quinn's chest rose in a tension-filled breath.

Francois turned to the beautiful brunette. "You may speak," he said, releasing her from his spell. "Where is the key?"

"It's . . ." Her eyes trailed to her breasts.

"Oh, bleeding mirrors," he cursed. "Retrieve it, please."

Under the siren compulsion, she complied. She slowly, tauntingly, pulled the key from her corset, almost as if she were seducing him—her small way of fighting his power. His eyes followed her every movement.

She held out the key to him as he said, "Don't speak."

Anger flashed in her brown eyes.

As Francois slipped the key into his pocket, Giselle bounded forward and punched him square in the jaw. She landed two more blows, and he fell to his knees.

Giselle mouthed something at him, mostly like a string of silent curses. She was unable to speak due to his spell. She moved to kick him in the balls as two things happened simultaneously.

A shadow cat emerged from the tattoo on Hadleigh's arm,

moving to attack Giselle, and Francois moaned, "Stop." He held up his hands in surrender. It was unclear if it was a siren spell, but Giselle complied. "You may speak."

Just as the cat was about to pounce, Hadleigh called it back.

"You are a bastard, lowly piece of shit, and I'll kill you if you spell me like that ever again," Giselle spat before sharing even more colorful and creative curse words with him. She slapped him across the cheek, this time with an open palm.

"As you wish, my vixen queen." A large smile painted his brown cheeks. Francois held up another staying hand to Hadleigh. "You really must tell me how you managed to unbind yourself."

"I have many talents," Giselle said, stroking the back of her knuckles.

He remained on his knees as if begging his queen. Blood trickled down his lips and tangled in his teeth, and yet he smiled brightly. "Where did you learn to land a punch like that?"

"I practiced on a boy in my youth."

Quinn narrowed her eyes at Giselle, who only glared down at Francois—venom coating her body. Typically, because they were so close, Quinn could predict exactly what her best friend meant, how she felt, and what she would do or say next, but this one caught Quinn slightly off-kilter. Was the boy from Giselle's youth Francois?

Because he was the fox?

It must have been.

The Fox was a friend from Giselle's past—a past filled with violence and gangs. It was clear that he didn't recognize her, but it was also utterly unclear why Giselle refused to acknowledge her acquaintance.

Francois brushed off his pants but didn't bother to remove the blood lacing his face. Instead, he climbed to his feet and towered over Giselle, stepping up close. The energy between them surged. "I think I would like to meet this man."

"I wouldn't bother." Her eyes stroked over him before she said, "He is a great disappointment."

Quinn tried to stifle a laugh but was unsuccessful. All eyes flashed to her. "I'm sorry, please don't mind me."

With a step back, as if Giselle just noticed how close they stood, she said, "Let us go, and I'll help you with the plans from the mirror."

"I don't have any idea what you mean by that."

"Yes, you do." She crossed her arms and licked her lips. His eyes tracked her progress. "You plan to break into the Pelican and rescue the Bullet, and now that Jane is dead, you're missing a key member of your team."

He raised an eyebrow, the blood from his split lip still streaking down his chin. "Are we?"

"I saw your plans, *Fox*." The nickname was spoken like liquid electricity. "I know you're planning a jailbreak, and based on your plans, you're going to fail."

Francois scoffed. "I highly doubt it."

"The Rock is inescapable. It is surrounded by wicked currents, sharks, and mirror protections. You cannot prance in the way your plans suggest." Giselle licked her lips again. "If you'd like to actually get the Bullet out, you'll need my help. Not only am I a trained acrobat, but I'm also an inventor; I can break into the system."

Francois cocked his head and examined her. "Why would you want to help?"

"You mean besides as a way to get you to let us go?"

"I don't trust you. Why would I want to work with someone I don't trust?"

Before Giselle could respond, Emrys fell out of the mirror with tangled limbs and a murderous look on his face.

In a flash, he was up and brushing off his suit. Emrys straightened his cravat before saying, "The second Blood Mirror is at the Royalle Ballet."

TWENTY-NINE

Quinn loosed a breath. Her plan to stall long enough for Emrys to return worked, but now she needed a new plan.

There seemed to be no good reason why the groups couldn't work together to solve the murders and find the mirror. After all, neither Francois nor Hadleigh's prints matched the killer's—she checked this morning—which meant they were most likely innocent.

"It seems like we all have the same goal," Quinn said. "Why don't we stop working against each other and start working together?"

Quinn didn't actually want their help. She couldn't trust them, but she needed to get out of this situation and to the Royalle Ballet.

She had no idea what to do once she found the mirror, but she couldn't let the killer get the paintings. It seemed like the best plan was to find the mirror and lure the murderer there. Get them to come to her and Emrys.

Francois glared at the prince. "Have you ever heard of asking politely? Your ballerina certainly knows how to."

"Where is the fun in that?" Emrys flashed a dimple. "It was far more entertaining watching the women break in. Little phantom here"—he waved at Giselle—"is quite a talented lockpick."

"I told you not to call me that," Giselle said through her teeth.

"So, the Royalle Ballet then?" Francois asked Emrys.

The prince nodded. "May I use your rotary phone? I need to call my family."

"Absolutely, the more vampires, the better!" Francois grinned with far too much delight.

"Wait, what?" Giselle raised her arms with a confused gesture. "That was far too easy," Giselle said, explaining what Quinn was thinking.

"Emrys and I are allies, even when he doesn't act like it." Francois prowled over to the brunette and ran a finger along her cheek. "I definitely don't trust you two, but I trust the vampire prince."

A firework of confusion burst in Quinn's gut. They acted like friends . . . more than friends—confidants. Then Quinn remembered the Russet and the blood bags.

The gang was running a blood ring to feed vampires. That was their main business.

Crimson light was painted across the sky as the group made their way to the Queen's Royalle Ballet. Unfortunately, they spent most of the day trapped in the mirror and lost valuable time to search the ballet without an audience.

It was the opening night of the winter ballet season, and the show was sold out. The place was filled to the brim with people, and it was the least opportune moment to sneak in and search for the spell-protected mirror. But if the killer had a blessed object that allowed them to observe Quinn and stay a step ahead, then the group needed to act quickly—during the show.

Quinn never thought she'd be thankful to the prince, but he

had the Royalle Box, and it didn't matter that the show was sold out.

The group—two gangsters, two ballerinas, an acrobat, a prince, and Jevon—entered through the private doors dressed like glamorous stars. The ballet was a place to be and be seen. It was a place where aristocracy, rich, and famous came to flaunt their wealth and success.

It was a game of fake smiles, polite compliments, and vicious gossip.

It was a den of sparkling lions.

Quinn wore a slick blue dress with diamond straps and a choker, and her mirror necklace was tucked into her corset.

The prince, as usual, dressed impeccably. Tonight, he was in a navy-blue suit with a waistcoat, silver vest, and black top hat. The silver accents were meant to match Quinn's dress. He was officially making it look like he was escorting her—like he was *courting* her.

Quinn didn't know how to feel about that or if it was even real. Was it for the publicity, or was it for her? And if it was for her, what did it mean? He'd made it so clear before that she was just another one of his girls.

Yet . . .

Was it possible she wasn't?

Either way, the press was going to have a field day with this story.

The room shimmered with gold and wild dreams. The walls had intricate carvings and crimson curtains. Marble white staircases stood at the center of the room, leading to the balcony seating and boxes. Flanking the room and stairs were giant golden statues.

As the group entered, everyone's eyes landed on them but specifically landed on Quinn and the prince who escorted her.

Violent whispers broke out, invading the room with toxic gas. The rumors created an almost physical fog that drifted through the room from person to person. Quinn's back tensed, and she held her breath. She'd always wanted to be famous, to have power, to have control, but the aristocracy looked at her like vultures. They wanted to devour her.

Devour the girl who dared to catch the prince's attention.

"Relax," Emrys whispered into her ear, his arm firm around her waist. "They mean nothing."

Perhaps they didn't matter to him, but they unsettled her—almost like the vultures could see underneath her skin.

"Come, we'll stop by the Royalle Box and get away from all of them. Besides, we won't be able to sneak anywhere until everyone is seated."

When she entered the Royalle Box, she nearly fainted from excitement. She'd only been to the ballet twice in her life. Quinn was too poor to afford it. The first time, she'd saved up all her extra money for three years to get a seat, and the second time, she won a dance competition for a ticket. But neither were box tickets. Both were in the very back, where she was barely able to see.

But now she had the best seat in the house.

The rest of the group filtered in and took their seats as the lights dimmed and the crimson curtains opened.

The group needed to wait until all the guests were settled before splitting up and searching.

The Blood Rebellion Ballet started with slow, elegant moves, with the dancers pretending to be the Vampire Gods. They depicted the total and utter control vampires had over humans. Humans were prey—victims—fully lacking power.

The dance was dark, alluring, and utterly captivating.

The Royalle Ballet's Mirror-Blessed dancers shined in the number, flying, hovering, and manipulating the stage. One of the performers had hair made of diamonds, and another shone like that of the North Star. Glimmering and gliding across the stage.

Quinn was transfixed, allowing the music and movement to fill her soul. But she felt the prince's gaze on her face like a phantom wind, and she turned to meet him.

"I wish I could see through your eyes," he whispered. Her

breath hitched, and her lips tingled with the memory of his kisses. "You see the world and all of its beauty." His gaze caressed her cheeks. "All of its possibilities. You study it, and you understand it."

She gulped.

A surge of passion built in her belly, and she leaned into him, his energy pulling her closer. A magnet needing to touch him, to feel his lips on hers. He was an intoxicating drug, and she wanted to get lost in him.

But then she remembered Constance's words from earlier. He still wanted her—longed for her. His roguish ways were due to his pain from losing Constance. Quinn didn't want to be a consolation prize or just another girl he played with. If she wanted him—which she absolutely didn't—she wanted to be more. She wanted to mean something.

She tore her gaze away and focused back on the stage, where there was a sudden flash of blood. Quinn gasped.

"Emrys, do you see it?" she said, tapping his arm and pointing at the stage.

At the back stood a massive two-story crimson mirror. It was a waterfall of sparkling blood, and it blended in perfectly with the coloring of the theater as if it belonged there—as if it had always been there.

She turned back to Emrys to see if he felt the same adrenaline surging through him at the sight, but he only glanced at her with crinkled brows. "I don't see anything."

"You don't see the mirror on the stage?" At this, everyone in the box's eyes landed on her, confusion lacing their faces. "None of you see it?"

Under her corset, her mirror necklace pulsed and burned. She pulled it out of the fabric, and the glass melted into liquid metal. Then danced a pas de deux in its cage.

"Has it ever done that before?" Emrys asked.

"Yes," Quinn whispered. "Once." Was the necklace the reason she could see the mirror, but others couldn't? Testing her theory, she looped the chain over her head and placed the chain in Emrys's palm. "Be careful not to touch the shard, but do you see it now?"

She was unsure if that was the correct answer because when she removed the jewelry from her body, she was still able to see the mirror.

"Yes," Emrys breathed. "I see it."

He passed the necklace to Constance, who passed it to Giselle, who passed it to Jevon. Within a matter of minutes, they all saw the sparkling liquid mirror at the back of the stage through the glamour.

Possibly because the Blood Mirrors were connected.

"How in the world are we going to get to it with a packed audience and dancers littering the stage," Giselle asked.

"Quinny, are you thinking what I am?" Constance said.

Quinn moaned. "We're gonna steal the dancer's costumes, aren't we?"

A mischievous grin painted Constance's face. "Yes, we are."

"What exactly is the plan?" Francois asked, raising a brow. "The cost of taking the paintings out is a soul, so we obviously aren't going to bargain for them, and the mirror is far too big to move during the ballet."

Emrys rubbed his forehead. "We need to guard it and maybe send someone in to ask if anyone has tried to bargain with it recently."

"I believe the killer has a mirror object that is allowing them to either watch us or be a step ahead. They might even be here now," Quinn said. "So, we need to make sure we keep them from getting what they've come for and then possibly figure out a way to lure them and trap them."

"We get as close as we can to guard it until the show is over or the murderer shows?" Jevon asked.

"Yes," Emrys and Quinn said in unison.

After slipping from the Royalle Box and using Emrys's vampire abilities, the group split into four groups. Giselle, with the gang, tried to get to the mirror from behind the stage. Emrys compelled two dancers to sleep in their dressing room so that Quinn and Constance could join the show. After helping the girls, he used his vampiric abilities to make himself invisible and get as close as he could, and Jevon watched from the stage wings.

Quinn never thought the first time she'd dance on with the Royalle Ballet would be in a stolen tutu in the middle of a murder investigation and vampiric conspiracy. But this was her life now.

The dance started within a croisé devant position and was full of tricky steps. Quinn knew the sequence, having performed the ballet once before, but it'd been a long time, and she was sloppy. She needed her fellow dancers to call out moves as they went.

Trying to position herself as close to the mirror as possible to keep an eye on it proved difficult while also trying to perform. Every turn she took, she spotted the mirror; every lift, her eyes watched the scarlet waterfall, checking and making sure no one approached it.

The music didn't flow through her like normal; it burned, singeing pieces of her. It wasn't beauty or passion; it was death and destruction.

But she didn't care. She had a mission. Protect the mirror. Watch the mirror.

As the ballet continued, more and more dancers and Mirror-Blessed performers flocked to the floor, making even the simplest of moves impossible. The stage became a labyrinth, and she kept getting pushed farther and farther from her task.

A dense, enchanted fog invaded the stage. It was ominous and full of deadly secrets, the mist too thick to see much of anything.

The room smelled of iron and broken hearts.

Rain poured from the ceiling, coating Quinn's tutu. The lights flickered as the music built into a crescendo, constructing a tense climax. Each strum of the violin echoed through her chest as she clawed her way to the mirror.

Something was wrong.

A drop of rain landed in her mouth, and it tasted like blood—real blood.

Quinn's heart stumbled, and dread licked at the back of her neck. This was not supposed to happen. Something had gone terribly wrong. She tore her way through the dancers, and as the song climaxed, and an explosion rattled the sky, sending shards of crimson glass through the air.

Sharp, massive shards sliced through the air, cutting everything in their path—including the flesh of the dancer's skin. Glass daggers.

Coming straight for Quinn. She threw her arms up to protect her face as she was about to be pummeled with the pieces of the mirror.

In a blink, Emrys appeared in front of her and pulled her into his chest, shielding her body from the shattering glass. The glass clinked against the ground, and time stilled. The sound was a thick, broken melody of death and destruction.

Screams burst through the glass melody, and chaos climbed into the night.

Quinn tilted her chin up and met Emrys's amber eyes which were coated in deep concern.

He'd saved her, taking the impact of the glass daggers—using his body to protect hers, and even though he was a vampire, it had to hurt.

"Are you okay?" she breathed.

His lips tilted up in a half smile. "Yes, Quinnevere. I am fine"—he stroked her chin with his thumb—"and so are you."

Quinn gulped. "You're bleeding."

"It's just a scratch."

The rotten melody played on while they stood frozen in each other's arms, but as the sound faded, the mirror glass evaporated into nothingness, leaving a scarlet stain across the floor—the sign of a dead magic mirror.

Quinn swallowed, her throat tight and aching. "We failed . . . again."

DAY
SIX

PRICE 2 CENTS

| BREAKING NEWS | # The New Swansea Times |

FRIDAY, NEW SWANSEA CITY, 95th DAY OF AUTUMN, 700AV

THE BALLET RUINED MIRROR DESTROYED

NEARLY NOTHING IS MORE TRAGIC THAN THE DEATH OF A MIRROR

During the Queen's Royalle Ballet's opening night performance, a mirror was horrifically murdered. It is unclear at this time who is responsible and if anyone is dead. Many people are injured—cont. on page 6

Day Five: Festival of Blood

As we count down the days until the Royalle Suitor Ball, we celebrate the Night of Carnival. The streets will be lined with revelry, masks, and loosened inhibitions. It's a time of fun and mystery—cont. page 2

Prince Escorts Ballerina Before Disaster

Sources say the prince and ballerina's romance is heating up. Some are even suggesting the two have kissed and others are saying they're lovers, meeting for midnight rendezvous. One thing is absolutely certain, the prince escorted the girl to the opening night of the Queen's Royalle Ballet—cont. on page 3

***Editor's Note: Prince Emrys is taller and more handsome than depicted.*

Thirty

Formalin and crusted blood laced the air. On the exam table lay a corpse with lacerations caused by broken shards of glass. A Mirror-Blessed dancer. The only person to die in the aftermath of the second Blood Mirror being destroyed.

A dancer like herself, except Emrys saved her, blocking all the shattered glass from impaling her, too. He *saved* her, but she didn't know how to feel about it or what to do with that information.

Quinn's throat worked.

At least no vampires died in the attack. Which was a blessing and a curse because it meant the killer must have gotten the paintings out before they shattered the mirror.

Quinn rubbed her eyes, tired from lack of sleep. It was hard to get any rest when adrenaline from the attack coursed through her body. She yawned as if to prove the point, and her uncle glared in her direction. He disapproved of displays of weakness, including tiredness. But at least Uncle Matias said nothing about their fight or the council meeting. As if ignoring the whole situation would make it disappear. Just another example of how her family avoided emotional conflict.

The family motto: *don't talk about it.*

Or perhaps he was too eccentric and busy to bother reprimanding her again. He'd been a surprisingly distant parental guardian.

Leaning over a table, Quinn checked and cross-checked the fingerprints from the council meeting *again* against the fingerprints from Jane's murder and the reporter. There was no match. She knew this, yet she couldn't help herself. She needed something to cling onto because anytime she got anywhere with the investigation, everything was ruined.

The murderer was truly one step ahead . . . always.

Quinn didn't know if she was still in danger. The murderer had destroyed the second mirror and gotten what they wanted. Technically, she'd played her part and led them to it. She had to assume they were watching her—following her. Somehow. Maybe with Mirror-Blessed magic? Quinn swallowed past the lump in her throat. It was all her fault.

All of it.

The victim on the table.

The dead mirror.

Everything.

The events also seemed to have shaken Emrys. He had held her trembling in his arms, protecting her from flying glass for far longer than was decent or necessary. Frozen in defeat. They'd failed. Spectacularly.

But currently, the prince sat in the corner reading a romance novel. It seemed that he also liked to suppress his struggles—with reading. The cover of his book read something like *A Rogue of One's Own* or *The Rogue Not Taken* or something similarly themed. She never imagined he'd be into romance, but he was so utterly confident, even in that.

After about twenty minutes of useless checking, Quinn huffed and dug her fingers into her temples.

"Find anything interesting?" Emrys asked, pocketing his novel, and pulling out a set of gloves.

"Nothing." She sighed. "We have nothing. Just like always. We take one step forward to take a thousand steps back."

Emrys examined the prints, his fingers shadowing her own—too close.

A bird in her heart fluttered against its cage, and she trembled. His closeness stirred sensations in her body, ones especially inappropriate in this situation. She needed to be impartial and not care —evidence required to be respected and cherished.

What she didn't need to do was imagine how his fingers would feel against her neck or how his lips would—

Pull yourself together.

Quinn gulped, and her breaths grew ragged. "Do you think it's vampires?"

"Yes." He pulled back and caught her gaze, misery pirouetting in his eyes. It was as if the weight of the Looking Glass rested on his chest. "It has to be. The illusions last night, blood rain, fog, and lights are all within our power of persuasive illusions."

Quinn's intestinal tract solidified, causing deep guttural pain. "I have no real suspects." She rolled out her neck and cleared her throat. "I am not sure what else to do. More people keep dying, and I am nowhere closer to the truth."

"I know the feeling." Emrys's voice cracked. "Maybe we're going about the investigation wrong. We've been looking for the murderer, but maybe we should try finding the last mirror and lure them into it."

Quinn tried her best to sound clinical and uncaring, but her voice had a slight tremor. "That involves finding the mirror."

"Perhaps your necklace or another mirror could help with that."

Quinn's mouth worked as Jevon opened the lab door carrying a package. Emrys stepped away from the examining table, putting space between them.

"Mr. Yale, you're not allowed in here," Uncle Matias said, eyes focused on his microscope.

Jevon flashed an innocent smile that oozed charm like magic.

"I'm deeply sorry, Dr. Thyssen. Someone left Quinn an interesting package, and I figured I'd bring it in. Of course, I'll leave as soon as I give it to her."

"Fine, fine." Uncle Matias waved him off.

Jevon strolled over to his friend and whispered from the corner of his mouth. "Find anything?"

"More of the same," Quinn said. "A package for me?"

"Yes." He handed her a box.

Stepping away from the samples, Quinn placed the package next to the sink before she removed her gloves and washed up. As she started to open the package, Emrys cautioned, "Wait. It smel—"

But his warning came too late.

Blood exploded all over Quinn's face and chest. She coughed, and it spilled from her mouth. Her whole body shivered, and she began to gag. It was caked everywhere, dripping from her chest and onto the floor, creating a river.

Quinn sucked in a breath and held her hands out, frozen. Shock cascaded through her bones, and she had no idea what to do.

Emrys was a stone statue. Inhumanly still.

Quinn turned to the sink and tossed water on her face and into her mouth, trying to get the blood off her skin and eyelashes. Appearing at her side, Emrys handed her a towel. She snatched it and scrubbed and scrubbed and scrubbed and scrubbed her face.

Emrys was only inches from her now, watching with preternatural stillness. "Has anyone ever told you that you look amazing covered in blood?"

She wasn't sure if he said it to break the tension or if he meant it. He stroked a finger along her collarbone, scooping up a stream of crimson. She shivered. Emrys placed his finger in his mouth, tasting the blood.

"Oh, god. I hope that wasn't diseased." She coughed and pinched her fingertips together.

"It wasn't."

"How would you know?" Quinn snapped before realizing that as a vampire, he must be able to tell from tasting the blood.

Emrys cleared his throat and crossed his arms, leaning against the table. "I just know. But if you don't believe me, you can live the next couple of years in terror if you would like."

"Right," she whispered, fiercely scrubbing her skin raw. "What in all the mirrors was that? Why would someone send me a box of blood?"

Emrys returned to the box with gloves and picked up a note wrapped in a plastic bag.

> *"Sweet Quinny, good work leading me to my prize. You have until the Suitor Ball to find the third Blood Mirror. If you fail to find it in time, I will murder one of your friends. And remember, I am always watching."*

Emrys read the note, his voice coated with a plague.

Her knees buckled, and she braced the sink for support. The walls felt like they were closing inward, trapping, and crushing her—the Mirror of Terror's warning. Four fears would come true. Her friends' dying was one of the fears.

She wanted to vomit.

"Fucking shattered mirrors," Quinn cursed, her fingers grabbing the sink so tightly her knuckles grew white.

"They're threatening you." Jevon appeared next to Emrys, glancing down at the note. Quinn shuddered. She'd entirely forgotten he was there.

The man truly was like air, impossible to see but somehow always around. If Constance was the wraith of the group, Jevon was the mist. She might have been able to disappear into the night, but Jevon was the night. Always hidden in plain sight.

Quinn inhaled sharply. "So it would seem."

Emrys set down the note, removed his gloves, and stepped away again, putting a significant amount of space between them.

"Quinnevere Igretta Ashelle, you better clean that up," Uncle Matias said, far more concerned about the mess than the fact that his niece was covered in gore. It would have been upsetting, except Quinn had once accidentally exploded bowels, blood, and stomach contents all over the place.

Emrys glowered. "Go take a shower, Quinn. I'll clean this up."

"Wait." Lightning struck her heart. She'd forgotten. "What time is it?" she asked, her eyes wide and probably wild.

"3:15 pm."

"Oh, *bloody mirrors*. Ballet auditions," she whispered as tears pooled in her eyes. The one thing that possibly wasn't going wrong in her life was about to slip through her fingers. Auditions were at 3:30 pm, and she was covered in blood, and the lab was a mess. "I am going to miss them."

"No, you won't. You will get cleaned up and go."

"No, you don't get it." Venom churned in her stomach—eating away her insides. "There is no time. I cannot wash up and get there on time."

Emrys's eyes lit up with pleasure, and a wicked smile played on his face. "Don't worry. I'll make you some time."

"How?"

"I am the Playboy Prince. I was made to be a distraction."

THIRTY-ONE

Quinn tiptoed through the studio door ten minutes late with soaking hair and a pristine tutu to find Emrys "entertaining" the room. He was having the male dancers teach him spins and jumps as the Royalle Ballet director glowered on. Shockingly, he had quite a lot of technique.

Did they teach heirs to the throne ballet at Castle Hill? Or had he learned to dance at some point in his long vampiric life?

Quinn walked to the side of the room as silently as possible, dropped off her pack, quickly slipped into her pointe shoes, and tied her ribbons around her legs.

"Are you okay?" Constance whispered. The girl was an empath and always knew when Quinn was upset.

"Yes, I am fine," she lied.

"Why is your hair wet?" Constance asked, her amused eyes fixed on Emrys doing a pirouette à la seconde.

"I received a lovely present filled with blood and threats that exploded all over my face."

"What?" Constance said far too loudly, causing the ballet director and the surrounding dancers to stare at them. Emrys paused his dancing, a look of triumph lacing his face. "Fuck, Quinn. Again?" Constance whispered.

"Yes, this time they're threatening you and Giselle and Jevon," Quinn murmured, her voice like the shattered blood glass.

Constance reached out a steady hand and comforted her friend. "We're going to be alright. I promise."

Emrys clapped, drawing attention back to himself. He embodied his role as a narcissist, needing all the limelight. "Well, thank you so much for your amazing instruction. I'd like to watch the auditions, if you would please." He waved his arm dismissively as if they were all his subjects and would all do his bidding.

It was an act, and perhaps it always had been.

Auditions continued as planned—almost. The director was supposed to observe their class for one week and then decide who would join the Queen's Royalle Ballet. With Jane's death, two of those days were postponed.

Today was another group number from *Midwinter*, the famous ballet always performed at the heart of the holiday season. Quinn danced the Waltz of Snowflakes, a dance normally performed on the stage as fake snow fell from the ceiling, causing the floor to become slick and lose all its friction.

As Quinn jumped a soubresaut, she imagined what it would be like to do that move on a slippery floor. It would be a tough move to pull off, which is why the Royalle Ballet only took the best dancers as apprentices.

The dance flew by quickly. At the end of the number, all the snowflakes fell to the floor in a heap. Quinn executed the movement perfectly, nailed all the moves in the dance, and even managed a tinge of emotion.

Slowly peeling herself off the floor, Quinn made her way to Constance, who had a glorious smile on her face. "That was incredible!"

"Thanks." Quinn tried to breathe, her lungs tight and stinging.

"Truly, if they don't pick you after that, it will be blasphemy, and we shall all revolt." Constance rolled onto her stomach and stretched her quadriceps.

Quinn held her toes and stretched her calves as Emrys approached. "That was great."

"Thank you."

"Would you like me to escort you back to the lab?" Emrys asked, holding out a hand.

Quinn didn't take it, instead she forced a smile. He was being so kind and helpful, but she needed space, fresh air, and to be able to breathe again. "Thank you for your offer, but I would prefer to be alone." From his concerned expression, she added, "For now."

He bowed his head in respect. "Let me know if you need anything."

Clutching her ballet bag, Quinn strode out into the crisp night air, trying to walk off the emotions that clung to her core. Movement always helped clear her head. So she simply walked and walked and walked, the icy wind her only companion as the sun drifted off to sleep and the fifth night of the Blood Festival awoke.

It felt like Quinn hadn't been able to breathe for days—like she was lost out in the ocean with waves crashing down over and over again. And she couldn't feel or think, too stuck in a pattern, begging for survival . . . and it was just all too much. She needed space and time to get herself sorted. She needed the air and distance from her friends, but especially from the prince.

Hours passed in a blur. Her thoughts melted together like a potion brewing in a cauldron.

When awareness finally hit, she was in the middle of the Marina District, surrounded by a parade of masks and secrets. But her thoughts were still a mixture of thick, clotted paint.

The threats. The mirror bursting. Her parents. Jane. People kept dying, and now, if she didn't find the last mirror, she might get her friends killed, too.

She was always seven steps behind the murderer and had no way of catching up.

It was hopeless.

As she walked, people sang odes to celebrate the end of the Vampire Gods and glorified King Emrys, the savior of the Blood Rebellion. Wine poured freely, and inhibitions melted to dust, leaving a maze of revelry, lies, debauchery, and sin. Wonderful sin.

People with visible mirror consequences freely walked the streets. There was a boy who cried tears of tar, a man who projected all his thoughts to walker's by, and a girl who disappeared for a moment every thirty seconds.

Gramophones played the blues, and masked acrobats in elaborate costumes walked on tightropes, dangled from rings, and floated on trapezes. Mirror-Blessed contortionists spun their heads in full circles; actors performed social satire to a crowd of adoring fans. On the docks sat a makeshift menagerie, filled with every creature imaginable—real and mirror-created.

The night lit up with enchantment—a night of dreams and make-believe.

The external celebration stood in stark contrast to the devastation in Quinn. The investigation was nowhere nearer to being solved than it was when Jane died. Quinn was a complete and utter failure, and now her friends' lives were on the line.

As she walked through the fantasy, tears trickled down her face, a light mist that turned into a river of feelings bursting out of her fractured heart.

Without realizing it, she'd walked all the way to the outskirts of the Nature District.

It was not a good place to be. The outskirts were filled with run-down buildings cobbled together from scrap wood, cardboard, and abandoned objects, creating an encampment that crawled with drugs and crime.

Passing under a bridge, Quinn glimpsed a shadow moving slowly and hauling something cumbersome. She should've continued on, but curiosity climbed up her throat. It was possible that Quinn's biggest flaw was curiosity. Because if she heard a whispered secret floating through the air, she needed to know all of it. She couldn't just drop it and let it go. Half of the trouble she'd gotten herself into over the past couple of days had come from eavesdropping. This knowledge should have stopped her and turned her around, but of course, it didn't.

It only made her want to find out more.

Following close behind, Quinn watched as a man dragged a human-sized lump to a massive bonfire before struggling to lift it up and onto the pyre. Quinn moved closer to gawk—or help, but then she noticed an arm hanging limply.

A body. *A lifeless body.* And then the stench hit her. Visceral and suffocating.

The smell of burning flesh and pine trees.

She gagged. Quinn was used to the smell of dead bodies, but burning flesh was rancid and all-consuming, and it wasn't something she was prepared for outside of a lab.

"What are you doing?" Quinn wrapped her arms around her stomach as if to protect herself. *Oh, you foolish girl. Get out of here while you still have the chance.*

"Burning him," the man grunted.

Horror stroked up Quinn's spine. "Burning him?" Her voice shook, and the horror intensified when her vision solidified, and through the embers, she saw that the bonfire was a pile of burning bodies, at least twenty deep. Twenty dead. "How did he die?"

The man shrugged. "Drink, drugs . . . who knows. I just burn the bodies so that they can move on to the afterlife."

"Have more people been dying lately?" Quinn asked.

"Nineteen this week. More than usual, but it's cold."

Without asking, Quinn examined the corpse's neck. There were too many bodies on the pile for them to be dying of natural causes or accidents. Someone or something was behind these deaths—first the mirror murders and now the homeless. Could it be connected? Possibly, if new vampires roamed the streets, they would need a food source.

"What are you doing, girl?" The man pulled the body out of her reach.

"I am . . . I'm a coroner. I just wanted to make sure he didn't have wounds on his neck." The body didn't. His neck had no visible markings, yet suspicion still tingled in her chest.

"People die on the streets every day from the cold, starvation, overdose, and disease. Fancy people like yourself have never cared."

"I'm not—" His words hit like a knife to her gut.

Quinn wasn't fancy.

She was an orphan who only lived off the goodwill of her uncle.

But she wasn't homeless. She had privilege in that sense, and she had a comfortable life for a sienna-less orphan. She always had a roof over her head and always had help. Even with everything going wrong in her life, she had Constance, Giselle, and Jevon.

And maybe even Emrys.

She had a safety net. *Options.*

This man did not.

Biting her cheek, she examined the body. "Let me help you burn him."

Together, they hauled the body into the funeral pit and placed him on the pile. As she moved to leave, the dead man's hand fell.

A bandage ran the length of his arm.

Recklessly, she reached her hand into the flames and pulled the bandage off. Her fingers sizzled as the fabric twirled off the man's wrist, revealing two puncture wounds.

Two vampire puncture wounds.

A sour taste erupted in her mouth. Her chest constricted, and breaths came in rasps. She started walking again, trying to process. She turned back toward the Marina, her footfalls aimless as her brain took over.

Vampires were killing people.

There was no denying it now. But how? The Blood Mirrors bound them, keeping them from murdering. Except . . . they didn't. Two mirrors were found and destroyed. The vampires bound to the first two were free—or worse, compelled.

Perhaps that was the motive.

Was a vampire trying to free their kind by destroying the objects that imprisoned them? It made perfect sense. But which vampires? She already fingerprinted the ones from the council meeting, unless . . . was it possible a newly created vampire was the kill—

A scream pierced the shadows of an alley. Quinn slid to a stop, and dust spread under her shoes. A woman squirmed against two people, desperately trying to escape them. One of the attackers was a man, and the other wore a cloak that covered their appearance.

The man's fangs glinted in a sliver of moonlight.

Vampires.

THIRTY-TWO

Adrenaline and endorphins spiked in Quinn's brain, and without thinking, she searched the ground and found a broken bottle. It would have to do as a weapon.

What are you doing, Quinn? You can't fight vampires.

A war raged in her head between fear, bravery, and logic. Logically, Quinn wouldn't be able to overpower two vampires. But if she did nothing, then the woman might die. But if she helped, then *she* might die. Glancing around, Quinn searched for someone else, but it was dark, and everyone partied in the high-end districts. No one was on the outskirts of the Nature district.

But Quinn couldn't walk away. The first rule of medicine was to do no harm. Walking away would be harmful.

Stupid, stupid, stupid.

Ignoring her thoughts, she charged the alley with her tiny, jagged bottle at the ready. One of the vampires leaned against the wall, a hood obscuring its face, watching the male sink his teeth into the woman's jugular.

"You need to stop drinking so much. You'll kill her if you don't stop," the cloaked vampire said.

"I won't stop," the male hissed.

Quinn stood transfixed with the bottle in the air. And it was then that she truly realized that she was no match against a vampire. Coming into the alley was so stupid.

What was I thinking, running into danger like a silent film hero? I'm no hero.

Attacking vampires was foolish, but Quinn also couldn't leave the woman here to die. There were no good options . . . but perhaps it was better to run for help. Get Emrys. Anyone stronger than her. Turning on her heel, Quinn ran to warn someone—to do something besides watch the woman die. Unfortunately, both vampires' had exceptional hearing, and their ears perked up. In a blink, the male was in front of her, blood dripping from his teeth. It wasn't lost on Quinn that this was at least the third time her lack of stealthiness had gotten her in trouble.

But then again, every time she'd eavesdropped before, she was also dealing with vampires. It was an unfair advantage.

Curiosity killed the cat . . . and Quinnevere Ashelle?

"Hello, pretty little thing, you smell divine," he said with a grotesque smile. "I wonder if you taste divine."

Three things happened all at once. The vampire lunged, Quinn raised the severed glass bottle, and the cloaked vampire screamed, "No."

Then, the world stilled.

The vampire yelped with pain as his fingers touched Quinn's skin. At the exact moment, she sliced upward at his face and took a nasty chunk out. With a guttural hiss, he lunged again, and his two porcelain fangs tried to strike Quinn's neck, but she turned into a pirouette-on attitude and kicked him in the side. His teeth scraped her shoulder. Coming out of the turn, she kicked the man in the face.

He stumbled back but jumped up far quicker than humanly possible—far faster than she expected. Black claws grew out of his fingernails, swiping and slicing at her.

She somersaulted and rolled back onto her feet, the glass shard at the ready. The creature was far too fast and strong. He pinned her to the ground, punctured her side, and sliced down her chest with his claws.

Crimson bubbled out of her corset and spilled onto the cobblestones. A burning pain radiated through her bones.

But Quinn didn't give up.

Clutching the glass, she stabbed him in the eye. He howled, and his claws pierced into the woman's neck, slightly breaking the skin as his fangs plunged at her carotid. Seconds after he tore out her throat, the second vampire grabbed him and swiftly broke his neck. The attacker crumbled to the alley floor.

Darkness and mystery cloaked the second vampire's face. Shadows and murder radiated from them as if they were the darkness itself. A beautiful, deadly darkness.

Even up close, she couldn't distinguish their gender, possibly because the vampire was obscuring her senses with their glamour. It studied her silently, a claw outstretched.

Quinn's heartbeat soared as the vampire slowly examined, taking in the human they'd saved.

But why?

They hovered above with preternatural stillness and grace. Without even seeing its face, Quinn knew that this creature was stunning. If not in their actual appearance, then in their enchanting essence. An essence as powerful as a shooting star.

At once, Quinn was fiercely drawn to and utterly repulsed by it—too much power in such a creature.

Quinn's breaths came out in ragged bubbles, blood filling her mouth. Her heart played a presto tempo in her chest—working far too hard. Fear licked her spine. Was this how it all ended? Would Quinn be the next body?

Forgotten.

No.

Placing the hilt of her palm on the ground, she pulled herself away from the vampire. Her hazel gaze caught on the woman who lay still and dying. Quinn had a choice: try to run or try to save her. She inhaled sharply, the process excruciating.

Pebbles and dirt spiked at her hands as she crawled toward the woman. Blood gushed from the wound in the woman's throat, and Quinn punched her fingers into the jagged skin, trying to feel for the rupture in the carotid artery, trying to halt the bleeding.

Success was an elusive dream. This woman was going to die, and there was nothing Quinn could do about it.

Failure coursed through her veins, and blood pooled between Quinn's fingers as the light in the woman's eyes faded. Only a couple years older than Quinn, the woman's life evaporated. Just gone. Just slipped into nothing.

Tears stung at the edges of her eyes. She'd performed many autopsies and studied many dead bodies, but she hadn't watched somebody die. Never seen the moment their spirit left forever.

Not even when her parents died, no, she'd hid under a table and squeezed her eyes shut—only seeing the dead bodies afterward.

This was the first time she saw death's embrace.

Shock bruised Quinn's soul, and her trembling fingers remained fixed on the dead woman's neck.

Their blood mingled together, pouring from Quinn's chest wound onto the victim. The longer she froze, the more blood leaked out and the more desperate her own situation became.

But she couldn't get her fingers to move. She couldn't turn to meet the vampire who still hovered behind her.

"Oh, Quinny." The vampire's sultry, wicked tone snaked at the nape of her neck, causing hairs to rise. "Quinny, Quinny, Quinn, turn around."

It had a voice of death.

Hot breaths heated the back of her neck.

Chills rolled down her spine. Rolling her shoulders back and holding her head high, she tried to be strong and face her death with bravery.

This creature would not see her beg or cry.

Cold fingers stroked her chin and tucked her blood-soaked hair behind her ear.

"You were not supposed to see this." The vampire whispered into her ear. "This was not supposed to happen." The vampire moved their hand over the fang marks on Quinn's shoulder, making sure not to touch her skin. "Move away from the girl, Quinny. She is dead."

Quinn was a granite statue, her limbs heavy and limp. Even if she wanted to move, she wasn't sure if she could. But she didn't even try to move. If her last living act was to defy this vampire, then that was what she was going to do.

They clicked their tongue. "Tsk, tsk, tsk, you're a bad, bad ballerina. Don't make me compel you."

"Then do it," she breathed with a tiny squeak.

"Move away from the body." The vampire's sultry voice slightly shifted to a hypnotic enchantment. One that she couldn't refuse.

It clawed at the back of her mind like an invasion.

A parasite.

And she had to comply. This magic was far more potent than Francois's siren song. This was an immovable wall.

Quinn's movements were slow and filled with agony. Every tiny shift shot jolts of pain through her. Heaving herself away, she left a streak of crimson in her wake. When she had no strength, she collapsed against the wall.

With a swift movement, far gentler than she'd expected, the vampire flipped her body over and leaned her against the wall. "I am sorry about this."

They slid a finger across her shoulder, dipping it in her blood before sucking it into its mouth. With this motion, their hood fell from its face, their expression pure agony like the blood burned its esophagus.

"Hmmm. You always taste sweet."

Always?

They'd tasted her blood before?

Quinn scowled and recognized the vampire. They looked slightly different, but—

"Forget my face," the vampire said hypnotically.

Suddenly, Quinn's brain fogged. She knew that face—she did —but now it was all a blur. Blinking, she tried to correct her vision. Yet, despite staring into their eyes, she couldn't tell what color they were. She had face blindness.

"You were never supposed to be involved," the vampire said, sorrow painting their words. "As soon as I leave this alley, you will forget our interaction. You will wake up next to a dead body, not knowing how you got here, and the next time you see me, you will know my face and have fond feelings." The vampire stroked her forehead sweetly. "Goodbye, little Quinny. Try not to die from blood loss. That would ruin everything." The creature glanced down at Quinn's ruined body and shook its head. "That will not do. I'll have to get one of your terrible friends to help you."

The words lingered in the air as a grey fog rolled into her mind, and blackness claimed her.

Thirty-Three

The world swam in a daze of shadows and agony. All 206 bones in Quinn's body screamed and pulsated with pain, and her muscles swam in a sea of sorrow.

All she knew was the pain.

But at least it meant life. It meant hope.

Without sight, Quinn couldn't know the extent of the damage. She needed to open her eyes. But even that task felt impossible. It was far more comfortable to drift into the land of sleep.

No, get up, move. If you don't, you'll die.

Fight. Survive.

And the first step, although very small, was to open her eyes. But her eyelids drooped and were heavy-laden. It took every ounce of her energy to open them enough to see. But what she managed to see was obscured by her thick black eyelashes.

Come on, Quinn. You can do this. You need to move.

Trying again, she gathered all the energy she could muster, and she fully opened her eyes. Within seconds of examining her wounds, she was hit by a burst of dizziness.

Blood stained her tutu so much that only tiny spots of the white remained. Claw marks ran down the entire length of her chest and torso. She'd been attacked by . . . by . . . a . . . Her mind emptied.

Focus. On your wounds, Quinn.

Oh, yes, her wounds. With a medical and precise eye, Quinn examined the injuries. They weren't deep, but they were numerous and gushing, and if she didn't stop the bleeding soon, she'd die from blood loss.

Quinn pressed her arm against her chest, desperately trying to compress and stop the blood.

It wasn't enough.

There were too many lacerations. She needed something to stop the bleeding. But her clothing was filthy and covered with germs and using it risked infection. But if she didn't do something, she'd die.

Holy fucking hell. It was bad.

A beautiful mixture of curse words left her lips.

Petticoats.

But she didn't have enough fabric under her tutu. She really needed to stop being late to ballet.

Quinn desperately crawled to the dead body beside her.

Waffling through the skirts as respectfully as possible, she tried to reach the woolen underskirt. The lowest petticoat was her best bet for both the cleanest and most efficient material. After much effort, she reached the skirt that she needed. With all the strength she could muster, she ripped and ripped.

But it took too much effort to pull apart, and her eyes . . . were . . . drooping. Sleep wasn't so bad. A couple of minutes of rest wouldn't hurt . . .

Sandpaper tickled her toes. It was scratchy and rather unpleasant. Quinn jolted awake.

She would not die here.

Not like this.

Not now.

Finding her feet, she realized that two flickering cat shadows licked her toes and kept her awake—Hadleigh's cat shadows. The magical familiars.

"Stop it," Quinn groaned as she sat up and began to wrap her wounds—very poorly. But it worked well enough to stop most of the bleeding.

But now Quinn needed to figure out how to get out of the alley and find help . . . in the middle of the night, amongst abandoned streets.

Focus. *You're a strong, athletic ballerina. You can do this.*

Pushing herself to her feet, she managed to take three steps before crumbling back to the ground. But Quinn didn't quit. When you fall in ballet, you get back up. When you fall in life, *you get back up.*

And that was what she did. She kept getting back up until . . . she hit a brick wall and toppled over.

Her body was too weak to move, so she let her head fall to the street.

This was how she would die.

Just like her second fear in the Mirror of Terror.

A thud hit her chest. One of the spirit cats pounced on her, and the other ran down the street. Quinn's vision blurred, her body hardening to ice. She was so cold.

Death was at her doorstep, ready to accept her into his realm.

"Hadleigh, get to a rotary and call him." A distant voice rang through the air. The face of a brunette man hovered above her head, and someone's hands were trying to staunch the blood. "Hold on, your prince is coming, and he will fix this."

Quinn's eyes fluttered, and her vision evaporated once again. She was just so tired, and she needed to sleep . . .

Death's cold fingers snaked up her body and invited her home. Darkness welcomed her like an old friend returning from a long, gruesome war.

"Quinn?" *His* voice seemed so, so far away. "Oh, fucking mirrors, Quinnevere, you're dying."

"That seems pretty obvious, prince charming." Her words were soft and barely enunciated.

Emrys's chestnut eyes appeared above her head, and they looked so . . . so concerned, like two pools of brown-coated fear. Her chest warmed, and for maybe the first time in her life, she was happy to see the Playboy Prince.

"Has anyone ever told you that seeing your face makes them want to die?" Her words slurred together.

Emrys chuckled, but the fear never left his eyes. "I should have guessed dying wouldn't change your feelings or your terrible sense of humor."

A bit too drunk from the blood loss, Quinn breathed, "Did you know you're so, so pretty? You're like a painting . . . a pretty, pretty . . . painting."

Her head fell sideways, and her eyelids fluttered shut.

"Quinn." He slapped her cheek. "Stay with me, you brilliant nightmare."

Quinn's eyes opened, and the disorientation flooded back in. She was staring at Emrys Avalon. The Playboy Prince, and richest man in New Swansea. A vampire. Her nemesis. Or maybe not a nemesis anymore . . .

"Humph. No. I have no interest in staying with you," she slurred and tried to roll away from him.

"Oh, god, your touch is revolting." Emrys pinched his eyes shut as he put pressure on her wounds.

"Very charmi—" Quinn's head tilted. It was too heavy to hold up. She would have been insulted by his words, if she weren't dy —blackness erupted through her mind.

With another jolt to her face, Quinn regained consciousness. "You need to stay awake, Quinn." Emrys fumbled, trying to find a way to save her, but he had no idea what he was doing, or at least that was what it seemed like from his franti—

"Quinn, please, stay with me." He held her limp head up by the neck.

"I don't think I have—" Quinn breathed, her body growing cold.

"Do you want to live?" Emrys asked. He was desperation—a man with no options.

"No." She tried to say it sarcastically, but with her throat so sore from strain and utterly dry, it came out as a sad and pathetic statement. Not at all how she intended it. "Yes, of course, I want to live."

Words were torture.

"Are you willing to accept the consequences?" He squeezed her hand, his gaze cutting into her.

"What are—" she trailed off, gray flowing back into her vision. She blinked to correct it.

"An eternity of dealing with me." He hesitated, despair spilling over a nonchalant mask he was trying to hold. "And possibly eternal damnation."

"Those are fun consequ—"

"Be serious, Quinnevere. We don't have the time for our usual and oh-so-pleasurable banter right now. You're dying." He clasped her face in his hands. "Do you want me to save your life? To mark you?"

"Yes. I—" She couldn't quite get the word to spill from her lips, but it didn't matter.

Emrys cut open his wrist and shoved it into her mouth, forcing her to drink his blood. It tasted of iron and strawberries. Oh, she was going a bit mad. Blood did not taste like strawberries.

The world danced a pas de deux filled with endless pirouettes, promenades, and piques. A melody of sickness and frailty sang in her body.

While she drank, voices swirled around her.

"What did you do?" Emrys seethed, his voice an abyss of darkness and rage, but it wasn't directed at her. "She's dying, Francois."

"We were doing our job. You asked us to find the mirror—"

"I didn't ask you to hurt—"

"What? *Your girl*?" There was a long pause between the words. "We had nothing to do with this."

"Then why were you here?"

"Because we had Hadleigh's familiars follow her."

Quinn was pretty sure Emrys growled at that, or maybe she hallucinated . . . The world flipped sideways as she couldn't hold her head up, and it slid down Emrys's arm. His steadying fingers gently held the nape of her neck and stabilized her, allowing her to see the hazy scene the right way up.

"Look on the bright side, she's incredibly talented. She managed to kill a vampire." A placating charm swirled from Francois's tongue.

Emrys grunted and shifted, but she was unable to see the message he conveyed with his expression. "That vampire is not dead. He's just incapacitated," Emrys said.

"Yes, well, I know—"

"You will need to bind him with silver and trap him. I want to have *some words* with him." The way Emrys said *some words*, it sounded like he would rip the vampire's throat out.

"Yes, we can do that."

The next thing Quinn heard was footsteps. Many, many footsteps.

"I'll also be having words with you, Francois."

"I would expect so."

Emrys made her drink for a long time. Possibly too long because by the end, Emrys had to clutch the wall for support. "This is weird, but I need to drink some of your blood. I can't get you to safety if I am too weakened. But I need your permission."

It was a weird request, but so was everything else that happened in the past week. "Yes, you can." It was all the words she managed to speak. Although she didn't think she would die, exhaustion tore at her and begged her to sleep.

"I should have listened to you," he said.

A small laugh escaped her lips. "Always."

"You're definitely not ginger. You taste like copper and cinnamon, Quinnevere."

She meant to respond, but instead, she rested her head on his shoulder. She felt him lift her and carry her half-conscious body. She nestled into his shoulder, drifting in and out of sleep. What had to be a door slamming jolted her awake. But she was still far too exhausted to open her eyes.

"I see you brought the ballerina from the papers," a woman said with a regal lilt that commanded respect. A voice frigid and unyielding.

Quinn managed to raise a heavy eyelid a crack. The queen stood at the palace entrance, oozing authority, and vampiric grace.

"Grandmother." Emrys used his arrogant, roguish voice. The one that either got him out of a lot of trouble or *into* a lot of trouble.

"Grandson." The queen smirked, her crimson hair streaked with grey, slightly bouncing with her movement. The interaction was tense and rang with falsities. "Why did you bring the barely conscious ballerina to Castle Hill?"

Quinn's eyelids drifted closed. She was far too tired to hold them open.

A silence followed before Emrys finally answered the question. "I found her covered in dirt and bleeding out in an alley with vampire wounds."

"How charming . . . just your type," the queen mocked. "And were you the vampire that attacked her?"

"I thought we agreed to stop antagonizing each other," Emrys said.

"Fine."

Emrys's tone softened, and he switched the topic. "Olivia, rogue vampires are killing people. Newly created vampires."

"That is problematic," the queen said. "So, we finally have the true motive for the mirror thefts?"

"I thought you would be happier to know why yo—" Emrys started and either trailed off or Quinn lost consciousness for a moment.

A deep, hollow silence split the air like lightning, immediately followed by thunder.

"What nefarious plans are you plotting, princeling?" the queen asked. "You must have something up your sleeve."

"Oh, Olivia, let the boy be." Another set of footsteps approached from behind. "You have far more important things to worry about than what Emrys is doing with his days." The voice was soft, feminine, and sparkling with kindness. The complete opposite of the queen's voice.

"And I would suggest that my more important duties are directly related to the plans stewing beneath his charming facade."

Oh, Quinn liked her.

Quinn lifted her eyes slightly. Emrys squared his shoulders and smiled at the princess. "Mother."

More footsteps clicked against marble, and a voice as wicked as the sea said, "Oh, blasted mirrors, why is that thing here?" The words belonged to Quinn's true nemesis, Countess Teagan Atwater. "Is it not enough that you force me to watch over her? Now, you must bring her into my home as well."

"I would watch your tone." Emrys's voice was liquid fire.

One of them sniffed the air.

"You marked her?" Countess Teagan's voice rippled with shock and a tinge of fear. "How? You're not dead."

"I don't know," he said defensively. "But she was going to die. I had to try something."

This time, the silence was thick and sticky like honey. But not nearly as sweet.

"Do you have feelings for the girl?" the countess asked, scorn soaking her tone.

Quinn slightly lifted an eye. She was far too curious about that question. Emrys flashed his claws and fangs, which caused her to shut her eyes tight, far too stimulated by the light and the weight of his anger.

Emrys's voice was coated with venom as he said, "Don't insinuate something so—"

"Woah, calm yourself, prince," the countess bit back. "I, of all people, know you could never care about anyone."

"I cannot have feelings for any woman. I have my duty." His voice was a midnight wildfire. "And if I did, it would not be—"

"Methinks, the Lord doth protest too much." Amusement lingered in the princess's words.

He bristled. Quinn felt his every muscle tense, but instead of denying it again, he changed the subject. "I think I've had enough of you three gawking, and I'll be on my way."

Quinn wasn't sure what happened next, but eventually, Emrys walked to a room. He gently placed her into bed before saying, "Leave us." Someone followed him.

"Should I be concerned about the lady's chastity?" the queen asked with a lilt in her accent.

Emrys growled again.

The door clicked, and the queen was gone.

"You can open your eyes now. I know you're awake," he said, stroking her forehead and feeling her temperature. Then he placed a hand on her neck as she opened her eyes. "Your heart rate is back up. But it's still low. Only forty-five beats per minute."

"That's normal for me." Quinn stared into his molten irises.

"Oh, good." He smiled, a finger lacing into her hair. "It will take two full days for you to heal. But in about twenty hours, your wounds will be gone. With no scars. Which I know will disappoint you since you believe beauty is in the imperfections."

She laughed, and it stung. The man didn't forget anything, did he?

"You're going to be fine." He poked her nose in a strangely cute and intimate way. Then his voice changed to a hypnotic and enchanting tone as he said, "Go to sleep now, pretty cinnamon."

Her mind emptied, and a wave of disorientation hit her. The last thing she heard was a man with a strangely familiar voice that she couldn't quite place say, "You will need to clean her up."

Then, a sleep filled with nightmares claimed her soul.

DAY
EIGHT

PRICE 2 CENTS

BREAKING NEWS

The New Swansea Times

SUNDAY, NEW SWANSEA CITY, 97th DAY OF AUTUMN, 700AV

THE DANCING PRINCE

Prince Emrys was seen at the Queen's Royalle Ballet for this year's auditions, showing his many skills. The fierce red haired dancer watched him with stars in her eyes before lacing up her pointe shoes and dancing herself. Is she the next Whitfield Wryte—cont. page 3

***Editor's Note: Prince Emrys is more handsome and taller than depicted.

The Seventh Day of the Festival of Blood Arrives

As tradition on the Seventh day of the Blood Festival all of the city's flags will fly at half-mast to respect the lives lost during the Blood Rebellion. People will also place ribbons and roses on lampposts, throughout the city, also known as the Day of Ribbons and Roses—cont. page 2

TWO YOUNG MEN FOUND DEAD

Two men in their twenties were found dead with puncture marks on necks. The bodies were not taken to the morgue because they were vagrants. Castle Hill and the Police do not have enough resources to investigate. However, it is belived that we have a serial killer on our hands who is pretending to use be a vampire —cont. page 8

Thirty-Four

Nails hammered at the back of her skull like someone constructed a building inside her head, her memory a blur of flickering images. A crimson river, spilling and flowing. Coldness. Emptiness. A midnight death. A shadowed prince. Claws, fangs, and broken screams. Blood. So much blood. Leaking through her fingers and dripping through her hair.

Her memories were a maze of cobwebs.

Complex and twisted.

A severed haze, like a ray of sun bursting through a layer of thick morning mist.

The last solid thing Quinn remembered was . . . a beautiful man, a manifestation of darkness telling her to sleep. And then nothing.

As she rolled over, her legs caressed a cloud—soft and silky. The finest sheets she'd ever felt in her life.

A blue velvet curtain hung around the massive four-poster bed. Gilded rose carvings decorated the wood above her. The curtains had golden roses embroidered into it.

Quinn opened the drapes and swung her legs onto the floor. Her toes scratched against hardwood.

But something was off. Her feet felt different. Pulling up a foot, she inspected it and nearly screamed at the sight. Her toenails were no longer bruised, and the pads of her feet had no calluses—perfectly smooth. She ran her fingers along her calf; the cut from the souvenir steamship was gone with no scar. Checking the rest of her body, Quinn discovered that every one of her scars had vanished.

Just like in the first chamber in the Mirror of Terror. It came true.

Her heart was a fast-flying hummingbird in her chest.

A sudden wave of memory hit. Compulsion and blood. And a vampire hovering over her broken body. Then, as the wave hit, it disappeared and was replaced by a wave of frustration gathering in her core. She had no calluses. Getting her feet into shape for ballet took years. Years of built-up muscles, broken toenails, and calluses.

She needed them to dance.

There were Royalle Ballet auditions to complete.

But if the first chamber of the Mirror of Terror came true, what was next? All of the chambers had gotten progressively worse.

Her stomach dropped to her toes, and her hands shook terribly. She was losing all control, and she needed to hold onto it tightly.

Control was freedom—it was safety.

Quinn rubbed her temples, desperately trying to remember. Only magic could heal and leave no scars. Had she gone to the healing mirror or some other looking glass? She'd been hurt. That memory was clear, but how did she heal? Had a mirror healed her but stolen her memory? Was that its cost?

Quinn stood and turned in a circle. Crystal sconces decorated with white roses lit the room dimly. Gold paint shone on the walls, glittering with expensive carvings. A violet armchair sat against the walls, and in the corner, was her massive wardrobe.

The bedroom door swung open with fury, and Giselle flew in and pounced on her best friend. Quinn grimaced and stiffened as pain raked through her body. She was magically healed, but her whole body felt unspeakably sore. "Ouch."

"Oh, sorry," Giselle said, releasing her arms.

Constance let out a low chuckle as she leaned against the doorframe. "Careful, Giselle, we don't want to break her."

Jevon strolled in as if on a breeze of wind and slowly slid into the violet chair. Always quiet, always assessing. Almost as if he believed that words were precious and only gifted sparingly.

Giselle plopped herself on the bed in a huff. "What happened, Quinn? You scared me half to death." A tear stroked down her cheek. "I wasn't sure if you would wake up. You were asleep for a day, and your entire tutu was soaked in blood. No human could survive a wound like that."

Quinn sank onto the bed. "I have no idea what happened. The last thing I remember is auditions."

Constance strolled over to the bed with the grace of a queen. A shock of heat sizzled up Quinn's arms as Constance said, "It's going to be okay. We will figure this out. All of it." It sounded as if she were trying to convince herself of that fact more than Quinn.

"We're here. No matter what," Giselle added.

"You scared us." Jevon steepled his fingers under his chin. "We thought you were dead. It was terrible."

A flicker of emotion came behind his normally kind eyes, almost as if a different, darker version of him lurked underneath. His protective and dangerous side. A side she loved about him. Jevon was cinnamon cake, warm, gooey, and lovely, but he also had a piece of him fiercely loyal and pure iron.

"You don't remember anything?"

"No." Quinn rubbed her temples.

A flash of trees and icy wind crept into her head. *The Nature District.* Memories sliced through the lobes of her brain. Disorienting and sharp. Burning bodies and a river of blood. White ballet tutus and vampires. And an attack. Emrys and blood. So, so much blood.

The memories faded. Quinn gasped, and her hand flew to her mouth. Fear and shock cascaded and coiled in her stomach.

Rolling her shoulders back, she tried to shake the fear and stabilize herself.

"What is it?" Constance asked.

Quinn's legs tingled as if her fear were a physical thing, piercing its talons into her entire being.

Upon her lack of an answer, Constance asked, "Are you okay?"

Quinn swallowed and passed the knot in her throat. "Yes. Where is Emrys?"

"Your uncle is blaming him for allowing you to nearly die," Constance said.

"Like it was Emrys's fault." Giselle jumped up from the bed and started examining items in the room as if she were deciding which of them she was going to "borrow." "I am pretty sure he is not responsible for every vampire."

The grandfather clock struck noon, and a rattle went through Quinn's bones as she remembered that she had to get to today's Royalle Ballet auditions.

"Oh, no. Auditions." Quinn rushed to stand but was stopped by Constance's arms.

Constance pushed her friend down with a hand on her shoulder. "Oh, no, you don't. You couldn't even dance right now if you tried. Give it a day, at least. You nearly died." Her voice shook as she said the last bit.

"But—"

"Emrys forced the Royalle Ballet Director to postpone yesterday, today, and tomorrow's auditions because he thought it was disrespectful to the illusion ceremony or some nonsense."

"He did what?"

Constance scrunched her nose and laced her fingers through the fringe on a throw pillow. "Our dearest prince canceled the Royalle Ballet auditions because you were unable to attend."

"He did what?" Quinn said again as the door opened to the prince and her uncle.

The two looked disheveled and like they'd just gone three rounds in the boxing ring, but neither one spoke.

"You canceled Royalle Ballet auditions?" she asked, her voice dropping in shock.

Emrys's mouth quirked. "Oh, yes, of course. The illusion ceremony is gravely important. Auditions cannot occur the day before or after it." He winked.

"Quinnevere Ashelle, what in the world were you doing in the Nature District?" Uncle Matias's voice dripped with disappointment.

Quinn's brow furrowed, and her shoulder blades drew together. "I—" She gulped. "I don't fully remember."

"You don't fully remember?" Uncle Matias's voice was a low hiss. "Get your things. You're coming home now."

"It is far safer for her here," Emrys said lazily. "We can protect her."

Uncle Matias's head whipped to the prince. "Like you protected her from the vampire attack?"

"I saved her life."

"After you put her in danger."

"Wait, what?" Quinn cut into the verbal sparring match. "Emrys wasn't with me. I sent him away after auditions."

"I thought you didn't remember." Her uncle crossed his arms.

Quinn sucked in a breath. "I don't remember the attack or how I got there, but I remember what happened before it."

"Precisely why you're coming home with me now." Her uncle pointed at the door. "He very well could've attacked you, and you wouldn't know it."

"Emrys didn't attack me."

"How do you know that?"

"I just do. And I am not a child." She folded her arms in a way that completely undermined her point, but she'd already done it, so she committed fully to the movement. "I have reached the age of majority, and you're no longer responsible for me." She paused, letting the fire in her voice settle. "I would like to stay here."

The blood rushed from her uncle's face, and a storm gathered on his features. "If this is your wish, then I'll leave."

As he reached for the door handle, Quinn said, "I love you, Uncle Matias, and I hope you can forgive me, but I have to see this through."

He hesitated with his back to her. Quinn's heart froze, and her mouth tasted like misery. Hurting the people she loved felt like eating poison. Guttural agony. Uncle Matias pivoted and tilted his head slightly before turning the handle and disappearing into the hall.

Silence dripped through the room like melting tar. Everyone was completely unsure what to say after that exchange. Especially Quinn. She'd never been so disobedient in her life. She was a rule follower.

Orderly. Precise.

"So, we have a problem." It was Giselle who finally cut through the tension.

Eight confused eyes landed on the beautiful brunette, but it was Emrys who answered in his practiced bored response. "What is that?"

"Vampires," Giselle said as if it were the most obvious thing in the world. "You have the Suitor Ball in two days, and it seems like a vampire is threatening our lives and possibly the humans at the ball. We need to find a way to protect them."

Jevon leaned forward in his chair, the noise catching everyone's attention. "What are your weaknesses?"

Emrys rubbed his chin, pondering the question. "We only have two. But only one you might be able to manipulate to your benefit."

"And do you plan on telling us what it is?" Giselle raised a walnut eyebrow, clearly annoyed by him dodging the question.

"Silver," he said, a devil-may-care smile dancing on his lips.

"Even the smallest amounts of silver can slow us down and incapacitate us, but it won't kill us."

Embers popped and crackled in the fireplace as the group contemplated the new information. "Would a lot of confetti laced with silver incapacitate you?" Giselle asked.

Quinn snorted, knowing exactly where her best friend was heading. Giselle was the inventor, but Quinn often helped with her experiments and pranks. One of her pranks was even integrated into the Viridian shows—her confetti bombs.

"Yes," he said.

A fiendish smile that matched Emrys's usual demeanor spread on Giselle's face. "Yeah, we can definitely make that work. Do you have a vacuum?"

He pinched his lips in confusion. "Of course, I have a vacuum."

"Do you have thirteen vacuums?" Quinn wrinkled her nose. She knew it sounded ridiculous, but Giselle needed motors, and one vacuum would not be enough. "Or access to motors? Vacuum motors would be the easiest to convert. Or possibly a camera. How many cameras and clocks do you have?"

Emrys stroked his lapel. It seemed to be something he did when he was nervous or confused or needed to center himself. "What are you going to make?"

"Silver confetti bombs," Giselle said.

"That could work," he said. "At least it would slow a vampire down long enough for any humans to get to safety."

"It's brilliant, Giselle. I'll help you make them," Quinn said.

"No, *I'll* be making them while you work out whatever it is you two need to work out." Giselle waved a hand, motioning between Quinn and the prince, her annoyance on full display.

"What do you mean?" Quinn raised an eyebrow, confusion licking at her core.

"Oh, come on, Quinn. You two obviously have a lot to talk about *in private*," Giselle said, cocking her head and examining the grandfather clock as if looking for the best way to gut it.

Emrys locked his gaze on Quinn as he slid his hands into his pockets. "We do have things to talk about."

Quinn knew this, but she didn't know if she was ready to find out the consequences of him saving her life again. The lack of callouses on her feet indicated she wasn't going to like what she heard.

THIRTY-FIVE

While Constance and Jevon helped Giselle create glitter bombs, Emrys and Quinn strolled through the palace in quiet. The only noise was the clicking of her heels against marble. But the prince's footfalls left no sound.

Eerie.

If the tension between the two were a noise, it would be a string quartet playing a somber melody at the climax of a ballet. A dark and bone-chilling song.

Emrys creaked open a door, the wood echoing old and forgotten tones. The ballroom was vastly different than the last time. Almost like the palace was sentient and in a terrible mood. There were seventeen well-known sentient buildings in New Swansea City. And given that when the Viridian's mirror was in a bad mood, the club's walls cried, Quinn was not counting against the possibility that the castle was alive.

Quinn's Mary Jane heels clicked against the marble floor as she glided through the room. The lights flickered in the wall sconces, singing a harmony of unease. The castle dimmed, and shadows danced with enchantment, some large and forbidding. Others were soft and small. And some a ghostly echo. The windows were covered in thick curtains, keeping out the light.

Whips of smoke lingered in the air like a myriad of candles had just blown out.

Emrys walked into the center of the room, but she didn't follow, preferring to stand at the edges of the darkness.

A chill licked Quinn's arms and down her spine. Eventually unable to wait any longer, she said, "What is it that we need to speak about?" Her chest rose with her deep breaths. "You look like you're leading me to my execution."

He chuckled. "I think it would be far more accurate to say it is *my* execution."

"Why?"

Emrys whipped around, and mist and shadows quickly engulfed him as he disappeared. A gust of wind stroked Quinn's skin, leaving gooseflesh in its wake. She reached out to the place he'd just been standing, and her fingers slid through thin air.

Vampire speed or something else?

Quinn pivoted, searching.

"Because you are going to hate me after I tell you," the shadows whispered. Emrys controlled them. They pulsed with each of his words. Was that a vampire power?

He appeared behind her, his breath mingling with her crimson hair. The distance between them felt like a physical, visceral thing.

It was a gnawing tension, begging to be released.

Quinn shivered, and her thoughts immediately drew to their kiss and how much she desperately wanted him to touch her like that again. Touch her with more than just his fingers.

"I had to mark you." His throat caught and brought her back to the moment.

She twisted around, placing a hand on his chest and digging her fingers into his cravat, keeping him from disappearing again. "Marked?"

He reached out and played with a single cinnamon curl, and she felt his body relax beneath her fingers. As if touching her in some way brought him peace—unlike every other time before when he'd winced.

Quinn gulped, dropped her hand, and averted her gaze. She was a coward. All she wanted was to kiss him again. Fuck him . . . possibly, but his reaction after their kiss scared her because she didn't know if she could handle simply fucking him. She'd want more, but he wouldn't be able to give it.

Quinn pulled away. She couldn't allow herself to want him. He was the Playboy Prince, and all he cared about was having a good time. And she wouldn't be one of his girls, not like that.

His kiss was . . . *wonderful.* But it would not happen again. Right?

Oh, fucking mirrors, it would probably happen again. Because the two sides of herself warred. The side that wanted to keep him at a distance and the side that desperately wanted to fuck him and experience the true pleasures in life. Ugh, she needed to think about something else, so she chose to focus on what he said.

"If I'm marked . . ." she started but didn't even understand enough to finish the sentence. "I need to know what that means."

"It's complicated."

"Uncomplicate it." The words lingered in the air between them.

"When I found you dying, I had a choice." He paused, like he was trying to figure out how to give bad news. "Either I let you die or save you, but in doing so, I had to mark you. Vampire blood heals, but it has high consequences."

"Wha—"

"But it's even more complicated than that. Based on the Vampire Accords, if I marked you, I would be breaking the agreement, and I would die."

Die?

He'd risked his life to save her. What did that mean? Did that mean he cared about her . . . or even *loved* her?

"You marked me, knowing that you could die?" Her indifferent mask crumbled and flaked like cracks in the molding of a decaying house.

"No, don't look at me like that," he said, waving a hand at her face, his usual uncaring arrogance sliding back into place.

"Like what?"

"Like I'm your chivalrous, charming prince." He cocked his head, his eyes as fearsome as a tiger about to strike. "I was fairly sure that I was no longer bound by my accord oaths because my painting was in the mirror at The Royalle Ballet. Given that I am not dead, it would see that I was right."

Still . . . that was a huge gamble—for her.

Quinn bit her lip, unsure of what to do with that information. "Please, tell me what being marked means."

He tilted his head. A gesture of respect. "When you die, you will turn into a vampire, and you will be drawn to your creator by a nearly irresistible force," he continued as anxiety crawled up her throat. "They will have sway over you, and the bond will make it hard for you to disrespect or disobey them. It's not a compulsion, but it's strong and lasting."

Quinn tensed. She wouldn't be controlled. Or bound . . . to him. Control was all she had. "Can a mark be overridden?"

"It's—" His eyes shifted, and a cloud of discomfort settled over him.

"It's what? Undo it," she snapped, anger pooled in her stomach. She was sick of being controlled and used like a puppet. Sick of being lied to and protected. "I don't want to be yours. I won't be your belonging to play with . . ."

He flinched. "I would never. I don't enforce the bond or try to control the vampires I've created. But I can't control if the bond makes you more . . . amenable."

"You mean obedient." Embers sparked in her blood; she knew Emrys didn't want to mark her, he'd even asked for permission, but she couldn't get over the intense frustration because she already wanted to kiss him so damn much. He'd already broken through her deep defenses, and now, she was magically bound to him, and it wasn't fair. "I will not be obedient to you." She said it more like a prayer than a statement.

He let out a low chuckle. "Now that I can believe. If it makes you feel any better, the bond should already be created, so if you don't feel compliant, it's possible it won't be strong."

Given that her first urge was to throw something at him—again. There might be hope that he was telling the truth because, at this moment, Quinn wanted to scream. She wanted to hate him. Not serve him, but still, this couldn't be true. She didn't want to lose her freedom. "Undo it. I don't want to be . . ." *A vampire.*

"It can't be undone." Guilt snaked in his voice, twisting and consuming.

"But—"

"You cannot be unmarked. Once marked, it cannot be undone. That's why we don't do it. That's why we have rules about it." He tried to explain, but she wasn't ready to hear it. She was still processing that no matter what she did, no matter how she died, she was destined to become a vampire.

A monster.

"No. I won't." Her eyes stung from holding back tears. "I don't want it."

"I know." He steepled his fingers and averted his gaze. It was clear he hated this conversation just as much as she did.

A memory crept into her mind like a spider sliding down silk. His words before he marked her. "An eternity dealing with you."

A sad smile played on Emrys's lips. "Yes. But I'll never force you to be a part of our family."

"How can I trust you?"

Emrys fidgeted with a pocket watch, clicking it open and closing it over and over again. But his pattern had no rhythm to it like Jevon's mindless tapping. But the sound caused her to remember a question that nagged at the back of her throat. "Does touching me hurt you?"

"It used to." He tapped his fingers against the table. "I should probably explain. Being a council member is a protection. Touching you is like getting jolted by a volt of electricity. It's excruciating. But now that I've marked you, it no longer affects me. Although now, other vampires will be repulsed by you. Being near you will be like smelling rotten eggs. And drinking your blood will burn and feel like daggers slicing open a vampire's esophagus."

"Oh." She gulped. "That's both horrifying and comforting."

"Yes," he breathed, and his lips were so close to hers. Butterfly wings tickled her stomach.

"It hurt you when you kissed me?"

"Yes." His eyes moved to her lips. "But sometimes there is pleasure in pain."

She inhaled sharply. Fuck. Her face fell, and her bones grew uncomfortably heavy.

"What's wrong?" He tilted her chin up while simultaneously steadying her.

"It's all my fault."

His eyebrows creased. "I am not following, Quinnevere."

"Jane's death," she said, "I thought we were equally to blame because you wouldn't kiss me, and you kiss everyone." His furrow deepened, but she continued. "It's about my Age-of-Majority Mirror-Rite. To complete my deal, I had to passionately kiss you, and you wouldn't comply. And because I failed, Jane died."

"Oh, Quinn, that's not your fault," he said, pulling her into an embrace.

Her head rested on his chest. "It's all my fault."

"Jane was murdered. Mirrors can't just make people murder someone else because of your deal. It doesn't work like that."

"How do you know?" She sobbed into his shirt. "No one truly understands how the deals work."

"What if Jane's death was simply a terrible consequence of timing?"

"It's not."

"Right." He said it as if he knew it was a fruitless argument he'd never win. "Who did you bargain with?"

"Beautiful Decay."

"Oh, hmmm," he said, and she could almost hear the gears in his head churning. "Nightshade would never kill Jane. If he did, his lover would gut him like a fish and hang him out for the world to see. Harlowe Merriweather is not one to trifle with."

"But what if the mirror didn't intend it to be the consequence?" Quinn murmured into his chest.

"Then that's Nightshade's fault, not yours." Emrys tilted her chin up to meet his gaze. "I know you like to control everything, but Jane's murder was because she was involved with the Blood Mirrors, not because of your rite." He stroked a thumb along her chin without a flinch or any sign of pain. "I promise."

She sucked in a breath. Much of their bodies were touching. Even when she was entirely distraught, Emrys was an electrifying force. "You truly don't feel pain anymore touching me."

"No." His eyes sparkled with mischief and dirty promises. She imagined the things he could do to her now that he wasn't in pain.

And she wanted all of it.

Quinn bit her lip. His kisses were passion personified. And oh, how she wanted a chance to experiment again. This time, she wanted to feel his tongue on a different part of her flesh. But—

She couldn't.

Because if she did, she'd want him to care about her—to want her. Rogue princes didn't care about their conquests.

"You can't kiss me or do more." She coughed. "I am not one of your girls."

He cocked his head, a reel of expressions playing on his face. He stroked one finger along her chin. "No, you are not."

The response stung more than she wanted to admit. He would never see her as desirable or as someone he could love. Not that she wanted that. Of course, she didn't want that. But . . .

She did want to be desirable.

She wanted someone to look at her the way Emrys looked at

his dalliances.

Emrys stepped back and slid his fingers into his pockets. The distance between them felt like a chasm, and she instantly regretted saying anything.

"What else would you like to know about me or vampires, Quinnevere?"

"Everything," she whispered. Before thinking, she blurted, "Can I study you?" She wished she could have taken the words back the second they left her tongue. "I mean . . . can I examine you? I would like to see how your . . . your body . . ." She gulped and bit the inside of her cheek. ". . . is different than ours. I just want to understand."

He didn't even flinch at the change in subject. Instead, he laughed softly. "And clearly, the only way to understand is to probe at it scientifically." It was a joke with the underlying message that *I see you, and I understand you.* And that act made her speechless. "I will let you study me if I can return the favor."

"What does that mean?"

"Everywhere you touch me, I get to touch you back."

Quinn's breath hitched, and wetness grew between her legs. Emrys was too talented at getting a reaction out of her body. It was utterly irritating and exhilarating. She ran her fingers along her lips as she thought and remembered the feel of him there . . . and in so many other places. But she had just promised herself she wouldn't be another one of his girls.

But did it count as being one of his girls if it were for science?

"Fine," she finally responded.

"Just fine?" he asked. "I would expect more excitement." She raised a rosewood eyebrow, and he chuckled. "Alright. I have a lab if you would like to do it now while we continue our conversation."

"Why do you have a lab?"

His cocky brow arched with amusement. "I enjoy science. Studying things and knowing how they tick. We're not so different, Miss Ashelle."

THIRTY-SIX

Ten minutes later, they were in his lab.

It had refrigerators stocked with blood bags, telescopes, medical equipment, and beakers filled with chemicals.

A chill stroked the back of her neck as she nervously fiddled with Emrys's equipment. Now that she knew vampires were still alive, her scientific brain wanted to probe at them. She wanted to know if there was a biological difference between them. She also needed science to keep her from thinking about everything that happened, from the murders to the threading notes to wanting to kiss Emrys Avalon.

Keeping busy and focusing on her insatiable need to understand things would keep it all at bay, and it would keep her lust at bay. Quinn would touch him, and she would let him touch her back, but the investigation came first.

Besides, she needed to know if blood flowed through vampires' veins, if they had heartbeats, and how their powers and reflexes worked.

It was science, and it was necessary.

One day, she would be one.

But this was the first alive person—creature?—she'd ever examined. It was different. For one, she had to ask permission to do things before poking and probing. But before doing that, she needed to set up the equipment and control the sample.

She needed her blood.

Being relatively used to pain—as a dancer, she pushed her body to the edge of pain daily—she decided to prick her finger for a sample rather than draw it from her veins. She placed four drops onto a slide, her mind whirling with disturbing thoughts.

She kept going back to the threatening notes.

If Quinn didn't find the killer or the mirror in the next three days, one of her friends would die. It wasn't an empty threat. She knew it. But she was nowhere near getting answers, and instead of trying to find the killer, she was studying a vampire.

Her heart crescendoed, the pounding rattling her ears, and her hands trembled.

"What's wrong?" Emrys asked. "I can hear your heart racing, and your face looks like you swallowed sour milk."

Quinn placed her slide down, causing it to clink. "The killer threatened to kill one of my friends if I don't find the third mirror, and instead of looking for it, I'm studying you . . . And I am going to let you study me. It's foolish."

"Do you think you can find the mirror when you're frantic and upset?" he asked, his tone calming and smooth like honeyed wine.

"No," she said softly. She could barely spell her name while in a frantic state.

"And what calms you down?"

"Dancing."

"What else?"

She raked through her mind and settled on. "Science. Figuring out how things work."

"Precisely." He smiled. "That's what you're doing. You're not wasting your time being here and studying me. You're exercising your brain."

"Oh." How did he have the ability to put her so at ease and calm her down when he'd only ever been an irritant before?

"And I promise, we'll find this monster before the ball," he said, his tone a dark conviction.

"You can't promise that."

"No, maybe not, but I can promise I'll rip out anyone's throat who tries to hurt you or your friends." He placed his hands in his lap, like he was waiting for her to proceed with her examination.

But instead of asking him to draw his blood, she said, "Are you still choosing a wife tomorrow?" She tried to flash a warm, supportive smile, but it came off more like an uncomfortable grimace, which matched his.

He nodded. "I have to."

"Why?" she asked as she gathered the serums needed to test blood type. "You're not bound by the accords anymore."

"But my family is," he said. "Some of the vampires that I'm responsible for are bound to the third mirror. If our secret gets out, they die."

"Oh," she breathed. "How does it work? Obviously, Kiara is not your mother."

He visibly swallowed and played with his cravat nervously. It was an emotion she'd never seen him wear before and went against his whole careless persona. "We agreed in order to keep vampires a secret every twenty-five years I would marry a new bride chosen by the council to be New Swansea's next ruler. A couple of years after the ball, my new bride announced her pregnancy, and she always had a baby boy whom we raised in Aberdare to keep him away from 'the corrupt city' until he turned sixteen. I use my glamour to age until I fake my death sixteen years after my son's birth. I then use my glamour to look sixteen while I return to the city and mourn my father's death. And so, the cycle repeats with different girls."

A new wife every twenty-five years, and he never got to choose them. He had no control over his destiny because he wanted to protect his vampiric family. It was a choice she didn't think she could ever make.

Quinn was too selfish. She needed to control her life and destiny.

"How does no one notice the pattern?" she asked.

"The mirrors erase people's memories if they get too close and don't know about the Accords." Now, her forgetfulness in the library made sense.

"Have you ever loved any of your wives?" she asked, not truly knowing why she wanted the answer. To satiate her curiosity?

"No, I do my duty." His voice was grave. "That is all."

"Are you happy?" When she was only met with silence, she asked a different question. "How many times have you been married?"

"Twenty-six."

Silence swirled around them in dark rivulets, matching his mood. The air in the room was filled with awkward tension. Somewhere in the last day, the nature of their friendship had changed. He'd saved her life and shared his deepest secrets with her, and she felt the urge to be close to him. To share with him parts of herself she didn't let others see.

But that also scared her.

To break the tension, she asked, "Can I sample your blood?"

"Yes," he said, and before she could get a needle to draw blood, he cut his hand, placing four drops onto a microscope slide.

Surprise laced her lips.

"It's fine." He answered her unspoken question. "It will heal in a couple of minutes. But if you stabbed me, it would take roughly an hour to heal."

"Is that an invitation?" she asked, grabbing a slide.

Emrys laughed. "Maybe another time." A devilish charm danced in his eyes.

She swallowed, concentrating on her work. "So, it takes an hour to heal from a stab wound?"

"Unless you expose the wound to the starlight." He tapped his fingers on the exam table he was perched on.

"What happens with starlight?"

"We heal at triple the rate."

Interesting.

Grabbing both slides, she added a drop of anti-A serum to one sample. To the second drop, she added the anti-B serum, and to the third drop, she added the Rh serum. The fourth drop she left alone. After waiting a couple of minutes, she checked the slides to see the reactions. Emrys's blood clotted in the anti-A serum and the B serum, meaning that he had type AB blood.

But the sample was strange.

The Rh clotted only partially. If Rh clotted, it would indicate a positive blood type instead of a negative. This might indicate that he had AB-positive blood, but there was something strange about the Rh sample. Quinn quickly turned on the microscope and peered at the blood on the highest magnifying level. There were A and B antigens and the Rh protein on the outer rim of the red blood cells. There was also another protein alongside, attached to the Rh. It was something she'd never seen before.

No one had an extra protein on their blood.

At least no *human* did.

Was she staring at the vampiric blood type?

Curious, Quinn checked her blood to see if it was normal. She anticipated that it would be. After all, she wasn't a vampire yet.

The results horrified her. She had type O blood, but her Rh matched Emrys's. Under the microscope, her blood also had the mutated Rh with an extra protein attached. Quinn's heart rattled in her chest. This was not normal.

Did her blood change as soon as she'd drank Emrys's?

Quinn dug her nails into her hair. She didn't want this.

As if sensing her dismay, Emrys asked, "What did you find?"

She told him everything.

"Interesting." He stroked his chin.

Wanting to focus on anything other than her sample, Quinn continued the examination. She strolled over to Emrys, who sat on an exam table and grabbed her stethoscope. "Can you take your shirt off?"

A cocky grin climbed onto Emrys's face. "I thought you'd never ask."

She didn't reward his arrogance with a response. Her traitorous heart marched to the beat of a war drum, climbing and racing in her chest. She noted it but refused to give in to her physical reactions.

He took off his shirt and exposed a chest of chiseled muscles. "That's a glamour, right? You're actually hideous."

"Tremendously so." He placed his hands in his pockets and dared her with his eyes. "Why don't you grab a mirror and see? It is the only way to see through a vampire's glamour."

She'd learned about vampire glamour in a picture book as a child. They were supposed to be stunning and draw humans in as prey. Just to wipe Emrys's arrogance away, she did just that and examined him through a mirror. The only difference was the scars etched across his face. But his abs, his perfect body, remained. Annoyingly, the scars made him more endearing and striking than his glamoured perfection.

But Quinn didn't understand. Her whole body healed when she was marked down to the calluses on her toes. "Why are they still there?" she asked. "Vampire blood heals. Starlight heals."

He averted his eyes as she placed the mirror on the table. "Every mirror has a cost."

He did not elaborate, and she did not press him.

"I think they make you beautiful." Quinn walked over to his shirtless chest, placed her stethoscope on a peck, and listened. The rate was very, very leisurely—just like him.

"What?" he asked, based on her reaction.

"It's so slow."

"Hmmm. And it's racing." Their eyes met, their breathing a bit ragged.

Quinn looked down and fiddled with her stethoscope and asked. "So, the normal heartbeat is even slower?"

"Yes," he whispered into her hair.

"But this is . . ." She counted the beats per minute. "This is twenty-five bpm. If this is fast, what is normal? A human's resting heart rate was between sixty and one hundred beats. "Are you even alive?"

He shrugged. "Hmmm, now that is the question, isn't it?"

Quinn ignored his mocking comment and continued the examination. She checked his muscles and reflexes. The latter, which she couldn't even see because they were so fast. All the while, she tried to ignore the fortissimo pounding in her chest and the wild carrion birds making havoc in her stomach. She found that keeping her eyes averted helped—a little.

Her hands studied his chest, and her toes curled because she knew it gave him permission to touch her there, too. But she needed to feel the muscles and see if they were different than human flesh. It would have been easier to study him if she could cut him open and see his muscles and organs, but she doubted he would allow that.

"Do you think becoming a vampire makes you evil?" Her voice shook. But it was what all of this was about—the examination. She needed to know what she was going to become. Would she be a monster?

He rubbed his fingers together as he thought. "I don't know. Possibly."

"I don't want to—" Her voice cracked like a rock hitting a windshield.

Emrys leaned forward and cupped her face. "I know."

"I don't want you to kiss me," she lied.

"I know." He dropped his hands, making it clear that he had no plans of kissing her. The absence of his fingers felt like torment. "I do believe you're the one fondling my abs. So, at the very least, you want me to touch you."

Glancing down at her fingers, which were indeed fondling his chest, she removed them as if burned. "I—"

"I wasn't complaining." His eyes sparkled with mischief.

After a beat, as if trying to settle her embarrassment, he asked, "What's my diagnosis, doctor?"

"Definitely not human," she said through a tense smile.

His answering grin was leisurely and toxic. It was the type of smile that would make her forget her aversion to kissing him, the type of smile that made her knees weak.

A distraction—she needed one badly. So she blurted the first thing that came to mind, "Can vampires turn into creatures?"

"No," he said. "It's just another persuasive illusion like the fog and blood rain at the Royalle Ballet."

"Will you show me?

"Yes," he said as his form melted away, leaving a golden peacock in his place. She jumped back, alarmed, and her hand accidentally stroked one of its feathers. The bird tried to nibble at her fingertips, and she stepped back again.

Emrys was before her again in an instant, and the bird was gone.

"I felt it," she said softly.

"It's a persuasive illusion. So real it's nearly impossible to see through." The smile on his face was brilliant, like looking directly at the sun without protection. It was too much in his shirtless state. She averted her eyes and changed the subject again.

"Do you also control shadows?" she asked.

"Yes."

"Is that something all vampires can do?"

"No."

She brought her eyes back up to meet his. "How does that work?"

"Some vampires have special abilities that others do not." He conjured a shadow tendril from nothing, wrapped it around her wrist, and moved it up her arm, leaving gooseflesh in its wake. "I have shadows, among other things."

But he didn't stop there. Quinn shuddered, and her breath hitched because, if it were possible, the shadow felt better than his hands. And for one moment, she didn't want him to stop. She wanted to fall into him, and she didn't care if it was real, if he cared about her, or even if it was their new bond that made it so—although she doubted it was the bond. She had wanted him like this long before, and Quinn knew that if she wanted to, she could say no, she could refuse his touch and push him away, and he'd respect it, but she didn't want to because she just wanted him for one moment of bliss.

Quinn pinched her eyes shut and let out a sigh as the tendril climbed her shoulder and spread up her neck and into her hair, splitting into more shadows as it went. Quinn grasped the lab table for support and stifled a moan. The sensation was just too powerful. If he wasn't careful, he was going to make her cum without ever even touching her core. And that was something she'd never experienced before.

"Oh, gods, more," she whispered, her knees growing weak. "I think I like your shadows."

One of the shadow tendrils caressed down her chest, stroking along the crests of her breasts and under her corset, and when it reached her nipple, Quinn let out a cry, and her knees buckled. She would have fallen, but Emrys was too fast. With vampire speed, he scooped her up and placed her in his lap. She immediately felt the hardness of his cock against her ass as his shadows continued their ministrations.

Her head fell back into the crook between his neck and shoulder, and her lips parted with a moan as his shadows circled her nipples and moved south. She spread her legs to him, her dress inching up as the shadows roped around them but still never touched her core.

"Emrys, I want . . ." *you to touch my clit. I want your full length inside of me. I want all of you.*

He let out a low chuckle. "You are a greedy ballerina."

"Yes." She sighed.

"I am not going to give you what you want. Not yet, because you're not done examining me, and therefore, I cannot touch you."

"It really feels like your touchin—" Quinn released a scream of pleasure as the tension inside her burst. She shook with her orgasm and leaned into him as he held her tight through it. When she finished shaking, she finally opened her eyes. The shadows had disappeared, and she was left in his lap, her head resting on his shoulders and her legs spread wide open to him.

How had he done that without touching her clitoris? Oh, gods, this man had magical abilities.

Embarrassment hit her like a ton of bricks. She'd been wanton *again,* and she knew it was all her and not some silly bond because she would have wanted that the night of her rite, and she did get a version of that the night of their kiss. But more than anything, she knew that wasn't the bond taking over because while she wanted to take orgasms from him, over and over again, she also wanted to punish him for marking her and calling her one of his girls after their first kiss, and a bond of obedience would never allow that.

However, even though that realization happened, she was still utterly embarrassed. Because that was twice now, he made her cum so damn easily. Twice, her body proved she wanted him. And that would not do.

Scrambling off his lap, she placed her feet on the floor and readjusted her dress, which the shadows had crumpled and displaced.

"Um, thank you for that demonstration." She swallowed hard. "I assume not all vampires have that talent."

"No." A way too satisfied smile stretched across his face.

Quinn suddenly understood why he was one of the most sought-after lovers in all of New Swansea. He made her cum without even touching her clitoris.

"So, back to studying me?" He wiggled an eyebrow. "There is one spot on my body you haven't examined." His eyes fell to his groin. "Are you sure you don't want to study that?"

Quinn inhaled sharply. *I want more than to study that.* Her cheeks warmed. Oh, he was going to be the death of her. Emrys was a dirty, hurtful, *talented* flirt. That was it. "Do you want me to examine your *corpus spongiosum*?"

"Is that the scientific word for my penis?"

"Yes."

He shook his head. "Of course, it is."

Quinn gulped, bit the inside of her lip, and picked up her notebook as if she were about to write some vital research in it. Quinn wanted so bad to fuck him. Especially since her heart and breaths hadn't calmed down from what he'd just done to her. But if she touched his cock, she knew they would fuck, probably on this exam table. But she wanted to mean something to him, and that would never happen. Emrys Avalon was an ancient, highly skilled vampire who probably slept with hundreds . . . if not thousands, of women. What was Quinn compared to them?

Nothing.

She was an inexperienced girl with a scalpel and dreams of being that kind of desirable.

But she never would be.

At least, not for him.

Quinn traced a finger along the side of her notebook. Quinn wouldn't fuck him today because, more than any of her other reasons, she wanted to prove that she could resist him—that being marked hadn't changed her. "I think . . ." Her voice was still too breathless and filled with need, so she paused to reel it all back in. "I am okay. I've read enough books. I know how that particular appendage works."

"Do you?" His eyes sparked as he raised a sculpted eyebrow.

"Yes, of course I do." She slapped her notebook shut. "I think we're done here." She averted her eyes and changed the subject again. "You don't have your shirt on." Her voice was mechanical and pragmatic.

"Well, I could remedy that for you."

"You should." Her heart quaked.

Emrys moved like lightning and was dressed in moments. Shaking out her shoulders, she sighed and let her body relax like a balloon slowly releasing air. Emrys disappeared in a blink before returning 2.5 seconds later. She counted, to be exact.

"There now, you won't be able to ravish me." He winked. "But I do remember you agreeing that anywhere you touched, I could also touch, and I don't think we're done with your lessons in passion yet for the day."

"I am fairly certain you just did way more than touch me."

"My shadows don't count," he said, exposing a dimple. "Besides, I plan to touch you with my mouth this time."

Quinn's breath hitched, and shivers snaked through her core. It took everything in her to say the next words, "Actually, no." A devious smile climbed Quinn's cheeks. If he could play with her, she could also play with him. "Let's take a raincheck on that."

"Ginger . . ." He raised an irritated eyebrow. "Are you telling me you're a liar?"

"Of course not." She wiggled her nose. "The first rule of bargains, dearest vampire, always specifies a timeframe."

"I highly doubt that is the first rule of bargains."

"You didn't specify when you would get to touch me, and so, I say, it is not today."

"As you wish, Ginger." He disappeared with his vampire speed and reappeared behind her shoulder, his lips at her ear. "But trust me, you will come to regret this." A shudder stroked up her spine. "One day, you will beg me to touch you again."

THIRTY-SEVEN

Emrys stole her breath and her sanity, which was precisely why she needed to postpone the "I touch you everywhere you touched me" session. Quinn needed to stop stalling and face her fears and her memories.

She *needed* to revisit the Mirror of Midnight.

The memories were the key to the case. Quinn recognized the vampire in the alley.

She knew it in her core.

Besides, she had promised to return, and the first time she visited the mirror, it wasn't all that bad. Her hand slid to the bald spot at the back of her neck. It wasn't too bad. It was only noticeable when she had her hair up in a bun, and even then, it was passable as done on purpose for fashion.

Emrys and Quinn walked back to her room to find Giselle sprawled on the floor, murmuring to herself, and completely ignoring everything else. She was surrounded by hundreds of tiny pieces from vacuums, cameras, and clocks. Jevon sat aimlessly, trying to help, but was more in the way than anything.

His head rose as they entered, but as per usual, he didn't say much, and Constance waved with a bright smile. But Giselle either didn't notice or didn't believe they required acknowl-edgment.

"I am returning to the Mirror of Midnight to ask her to restore my memories from the vampire attack." Quinn's words were met with three different versions of surprise.

Giselle dropped a wrench on her toe and mumbled, "Ouch," Jevon rose from his seat silently, concern etched into his roguish features, and Constance just stared at her with large, terror-riddled eyes.

"But you hate mirrors," Constance said, a wisp of air swal-lowing most of her words. "Are you sure you want to risk it again?"

"I have to," Quinn said.

Constance nodded, but all the blood leeched from her face. "Alright."

A couple of hours later, the group boarded a cable car leading to the Spirit Sector and the Mirror of Midnight. Everyone was there except Constance, who had to go to the Viridian for dress rehearsals.

As Quinn slid onto the bench, Jevon asked, "Quinny, can I talk to you for a moment." Unease rippled in his eyes.

"Yes, of course," Quinn said, sliding over and making room for him.

"You seem to be getting close." The words were encouraging, but something grim lingered in his voice.

"You seem upset."

"I . . ." He started and stopped as if not knowing what words to use. "I just don't want to lose you like I lost my brother. He was so obsessed with finding answers that he lost track of the things that mattered."

Quinn squeezed his hand, remembering their conversation at the Russet. "I am not going to be like your brother. I want to find the murderer."

"But you're already changing," he said. "You're doing things you never would've done before, like leaving home, whatever it is you're doing with the prince, and standing up to your uncle."

He had a point, but she didn't necessarily think that those were bad changes. She didn't feel any different. "Those things were always bound to happen at some point, but I promise, I won't change that much, but I have to continue this through. The murderer is threatening you, and I need to keep you safe."

He sighed and leaned back into the seat, his eyes on the city passing by. "I know, and I want to find them, too. I'm sorry, I worry about you."

"I appreciate it, Jevon, but I promise it will be okay." The words were not convincing, but if she said them out loud, maybe they could be true.

Twenty minutes later, they finally reached the Mirror of Midnight, where twilight lit up the sky in crimson watercolors.

A sea of ribbons whipped in the wind, and rose petals rained down the street. It was a treacherous time for the Day of Ribbons and Roses, the seventh day of the Blood Festival, because the city was on the edge of a storm. Yet the chaotic weather made the imagery more beautiful.

It was like a dance of color and remembrance, each bow representing a life lost not just in the Blood Rebellion but from any vampire attack.

Quinn even brought her own ribbon to tie to a streetlamp to represent all the lives lost in the Ashelle and most recent murders.

"Are you ready for this?" Giselle asked.

"No," Quinn whispered. "But that doesn't matter."

She stepped up to the swirling surface of the mirror, but Emrys grabbed her hand and pulled her back. "Do you want us to come with you?" he asked as if sensing her fear. "This isn't your rite. You don't have to do it alone."

She blinked, taken aback. She wouldn't have to do it by herself? "Yes, I would like you to come."

Wasting no time and not wanting to think about what she was about to do, Quinn moved into the liquid. It was as uncomfortable as the first time, like gelatin crawling up her flesh.

Gasping for air, Quinn entered a wonderland of living soap bubbles. The place was still composed of midnight dreams, but instead of being in the expanse of space like last time, she was in a black void, filled with bubbles holding galaxies and stars. And it rained golden stardust.

Emrys followed her, his usual ease painted on his face as he leaned against a bubble filled with stars. Giselle walked in the darkness with her mouth hanging open, but Jevon was nowhere.

Before Quinn could ask, Giselle said, "He didn't want to come. He's not very fond of—" Giselle nodded at the world around them.

One of the bubbles burst into pieces, sending more stardust flying, and Midnight stepped out with a saccharine smile coating her cheeks. Her pink hair glowed and danced on a phantom wind. "Hello, Quinnevere. It is good to see you again, and you brought me friends!" She clapped and jumped with joy, her words gilded with dubious intent.

Quinn's necklace buzzed, forcing her to pull it out. Once again, the crimson shard melted into liquid scarlet as it did piqué manege turns out of its cage. When it finally stopped dancing, the liquid metal solidified before shattering into tiny pieces and leaving the brunette woman, Blood, once again standing before them.

"Hello, Quinnevere." Blood smiled, and her eyes were green pools of love. It was as if she were seeing an old friend after years away.

"Ugh, you brought her again." Midnight's voice was a tantrum. "She's absolutely no fun. No helping this time unless I say so, Blood."

Before the two could get into a fight, Quinn cut in, "Midnight, I would like you to give me my memories back from the night I was attacked by a vampire."

"That's not my name," the teenage mirror with the baby-like voice said.

Quinn rolled her shoulders back, preparing to deal with the tricks Midnight would play. "What is your name?"

Midnight tapped her nose in thought. "Umm . . . I like periwinkles."

"Your name is Periwinkle?"

"Sure . . . Yes, I like that. Call me Periwinkle." She dropped her hand and smiled brightly. "So, you want your memories back. I could do that for a price, of course."

Of course . . .

During the exchange, Emrys leaned with his arms crossed in silence, amusement lighting his tawny cheeks. Giselle seemed fascinated. She followed each word as if she were cataloging it for later. The girl always responded to dangerous situations in adverse ways.

"What would you like for my memories?" Quinn asked. "Hair again?"

She didn't particularly want to give more hair, but she was willing to sacrifice her life to save people's lives. Especially her friends' lives, who would most likely be the murderer's next victims if Quinn didn't find them.

"No, not hair. I already have yours." She pursed her lips. "It would be no fun to take more."

Quinn heard the girl's words but was too stuck in thought to acknowledge them. *The mirror.* How much would that information cost? She vocalized the question out loud.

Periwinkle frowned. "Unfortunately, that cost would be quite steep. It's not quite soul-steep, but for me to give that information, I would have to defy another mirror, and it would cost me quite a lot, which means your cost would have to be as emotionally or physically high as mine."

Not quite soul steep.

It was *too* steep.

So, she would focus on finding the mirror a different way . . . possibly using her necklace?

But for now, she focused on the killer first.

"So, how much for the memories?" Quinn asked.

Periwinkle tapped her nose again, her face bright with mischief. "You could give me five days of your life or your necklace or a gallon of your blood."

That would be nearly all of it. No one would survive giving a gallon of their blood. An adult human had roughly 1.5 gallons of blood in their body. Quinn opened her mouth to respond when the Blood Mirror spoke.

"You must be very lonely," Blood said, her head tilting empathetically.

Quinn narrowed her eyes, unsure if the brunette was compassionate or faking it. Both mirrors were gutturally unsettling, but at least Periwinkle's motives were clear. On the other hand, Blood was a shroud of darkness and mystery.

A shiver skated down her spine.

"I am an endless abyss of isolation," Periwinkle said with a sigh, her voice light and filled with childlike awe.

"And hyperbolic." Giselle tittered, enjoying herself far too much.

"Yes, yes, that big word, too," Periwinkle agreed.

Quinn cleared her throat, trying to get them all back on task. "We're discussing payment for my memories."

"Oh, yes." Periwinkle rolled her eyes. "You're about as much fun as Blood. But I like your friend, Giselle Catalina Reyes-Vega, daughter of—"

"Yes, I like you too." Giselle cut off the girl before she would give away any of her personal information.

"You could give me some of your hair," Periwinkle told Giselle. "Or maybe a toenail."

Before Giselle could offer to rip her toenail off—something

she would definitely do—Quinn said, "I think I'll be paying the cost."

The one controlling the situation.

"Oh, fine." Periwinkle loosed an exasperated breath. "Maybe I could give you something as a cost, Quinnevere. How about acne? Your face is way too pretty. Or maybe I could give you bad luck for the day. Or I could break your leg. That would be a nice present."

"I think you need to redefine your concept of presents." Giselle laughed, enjoying this far too much.

You must be very lonely. Blood's words rang in her ears. *Lonely.* It was a hint. Quinn's gaze caught on the brunette, who nodded and smiled softly as if she knew precisely Quinn's thoughts. She was beginning to realize that Blood didn't speak unless it was useful.

But why?

Something about the way the mirror looked at her made Quinn's unease melt away. It was love—pure love.

An uncomfortable emotion. Quinn gulped. "What if we stayed with you and kept you company for the day?"

The violet pools in Periwinkle's eyes shifted from amusement to sorrow at the words. Vulnerability was painted across her face. It was the expression of a lonely little girl, trapped and desperate for friends.

Periwinkle visibly swallowed. "I'll accept this cost if you also promise to come back to visit me again!"

Quinn felt for the mirror. Her heart was fragile glass, moments away from shattering. Quinn hated seeing others in pain. "The day is to be taken immediately and only the normal twenty-four human hours of our day."

It was a gamble. Quinn needed all the time she could get to solve the case, but if she had her memories back, she might be able to find the killer before they struck again. A lost day would put them just before the Illusion Ceremony and the day before the ball.

It would work.

"Yes, I agree," Periwinkle said.

A day later.

Shock shackled Quinn's brain as she fell out of the mirror and hit the ground hard on her uncalloused hands and feet. She let out a groan and leaned back on her knees. Her breaths came in waves of tension. Her memories suffocated her and processing them seemed impossible.

Emrys gracefully stepped out of the mirror and crouched beside her, watching.

She leaned back on her feet, her mind a splattered painting. Splotches upon splotches of information danced and pulsed at her brain and gave her a piercing headache. Quinn rolled her knees into her chest and hugged them close.

You were never supposed to be involved. The words hit like wildfire. Consuming and inescapable.

It's what the vampire said in the alley. The truth hit with the force of a nightmare. Everything from the ally rushed back in with the weight of a cable car. And the vampire's slender face formed and burned into her mind.

Constance.

DAY
TEN

PRICE 2 CENTS

| BREAKING NEWS | # The New Swansea Times |

TUESDAY, NEW SWANSEA CITY, 99th DAY OF AUTUMN, 700AV

THE PRINCE WAS SPOTTED WITH THE BEAUTIFUL UNCONSCIOUS BALLERINA

****Editor's Note: Prince Emrys is much more handsome than depicted.*

Prince Charming was seen holding the unconscious ballerina in his arms. It is currently unknown what happened to the stunning dancer, but the prince's face looked like murder. Could he possibly be in love? Or did the ballerina simply swoon for the attention—cont. page 3

UNCONSCIOS BALLERINA

The Ninth Day of the Festival of Blood Arrives

As is tradition on the ninth day of the Festival of Blood, the funeral ship will be lit, and mirror illusions will glow for every human death during the Blood Rebellion as a remembrance. Three-hundred-and-forty-two lives were lost in the war for humanity, and each one of them will have illusions burn against the sky. Prince Emrys is expected to light the first floating funeral pyre tonight for the first time instead of Princess Kiara— cont. page 2

Thirty-Eight

onstance was the murderer.

Betrayal's talons scraped down the back of Quinn's skull. Constance was one of her closest friends. Someone who had always been there for her, so this was utterly unfathomable and deeply hurtful. Did Constance kill Jane?

Quinn felt like vomiting.

The betrayal tasted awful, like shattered hearts, poisoned tears, and melting pearls. Things that never should happen. Things like this.

And as much as Quinn didn't want to believe it, she scoured over the evidence in her mind, and all the pieces aligned. The glitter, the silver sequins from the dress she wore the night of Jane's murder, and the fang markings on all the victims. The feathers found on Jane's body probably came from Constance's Viridian costume. In Giselle's pictures, Constance was watching Jane on the night she died. The reporter died minutes before they arrived on the scene. Constance had both time and opportunity to use her vampiric speed to kill him before everyone else made it up to the room.

And the reporter's body was still warm.

It was possible.

And she had a motive. All the vampires did. Maybe Constance didn't like being under the restrictive Accords and decided to kill in order to free her painting.

It must have been in the first Blood Mirror. That's how she'd been killing for the last nineteen years.

And she created more vampires.

It all pointed directly to Quinn's best friend. Even the shooting star comment made sense. She could move faster than human sight could measure.

Despite knowing all of this. Quinn still wanted irrefutable evidence. Everything thus far was circumstantial. Constance could've been in the alley for an unconnected reason. But if they had her fingerprints, they might be able to match them to the crime. Maybe her past sample from the council meeting was manipulated . . . after all, Constance had access to the prints. She could have easily tampered with the evidence.

But to get a new sample, they needed to break into her rooms in the Courtesan Wing of the Viridian.

Quinn jumped up with ballerina reflexes and dashed up the street, but before she got far, Emrys appeared in front of her with worry swirling in his chestnut irises.

"What is it?" he asked.

"It's Constance." Quinn's voice crumbled to ash.

Emrys stepped back as if slapped. "It can't be."

The words were echoed by her friends who stared wide-eyed at the unfolding scene. Jevon tapped his fingers on his thighs for comfort, and Giselle let out a low curse.

"It is," Quinn breathed.

"You don't understand." Emrys reached out and clutched her hand. "The Viridian is a sanctuary for the lost and broken. Constance opened it with Kordelia to give people in desperate circumstances a safety net. She'd never kill your parents or Jane or even search for the Blood Mirrors. She has no motive. She wants vampires to be bound. Unless . . ."

"It's her." Quinn's voice trembled, and her heart thundered.

"I remember her face. She was one of the vampires who attacked me in the ally. *It's her.*" Tears rolled down Quinn's cheeks like patterning rain. "I can prove it. We just need to break into her rooms at the Viridian."

"I believe you," Emrys said, stroking a tear from her cheek.

They entered the labyrinth of the Courtesan Wing, and everyone but Emrys was disguised as performers. Quinn wore a tutu that flowed like a river of feathers from her hips to the floor—like a peacock resting in a tree, letting its tail dangle in the wind. Her face was painted with birdlike makeup, and her hair dusted with blue glitter.

Giselle wore her acrobatic costume, and Jevon was dressed for temptation—or, more correctly, not dressed. He wore trousers and a white unbuttoned undershirt, exposing his ivory-muscled chest to the world. The outfit was complete with a peacock blue cravat and top hat.

Traveling through the Courtesan Wing was difficult because the walls and halls were enchanted. They twisted and danced, and none of them went where she thought they should. Every night, the corridors changed directions and played tricks on the mind. The closer anyone got to the Courtesan Wing, the more the walls danced and moved. Almost as if they were purposely trying to keep a secret—trying to keep people out.

After all, the wing was forbidden.

The task of navigating was made slightly easier with Giselle and Emrys guiding them.

The walls responded to Emrys differently than the rest of the group. They reacted like an old friend, coming to visit after years of being away. They liked him. Which is why he led the group through the twists and turns and magic.

Unfortunately, Quinn was the slowest of the group, having pointe shoes strapped to her feet. Giselle, being an acrobat, wore no shoes at all with her costume.

Five strides ahead, the group turned the corner just as a wall solidified in front of Quinn, trapping her away from her friends. She pounded to no avail. The Viridian hated her, and it didn't want her to know its secrets—to be allowed into the depths of its soul.

"Dirty mirror." She groaned.

Twirling around, she tried to get her bearings. Randomly, she chose a direction and started walking. At every turn, the walls shifted and obstructed her way.

Perhaps cursing at the mirror was a mistake.

The shadows tracked her movements, and it felt as if someone were watching her. But only curtains and an explosion of red greeted her. Continuing her path, she walked through three more doors with still no sense of direction. She doubled back and tried to follow the way she'd come, but it disappeared into dust.

"Hello, Cinnamon," Emrys cooed in her ear as she jolted out of her skin. "Did you get lost?" Quinn slowly twirled around and stared up into his eyes. Transfixed. "Are you in need of rescuing?"

"This place hates me." She huffed.

"It protects its secrets." Emrys smirked and clasped her hand. "But you're with me, and I know all of its secrets."

"Of course you do." Quinn sighed and allowed him to navigate her through the maze. "Where are Giselle and Jevon?"

"Searching the rooms."

"Oh, good."

Emrys grimaced. "I know I promised I wouldn't do this again, but—"

He gently pushed her into the wall and planted a falsely passionate kiss on her lips. A kiss for an audience.

A show . . . until it wasn't.

It started as locked lips and guarded disguises. Emrys did his best to not actually kiss her—not like before. It wasn't a kiss for him or for her. It was an escape route. A way to distract the person coming down the hallway.

For the scandal that it was, it was the tamest, most respectful of stage kisses.

And it wasn't Emrys who turned it into more. It was Quinn who opened her lips with a sigh and deepened it into passion. It was Quinn who laced her fingers into his hair and pulled him closer. But she wasn't alone. He matched her fire with an inferno of his own, and soon he was teaching her so, so much more about kissing.

He was teaching her about lust and pleasure and devastation. For what they were doing would only lead to devastation. But Quinnevere Ashelle didn't care anymore. She was done fighting her physical attraction to him. Now, she just wanted all of him.

Someone cleared their throat and said, "Get a room, Princeling."

Breathless, his lips left hers, her heart beating a symphony of excitement.

Emrys glanced behind him, still shrouding her with his tall, muscled body. "With pleasure."

"And see that she makes her way back to the show." The sharp soprano voice belonged to the owner of the Viridian.

"Of course." A smug smile graced his swollen, just-kissed lips. He pulled her by the hand down the hall and into a room, his breath heavy as they waited for Kordelia to leave the hall.

"Well, that wasn't exactly as I'd planned it," Emrys said.

Embarrassment cried a river from Quinn's head to her toes. "We are not gonna talk about it."

"We're not going to talk about how you just attacked me?" Amusement colored his voice.

Quinn scoffed. "Who attacked who is debatable. Now, seal your lips, Prince."

"Are you sure you prefer them sealed?"

"Do you think it'd hurt if I punched a vampire?" she asked.

Emrys chuckled. "It would hurt, but not the person you intended it to."

"Silence, Prince."

Emrys mimed, sealing his lips before grasping her hand and leading her out of the room and farther into the Courtesan Wing.

With each step she took closer to Constance's room, more anxiety stroked her core. Quinn was about to discover if one of her best friends murdered her family. Maybe she allowed herself to get lost in the halls because she wasn't ready to handle the truth.

The pressure was dense.

Her brain wouldn't quiet. It kept circling through all the information over and over again.

Betrayal split her skull, filling her cell nuclei with chaos. A myriad of feelings circled in her baffled mind. Emotions she worked so hard to avoid and keep at a distance flooded through her bones. And she needed it to stop. She needed an experiment, a body or something to study, or to dance. Anything that would take her mind off Constance DeWinter.

She needed—

All of Quinn's thoughts froze in place.

Emrys hadn't led her to Constance's rooms. He led her to Constance and to the discovery of why the Courtesan Wing was forbidden. Quinn expected naked bodies in carnal acts, but what she saw was far more horrifying.

Five men were attached to blood bags, fully clothed, and completely dazed—drugged.

The women who performed the blood draw were famous Viridian Ladies, and they stole men's blood. Not . . . not seducing them. One of the girls—Ainsley, the singer—went from man to man and used her retractable claws to take a sip of their blood before saying, "You're having an erotic and pleasurable time. You're experiencing all your greatest fantasies. You will wake up feeling more than satisfied and wanting more."

Another girl drank directly from one of the men's wrists. The

Viridian Ladies were vampires—beautiful, flawless creatures of the night in more ways than one.

And Constance sat in a gilded chair that could've been a throne, licking blood off her claws.

Quinn stepped backward, trying not to make a sound or a fast movement, and she held her breath. Confronting vampires was a terrible idea. Confronting a murderous vampire was suicide, even if she had Emrys by her side. The best option—the only option— was to flee. She slid her foot through the air and tried to place it without noise. Unfortunately, Quinn was fucking human and had no ounce of stealth in her body, and once again, for the fourth time in a week, she made too much sound for vampires' ears because the floorboard creaked beneath her toes.

She squeaked as all eyes in the room turned on her.

Fuck. Again. This was getting pathetic.

Thirty-Nine

Every muscle in Quinn's body was as taut as a harp string.

"I see you are shocked and horrified, little dancer, but in fairness, you aren't allowed in this wing." Kordelia lounged on a chair, her feet dangling in the air. "And you brought her here, Princeling. Is she your sacrifice?"

Quinn cringed. She felt the vein in her neck budge as she took another slow step backward. "I—" she started, but she had nothing to say.

There was nothing to say.

Before Quinn could think, run, or do anything, a vampire moved with inhuman speed and trapped her against the wall, and two other vampires were on Emrys, who didn't fight back. They held him up against the opposite wall as he watched the scene unfold silently.

Shock spiked in Quinn and ripped through her flesh. Another person betrayed her. Again. And it was all too much. Had Emrys brought her as a sacrifice? Were they all working together to free their paintings and take over the city? Was it all lies?

Fear captured her tongue, and she couldn't say anything or do anything but hear the pounding of the beast in her heart, begging to break free of its cage.

Kordelia sauntered up beside them. "What should I do with a human girl who won't listen?" She clicked her tongue. "Naughty, naughty, naughty."

The vampire holding Quinn flashed her retractable fangs before biting down on one of her claws. It was sultry and disturbing all at once.

A trail of gooseflesh licked up Quinn's arms, and she felt the blood leech from her face.

"The men," Quinn uttered, not meaning to say it. Fear cut her stomach and stole her rational thoughts as her eyes rested on the blood bags.

Kordelia clicked her tongue. "Oh, don't feel bad for these men. They are all predators, every one of them." She picked at her fingernails. "We research and vet them. These are the dishonorable ones. The men and women who treat the people respectfully aren't taken to these rooms. We only do this to the vilest of men and women—although that's a much lesser number. The ones who abuse and assault innocent people. We would never do that to someone who didn't deserve it. But you aren't bad. You're a nosy human. What should we do with a nosy human?"

Quinn's heart hammered, and a tear of sweat rolled down her forehead. "Please, I—"

"Leave her be," Constance said with the steely timbre of a snake. "Although, I don't mind if you compel her to leave."

Kordelia treaded backward, obeying Constance's command, and the vampire holding Quinn loosened her grip but stood blocking the way out. "You will—"

"There is no need to compel her. She already knows about us and the council." Emrys cut in. "We came here to ask you, Constance, if you killed Jane?"

"Of course not."

"Are you willing to let us sample your fingerprints?" he asked steadily.

"Of course!" she said. "I have nothing to hide." Constance

seemed to get the irony of her statement because she amended it. "Well, nothing besides this."

"Really, you have nothing to hide?" Giselle scoffed, stepping into the room from the hallway. Jevon strode in beside her, tapping his fingers on his pants. The tapping became more frequent when he was upset, and his expression painted a thousand pictures of distress.

"Then explain how we just found this hiding in your bedroom?" Giselle held up the silver sequined dress between two fingers as if it were the plague. The dress was drenched in blood, almost as if it bathed in it.

Quinn clutched the wall, her knuckles turning white. "Oh, fuck," she whispered and fell to her knees, her body crumbling under the weight of this knowledge.

There was no denying it now. Constance killed Jane. The evidence was unshakable.

Quinn's body trembled and couldn't make it stop. Everything was obscured with far too many useless feelings, and she didn't know how to think anymore or find the reason. Constance didn't just kill Jane—the closest person Quinn had to a sister—she also threatened Quinn—and had tortured and tried to kill her.

There were no words for that level of betrayal and heartache.

Quinn smashed her hands into her face, clawing at her cheeks. She hated emotions so much. Sometimes, she wished they could be removed altogether.

The second and third fears from the Mirror of Terror were coming true: public emotions and a friend's betrayal.

Shit. Shit. Shit.

But more importantly, Constance was a monster and a murderer. *Jane, her parents, the girl in the alley, the reporter.* So many people died at her hands.

Quinn's breaths quivered. "How could you, Constance? You're one of my best friends. And all this time we've been investigating Jane's murder together, you were responsible."

Constance took a step back, her eyebrows performing a grand

jeté. "Quinn, I haven't been investigating Jane's murder with you, and as much as I love you as a friend, I would never consider you my best friend. I only dance ballet with you and only sometimes. I mean, I haven't even been at class in weeks."

"I . . . what?" Quinn flinched, confusion lighting up her core. "You've been at auditions all week, haven't you?" Was Quinn going crazy, or was Constance lying again? "I've been with you every day this week. I've known you for three years. We do almost everything together."

Quinn held her breath, her insides melting into ash. Nothing made sense. Constance was her friend . . . her best friend . . . something was wrong, and Quinn didn't think it was just an effect of the Viridian mirror anymore.

"Oh, well, that answers my suspicions." A delighted smile climbed Kordelia's porcelain cheeks. "Seren's back."

What the fuck did that mean? Quinn swallowed hot coals.

"The only thing that is relevant here is that you killed Jane and betrayed us," Giselle said. "And we have proof." She handed the pictures from the night of the murder over. "You were wearing this dress." Giselle held up the dress between her fingers. "And it was found covered in blood in your rooms."

"Like she would keep it in her rooms," Kordelia scoffed.

Constance stared down at the pictures between her fingers, her face a stone statue, unmoving, and her emotions masked. She turned her gaze to Kordelia and said, "It would seem I must apologize. You were right."

Without saying anything else, Constance handed over the photos to her sometimes-lover.

Kordelia—whose face was poison—glanced at the photos and said, "Yes, Seren is back and apparently more destructive than ever." Kordelia pointed to the picture. "That is not Constance."

"My camera," Giselle started.

Kordelia held up a hand, silencing everyone. "Before you argue with me, just know that I am not foolish enough to mistake my lover's twin sister for her more than once."

"So, it did happen once?" Emrys raised a cocky, far too interested brow. "I'd love to hear that story."

"And I'd love to put a knife through your heart. I know it wouldn't kill you, but I imagine it would hurt quite a bit," Kordelia purred like a hunting lioness.

Emrys loosened his cravat. "Maybe we can play that game another time."

"Wait." Quinn's voice quivered. "Constance, you have a twin sister?"

"It would seem that her twin sister, Seren, has been impersonating her for some time now." It was Kordelia who responded. "This one is Seren." She held out a photo of Constance in a silver sequined dress. "And this one is Constance." She held out the second photo, but this time, she was in a silver velvet dress that barely sparkled.

Constance lowered herself into a chair and sighed. "Your murderer is my sister."

"Oh, holy mirrors," Quinn gasped and stared at the photos closely, her heart rupturing. Lies. So many lies. She didn't even know what to believe. Looking at the pictures now, even knowing that they were two separate people, it was hard to tell them apart. Quinn couldn't find a single difference between them.

Kordelia returned to her throne-like chair and clicked her heels. "They may look identical, but trust me, they are worlds different. Hanging out with Seren is like hanging out with a party full of people high on Summer's Dust—" An upper drug known for giving people false happiness and far too much energy.

"Seren disappeared over twenty years ago, leaving New Swansea and everything she'd known behind. Kordelia told me she thought she might be back, but I didn't believe her." Constance sat up quickly, crossed the room, filled a glass with bourbon, and returned to pacing faster than Quinn could blink. "But I should've known. Seren is dynamite, waiting to explode."

"You're drinking?" Kordelia raised a concerned brow.

"Yes," Constance said. "It seems like a good time to start up again."

Kordelia let out a long-suffering sigh. "You should've grabbed me a glass," Kordelia pouted before standing up and grabbing one for herself. "Anyone else want a drink?"

Everyone shook their heads.

Kordelia turned to her sometimes-lover and said, "See, that's the proper way to get yourself a drink."

Quinn didn't know how to process any of this information, especially the lies, so she stood in silence, her heart tumbling.

"I should have known too," Emrys said, pulling his cravat from around his neck and removing his suit jacket. "Twenty-five years ago, Seren fell in love, but her romance ended very poorly. Her betrothed was a council member, but he wanted to have eternal youth like Seren, so they went to a mirror and bargained. The mirror gave him eternal youth, but it turned him into a monster. Or at least part of him into a monster. He was split in two—one half of him remained himself, and the other half only wanted chaos and destruction."

"It was like a demon lurking under his skin," Constance added. "Gideon held the demon at bay for a long time—"

"Until he didn't." Kordelia took a sip from her glass. "But I always thought he traded his empathy to a mirror?"

"He did, eventually," Constance said. "Or at least parts of it."

"What happened to him?" Jevon asked, leaning against the wall, tapping his fingers on his knee.

"He died at the hands of the council," Emrys said. "Seren vowed her revenge, and then she disappeared. I honestly thought she was more likely to refuse to drink blood and turn to stone than do anything to hurt anyone. She was depressed, not murderous. She was always a bit erratic, but she was kind and gentle at her core."

"So, now she is back and taking her revenge? What does that mean for the mirrors and your paintings?" Jevon asked.

"That's the true question," Emrys said. "What does she want, and why has she been so desperate to get it?"

"Maybe she just wants chaos." Kordelia bit at her fingernails in a far too seductive way. "For revenge."

Constance shifted uncomfortably. "She wants to destroy the Accords. That's always been her goal to destroy the laws that bind vampires."

Emrys rubbed his chin and stared at Constance, taking in her every micro movement and every one of her features, almost as if he were trying to paint her correctly in his head. "We have another problem."

"What?" Four voices said in unison.

"Seren knows all of our plans." He closed his eyes and sighed, almost as if he were mad at himself. "I should have known." His face fell into a mask of shadows. "She's been with us all along. Always one step ahead."

Quinn curled her fingers into the feathers on her skirt. Still too frozen in shock to do anything but listen. Her best friend wasn't who she said she was. She was a murderer, and she killed Quinn's parents. It was too much to process.

Tears fell freely from Quinn's eyes as she shook and shook and shook. Everyone was too preoccupied with their schemes and conversation to notice her.

"That means she knows about the glitter bombs." Giselle squeezed her fists tight, her face red with fury. While Quinn froze, Giselle fought. "She has the upper hand."

"No, she had the upper hand," Emrys said. "She has no idea where you were going to place them or how they work, and now that we know her plans and what she's been doing, we can stop her."

"So, what do we do now?" Giselle asked, worry twisting her normally brave features.

Fear, unease, and exhaustion painted the room. Quinn was still a statue of silence.

Eventually, Emrys glanced at her distressed expression, walked over to her, and placed a soft, gentle hand on her shoulder. "It's a lot to process. You're allowed to be afraid and feel betrayed. You're allowed to take a moment."

"We don't have a moment," Quinn breathed. "We need to find the third Blood Mirror and lure Seren into a trap."

"Yes." He stroked her cheek. "But first, we have to keep up our appearances and get to the Illusion Ceremony. The entire city is waiting for me to light the pyre. And I need to be there, or it would raise questions we don't want to be asked."

Forty

The diamond stars twinkled above, whispering secrets across the vast, shadowed expanse. The church bells of St. Grace Cathedral struck midnight, and Emrys stepped onto the dais to give his speech celebrating the loss in the Blood Rebellion at the Illusion ceremony.

The ceremony was a moment of breath for Quinn. A moment to process her reeling emotions and the fact that the last three years of her life were a lie.

The last nineteen years.

The ground shifted, and everything was hanging off-axis.

She didn't know how to move forward.

Quinn stood with the palace's retinue behind the gilded dais between her best friend and the girl who made life torture. Giselle and Countess Teagan. Quinn was utterly confused about why the prince wanted her to be among his palace's guests.

The violet-capped train of Quinn's dress swayed in a frigid late autumn breeze. Draped from her shoulders was an onyx velvet dress with a sweetheart neckline. The violet train flowed from the dress's back, adding a pop of subtle color. Despite its simplicity, the dress had a seductive shape. Emrys dressed her as a modest princess who shined more brilliantly than the elegant, uninvolved dress she wore.

Giselle and the countess, on the other hand, wore over-the-top designs. The countess in a canary yellow ensemble, complete with an armored bodice, and Giselle in a red sandstone piece that made her look like a gilded sculpture.

Jevon, per usual, managed to make his suit look loose, ruffled, and worn.

As Emrys's speech drew to a close, he held out his arm, inviting his retinue onto the stage. The group slowly gathered by his side, Quinn trying to hide in the back and out of the view of journalists, who'd been enjoying writing salacious articles about her and the prince.

There was no need to give them more cannon fodder.

No. Little ballerina, by my side. Emrys's honeyed voice echoed in her mind, and she jolted. She tried to keep a happy mask on her face despite the emotions rolling up her spine. Hearing voices in her head was utterly impossible, jarring, and crazy-making.

It must have been a vampire ability that she'd never known about before.

On the inside, she let out a very elaborate cuss and stared at him like *you have to be kidding me.* He couldn't have warned her about this before.

He winked. *By my side, little ballerina. Let's give them something to talk about.*

I hope you're not serious.

I always am, except when I am not.

He'd heard her thoughts too. What in the world?

Not now, I'll explain later. He held out his arm, waiting for her. And now everyone seemed to notice the silent looks between them. She searched the crowd, the camera flashbulbs raging as journalists frantically wrote on their notepads. Now, if she didn't comply, it would look horrible, so she forced a sweet, candy smile on her face and strolled over to the prince and took his hand.

I am going to kill you later for this. She flashed a twinkling gaze before turning back to the crowd.

I am sure I'd enjoy you trying, he said in her mind before turning to the crowd. "We honor all of the fallen, all of those who gave their lives to make New Swansea a safe country, free of the tyrannical rule of vampires."

Even this was a lie.

That's all vampires ever did. *Lie.*

A life built on lies. Constance—Seren—whatever her name was, was made for this life. She flawlessly performed deception, trickery, and murder.

Quinn's mouth tasted like acid, and she rolled her free fingers into a ball.

Emrys dropped her hand and motioned to a footman who handed him a bow and arrow. Once he nocked the arrow, he held it to the footman, who lit it on fire. Pulling the string back to his anchor point—his perfect mouth—he said, "Be with peace." Then he let loose the arrow, which cut through the air and perfectly hit the center funeral pyre floating on the lagoon.

Echoes of "be with peace" traveled through the crowd as more and more arrows flew through the air, hitting the 342 miniature funeral ships spreading across the lagoon. At that exact moment, the Mirror of Aurora awakened and released illusions into the midnight sky. Ten for each person lost in the war, each uniquely representing them. Some of the illusions were animals like doves and lions, others were lilies and roses, and others still were diamonds and lanterns. They climbed the night like fireflies dancing to the heavens, covering the horizon with speckled glowing paint.

The night sang with a somber beauty. A melody so soul-touching stole the sound from the festival, and people were so transfixed they refused to speak.

I like you in simple dresses, Emrys whispered into her mind, his focus on her instead of the brilliant spectacle in front of them.

She bit the inside of her cheek and averted her eyes, watching anything but the prince. She wouldn't like him. She couldn't want him because he'd never want her back. He'd never want only her—only one paramour.

You shine more when covered with elegance than feathers and sparkles, he said.

Why am I here, Emrys? she asked, still refusing to look at him.

He grinned and placed a hand on the small of her back—his touch electrifying. *Because the world needs a distraction from the truth, from bodies with vampire markings and break-ins, and broken mirrors, and the papers have always been obsessed with me.*

So, I am a distraction? She gulped, and an unfamiliar feeling raged in her bones. *What's your purpose for me being here?*

Tell me a secret, Quinnevere, he said, changing the subject.

"No," she breathed and finally opened her eyes to his.

I'll tell you a secret, not about who or what I am, but about me. His chestnut eyes glistened and reflected the dancing fire. *My secret is that I don't want to want you. I'd prefer to have no feelings or desires altogether.*

Confusion clenched her stomach. What did that even mean? Was he confessing to having feelings or just promising that he never would? Her palms grew clammy, and her mind fell into a spiral.

Anger prickled at her spine. He was using her—always using her. And she shouldn't have been surprised. He was a vampire, just like Seren. He used people for pleasure, for company, for answers, for a distraction. Quinn was no different.

She'd never be different.

And he'd used her earlier in the night, too. He brought her to the lion's den instead of taking her to Constance's room. He brought her to the vampire blood smuggling operation because he wanted answers from Constance. Emrys Avalon didn't care what Quinn wanted.

He only ever cared about himself.

If he was going to be cruel, then she didn't have to be friendly either.

I would also prefer to feel nothing for you. Her nose flared, but she didn't pull away from him.

"I know," he whispered into her ear, the touch of his lips sending shivers through her body. "Your feelings for me are written all over your face and in your words. You like science. You desire to experiment with me, but you'll never desire me."

"Good. We understand each other perfectly," she said, focusing back on the festival.

When they were safely inside the palace after the festival and out of earshot of everyone except Giselle and Jevon, Quinn rounded on the prince. "You can read my mind?"

"No," he said, a wicked and frustratingly arrogant smile lingering on his mouth. "I can hear the thoughts you project at me and vice versa because I marked you."

"And you thought instead of warning me or telling me you can do that, you'd surprise me in front of a public audience and news crews?"

His following six words were simple and made her want to murder him. "I wanted to see your expression."

Oh, she was angry. He'd used her, tricked her, and paraded her in front of New Swansea just to satiate some sick need of his to get a rise out of her—to play with her. And now she would be bonded to him for all eternity. This condescending, haughty, devilishly handsome prick. Nothing he'd done in the past few days had truly changed him. He only helped her solve Jane's murder for selfish reasons.

Always just about the paintings and the vampire agenda.

Emrys Avalon always was and always would be the arrogant, roguish prince. And she was so foolish to have let his stupid kisses soften her feelings toward him.

He chuckled softly. "Well, at least you think I am devilishly handsome."

"You heard that?" she asked, a vicious snake coiled in her stomach, waiting for the right moment to strike. And Quinn wanted to strike him.

"I can't help hearing it when you're shouting at me." He leaned against the wall and slid his hands into his pockets.

Quinn stepped in, about to confront the prince, when Giselle cleared her throat and reminded them of her presence. "As much fun as it is watching whatever this is"—she waved a hand at the prince and ballerina—"I need to set up the confetti bombs in the decorations along the walls and the lever release packages on the ceiling and the ignition spots, which could take me all night long. I need someone to help me do that."

Emrys wiped off his lapels. "We can help you."

From the shadows at the edge of the hall, appeared Teagan as if she had been summoned by magic. Given that Emrys could talk to his marked from mind to mind, she probably was indeed summoned.

"Do watch out," Emrys said, his eyes on his friend.

Giselle crossed her arms. "I am sure I'll be absolutely fine."

"Oh, I know you will be." His gaze touched Giselle's for a moment. "I was warning her about you. I've seen the way you talk to and about gangsters. Spoiled old Teagan doesn't stand a chance."

Teagan scoffed but didn't say a word.

"You're not staying," Quinn said with one hand on her wardrobe. She intended to get ready for bed after spending three hours helping Giselle in the ballroom, but Emrys wasn't leaving.

"I am." Emrys's mouth flattened into a hard line. "Someone has to stay in your room. Seren is danger—"

"I am well aware of the situation." Quinn crossed her arms and glared at him.

"Then you know exactly why I am staying in your room." He gracefully fell into the armchair.

She glowered at his perfectly quaffed hair and divinely styled suit. "Stop acting like I'm some defenseless doll you can play with."

He refused to answer. Instead, a taunting smile laced his lips, and he picked lint off his shirt.

"It's safer for me than it is for you," Quinn said. "Seren has your painting, but I don't hear us discussing your safety."

He squinted, his eyes whispering an emotion she couldn't read. "I am an immortal. I can handle it, and you are—"

"A fragile little human?" Quinn scoffed.

"Precisely."

A snake coiled in Quinn's stomach at his hurtful word as chills caressed her spine. "I am not as fragile as you believe."

"Every human is as fragile as I believe." He disappeared and reappeared at her side, leaning on her wardrobe. She tried not to flinch. She didn't want to prove his point. "I could snap your neck in a second, and you'd never see it coming." He reached out his arm to grasp her neck, but she swatted it away.

"Well, apparently, it doesn't matter because I am marked, and I'm gonna become a vampire whether I like it or not." She tilted her head up, her gaze a bloody machete.

A silence crawled between them—prickling and uncomfortable. Quinn reached out and grasped his hand and placed it around her neck. "So go ahead, snap my neck."

His fingers curled into a gentle caress as he drew his hand away. "Stop being so . . ."

"So . . . what? Cavalier? Like you always are?" she snapped. "I am sorry if I think it is funny that you of all people are lecturing me about my life when you're the one who stole it from me."

That was not fair, and she knew it. She also knew that he'd asked for her permission. She was just lashing out because of everything. *Seren*. The murders. Her feelings. And the last thing she wanted to be was a vampire. If she were honest, she also lashed out because she felt herself getting too close to him. Feeling too much. And that *couldn't happen*.

To love someone was to give up too much control.

Intimacy, connection, friendship . . . it was a plague to the heart. So, she choose antagonism.

She breathed in a slow, steady breath, trying to calm herself.

"At least turn around so I can get dressed," Quinn said, pulling out the least glamorous négligé she could find, but this was the palace, so they were all glamourous.

When he'd fully turned around, she quickly undressed and threw on her sleeping attire. "What about Giselle and Jevon? Who is watching them?" she asked, closing her wardrobe.

"Teagan is staying in Giselle's room, and my second is with Jevon. They're safe, just like you." He emphasized his last words, making his earlier concern abundantly clear.

"Fine." She sighed, walked to her bed, and slid under the covers. Emrys returned to the armchair, and she felt his gaze on her like a living breathing thing.

She lay there and stared at the carved bedframe, trying to avoid the electric tension in the room.

Eventually, she said, "Are you going to sit on the chair all night?"

"Yes," he said slowly.

"Are you going to sleep in it?"

"Yes."

"That's foolish. Do vampires get kinks in their necks?"

"Yes."

Quinn shut her eyes tightly, knowing that she was going to regret her next words. "Sleep in the bed. Just don't touch me."

He chuckled. "If you insist."

"I do."

He slowly laid down on top of the blankets as if not wanting to disturb her. For a while, they both stared up, neither wanting to say anything. Turning on her side, she made sure her back faced him.

His body felt close—too close. He tensed, clearly as uncomfortable as her. Quinn counted his rhythmic breaths. A soft, slow tempo. Controlled and steady. They were in contrast to hers, which were ragged and tight. Wild heartbeats pounded in her ears, and she knew he could hear them.

A flush crossed her skin.

Desire rippled through her stomach like eagles taking flight. She felt the phantom sensation of his lips on hers and how absolutely glorious he could be with his hands and tongue. And she wanted to feel it all again.

Her fingers hovered over her lips, desire a beast in her belly.

She wanted to roll over and kiss him, but instead, she said, "I'm sorry about the marking comment. That was not fair of me." She tensed, still on her side. She could apologize, but she couldn't do it while meeting his eyes. "I know that you saved me and extended my human life. I know that you asked before you did it." She sucked in a deep breath. "I—I lashed out."

He turned, his body warm and reassuring next to hers. She wanted more than anything to lean into him. To feel him against her. To let him comfort her.

"I was an overprotective asshole," he said, all his usual swagger gone. "I just—I don't want anything to happen to you."

Quinn inhaled sharply and rolled over, her eyes locking onto his. "I know. We were both being assholes."

"So, our normal?" He laughed, a brilliant, low sound that reverberated through her heart.

"Yes," she breathed.

The tension between them crescendoed. He leaned in and rested his forehead on hers, caressing her chin. A shiver ran through her whole body. Her want was slowly killing her inside. It was a living force, hungry, and demanding. But she wouldn't be the one to kiss him. He had to do it.

"Emrys." Her voice was soft like seduction, but she had no idea if she was seductive. "Will you touch me everywhere I touched you?"

A tense, needy silence lingered between them, and his eyes darkened to the shade of shadows, but he refused to lean in or say anything until . . .

"I promised I'd make you regret it." He flicked her nose softly and ruined the moment. "Go to sleep, Quinnevere. You have a big day tomorrow. We will find the mirror and capture our murderer. We'll have plenty of time later for me to ravish you."

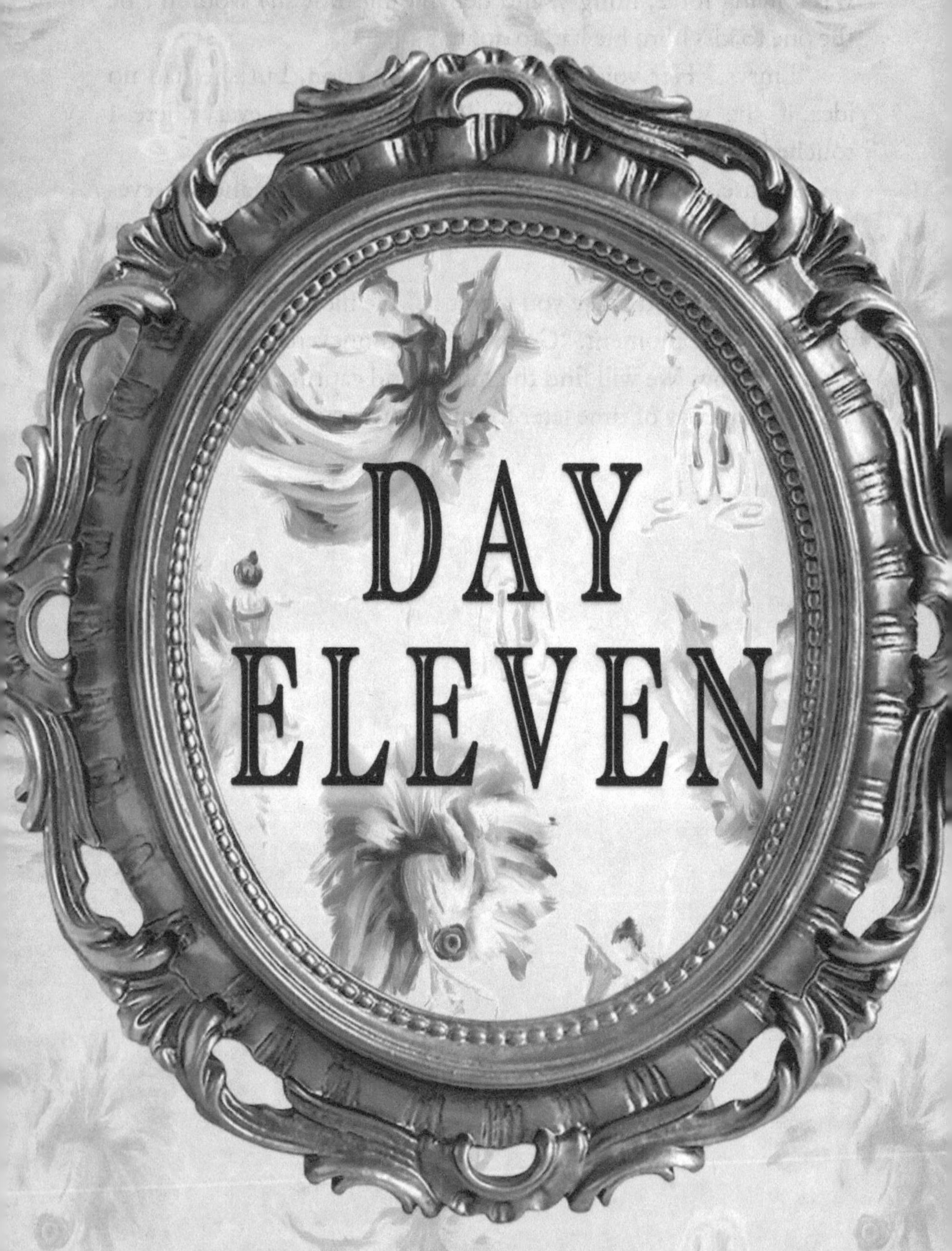
DAY
ELEVEN

PRICE 2 CENTS

BREAKING NEWS

The New Swansea Times

WEDNESDAY, NEW SWANSEA CITY, 100th DAY OF AUTUMN, 700AV

PRINCE KISSES BALLERINA

While we have long suspected that Prince Emrys and the Ballerina have been sharing intmate moments, last night it was confirmed. The two were seen kissing in the Courtesan Wing at the Viridian. A source says the two then retired to a private room for some *alone time*. We have long known of the prince's prowess under the sheets, but it seems that the Ballerina has experienced it as well. Is the prince in love or is it simply lust?—cont. page 3

The Night of the Royalle Suitor Ball Arrives

All the preparations are set for the 27th Royalle Suitor Ball and girls from all over the kingdom are hoping to be chosen as Prince Emrys's bride. We here at the New Swansea Times believe the Prince will choose his new lover Quinnevere Ashelle as his betrothed. She is beautiful and feisty, just what the prince likes—cont. page 6

FORTY-ONE

By the time Quinn rolled out of bed, Emrys was sitting in the armchair and dressed in a different suit, with a mustard vest and purple cravat. He always wore purple in some form. But usually, he preferred it in his vest.

"Good, you're up. You need to get dressed." Emrys pointed at the pile of clothing he'd picked out for her.

It was a ballet leotard and a simple skirt. Quinn stared at him, confusion pooling in her stomach. "We have to figure out where the mirror is and find a way to stop Seren. The ball is tonight. The threat. There is no time for—" *Ballet auditions.*

She swallowed the last words, unable to get them out. They hurt too much. But she was willing to give up her dreams if it meant saving her friends and all of the innocent people who might get caught in the crossfire.

"We have to go back to the Mirror of Midnight and bargain for the Blood Mirror's location," Quinn said, no longer caring about what the cost might be. If it would protect her friends, she'd be willing to pay the cost.

They'd discussed searching for the second mirror by strategically walking through the city and seeing if the blood necklace reacted, but that could take forever, so the mirror was the only way.

"We have time, Quinnevere. You don't have to give up your dreams to save your friends," Emrys said. "You can have both."

"Your lack of urgency is unsettling—"

"We have a plan, and we will find the mirror." He stood up, and in three strides, he cupped her cheeks tenderly. "You don't have to give up what you want for anyone." Her heart beat wildly. "Put your clothing on, go to auditions, and then we can get our answers."

She nodded, unable to say anything. The man was too confusing. One moment, she hated him, and then he did things like this. Things that made her believe he might actually care about her.

His fingers gently caressed her cheeks as they moved away. Then he excused himself, saying that he would be waiting in the hall. She quickly pulled on the ballet leotard and the skirt. The pas de deux she was to perform did not require a tutu. *Lover's Lost* was a ballet developed from ancient myths, and therefore, the ballet had more flowing costumes than the typically stiff and structured tutu.

Swinging open the door, she met Emrys in the hallway. He escorted her from the floating gondolas to the Gold Quarter.

For what felt like the first time, Quinn arrived at auditions on time. Emrys strolled behind her and let the Royalle Ballet director know that he was going to watch auditions again.

But when it was time to perform her pas de deux, her partner was missing. Apparently, he broke his foot during the Illusion Ceremony. Quinn walked to the center of the room, at a loss for what to do. She couldn't dance without a partner. But just as she was about to give up and ask the pianist to play the music for her solo variation, Emrys stood, walked to the center, and held out his hand. "Miss Ashelle, would you honor me with a dance?"

Through her teeth, she asked, "Do you know it?"

"Of course I do." He smiled, his hand lingering in the air between them. "Are you ready?"

No.

But she slid her fingers into his, anyway. Music played a three-four-time signature.

"Try to keep up. This dance is complicated." He pulled her sharply into a hold.

She scoffed. "I hope you're kidding."

At first, she was stiff and unfeeling—afraid—moving as if she had cinderblocks connected to her feet.

Emrys whispered, "It's okay, Quinnevere. Let go. I'll catch you."

The veins in her neck budged, and her shoulders were tight and unyielding. She didn't know how to let go, how to let someone catch her. Let someone else take control. But she wanted to try.

The piano sang a somber and hollow melody as their bodies slipped into a rhythm. Her heart hammered, so scared, so resistant, in her chest, but she ignored it and plunged in the dance with the prince.

With *her* prince.

But it was different than any other dance. It was intimate, connected, and emotional. Quinn enjoyed the feel of his fingers resting on the small of her back and their interlaced hands. The simple way he guided her body.

Untamed emotions flowed through her, along with the music and dance. Butterfly wings flapped and caressed her heart with every beat. Nerves jittered through her bones. Not the normal jittery nerves she'd get before a show. No, these were the nerves that made her fear messing up, the nerves of getting too close— the nerves of losing the things she loved.

And she did not want to mess up, not with Emrys.

He twisted her around and pulled her into a tight hold.

It was a dance for enemies and lovers. It started with an intense hatred for each other with quick and sharp tango positions. But at the halfway point, the story changed and softened. And turned intimate and close.

"So, you *can* follow," he breathed into her hair.

"Of course I can."

"You're normally so controlled. I wasn't sure you would let me lead for once."

Emrys whipped her out like a lasso before slowly, sensually reeling her back until the sides of their noses touched. His scent made her insides quiver. And she wanted nothing more than for him to tilt his head slightly and brush their lips together.

She was hungry in a way she never knew she could feel.

Tango was defined by its sharp and precise feet movements. Quick, quick, slow. Quick, quick, slow. Passion. Hatred. Heat. Lust.

Their tension was a tightrope. Electricity sparked between them. He slid his hand up her thigh, and she shivered. Her whole body felt alight with fireflies, buzzing and warming her soul. She told a story with her feet. A play of seduction and yarning. She tracked her fingers along his chest, curling into his chiseled pectorals as she twirled around him.

The movements became quick and heated. Angry and burned. Fast. Whip. Fast. Whip. A play of interlocking feet. Synchronized enemies and warring nations. Fire split the air between them, consuming their motion.

Pain rippled through Quinn's feet. The lack of calluses made the dance incredibly painful. It was like running a marathon in slippers.

He pulled her into a twirling lift. Holding. Supporting. Controlling. A move that required total trust. Total release. It ended in a fish dive, and if they messed up, she would fall on her face. But he held her tight—safe.

Passion surged between them.

As the dance progressed, the movements grew slower and slower. In their final step, he dipped her before drawing her by the nape of her neck. Their eyes met, their lips hovering, nearly touching each other.

A spark burst between them.

She wanted more than anything for him to lean in and kiss her. But instead, he said, "I don't think anyone could say your dancing isn't passionate now."

"I think you're a little like poison." She panted, her chest rising frantically with every gasp. "You wreak so much havoc in my heart."

"Funny because I was thinking the same thing." His fingers laced into the hair behind her ears, and she shivered beneath his touch. "You make me want to give you want you want." He paused, his lips gliding along her jaw. "You make me desire nothing else."

She couldn't take it anymore. She wanted him. Her fingers curled into the fabric of his shirt. Desperate and hungry. But he didn't move to kiss her.

"You destroy me." His lips stroked her ear, and her whole body quivered.

"It seems mutual." Her breath hitched.

"Yes." He cupped her face and moved in to kiss her, their lips barely touching—

Shocked gasps forced them apart, ruining the moment. Still panting, a twinge of frustration stroked through her bones. The passion inside Quinn wilted like a dying rose, and she jolted back and stepped away from Emrys as she noticed their audience.

"Wonderful job, dancers," the Royalle Ballet director said, trying to break the tension and shock cascading through the room. "We will announce our new apprentices in tomorrow's newspaper."

FORTY-TWO

The molten surface of the Mirror of Midnight beckoned, shining brightly in the midday rays as it escaped from the thick fog.

"Alright, we do it together," Quinn said, holding Emrys's hand.

Giselle barged in first. Quinn followed closely, but as she stepped, a distant voice called, and Emry slipped his fingers through hers.

She sucked in a breath as coarse sand slithered across her skin, feeling like tiny pieces of glass cutting lacerations into her flesh.

The girls stepped out into a sea of midnight butterflies that formed galaxies and constellations in an ocean of night. Periwinkle sat crisscrossed, braiding red hair, and waiting for them.

"You came back!" She wiggled her nose with glee. "Look, I am braiding your hair. Isn't it beautiful?"

The girl held up an intricately crafted braid with three different styles mixed together. It truly was artwork. The mirror was strange and terrifying, but Quinn had to admit the girl was growing on her. "It's beautiful."

"Thank you." She smiled brightly. Quinn whirled around, searching for Emrys, but he was missing. "He's not coming."

"Where is he?" Quinn asked as her necklace vibrated and melted into liquid ruby once more. The Blood Mirror formed into the brunette woman.

"That's a question." Periwinkle held up one finger in the air.

"He's held up outside dealing with a situation," Blood answered quickly.

Periwinkle groaned. "Stop that, Blood. This is my domain."

"Sorry." Blood shrugged completely unapologetically.

Periwinkle sighed, her lips forming into a line. "So, you've come for the location of the final Blood Mirror."

"Yes, what would that information cost?" Quinn asked, dreading the answer.

Periwinkle twirled the hair between her fingers. "You could trade your soul."

"No, she will not." Blood's voice was liquid wildfire.

"Yeah." Periwinkle sighed. "I don't think I could go through with it anyway. I am not like the other mirrors. I remember what it was like to be human, and I find myself not wanting to extract that kind of cost."

"You were human?" Giselle asked, the thrill of new knowledge dancing on her face. Giselle loved learning and discovering new secrets.

Quinn's heart tumbled, her scalp tingling as the information rained over her. If the mirror was once human, it meant that Periwinkle was a human soul trapped inside. It was all at once tragic and fascinating.

Which meant Blood was also once a human.

"Yes, I sometimes forget that," Periwinkle answered. "It was long, long ago, maybe eons, maybe days . . ." She shrugged. "I was human before my glamoured beauty and endless hunger . . . but I was a human." She was lost in thought, and no one was willing to interrupt her. For the first time, maybe ever, Periwinkle was giving information for free. "Every time we die, magic morphs us, and we grow stronger. We don't reach our most powerful state until the end. Like the motto of the Grand Library. Some of us glory in the power, but others wilt. I think I am more of a wilting rose. What do you think? A rose? Or maybe a lily? I am also partial to periwinkle."

"Every time you die?" Quinn asked at the same time as Giselle asked, "How many times have you died?"

"Oh, two, I think . . ." She counted on her fingers, holding up three and then rethinking it, resting on two. "Unless you count every day in here."

It was her prison. How sad and lonely it must be to be stuck inside a magic world all alone. Could Periwinkle communicate with the other mirrors? Mirrors were capable of watching humanity, but watching was far different from living.

"I'm sorry," Quinn said.

Periwinkle shrugged and changed the subject. "So, your cost. It has to be something big because the information is protected. So, I would like all your negative emotions. I want to take your sorrow, pain, suffering, and betrayal. The devastation of watching your parents die. You will never feel a negative emotion again. Give them to me, and I'll give you the location of the hidden Blood Mirror."

Quinn stepped back as if punched in the stomach. It offered what she'd always wanted. After her parents died, she never wanted to feel again. She wanted every bad emotion stripped away. To control the storm inside. It was the reason Quinn spent so much time in the morgue and dancing. Dead bodies, science, and dance kept her from being able to think about her pain, and if she didn't think about it, she wouldn't feel it. And if she didn't feel it, she could control it.

There was a time she would've given anything for this offer. *Anything*.

Maybe it was a good offer. The mirror only wanted her negative emotions. It only wanted her sorrow and anger and pain. It would leave her positive emotions. She could still be happy and love and care about people. It sounded like the perfect deal.

Except all mirror bargains had hidden costs that never ended well for humans. If Quinn couldn't feel negative emotions, would she be able to have empathy? How could she feel for others when she wouldn't know what pain felt like? If she lost her negative emotions, would she know what it meant to care? Would she know the strength of happiness?

Or would she become a shell? A facade. Externally beautiful but internally empty.

"No," she whispered.

A butterfly fell from the night sky and turned to ash. "It is everything you have ever wanted," Periwinkle said.

Quinn rolled her shoulders and forced herself to face the girl with strength. It was mostly a mask, but that was okay. Sometimes, one needed to wear a mask. "Maybe I shouldn't have wanted it."

Periwinkle's face lit up with a magical smile. "Good. I thought you would say no to that." Her eyes landed on Blood, and she nodded slightly as if the two were colluding. "Instead, I want you to have what you've always feared. I want everyone to be able to see your emotions." At Quinn's horror, Periwinkle said, "It won't hurt much. Well, it won't hurt physically at all."

"What are the hidden costs?" Quinn asked.

"There aren't any . . . probably. When you are upset or sad or happy, people will be able to see it."

"How?"

"I think I'd like to surprise you with that." Periwinkle wrinkled her nose.

It was a terrible cost. One of the worst things she could possibly imagine, but then any cost for this level of information was terrible. Although it was a far better cost than giving her soul or losing her ability to feel.

She'd never, ever be able to wear a mask again. Everyone would always know all the deepest secrets of her heart.

But her friend's lives were on the line. "Okay," Quinn breathed. "I accept the cost."

"Oh, goody." Periwinkle clapped. "I think you'll find that

you'll enjoy this." Periwinkle smiled at Blood. "She's grown up to be quite wonderful."

"Yes, she has." Blood's voice was a warm embrace.

"The third Blood Mirror is in the Ruins District at the castle ruins." Periwinkle clapped again. "Oh, today is a brilliant day!"

FORTY-THREE

Quinn strode out of the mirror, not feeling any different. A guttural sense of unease lingered but not much else. No new magic or horrible curses . . . yet.

Periwinkle said Quinn's emotions would display externally so everyone could see them, but so far, nothing seemed amiss.

But dread sank like an anchor in her stomach as she took in the scene on the street. Countess Teagan, Jevon, and Emrys stood stoically in a line.

Something was wrong.

Emrys hadn't gone into the mirror, which was strange given his sense of profound duty and desire to help.

"What's wrong—"

"Quinn, is there a reason your hair and eyes are suddenly a dingy yellow?" Emrys cut her off, asking a question of his own.

"What?" Quinn stammered as she glanced down and noticed a strand of dirty blonde hair dangling from her head. "Oh, filthy mirrors."

What was Periwinkle's obsession with hair?

Just as the thought poured into her mind, Quinn's fingernails morphed to a bright orange while all the color leached from her hair leaving it moon white. Quinn pulled out a mirror and watched as violet painted her irises.

She changed the colors of her nails, hair, and irises with her mixed emotions. Orange burned with surprise, white sank into terror, and blue danced with sorrow.

"Oh, *filthy mirror*," Quinn cursed under her breath.

"I think it's fascinating," Giselle said, appearing at Quinn's side.

"You don't have to live with it." Quinn's hair and fingernails dimmed to the dark-somber-blue of her eyes.

"But I do have to watch it." Giselle smiled, finding the situation far more amusing than she should. "Considering the other options were not feeling anything or giving up your soul, I think this was the better option."

"The mirror cursed you?" Emrys stepped up, his fingers hovering like he was unsure if he should touch.

"Yes." She sucked in a breath and stepped into his embrace.

His arms tightened around her as he rested his chin on her head. "Are you okay?"

She nodded into his shoulder.

"I hate to cut in . . ." Jevon coughed uncomfortably, tapping his fingers on his pants. "But what did the mirror tell you?"

"Oh, yes." Quinn stepped out of the hug. "The third Blood Mirror is in the Ruins District."

Emrys's hand lingered on her shoulder tentatively. A muscle in his cheek ticked, and he looked like he'd swallowed glass.

"Then we should go find it before Seren can!" Jevon said.

"Yes, that sounds like a good enough plan," Emrys said through his teeth. His hand was still on Quinn's shoulder, and his eyes a deep ocean storm.

What's wrong? She tried to send the thought through their minds, but she was still unsure how it worked. Her hair reverted to the dull, uneasy blonde color, her nails remaining midnight blue.

Emrys smiled brightly. *Everything is fine.*

"So we go to the Ruins District?" Countess Teagan asked. "We only have a couple of hours until the ball."

Quinn narrowed her eyes, not trusting the countess at all.

After the fifteen-minute walk, the group rested in front of the towering mermaid gates. Beautiful yet rotten, unlike the dragon gates of the Gold Quarter.

Quinn's hands shook, and acid crawled up her throat, her hair the midnight black of unmitigated fear—a torrent of it gripping her in a vise.

The viciously beautiful statues on the gate whispered to life, their tails flicking, hair waving in the crisp wind, and their eyes carving a hole into Quinn's chest. The hair on the back of her neck and arms stood at readied attention.

"Enter at your peril, wicked humans and creatures most vile," the mermaids said in sinister unison.

The group hesitated until Giselle held up her skirt and dashed through the gates. Everyone followed.

Two things happened simultaneously. An ocean of screams and curses came from the Mirrors of Trapped Souls, and a chilling invisible barrier attacked the group's bodies. Once they stepped through, night claimed the sky, casting the entire plane in chilling shadows.

Oh, wicked mirrors. Was this how the souls were trapped? People walked through the barrier and were never allowed to leave.

Panic clawed across her back, leaving scars of sorrow in its wake. She couldn't be stuck in a mirror? There was nothing worse imaginable. So, she leaped backward, and the barrier gave away, causing her to crash onto the paved street.

She loosed a breath and thanked the stars that they'd have an escape.

Around her neck, the necklace vibrated and glowed with red fire—the mirror shard liquefying and dancing.

They were getting closer.

With pure resilience and utter grit, she stood back up, wiped off her hands, and barged through the barrier once more. Bile rose in her throat as the caged souls shrieked, filling the air with nothing but terror, torture, and turbulence. They were restless and chanting such evil that even nightmares would cower in fear. As the group moved, the mirrors started telling unknowable truths mixed with unimaginable lies.

They said things like: "We want to taste your soul," "Quinnevere Ashelle fears emotion more than is wise," and "Your heart is evil and full of hate." They went on and on, whispering cruel and damaging words into the blackened night. "Magic rests inside. Use it, and you may prevail," said a mirror with kind gray eyes.

A particularly vicious one screeched. "One of your friends will betray you, little ballerina."

But that had already happened.

All the while, Quinn's hair paled to snow-white, and her nails wept midnight tears.

As she trekked farther into the fray, she began to find warm souls that split the wretched with hope. They cheered them on and helped them to continue through. At the edge of the cluster, rested a mirror with a thirty-year-old woman who had sweet eyes, a kind soul, and silky black hair. So much about her was familiar.

Blood. It was Blood.

Quinn clutched her necklace.

Blood whispered, "Stay the course, and only trust the human without magic."

When they finally reached the clearing beyond, it was like breathing for the first time. All six of them gasped for air. Their reactions ranged from clutching their knees to holding their sides to staring straight ahead at the next obstacle.

The towering vampire ruins.

Stone crumbled at the seams of turrets and looked like the jagged edges of a shattered stained-glass window. The once beautiful, majestic castle festered and rotted like the bowels of a river-soaked corpse. Darkness's wings surrounded the place and covered it in death. Vines snaked up the shattered stone, and mold grew along the walls like parasites feasting on flesh. Moss and mildew covered the ground, and everything about the place screamed, "Get out!" Including Quinn's gut.

Monsters worse than death haunted the grounds. Decay breathed life into this place, and nothing was free from its chokehold.

Above the entrance were dripped words written in blood.

It took several moments for Quinn to organize the letters and make sense of them. *If you wish to enter the ruins safely, a blood sacrifice must be freely given.*

"What does that even mean?" Giselle asked, her eyes wide with excitement or fear. It was hard to tell the difference with her.

Emrys cocked his head. "I think it means we need to offer it some of our blood if we want to enter."

"Any volunteers?" Jevon asked, kicking a piece of severed stone away from her.

"This is your foolish mission, *Quinnevere*. Why don't you go first?" Countess Teagan said the name like poison.

"Sure, if you're too afraid. I'll certainly go first."

Without hesitation, Quinn stepped up to the castle, picked up a sharp rock, and pulled it against her palm. It was an incredibly foolish choice, but her friends' lives were on the line. The third Blood Mirror was inside.

Quinn rubbed her palm against the stone, not knowing what else to do. Immediately, the ink leeched from her arm and cried a river of tears flowing into the crevices of the stone. It stole her tattoo, and it tore all the magic clinging to her fingernails and hair.

"Enter if you dare." A faceless voice whispered in the wind.

Quinn glanced back at her friends, white painting her face.

They all stepped up and repeated the process. As the vampires touched their hands to the wall, wisps of shadows leaked out of their bodies. And from Jevon's body, white light drained. Giselle was the only person not affected by the castle's strange magic.

"It took my healing," Jevon said, staring down at his bleeding hand, tapping his free hand on his chin.

"And our speed," the countess echoed.

"All of our abilities." Emrys's face leeched color.

Teagan straightened her spine. "Then, we shall have to face the unknown as mere powerless mortals."

"Broken mirrors, that must be terrible for you." Giselle rolled her eyes, folded her arms, and stepped through the entrance. Always blazing the trail.

The group tentatively followed. Nothing happened. Quinn wasn't sure what she expected, but it certainly wasn't anything.

The inside of the castle stared upon the cursed night sky. Stars leered down with wicked intent, the rays burning and glowing with cruelty. They were disturbing like possessed humans turned into fiends. The room shined with crimson light that illuminated the shriveling castle. At its center stood a scarlet mirror. A ruby the size of a boulder.

The crown jewel in a sea of rot.

"Thank you. You've done very well. I have to admit I almost lost hope when you decided to spend too much time with that stupid prince," Jevon said, his voice changing and lowering into a dark caress.

His friendly facade tumbled to the floor like a snake shedding its skin and was replaced with something truly wicked. He stood straighter, taller, and completely stopped fidgeting. Everything about his body language shifted. Where his face once glimmered with compassion and a quiet knowing, he now radiated a dark cruelty. It was almost as if he were possessed by a completely different Jevon.

Quinn's body grew as taut as a harp string. She didn't move a muscle. Confusion and betrayal hammered at the back of her skull.

Sweet, harmless Jevon was a lie.

A lie that was nearly impossible to process.

It was supposed to be Seren. The evidence pointed to her. The dress and the alley disappeared after Quinn remembered the attack. It all pointed to Seren.

But what if this whole time, it was them both?

Quinn's brain tumbled with all of the evidence.

The fingerprints from the feather found at the crime scene matched the killer's, and Jevon had picked it up without gloves. Jevon and Constance were in the reporter's apartment first. He brought in the threatening note to the lab, and he even disappeared at the Queen's Royalle Ballet.

It was them all along.

Jevon was always one step ahead because he was always there, silently observing. Seeing everything.

"It was you," Quinn breathed. A hand raised to her lips. A draft of icy air slapped her in the face, and she nearly buckled, but Teagan steadied her arm.

"Yes," he hissed. "Emrys, if you would." Jevon removed a handheld mirror from his coat pocket when Emrys didn't respond. "Do it, or I will instantly kill you, Teagan, and all of your friends."

Before anyone could react, Emrys strolled over to Giselle and placed a blade against her neck. Did Jevon have Emrys's painting inside his mirror, or was the mirror used to compel Emrys? Either way, it was clear Emrys was under the other man's spell. And even without vampiric strength, Emrys was intensely strong. Giselle tried to fight, but she was no match for him.

"Emrys," Quinn breathed, her eyes begging him to stop, but he remained uncharacteristically silent.

"Retrieve my paintings, Quinny." Jevon's eyes tore to the mirror. "I'm a bit of a collector."

Emrys jerked at the words, his eyes a liquid inferno. The vein in his jaw pulsing from holding it too tightly. "No."

"Quiet, Princeling." Jevon waved the mirror.

A vile sickness rose in Quinn's esophagus. "Why?"

"Because I can," he said. "Now, get my paintings, or Emrys will kill pretty Giselle."

Giselle stood still, her nostrils flaring. She was unable to talk because the knife was so tight against her skin.

"Stop this," Quinn said. "We're your friends. We love you." Her voice broke.

"Are we?" Jevon asked, walking over to Emrys. Jevon roughly gripped Giselle's chin and tilted her head closer to the blade, drawing blood with the action. Emrys visibly swallowed but did nothing.

Ash burned in Quinn's blood. Teagan stiffened, an unreadable expression on her face.

"Careful." He clicked his tongue. "We could kill her in a second. Humans are such fragile creatures."

Was he not human, then? Was he a vampire?

He kissed Giselle's neck and laced his fingers into her hair, pulling her neck backward and out of Emrys's grip.

"If you would, Emrys?" Jevon held out his hand for the knife, but the prince hesitated before handing it over.

During the exchange, Giselle shifted. Then she turned sharply and kneed Jevon in the jewels. He howled and fell to the ground, his scream a dark promise.

Giselle dashed away, but Teagan blocked the way and punched her in the face. "He will kill us all, girl." Teagan shook out her fist as Emrys grabbed Giselle by the shoulders.

"I'm sorry," the prince whispered. "I can't have him kill my entire family."

Jevon sat up, holding his core, his fingers circling around the mirror, and hissed, "You're going to regret that." After a moment, he stood, gripping the knife tightly. He raked it down Giselle's face, and blood pooled in a river down her chest. "Try to escape again, and I'll put it through your heart."

Giselle gritted her teeth and held her head high despite the blood still pouring from her wound.

Jevon licked some of it off her cheek. "I wonder if it tastes different to a vampire," he said. "A question for a different day. Get my paintings, Quinny."

Quinn's eyes shifted to the vampires, sending a silent plea for help.

"Oh, they won't help you." Jevon's mouth curved with fiendish delight. "I control them. I could make your pretty prince slit his own throat if I wanted to."

She turned back to the mirror, her veins on fire, and her intestines twisted into knots. There was no time to waste, so she inhaled sharply and darted to the surface—

"No!" Emrys's cry was suffocated by the consistency of the mirror.

As Quinn stepped deeper within the barrier, she glanced down at her arm, and magically, her tattoo returned as if the magic that affected the ruins held no sway here.

This mirror felt different than Periwinkle. It felt like flower petals brushing along her skin. Smooth, soft, and calming. Like a relaxing bath or a sweet garden. But it was also wet like rain. When a drop landed on the center of Quinn's palm, it was red and thick.

Blood.

FORTY-FOUR

Blood gushed from the sky, oozing down her face, and covering her body in crimson. Quinn pinched her eyes tight. As she stepped fully into the mirror, the blood rain ceased, but it still clung to her dress, hair, and skin. She cleared her eyes with her palms, and a woman stood at the center of a deep crimson room. Red from the floor to the ceiling with blood crying from the walls.

The mirror's face and arms were shaped out of puzzle pieces, and her hair was sculpted from white flower petals. The petals from magnolias and roses draped past sharp cheekbones, full lips, and a chiseled jawline. The bodice of her gown was formed out of angel feathers. Blood dripped from both the petals and the feathers down her body like wet watercolor paint. Porcelain butterfly wings stretched from her back like a carved statue. Her scarlet, glowing eyes repeatedly blinked like a doll, and red smoke tendrils slithered from them. Blood dripped from her mouth, and she licked her lips as if savoring the taste. It was like a vampire, and an abstract painting melded and created a new creature altogether.

A new and far more terrifying predator.

The creature's eyes raked over Quinn's necklace, staring covetingly at it as it waltzed out of its cage and formed into the brunette woman.

Neither mirror spoke, and Quinn didn't have any words.

"You have come for my paintings, Daughter of Blood Glass." Her voice was like a beautiful white swan. Enchanting and dangerous. "There is only but one trade, but are you brave enough?" she asked, waving her arm as seven paintings appeared.

Shockingly, they looked normal and as if they were created seven hundred years ago. They were small, the size of two books lengthwise. If she rolled them up, she'd be able to hide them under her skirt.

Three of them were familiar. One was a dancer from the Viridian—Constance, or Seren—and another was Emrys's second.

Quinn finally answered. "What's the trade?"

The mirror slowly blinked and cocked her head like a snake. "A soul."

"No," Quinn breathed.

A petal wilted and fell from the girl's temple. "It's the only way."

"I'll give something else, anything else." Quinn's voice shook.

"Only the soul trade is sufficient." The creature's voice was a wicked enchantress.

Quinn bristled, and the chambers of her heart filled with petrified wood chewed by termites. There was no way Quinn would trade her soul to a mirror. "I won't give you my soul. There has to be something else."

"You misunderstand me, girl." The mirror cocked its head. "The Accords require a soul trade, not me."

"A soul?" Quinn's voice decayed like the ruins outside.

It was the worst trade imaginable. Her soul was the only thing she truly owned. The one thing that was undeniably hers. The only thing she had true control over. Quinn trembled, her body convulsing under the weight of this decision.

Either she gave up her soul or her friends' lives. It was an impossible choice.

"What happens when a person trades their soul to a mirror?" she asked.

"The soul inhabiting the current mirror is freed, and the person trading their soul takes their place." It was Blood who answered.

Quinn swallowed, the knot in her throat tightening. "Instantly?"

"Not necessarily," the puzzle mirror said, the pieces of her eyebrows creasing together.

It didn't have to be instant. So, it was possible for Quinn to trade her soul at a date in the future. If she could set it so she'd have a long life, possibly trading wouldn't be all that terrible. Yes, it would be horrible to end up in a mirror regardless, but the alternative was allowing the people she loved to die.

Allowing Giselle to die.

The image from the Mirror of Terror flashed into Quinn's mind. Clutching Giselle's lifeless body, blood dripping in a sea around her. Imprisoning her in endless sorrow. Her mouth ran dry, and her spirit ached. Giselle was the one person who always had Quinn's back. She was family.

There was still one fear still yet to come true, and she would not let it be Giselle dying.

Quinn would never let it happen. She'd rather give up her own life to save her friends than watch them die.

This was the ultimate choice. There was no use resisting. She'd passed the point of no return a while ago. Quinn's voice crumbled as she said, "I'll trade my—"

"No!" Blood screamed, cutting her off. "Quinnevere, you cannot do this."

Every muscle in Quinn's body felt weak, and she shook with fear. "Perhaps the bravest thing I will ever do is accept that I cannot control everything." Her voice trembled with her body. "Perhaps all I can control is my mind and how I respond."

"No, Quinnevere, you cannot give up." Blood sobbed.

"I'm not giving up," Quinn said and cupped Blood's face. Tears painted her cheeks. "I am not giving up. I am making the choice for my family. You must understand that."

"You can't. You're too young." Blood stroked away one of Quinn's tears.

"Seren once told me that she would do anything for love," Quinn said. "I didn't understand at the time, but I do now. I have to save my friends and New Swansea from Jevon."

A surge of warm conviction spread over Quinn, and she tingled. She had to trade her soul for the paintings, but what if she got more? What if she found a way to live both a long life and protect the paintings—a way to keep them from Jevon, a way to live long enough to defeat him?

Her chest rose and fell in devastation, but she would be resilient. She would do this. Fear was a weight constricting her chest. Fear of the unknown. Fear of making a mistake. Fear of losing all control and losing herself.

But her greatest fear of all was being powerless and unable to save the ones she loved. Not again. Not like when her parents died. She was damning herself forever to a glass cage, but it was the only choice she felt comfortable making. It was a choice formed out of love.

"Here is my proposal: I'll trade my soul for these paintings." Quinn waved at them. "And exact duplicates of each one. Additionally, I won't surrender my soul until I have lived a long vampiric life with no hidden consequences."

"You're a clever one." A petal on the mirror's face rose in a delighted smile. "But I cannot accept your trade. It's too long of time. I can give you six months."

Quinn sucked in a breath. "Agreed."

"So it shall be." As the last word left her mouth, the facade slipped from her body—all the flowers and puzzle pieces, leaving a girl with honey-brown hair and golden eyes. She walked over to Quinn and held out her hand.

Hesitantly, Quinn slid her fingers into the mirror's. When their skin met, a flush cascaded through her body and on her back, a carving etching into her skin.

"You have until the last leaf falls on the tree," the mirror said with a nod.

Quinn sucked in a breath and rolled her shoulders back. This was a worry for another time. But now she needed to get to work.

She focused on her task and greeted the real paintings. Quickly, one by one, she popped them from their frames, placed them into a pile, and once all of them were out, she gently rolled them up together. Then she ripped a long piece of her petticoat and tied the paintings to her leg, hiding them under the pouf of her bustle and skirt.

When she was finished, out of mist and magic, she swirled duplicate matching canvases.

The fake paintings she took from the frames and rolled together as well, but she kept them in her hand.

"Time to go, my Quinnevere," Blood said. "Make sure you keep your necklace on at all times. It will protect you against mirror magic from now on." She smiled and ran a finger through Quinn's hair. "For your sacrifice, this is a gift I will give to you."

"Thank you." Quinn hugged the mirror. "I will miss you."

"And I you."

Quinn pulled away, and with one final glance, she whispered goodbye before stepping back out of the mirror.

Her tattoo vanished from her arm and her back, and she was met with a seething monster.

FORTY-FIVE

"That took too long," Jevon said through his teeth as he pressed the knife into Giselle's neck, causing a drop of blood to run from the wound. Painful but not deadly, but her face paled from his original wound.

Fire seethed in Quinn's stomach. She wanted to murder him for even touching Giselle—her one loyal friend. But instead, she walked over to the monster and held out the fake paintings. "As you requested."

He didn't take them. Instead, he asked, "What took so long?"

Emrys cut in. "How did you do it without losing your soul?"

"Who says I haven't?" she snapped. Instinctively, she knew none of this was his fault, but it was incredibly hard watching him do absolutely nothing or, worse, hurt Giselle. Quinn knew he was compelled to do it because Jevon had his painting from the second Blood Mirror, but she still couldn't help as anger bubbled out at the entire situation.

"What took you so long?" Jevon asked again.

The vein in her neck pulsed, but she laced a false smile on her face. "I had to convince the mirror not to take my soul immediately. It took a while." A half-truth.

The answer seemed to appease him. "Hand me them over, and I'll let Giselle go."

Giselle's life meant way more than trying to resist him—Quinn had given up her soul for it—so she handed over the fake paintings without hesitation. Once the scrolls slipped into his fingers, Jevon threw Giselle with a force that nearly knocked Quinn to the floor.

"Are you okay?" Quinn asked, examining her friend's facial wound.

"Mostly," Giselle said. "Just another interesting day." She forced a smile.

Jevon sauntered to the mirror. He lifted a wine-bottled rock and hurled it, shattering the mirror into pieces. The room rained lifeblood—filled with red dust and jagged stained-glass splinters.

"No!" Quinn screamed and fell to her knees, scrambling to grab one of the shards before they disappeared into nonexistence. What happened to the mirror's soul when it died? And if the mirror disappeared, would Quinn die? There was no way of knowing what would happen to her soul once the mirror finally took its cost.

The world was too dark to believe that destroying the mirror would destroy her bargain. But she had no way of knowing.

Would it destroy her? Her hand circled a piece as a sob escaped her throat. "No."

Javon cleared his throat and stepped on her hand, holding the slice of glass. "Drop it, or I'll kill her." He had Giselle by the hair again with a knife to her throat.

"No, please," Quinn begged. "Please." She thought if she held onto a piece as she had with the original blood mirror, it could save her.

"Don't test me again." He released his foot and pressed the blade against the skin, causing a trickle of red to appear on Giselle's throat. "I don't care enough about her to keep her alive, Quinnevere."

Quinn's heart pounded in her ears. She felt its angry pulsing in her veins, as she opened her hand and let the shard fall to the floor, clinking as it bounced off the stone. The sound of her devastation. Her life. Her future. A sound that would forever haunt her soul.

Jevon tossed Giselle to the ground, and her hands scraped against the glass as it dissolved. A crimson shadow painted the floor where the pieces once were, and Jevon's fingers were stained red. The sign of a mirror murderer.

"Teagan, restrain her," Jevon glowered.

The countess grabbed Quinn's hands and wrenched them behind her back before dragging her after Jevon. Quinn didn't fight back. Instead, she went completely limp and forced Teagan to carry her as if she were a dead body—making it extra hard.

As they reached the exit, Quinn changed her tactics and started to struggle. Unfortunately, it was a little too late because as soon as they managed to pass the threshold, the vampires gained their strength back, and her tattoo seeped back onto her arm. Jevon's hands also magically reverted to pale ivory, showing no sign of the red staining from murdering the mirror.

"Make her sleep," Jevon said, seeing Quinn's struggle.

"Go to sleep," the countess said harshly.

It was a compulsion.

No.

She couldn't fall asleep. She needed a plan.

Quinn tried to fight it. But the struggle was useless.

Darkness descended into her every pore, and she passed out, crumbling to the ground.

Fairy lights twinkled. Buzzing and floating. Shapes painted in her mind in shiny yellow and periwinkle. She blinked, and a room made of pink surfaced. It looked like a fairy had vomited on every surface. Quinn loved girly things, but this was a completely different thing. This was a nightmare made manifest.

Pink, puffy, and overwhelming.

Jevon was nowhere to be found.

Some of the tension released from her shoulders because she was happy to get a reprieve from his dark machinations.

However, she wasn't free. Seren lounged on a periwinkle-pink sofa and refused to look in Quinn's direction. So, they were working together, after all. It was impossible to decide which betrayal hurt more. She loved both of her friends. But they were never real. They were ghosts. Illusions of love. And that was the most heartbreaking of all. Quinn's hair matched her pain, turning a somber midnight blue, while her nails were a fearful white. Ropes chafed at her wrists, which seemed like overkill because no human had a chance of outrunning a vampire.

In the corner, the compelled countess helped Giselle into a massive ballgown, and a couple of vampires Quinn didn't know were sprawled out on the sickening decor. But an anchor dropped in Quinn's stomach. Emrys was missing. Despite everything that happened over the last eleven days, the one positive thing in a sea of rot was her newly established *friendship*—or whatever it was with Emrys. A truce?

A sickness festered in her stomach. The night had only just begun to sour, and it would certainly get much worse. But she wasn't powerless.

She had the real paintings.

She rubbed her legs together, and they were still fastened there. Thank the stars.

The vampires were preparing for the ball, and very soon, Quinn would be forced to undress and get into a gown.

Jevon's plan clearly involved the ball, and he wanted them all to see whatever was going to happen. He wanted an audience. But it was still unclear what he wanted. He had the paintings. Now what?

"What is this?" Teagan asked.

Giselle snatched whatever it was back out of the vampire's hands. "Oh, that's my lucky gemstone, and I would appreciate it if you didn't touch it."

Giselle didn't have a lucky anything.

But Quinn didn't get an opportunity to ponder that riddle because Seren noticed a movement out of the corner of her eye and snapped her gaze over.

Quinn's heart lurched as the semi-unstable vampire's attention locked fully on her. A tension sucked the air out of the room between them, and Seren's eyes grew to a shade darker than black, yet she didn't say a word.

Nothing.

It wasn't logical; it was all emotion, and Quinn didn't know what to do in a situation that defied reason.

She opened her mouth to say something, to break the tension channeling through her body, but as she did, Seren dropped her eyes back to her book and continued to read, her feet dangling over the chair's side.

Shit. What did that even mean? Was it a psychological game?

Quinn needed a moment to think, to plan, and not be seen, but her hair shifted to a scheming forest green. *Fucking Periwinkle*. This was a horrible mirror cost because everyone would know the precise moment when she thought it changed to something else. She'd become as easy to read as one of Giselle's many fiction books.

Fuck. Fuck. Fuck. *Pull yourself together*. Quinn's nails bit her palms, and she sucked in a deep breath, steadying her emotions and turning her hair back to red. Her hair color was locked to her emotions, not her mind, so she needed to control the former so that no one would discover the latter.

Quinn's plan needed to be A) figure out what Jevon was doing and B) thwart it. *You know, easy shit*.

It all revolved around the ball, and Quinn would figure it all out, but she let the problem stew in the back of her mind as she decided to help Giselle.

Reaching into her pocket, Quinn pulled out her medical kit —she never went anywhere without it. Balancing the scalpel, she sawed slowly along the strings of her binds, until they all fell loose. The whole time she worked, Seren refused to look over, yet she paid full attention.

From the way her ears perked up at attention, it was clear she knew exactly what Quinn was doing but didn't stop her, and that didn't bode well. Because the wickedest vampire in the room didn't even feel like Quinn was a concern.

And maybe she wasn't, but she refused to give up.

Once the ropes were removed, Quinn walked to Giselle without being stopped. In the vampires' arrogance, they thought two humans weren't a threat. An assumption she'd make them pay for. But that would come later. Giselle had her glitter bombs, and Quinn had her brain and the paintings.

They'd figure something out.

"Would you like me to stitch that?" Quinn pointed at Giselle's face wound, which was covered with cotton.

"Yes."

"It's going to hurt."

"I know." Giselle twitched but placed a resilient mask on. "I like pain."

Shaking her head, Quinn made her friend sit. In a matter of minutes, she poured saline on the wound, cleaned it, and stitched it. The whole time, Giselle gritted her teeth but refused to whimper.

"It'll leave a scar." Quinn frowned.

"All the better." Giselle winked. "Now, maybe people will stare at my face instead of my—"

"Oh, shut it." Quinn laughed. "They're still definitely going to look at your chest."

"And ass," Giselle added.

"You're very good at stitching wounds," Seren said, finally locking eyes with Quinn.

"I've had to be, considering I was raised in a morgue." Quinn's voice was poisonous gas.

Seren visibly swallowed. "I'm sorry."

"For what? For Jane's death? Threatening me? Killing my parents?" Quinn's words were filled with a resolve that snapped every bone in her body, turning them into unbreakable diamonds. She wasn't flesh anymore. She'd be stone. But not just any stone, diamonds.

"All of it," Seren said without hesitation. "If it makes any difference, I never wanted you to play any part in this. But—"

"But what?" Quinn shook her head, disgusted. Her dress turned a lime green, but her hair remained dark crimson. "You cannot blame Jevon for *your* actions." Seren wouldn't be absolved just because it wasn't her intention. She betrayed her friends in the worst way imaginable.

"I know. My actions are my own," Seren said, her brown eyes swelling.

Anger spiked through Quinn's blood. Seren's betrayal felt like thousands of shards of shattered glass slowly slicing away at the skin—slowly bleeding to death. The friendship was a lie.

A dirty, broken lie.

Having deep relationships was hard for Quinn, and she only recently allowed herself to get close to people. She was rewarded with this. Two of the people she thought of as family had been using her for three years, and worse, they killed Jane—Quinn's only true family.

"You've been playing with me for three years." The words tasted like violation and empty promises.

"I—I never toyed with you," Seren bit her lip. "I always thought of you as my friend. Possibly even the best friend I ever had."

Quinn's nostrils flared, and her heart felt like melting icicles. "Best friends don't lie. They don't pretend to be someone else, and they certainly don't kill their friends or kidnap them." Her eyes stung, but she refused to let Seren see her cry.

"There is nothing I can say to make up for all of this." Seren's shoulder slumped. "But I wish I could. You *are* truly my best friend, Quinny. Even though I would have never imagined it at the start, I love you."

Giselle scoffed again. "I think you need to learn how to treat your friends."

Seren ignored the comment. "You're angry. I understand that, but we have eternity. You will forgive me."

Nails bit at the center of Quinn's palms. "I won't."

"And not that it matters," Giselle said. "Since you seem not to care about our friendship at all, I won't forgive you either."

Tension cascaded over the room, circling and invading Quinn's body. It choked her and clawed its way down her spine.

Eventually, Seren said, "You need to get dressed."

There was no use in arguing. If Quinn didn't comply, she'd certainly be forced. But she needed to figure out a way to get her new undergarments without anyone noticing the paintings. "Fine," Quinn said. "But I have to use the lavatory."

"Sure," Seren said.

Quinn stalked into the powder room, thinking. What were the chances that the painting attached to her leg was Seren's and not Constance's?

Low.

Could be possible that Jevon was the murderer all along and not Seren.

It was worth a try.

Finding a soap bar, Quinn turned on the sink, wetted it, and wrote on the mirror, *Tel Teagin and the other vampirs to leeve.* Then Quinn called, "Seren, can you come help me in here?"

As Quinn waited, her fingers absentmindedly hovered over the paintings. Seren opened the door, and Quinn pointed at the mirror.

"Do it," Quinn said as commandingly as possible. She held her breath, waiting, hoping.

Seren stepped back as if slapped, and she gasped, holding a

hand to her mouth. But then she said, "Teagan, Veronica, and Charlie, I need you to do me a favor and go find Marcus, and please go now. It's vitally important." Now, speaking directly to Quinn, "You have—"

"No, don't. I have nothing." Quinn cut her off, knowing that whatever Seren said would be heard by the other vampire still leaving. "Don't talk about this."

Seren's mouth moved but she was unable to form the next words.

Quinn ran a finger down her dress, hovering over the canvas. "It's yours."

Seren's mouth worked and was blocked. Emrys said that whoever held their paintings could control them.

An anchor dropped in Quinn's belly. It was a sickening feeling to control someone else. To command them, and that feeling spread to Quinn's hair, which darkened to a sickly deep green. The idea of controlling someone else made her want to vomit but it also might be the advantage she needed.

"You will tell no one that I have the paintings." Quinn's voice was laced with an unbreakable command.

Seren nodded.

"Why do all of this?" Quinn asked, stepping out into the room.

Seren followed. "Because I love Gideon." That was all the answer she was willing to give unless forced. Quinn opened her mouth—

"And what does Jevon want?" Giselle asked the question that was bubbling at the back of Quinn's mind.

"Revenge," Seren said. "The council condemned him to death for trading with a mirror and becoming a monster, so he vowed to get revenge. He wants to release the vampires at the ball and expose the prince as a blood-sucking devil in front of the entire city."

Quinn let the words sink in, and a plan stirred in her stomach.

It was a foolish plan and had little chance of succeeding, but it could work.

If they were very lucky.

"Alright, here is what we are going to do. First, Seren will tell us the logistics of Jevon's plan. Second, Giselle, you'll get the Fantômes and ask for help. And third, we're going to find the rest of the vampires who belong to these paintings."

FORTY-SIX

One hour late to the ball.

The party was in full swing, and the room smelled sweet, like lavender and honey, but it tasted like rotten wishes.

Quinn hated it. Jevon's plan for utter destruction was to take the jubilance floating through the air, turn it sour, and make it decay.

The anticipation of it all caused Quinn's hair to fade into a shade of midnight black as terror danced along her spine. Bad luck fizzled in her stomach, and she knew, despite her best-laid plans, something would go wrong. But even knowing that, Quinn marched on. She had to follow the plan and see it through. If she didn't, people would die.

So, with no other recourse, Quinn swallowed her fear and walked on.

As she reached the top of the stairs, the music crashed to a halt, and a footman announced her presence. "Quinnevere Ashelle, the prince's personal guest."

Her attention snapped to the footman. What in all the *fucking* mirrors did he just say? *Personal guest?* Where the fuck was Emrys, and what did he mean by that fucking title? He couldn't be going through with this suitor ball, could he? And he certainly was not going to choose her, right? That was a terrible idea. She would make an awful princess. *Truly terrible.* Besides, they had far bigger issues to deal with than a foolish marriage proposal.

Every eye in the room latched onto her as they, too, heard the title the footman had given her. *Personal fucking guest.*

Quinn felt naked, despite wearing a ridiculously large ballgown that fell off her shoulders in a wave of golden fringe. The dress looked like stars crying molten teardrops. The golden bodice clung tightly to her curves with its embroidered crystals and translucent lace set to a pattern of mermaid scales while the sleeves swam with cerulean tassels.

It was beautiful, but danger lurked beneath its pristine elegance. A scalpel was sewn into a pocket, and the paintings were fastened to her leg.

"Quinny!" Seren whispered, gripping Quinn's arm and keeping her from walking down the stairs. "I know you have a plan, but it's not going to work. Fighting will only make him stronger. Jevon's power feeds on chaos."

Quinn gulped. If Seren were telling the truth, the plan would definitely *not* work. Quinn planned on using the vampires to fight back until Giselle could set off the glitter bombs, and the gang could get the humans to safety.

In the chaos, they were meant to get ahold of Jevon's mirror, but if his powers fed on chaos then the whole plan *was doomed*— because she had been planning on chaos, too.

However, her one advantage was that Jevon didn't know. He thought she was compelled and doing his bidding.

Quinn grazed her fingers against the handrail and methodically stepped to a four-four rhythm, and her dress danced with every movement. Quinn swallowed as her slippers clicked against the marble. A crowd of eyes tracked her, but only the chestnut ones mattered. Emrys had finally come into view, and he took a subtle step forward, signaling to everyone on the dance floor that he was paying extra attention. His jaw was set in a hard line, but his eyes sparkled with an emotion she couldn't quite place . . . maybe desire.

She shook out her shoulders, trying to release tension. But it didn't work because everyone else in the room was focused on her —Quinn, the poor, pathetic orphan with very little to her name. The girl who'd captured the prince's attention, and in the crowds' minds falsely so. There was nothing special about her. Nothing worthy of the golden prince's heart.

A young, twenty-something girl in a pink dress whispered to her friend, "She's not even that pretty."

"Yeah, she has a lovely enough face, but she is so skinny," a girl in green responded.

The crowd found her wanting and whispered unkind words as she passed, jealousy, confusion, and resentment coating their poisoned tongues. Their words caused a surge of shame to rupture through her core, and she was left feeling exposed, vulnerable, and dumb—the way she felt reading. Especially because while the prince showed her favor and would possibly choose her to be his bride, they had no idea that it was all for show, all fake.

Because Emrys was all show.

And it was that fakeness that killed Quinn. Because, for once in her life, she just wanted to be truly chosen. Not for her family connections, necklaces, or council tattoos. Or her ability to hunt down a killer. She just wanted to be loved and seen for *who* she was, not what she could do for someone. She wanted to be worthy of more than quick kisses and useful skills.

Nothing about the moment felt happy.

She was a porcelain doll on display, ready to be toyed with or broken. That was it. But those jealous whispers would never know it.

Quinn tried to calm herself and not focus on them. Counting had worked in the past, so she sucked in a breath and listened to the clicks of her heels. *Click: one, click: two, click: three. Breathe. You can do this. Click: four. Breathe. Click: five.*

It helped keep her emotions in check—sort of—but her hair was still a solid black. At least it was better than a sea of colors.

Reaching the center of the room, her heels stilled, and she stopped eight feet away from *her* prince. Silence stretched between them as they locked eyes. Even with all the pain and the fakeness, she couldn't help but seek comfort in him. And maybe that was enough. Because although it wasn't real, he *had chosen* her.

Perhaps the Playboy Prince wasn't capable of being real. Perhaps this was all he could give. And maybe, just maybe, that could be enough for her—at least for now.

Emrys wore a perfectly tailored tuxedo and gold cravat—matching her. Again.

In three long strides, he reached her and tilted her head up to meet his brilliant eyes—the color of the forest bark just before sunrise.

He was so beautiful, this stupid, glorious vampire.

Sound faded away—the music, the chatter, and even the clicks of glassware were gone, and only he existed. The world stilled for a perfect moment, and it was just the two of them in a blur of color. Tension licked her insides, and it wasn't just coming from the fear and anticipation of the soon-to-be fight; it was also coming from her desire for him.

Because as much as she denied it, she needed this man in so many ways.

"A dance, Miss Ashelle?" Emrys held out his hand.

A dance would give them a moment alone among the sea of revelry. It would be the best moment to warn him.

"Why, yes, of course." She smiled and slid her fingers into his.

Quinn sucked in a breath as he pulled her into a tight hold, and in his arms, her hair morphed back into its typical red—her hair liked him just as much as she did. Emrys's scent was intoxicating and calming. He smelled of sandalwood, cinnamon, and safety.

With his eyes, Emrys asked the question, *Are you okay?* And then she heard it in her mind.

No, her insides screamed. *Where have you been?*

Confined to the castle, his words rang in her head. *Compelled to stay. I've been so worried about you. Jevon—*

"I know," Quinn whispered right before he spun her out and then pulled her back in. Their steps were perfectly in sync because they had trust and a true partnership. *Jevon plans to break the Accords in front of all of New Swansea and take control of the city.* Quinn sucked in a breath. *He also wants to destroy you . . . to expose you as a vampire in front of everyone.*

How do you know all of this?

They froze in the middle of the dance floor, their eyes on fire for each other. Skirts swooped around them, and the sounds of clicking heels and the strokes of violin bows cut through the sizzling air between them.

She inhaled sharply, afraid of her next words. *When I traded my soul to the mirror, I also traded for duplicates of every painting in that mirror, and I gave him fakes.*

His body tensed, and his face paled. *Oh, Quinn, your soul—*

You couldn't have protected me or taken my place.

He squeezed her hand. *I'll fix this. We will find a way to fix it.*

Quinn simply nodded. She didn't believe she could be fixed. A deal was a deal. That's how mirrors worked. But she smiled at him because he needed it.

Moving back into the rhythm of the dance, they twirled as they continued their conversation.

If you have the real paintings, does that mean you can now compel the vampires?

A soft smile rose on her lips. *I didn't need to compel the rest, but yes, I am compelling Seren. Jevon plans to start his terror during the midnight bells. We need to get as many people out as possible before then.*

The dance ended, and Emrys kissed her hand. "Miss Ashelle."

"Your Royalle Highness."

Without hesitation, Seren swooped in and stole Quinn from his fingertips. Quinn flashed a fake, desperate glance back as she was pulled into the crowd. "Why did you do that?"

"You need to keep up appearances, Quinny," Seren said. "Jevon controls nearly all the vampires in this room, and I think a few of them are start—" She cut herself off and smiled at a party guest passing nearby. "Smile. They can hear your heart beating. You're having a good time."

Quinn heard the hidden message in the words, too. *They hear any command you make or anything you say.*

Glancing around the room, she noticed the sheer number of people staring at her. She couldn't tell if they were staring out of envy because they thought she would be chosen as Emrys's bride or because they were vampires watching to make sure she didn't step a toe out of line.

This was the most annoying part of her plan. She was unable to do anything to help the humans and vampires get out because she was the decoy. The pretty toy on display to make their enemies think that everything was going to plan.

She shivered, and for a brief moment, her gaze landed on an ignition spot for the glitter bombs. Hopefully, Giselle and the Fantômes were ready to set them off. They didn't want to do it too early and expose the vampires. The plan was to keep the secret and confront Jevon in a private room, but unfortunately, he was nowhere to be seen, and they were quickly running out of time to find him.

"Do you know where J—"

Intoxicated giggles forced Quinn not to say anything else. A couple stood on the opposite side of a room divider.

Seren tensed.

"We could find them, or we could simply enjoy each other's company," Kordelia purred.

"What were you thinking?" Constance asked.

Kordelia whispered something, and the parts that could be heard made Quinn blush.

"As much as that sounds like an enjoyable time, I can feel something dark in the air. Seren is up to something, and we have to be prepared," Constance said.

Kordelia crossed her arms and pouted. "Sometimes, you're absolutely no fun at all."

"Yes, it is terrible that I am the reasonable one." Constance giggled.

"Oh, wicked mirrors, please don't make me watch this," Seren whispered to the ceiling.

Constance immediately pulled away from Kordelia, and her face soured as she faced her twin. "Seren." In an instant, Constance was on her sister, slamming her into the wall with her hand around her throat. "What are you up to?"

"As much fun as this reunion is, I have no time for you, *sister*." The last word was a deadly curse. Seren flicked her eyes to a grandfather clock. "You're too late."

Quinn whispered out of the corner of her mouth. "Constance, get out and get humans—"

Midnight bells cut through the ballroom, causing chaos. Dozens of vampires slammed, blocked, and guarded the doors, and it all happened too quickly for her human eyes to see.

The music came to a crashing halt, and fifteen vampires held fifteen humans hostage. Quinn recognized two of the humans. The girls in the pink and green dresses from earlier who jealously commented on her looks. Now, they were at vampires' whims, with silent tears stroking down their faces. Despite how cruel they'd been to her, Quinn felt for them, and she wanted to help them. But Quinn never got the chance.

Because in an instant, all fifteen of the vampires, as if in a choreographed dance, slit the throats of their hostages. The girl in the pink dress fell first, crumbling to the ground like a used tissue paper. The green-dress beauty followed her friend in death, her blood spurting all over the once-pristine floor.

Quinn let out a scream.

The ball went from a glittering tapestry to a decaying catastrophe in a matter of seconds.

A river of gore painted the floor, pouring from the throats of dying humans. It was gruesome and too horrible to look at. They didn't even have a chance to escape, and they had no warning. They were simply gone in the blink of an eye—at the snap of Jevon's fingers.

Quinn's white hair fell into her face and shock dangled in the air like a hangman's noose floating on a wicked wind. A moment of stillness was preceded by utter chaos. Horror stroked Quinn's esophagus, pain burning up like heartburn. "You didn't tell me . . ."

Seren's eyes went wide. "I didn't know."

"Liar," Constance hissed, still holding her sister by the throat.

Constance, Seren, Kordelia, and Quinn were the only still figures in an ocean of mayhem. Humans ran for the exit while Jevon's newly made vampires attacked anyone in sight, ripping out throats, pulling out intestines, and sucking up a brilliant feast. The compelled vampires also joined the fight, forced to kill humans as well. But they did it in a more dignified manner. It was only ten vampires who resisted. Quinn's ten whose paintings she'd rescued from the third Blood Mirror.

In the disorder, Seren freed herself and clutched Quinn's arm, pulling her away from Constance. Blood and guts soaked the ground. They walked over the gruesome floor as Seren tried to say something, but her voice didn't carry over the destruction.

"What?" Quinn yelled.

Seren paused and turned around, her wrist still on Quinn's. "I truly didn't know, Quinn. I never wanted innocents to die." The last bit was a plea. "You have to believe me."

"I don't have time to care about you right now." Quinn ripped her hand free, and she forced her mind to still and focus on the battle. She needed to find Jevon and get the handheld mirror from where he kept the other paintings. She needed to free the compelled vampires because they were far outnumbered.

Through a sea of blood and battle, Quinn spotted Giselle pulling the princess out of the fray and to relative safety. Francois was also by her side, helping.

Oh, thank the mirrors.

Possibly compelled, Emrys stood frozen at the center of the ballroom, watching in horror—unable to do anything. Quinn couldn't imagine the torment that caused because, despite how much he had used her, he had done it all for his people. And his people included all members of New Swansea from vampires to humans to Mirror-Blessed. This must have destroyed him.

Jevon stood in front of the massive windows, silhouetted by the moon, watching in delight. The monster inside him clearly enjoyed bathing in blood and death.

"Everyone stop," Jevon commanded.

Every person in the room froze except Quinn's vampires. It was the only shot they had, and they took it. Three of them immediately snapped the necks of the vampires they were fighting. A smile rose on Quinn's lips. Maybe they could win this after all.

Except her glee was short-lived. Because when Quinn's vampires didn't respond to Jevon's command, his face grew tense, and the vein in his jaw feathered. He yelled the command again, to no avail, and his confusion was replaced with a dark, wicked rage.

Then he spotted her. "You," he hissed. "You're responsible for this. How did you do it?" He chewed on the question for a moment. "No matter, let's do this the hard way."

With a snap of his fingers, the dead bodies slowly rose from the floor, blood soaking their clothing, and some even had intestines hanging out of their torsos. It was disgusting. The newly animated corpses grabbed more humans, holding them hostage. With the second snap of Jevon's fingers, Quinn's body froze, her muscles growing heavy and impossible to move.

What the fuck?

Her eyes tracked to Jevon, who had a wide, evil smile on his pale, hollow face. In this moment, he resembled a corpse. He could control bodies—not just dead ones but all living and dead flesh.

Instantly, all of Quinn's plans melted because if Jevon was fueled by the chaos, they were all fucked. Because his power—whatever it was . . . possibly Necromancy—was growing to unimaginable heights.

He was unbeatable.

From the looks on everyone else's faces in the room, they all knew it, too. Quinn saw the precise moment when hope faded into ash and was left with only despair.

Every human and vampire in the room was frozen, stuck under the weight of his power.

How could she fight this? How could anyone?

They were all going to die. Quinn's throat grew dry because she had nothing left, nothing to do but accept her fate. Quinn pinched her eyes closed and waited to die—or for whatever the monster would do next.

But hope came in the most unlikely place.

Seren squeezed Quinn's hand. "Calm your heart. His power feeds on chaos. On your chaos."

Quinn opened her eyes and met the gaze of her ex-friend. *What?*

"You can fight him. Fight the chaos in your heart." Seren squeezed Quinn's hand again and nodded. "You can fight him."

"Now that I have your attention." Jevon sauntered to the center of the room and stepped in front of Emrys, who shielded a human girl from the vampires and animated corpses around him. "Let us have a public execution."

From his inside pocket, Jevon pulled out his hand-held,stemmed mirror. Quinn wasn't sure why the mirror did Jevon's bidding when the Mirror-Gods were far stronger than the creatures they created, but there had to have been a bargain between them.

From Jevon's mirror floated a large scroll, and he caught it in mid-air before placing his hand-held mirror back in its pocket. Jevon unrolled the scroll and exposed Emrys' vampiric painting.

His life force.

"You really shouldn't have tried to kill me." Jevon's face magically shifted. His freckles slid away, and his blond hair flaked into a soft walnut. His blue eyes were now a bright, mint green. Clearly, his power allowed him to completely manipulate his body . . . and others.

"You won't move." Jevon's voice was laced with compulsion, freezing Emrys in his tracks.

"Gideon," Emrys said with wide, disbelieving eyes. "Or is it the monster who lives inside you speaking?"

FORTY-SEVEN

In a battle between a vampire and a monster, who would win?

Quinn didn't know.

But they would all soon find out.

Jevon's lips turned up in a feral smile. "Hello, old friend," he said to Emrys. "I believe Seren once promised to destroy you and your family, but I thought it would be more fun if I did it. Since you were the one who stabbed a knife through my heart."

"I clearly missed." The muscle in Emrys's smooth jaw pulsed. "I'll try not to miss next time."

Jevon let out a fit of chaotic laughter. "You will not get a second time. You're minutes away from death."

"You killed the man you once called brother when you destroyed the first Blood Mirror. You've had your revenge on us. What more do you want?" Emrys asked.

"I want to finish what I started," Jevon said. "You allowed vampires to be shackled, manipulated, and limited by the Accords." He clucked his tongue. "Imagine what it could be like to be unlimited? Imagine the chaos."

Quinn's bones quaked. At the mention of breaking the vampire Accords, the crowd visibly responded. Some screamed, others wetted themselves, and others turned solid white with fear.

Quinn would have thought that it was obvious that vampires were back, considering how many of them had just attacked, but brains were fickle muscles. They often made people believe what they wanted to—tricked them into believing false truths.

No one wanted the return of the Age of Tyrants, so any other truth was preferable.

"I don't have to imagine," Emrys snapped. "I've lived through the horror vampires can unleash. I know our villainy and cruelty firsthand." He dropped his glamour and let everyone see the claw marks raked across his face. "Your vendetta is wrong."

Jevon played with the scroll in his hand and pulled out a dagger. "I am not your villain, dearest vampires." Jevon waved his knife at the vampires littering the room. "I am your liberator."

Emrys's lips fell into a flat line. "Vampires are not chained; we live at the highest levels of society. Peacefully. It is our cruelty that was bound. We merely abide by laws just like humans."

"But I have unbounded them, and isn't it fun?" Jevon ran the tip of his dagger across the painting of Emrys's face.

The real Emrys flinched. "No, it's not fun to watch the world burn."

"That's where we differ. Sometimes, the world needs to burn." Jevon's sadistic grin widened as he pocketed the knife. "Speaking of burning. Teagan, darling, do hand me my lighter."

With hard features, Countess Teagan handed Jevon a lighter, and his fingers circled it before he ran his thumb along the grooved starter. A small flame danced at the end.

Emrys straightened his spine and faced his death with dignity. Quinn quivered, and killer hornets hummed in her stomach, threatening to strike. Her muscles were tight and immobile. The world silenced, save for the taunting clicks of a grandfather clock.

Tick.

Tock.

Jevon tauntingly raised the flame closer to the painting.

Tick.

Tock.

It danced along the edge, slightly browning the canvas paper.

Tick.

Tock.

Panic crawled up her throat and ate away. If someone didn't stop Jevon, then Emrys's painting would burn. Quinn begged her mind, her necklace, anything to fight the power. *Please unlock and work like you promised, Mother. Please. You promised protection from Mirror-Blessed.*

Quinn was so foolish.

She couldn't fight vampires or Mirror-Blessed. She couldn't even fight a textbook. She was weak, helpless, and alone. Her parents were dead, and her best friends were traitorous murderers.

She'd never be able to live in this immortal world and be enough. Quinnevere Ashelle was utterly useless, and she always had been. No one should trust someone illiterate. She was never going to be strong like Emrys or Giselle.

She was a mouse in a trap, whimpering as it died.

Quinnevere, I—a hollow scream played in her mind with the voice of an angel. She closed her eyes and let the pain flow away, and the world caved in on her. But that angel's voice sang in her head to the melody of a lover and friend. *I'm happy I got to know you.*

Her eyes flicked to Emrys.

Terror licked her spine.

Jevon was going to kill the prince. Quinn needed to save him. She needed to help, and she needed to find the strength to fight the necromancer. Her body trembled, but her foot moved. Seeing it, Seren pulled a pistol out of her pocket and handed it to Quinn.

"I never wanted this to happen. Not all the death. I just wanted him back. I love him," Seren whispered, seeming completely shaken by the devastation coating the room. "But I love you, too. I'm so sorry I can't kill him, but—" *You can.*

As Jevon lifted the flame fully to the paper, the dam inside Quinn disintegrated, and her necklace burned on her chest. "No," she shrieked as she ran forward and tackled Jevon. They fell to the floor, and in the mayhem, she aimed the pistol at the largest part of Jevon's chest and pulled the trigger. Blood poured out of his stomach. In a blink, Countess Teagan restrained her and pulled the gun away, tossing it to the floor.

As if not injured at all, Jevon rose to his feet, cracked his neck, and turned his poisonous gaze on Quinn, blood still pouring from his stomach.

Oh shit. His power, at least the power that she knew of, was near instant healing.

"Give her over," he said. The countess complied.

Fear coiled in Quinn's stomach, and her snow-white hair fell onto her face. Jevon's hands encased her neck and squeezed. "Actually, Prince, I think I'll torture your pretty little ballerina first and make you watch as I slowly kill her."

Quinn's breaths halted as the fire climbed her esophagus. Jevon's fingers indented into her skin and her fingers clawed at his grip.

Her eyes scanned the crowd as she slowly choked. Constance and Kordelia were frozen statues holding each other's hands. Kordelia looked like she wanted to rip someone's head off, pure fury etched into her face. Giselle stood on the stairs at the side of the room with the princess and Francois. The queen was nowhere to be seen. Every face in the crowd was coated with its own mixture of terror.

The whole city was watching a massacre and could do nothing about it.

When Giselle met Quinn's eyes, she slightly moved. Almost as if she was growing the ability to fight Jevon's powers. In her hand was a crimson stone. Slowly, centimeter by centimeter, she tried to reflect light.

Giselle shouldn't have been able to move, but she was somehow fighting. That fixed Quinn with a resolve.

Her throat burned, and she tried to knee Jevon in his jewels. He released her neck. "Teagan, darling, break her wrist."

The countess visibly swallowed, and with leaden feet, she forcibly walked over and snapped Quinn's wrist.

Her hand hung sideways from her arm, and an agonizing scream escaped as she cradled it to her chest. Red streaks pulsated through her hair at the pain. Her fingernails were pure crimson. The agony echoed through her bones, and she wanted to crumble to the floor.

Tears leaked from her eyes, and her chest fell to her knees, one hand clutching her kneecap. Using the distraction, Quinn slipped the scalpel from her dress.

She sucked in a deep breath, and her body trembled, but she needed to do something. She couldn't allow the pain to jolt her. She'd danced through worse agony. She could fight through it, too.

I'm not a mouse in a trap.

She rolled her shoulders back.

I'm a lion.

How do you beat chaos?

By cheating.

Jevon pulled her up by the chin, and she let herself get close because now he was *her prey.*

Her eyes locked with Giselle, who'd somehow managed to break free of the magic. Almost as if they were psychically linked, Giselle pushed over a massive vase, creating a distraction. At that exact moment, Quinn thrust her arm up and released the scalpel into Jevon's throat.

"Seren, now," Quinn yelled.

Three things happened instantaneously. Jevon crumbled to the floor, as did the reanimated dead bodies, and everyone was released from the magical hold. Seren plunged forward and tried to reach Jevon's mirror, but she was knocked off track by an attacking vampire. In the madness, Quinn snatched Emrys's painting from the floor.

A battle started between the newly created vampires and the originals loyal to Emrys.

With a quick pirouette and a grand jeté jump, Quinn dodged an attacker. With another jump and a somersault, Quinn avoided a vampire who had his sights set on her. In doing so, one of Emrys's vampires was able to intervene.

It was a clash of immortals.

And humans were stuck in the middle as collateral damage.

Quinn fought well. Ballet was a handy skill to have while fighting vampires. She ducked and pliéd, avoiding another vampire. She was trying to get to the wall and to a painting of Emrys displayed on it. To save the prince, she'd switch out his painting and hide it somewhere.

Reaching the wall, she pulled the artwork off with her good hand, ran, jumped, slid on her knees across the room, dodged vampires, and slid under a table concealed by a white tablecloth as fast as she could. Quinn plucked off the frame with her good hand, clutching her bad one to her chest and begging away the pain still shooting through it. Quinn clumsily rolled the art into a scroll. Then she flipped her skirts up, untied the other paintings, and added Emrys's to the pile before rolling them up again. With one hand filled with scrolls and the fakes in the crease of her elbow, she peered out from under the tablecloth.

Across the room was a gilded vase big enough to stash the real paintings. If she put them there, she could give the fake of Emrys back to Jevon. She shoved the real paintings underneath her stays before sliding out from under the table and navigating around the battle.

Quickly, she got to the vase, and with her broken, useless hand, she parted the white feathers stashed inside. Blocking the sight lines with her body, Quinn stuffed the paintings between the feathers.

Hopefully, that worked, and no one saw. Because if anyone noticed, she would be caught and in a far worse position than before.

But for now, the paintings were safe. Emrys's painting was safe! And that was all that mattered.

The only problem was that in hiding the real paintings, Quinn was forced to let go of Seren's, and she was now free and able to fight her. Quinn hated losing that control, but it had to be. It'd be worse if Jevon got his hands on that power. Besides, she hated the idea of taking someone's choices from them.

With her task complete, Quinn was finally able to breathe and clutch her broken hand to her chest.

But the battle wasn't over. Across the room, Giselle frantically searched the floor for something until . . .

Until her fingers slid onto an object. Quinn's heart leaped into a sissone jump as her best friend maneuvered the reflective stone and chandelier light. But the stone must've been too bloody because she frantically wiped it on her dress.

Finally, reflecting the light, she dragged it to the ignition spot, her fingers visibly trembling.

Quinn's heart exploded . . . or maybe it was the bombs because silver confetti erupted from the walls and fell from the ceiling like snow.

Giselle was successful, and warmth spread through Quinn's chest as pride swelled.

The effect was instant. As soon as the silver touched the vampires' skin, they screeched in guttural pain. It incapacitated the majority of them, but some tried to crawl and stumble away. Some passed out from the pain.

Every movement wrote agony across their faces.

Humans, on the other hand, were gorgon statues. Frozen in terror. Some even had puddles running from their suits. But they needed to get out. They needed to move. This was their chance—the chance to live.

Quinn screamed. "Everyone, run. Get out. You only have a short time." She yelled at the top of her lungs, her voice cracking with the effort. "Get out."

Almost as if waking from a dream, the humans snapped out of their daze and ran for safety. Quinn breathed. She did it. She couldn't save herself, but at least she could save them.

But her victory was short-lived by some terrible fate. Jevon stirred and clutched Seren's revolver. His neck wound was almost fully healed, and he pointed the gun first at Emrys and shot him through the chest.

The world stilled as Emrys crumpled.

Oh, wicked mirrors. Did it hit his heart? Did it matter if it had?

Quinn gasped in a quivering breath and stumbled over to him, dropping his fake painting at their feet. The bullet barely missed his heart, and Quinn rested her forehead against his as relief flowed through her. He was alive. The Playboy Prince, the bane of her existence and her friend and maybe more, would live.

He'd live. Thank the mirrors.

"Is he okay?" Giselle asked, appearing at Quinn's side.

Quinn gulped and stared at her best friend. "He'll live, but you have to get out of here, Giselle."

"I'll leave if you do." Giselle wiggled a brow at her best friend.

"You both need to leave," Emrys said, blood pouring from his mouth.

As Quinn clutched his agonized face with her good hand, Jevon let off another shot. This one hit Constance through the neck.

Kordelia screamed. As if urged by magic or an increase of adrenaline, Kordelia grasped Constance by the shoulders and slowly—painfully slowly—dragged her, presumedly to get her to starlight to heal the wound.

A third bullet rang through the room this time, hitting Seren in the forehead. Quinn's heart dropped to her toes. Could a vampire survive a silver bullet to the head? It wasn't her painting, so most likely, she'd be fine. Jevon aimed the gun at Giselle, and he slowly pulled the trigger.

"No," Quinn screamed, and without thinking, she pushed her best friend out of the way and pinched her eyes tight, bracing for impact.

Time stilled as the bullet sliced through her stomach before exiting and lodging into Emrys. At first, she felt nothing, just shock's tingles. Then the pain burst with a vengeance as it clawed at her insides. Fire filled her stomach, hot and wicked—an unlivable wound.

She clutched the bullet hole in her core, blood leaking through her fingers.

She needed to clog the bleeding, or she would certainly die from blood loss. Slowly, with her good hand, she pulled Emrys's cravat from around his neck and clumsily stuffed it into her bullet hole. It was excruciating.

"No." Jevon coughed in pain. "Not you."

Jevon's face paled, and his entire demeanor changed. As if a switch was pulled, and he was back to the version of himself that was her friend. He tapped his fingers against his thighs as horror settled into his features for a moment. "What have I done?" he asked, taking in the destruction. But like a light switch, the man turned, his body morphing again, allowing the monster inside him to have free reign. He cracked his neck and said, "So be it."

Quinn's focus turned back to her wound. There was nothing she could do to stop death's beckoning call. "Giselle, you need to leave, please."

"No," Giselle breathed.

"Find Francois and find safety, please. I beg you."

Sorrow played on Giselle's face as she nodded. Giselle wasn't foolish; she knew that she was a liability. She was the only living human left in the room and Jevon's only leverage left. "I trust you, okay." Tears leaked from her eyes. "I trust you to do what you need to do, but you better come back, or I'll travel to the afterlife and pull you back myself, and then I will kill you for doing this to me."

Quinn choked on a smile. "It's a deal."

"I love you, you foolish, awful friend."

"I know." Blood bubbled through Quinn's lips. "I love you, too."

But as promised, Giselle quickly disappeared, as it was the only recourse left.

"Quinn." Emrys stroked her face with the back of his fingertips. "Drink, please."

"I—" Quinn started, but her head lulled to the side, too weak to drink anymore. Blood bubbled out from her wound too quickly, staining Emrys's expensive suit in crimson.

Emrys lifted her head back up to his wrist, but when she tried to drink again, she choked, no longer able to consume it.

"No," he breathed. "Not yet.

Quinn's eyes grew heaving, and her body began to hum with . . . magic. The blood seeping from her wound turned into liquid fire and gathered into magical cords that looked like thick yarn. The cords streamed together, folding, and forming and braiding into a picture of Quinn's face, dripping with a scarlet-iron liquid.

A blood painting.

"Stay with me, Quinnevere." Emrys's chestnut eyes stormed with a symphony of emotions, none of which she could decipher.

"I can't." Her lips touched his for one moment—one glorious moment—a sweet, broken kiss before her head lulled and became far too heavy to lift again. "It's rather unfortunate that I am going to die a human virgin."

All her energy evaporated as she collapsed into his chest.

A whimper escaped Emrys as his fingers held her limp and dying body. "Quinnevere, please stay with me." She was too weak to respond. "Stay with me, and I promise I will remedy your problem." They both knew his words were useless. They both knew it was too late for her human life.

Quinn let out a pathetic blood-coated laugh as her mind flooded with Emrys's pain—his thoughts—everything he wanted to say to her as her life force bubbled from her, and her breaths slowed. She pinched her eyes tight and fell into the comfort and warmth of his chest.

Emrys, I switched out your painting and hid it in a vase. She tried to send the thought through their connection, but she was unsure if it made it.

So was just too damn weak.

Too weak to do anything save count his heartbeats.

Beat . . .

Beat . . . beat . . . beat . . . beat . . .

Then shadows and death's cold, dark shackles consumed her.

And Quinnevere Ashelle was dead.

FORTY-EIGHT

Death's haunting voice played in her mind, and his fingers curled into wisping shadow ropes. They snaked around her body and imprisoned her. Ice slid into her veins. Cutting and freezing. Changing her.

Rebirthing her.

Her body shifted and melted into something new—something stronger. *But not better.* This body had a constant hunger, an all-consuming appetite that ate away at her rational thought. It sank its fangs into her core. Hunger boiled and bubbled.

All she wanted to do was devour a human, taste the rich, thick, intoxicating liquid. She wanted to soak in it. Bathe in it.

Her gums hurt, and she opened her mouth, sensing and smelling the iron coating the room. Even the air tasted like blood.

And she needed to consume it now.

Her eyes flared open, and she sat up quickly. Pain pricked at the back of her neck and turned into agony, encasing her entire body.

"Silver." She growled.

A guttural hissing feeling rose in her belly.

Bodies caked the floor, mingling with a river of blood and

silver rained from the heavens—no, not the heavens, the ceiling. It would have been beautiful if it wasn't so agonizing.

With a cupped hand, she swiped blood from the floor and poured it into her mouth. It tasted like heaven and crushed fantasies. Her hunger became frantic as she tried to get as much blood as possible, drinking from the floor and dead bodies both. She didn't care. The hunger was untamable. Nothing would be enough.

Nothing would satisfy—

Fingers clutched her face. Who was that pretty, perfect man with the brown eyes and horrified expression?

Quinn knew that man . . .

And then it hit her. Everything. Every memory stolen from her by compulsion, her life, her dreams . . . everything danced in her mind.

"Oh, Emrys," she breathed and cupped his face between her hands. The man was *her* Emrys.

Well . . . maybe not hers—not now. But maybe one day he could be hers?

"Emrys," she whispered again, meeting his eyes. "I—"

"Come here, Quinny," Jevon demanded, holding her blood painting—created when she'd died. He twisted its compulsion powers and made her do his bidding. She felt it in her bones, but instead of fighting it, she let it sink in. She would comply, just not quite yet.

First, she wanted her Playboy Prince.

Facing Emrys for a final time, she pulled his lips into hers and kissed him with all the fire and passion in her heart. He tasted of sorrow and broken promises. It was not a kiss to end all kisses, but it was hers. For one moment, be it a tiny second in a sea of entirety, she would have Emrys Avalon. He'd be hers, and she'd be his. And it would be the memory she held and grasped onto in the darkness to come.

But the kiss didn't last long. It couldn't. She was not his. And she would never be if Jevon had anything to do with it.

"I'm sorry." Her voice lingered in the air.

Emrys looked like death. His expression said a thousand words: *I am sorry. I ruined everything. I am a monster.*

Quinn turned and slowly and painfully crawled to Jevon. In the process, she passed Seren's unconscious body. But her chest still moved up and down despite the bullet piercing her skull.

She would survive.

And that bred hope.

Because somewhere deep down inside, Quinn knew that Seren could change, and maybe she already had.

When Quinn finally reached Jevon, he leaned down and hauled her up by her chin. "You are such a troublesome brat, but perhaps you'll be a useful one of these days. But first, I am going to make you watch your lover die."

What?

Jevon tipped her chin to catch Emrys's gaze. He was bound at their feet, blood still pooling from his wounds.

Quinn's heart burst, and she turned a begging gaze on Jevon, "No, please."

Jevon dropped her chin. "You will not intervene." The compulsion captured her bones, her body, and her soul, and she could do nothing but watch what happened next.

Jevon—or Gideon or whoever he was—pulled out his hand mirror and placed her painting inside while trading for Emrys's painting. Wasting no time, Jevon ripped the prince's painting in half. Emrys jerked, kneeling among a sea of death, blood still streaming from his wounds. With a feral smile, Jevon ripped it again and again. Emrys clasped onto all fours, his suffering immense.

It couldn't be real. She'd switched his painting. Hadn't she? Had Jevon discovered the vase? Emrys was just faking it, right? It had to be, but it felt so real. It seemed so real.

Was it real?

She didn't know anymore.

She had no idea how long she'd been dead. Jevon could have

found the real paintings. An anchor dropped in her stomach, and the vein in her neck pulsed.

Once Jevon sprinkled the pieces of the painting on the floor, he set them on fire.

"No!" Quinn screamed and fell to her knees watching, unable to do anything. Every bone in her body ached, and silent tears cascaded from her cheeks.

The room smelled of smoke and curses.

Emrys dissolved slowly into ash as each of the pieces of his painting disintegrated. The ash from both the canvas and the dead body swirled into an enchanted tornado and crystallized. Sparkling and glittering with glory and power.

It crystallized into silver-glass, forming a—

Quinn gasped, and her body trembled.

It couldn't be, but there was no denying that where Emrys's body once lay was a sparkling mirror. An enchanted mirror.

Shock radiated through her.

Vampires became mirrors when they died.

"Destroy it, Quinny," Jevon said, hovering above her ear. "Destroy his mirror. End him forever."

Quinnevere Ashelle fought the compulsion with every ounce of her energy, with all her strength and all her soul, but even she was no match for a painting compulsion.

The beast in her chest returned and captured all of her strength. The sound of her heart's furious beats was the only thing she heard and focused on as she hauled the mirror up with her vampiric strength and hurled it to the floor. As it shattered, she fell to her knees, her glass heart shattering with it.

Slyly, she grasped a piece between her fingers and slipped it into her corset as the mirror shards vanished into the night.

Quinn glanced down at her fingers, which were now stained azure blue—a murderous blue.

Five prophecies were now true. The Mirror of Untamed Terror's prophecies were written into existence like a curse.

Her feet bore no calluses.

She publicly showed her emotions to all who could see.

She died.

She was a vampire.

And Emrys Avalon was dead.

Quinn's hair wept a dark indigo color and was coated with her devastation. The curse from Periwinkle was still fully intact even though she was a full-blooded vampire.

Then it hit her: Periwinkle's six nonsensical words about the vampire motto suddenly made sense.

Vampires were Mirror-Gods, and Peri had been trying to tell Quinn all this time.

With Every Death, We Grow Stronger.

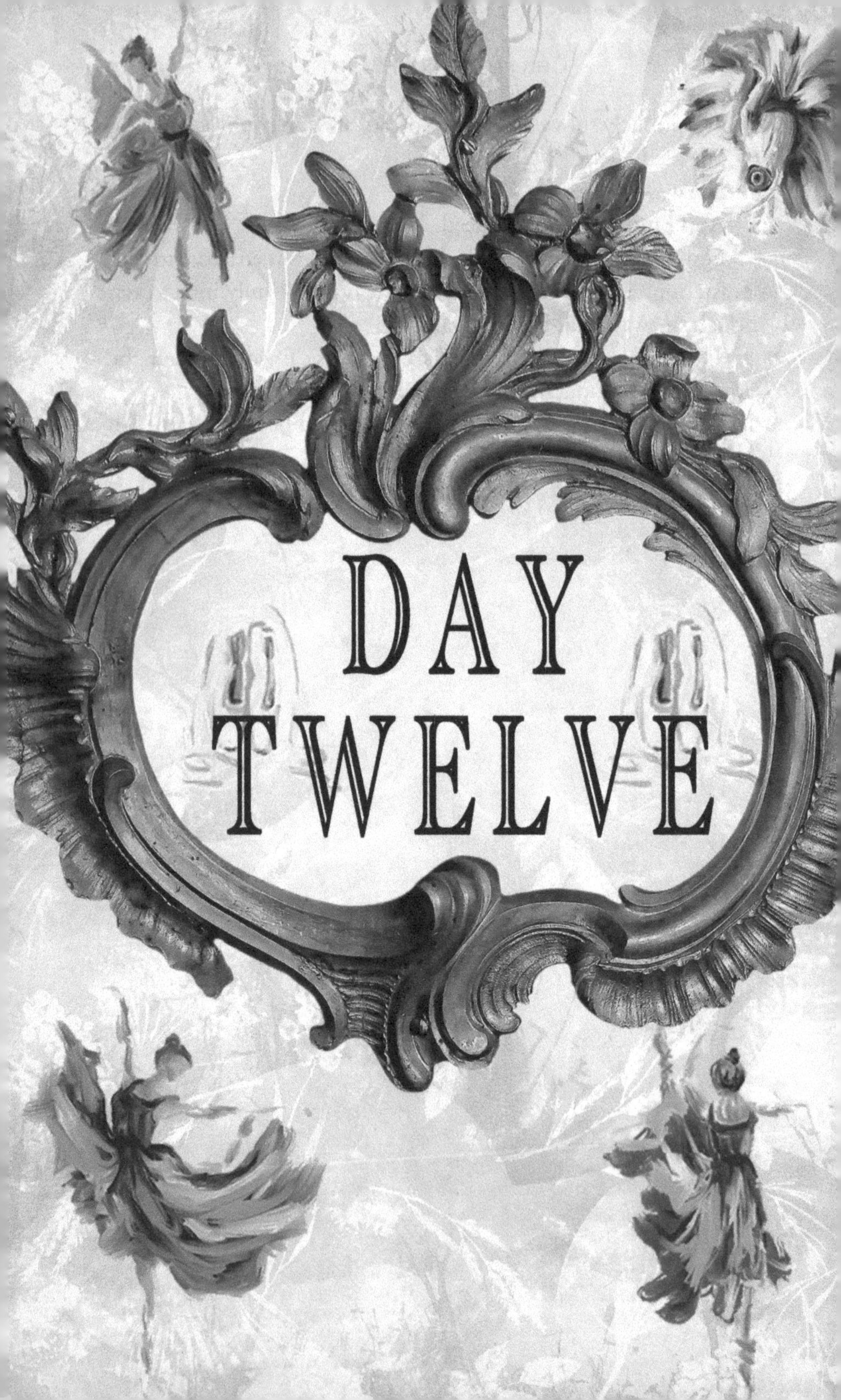
DAY
TWELVE

BREAKING NEWS

The New Swansea Times

THURSDAY, NEW SWANSEA CITY, 1st DAY OF WINTER, 700AV

Horror grips the city as the news spreads. Vampires are back and have taken over most of New Swansea City under the tyrannical rule of the infamous Gideon Hale. Many humans were murdered at the ball. Among the dead are Prince Emrys Avalon and his mysterious ballerina—cont. on page 2

QUEEN'S ROYALLE BALLET Announces New Apprentices

- Arthur Florence
- Aylin Autumn
- Quinnevere Ashelle

VAMPIRES ARE BACK!

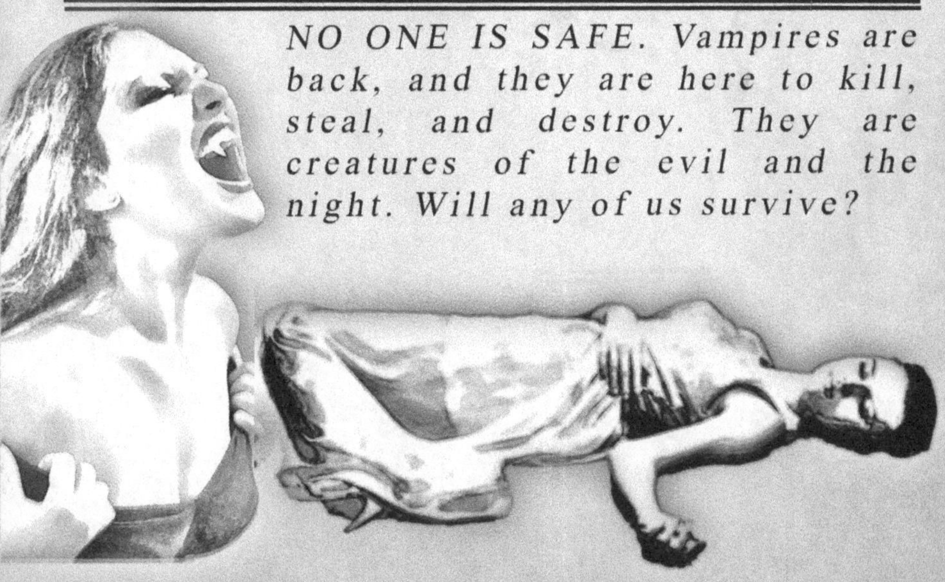

NO ONE IS SAFE. Vampires are back, and they are here to kill, steal, and destroy. They are creatures of the evil and the night. Will any of us survive?

Acknowledgments

First, I want to thank my readers. I am so beyond thankful I get to share my worlds, and stories with you. I wanted to give a special shout-out to my earliest readers. I love you all so much! I wrote the first draft of this book in 2019, and in 2020, I got an agent, but in 2021, Gilded Wicked Mirrors died on Submission, and I thought it would never see the light of day, but your early support convinced me to publish this book after Courting War. So thank you so much!

Mom and Dad, thank you for everything. You are the best parents a girl can have. I would not have been able to follow any of my dreams without your continuous support. I cherish every moment I get with you and want a million more. Dad, thank you for being my first reader and reading this book before it was dirty.

I want to thank my siblings, Jennifer and PJ, and their spouses, Jace and Nichole.

Bacardi, Bella, and Loki I love you so much it actually hurts me.

Joseph, Carina, and Aylin thank you for teaching me true friendship and love. I love you much more than words can express, and since I suck at love letters, let me just dedicate Quinn and Giselle's ride-or-die friendship to all three of you!

Michelle, thank you so much for your continued support and love, and thank you for proofreading this book!

Jamye, Brittany, and Amanda, I could not publish without your constant support. I would barely be able to function without you three hiding things from me and lying to me when I am upset, and I love you so much for it! Truly, I am so thankful to have you three in my life.

Donna and Rachel, you STILL make me buy too many pretty books. Your influence is strong. Thank you for being my BFFs. I love you as much as I love Shadow Daddies.

Ellie, this book would not exist without your support and guidance. I love you so much.

To my first agent, Kristy. Thank you so much for taking a chance on me and this book. It sucks it didn't sell, but I still believe so much in this world and characters.

Giulia F. Wille, thank you so much for being the best artist a girl could ask for! You are so easy to work with, and you make collaborating fun and exciting! I love your work more than words can describe. This cover is beyond STUNNING. It is truly perfect. Cheers to all the future projects we work on together!

Chinelo, Michael, Carrie, Val, Sienna, Dianna, Angela, Sarah (SK), Audrey, and Anni, thank you all so, so, so much! I could not make it through this rough industry without you. You all mean so much to me, and I am so lucky to have you in my life!

Thank you to all of the following people for being amazingly supportive! Melissa, London, Jaime, Stephanie, Nicole, Skyler, Natalie, Lily, Shelly, Nadine, Michelle, and Rosebud (Emily). I also want to give a special shout-out to everyone from the forge (there are too many to name), especially Kelly, Mandy, Ruth, Amber, and Jen. Also, thank you to all my Clubhouse friends. Thank you for everything. I could not do this without you.

To Rie, Rosanna, Becky, and Victoria, you were my first writer's group and the reason I've gotten this far. We need to hang out again.

To all my Instagram followers who constantly watch my procrastination stations, even when there are thirty meandering videos, know that I love you SO MUCH.

To my fantastic editors, Jennifer, Connolly, Rebecca, and Cindy, thank you for helping me fix this story and these words! You are amazing!

I couldn't mention everyone here, and I am sorry. I am so blessed because I have so many amazing people in my life (many not mentioned here). Thank you all!

Finally, I want to thank God for being there for me in all things. Thank you for giving me grace and love even when I don't deserve it. I have a beautiful, joyous life, and it's all because of you.

Love, Hazel

About the Author

Hazel St. Lewis is a Northern California-based Fantasy Romance author. Diagnosed with dyslexia at a young age, she struggled to read and write, but fantasy stories inspired her to start storytelling. Unfortunately, now, she is a little too obsessed with Dracula. When she isn't writing, she can be found playing with her hoard of cats (too many to count...it's a problem), singing songs to said cats—like Cinderella—or painting.

Facebook Group: Shadow Daddy Books, TikTok @hazelstlewis, Instagram @hazelstlewis

Newsletter Sign-Up

Sign up for Hazel's newsletter on her website to be the first to receive exciting news, updates, and bonus content.
   https://www.hazelstlewis.com

Please Leave a Review!

If you enjoyed this book, please consider leaving a review. One of the best ways to support authors (especially new ones like me) is to leave a review!

Danger is a
beautiful
bedmate